Into the Night

Into the Night

By

Shannon Pearce

Strategic Book Publishing and Rights Co.

Strategic Book Publishing and Rights Co.
12620 FM 1960, Suite A4-507
Houston TX 77065
www.sbpra.com

ISBN: 978-1-62212-337-7

For Aunty Angie,
always in my thoughts, forever in my heart.

CHAPTER ONE

Dear Misty,

Sorry I didn't call. I knew how you would have reacted if I had, and I didn't want to fight with you. I know how you feel about this but I think we both know it's for the best; besides, my expertise is needed urgently. I know I haven't been home in a while. It's been hectic and these things never rest, but I have some good news: I've dealt with this before so I know what I'm doing and it shouldn't take too long to finish up. I promise I'll try to get home this time, but you know how it is sometimes; things just come up. I can't wait to see you again. I'll have to show you all the new battle scars I've gotten and before you freak: I'm just kidding, there aren't that many. I miss you, little sis, and trust me, if I didn't think that people would die without me being here I would be home right now, instead of sitting in a crappy motel room, writing you a letter.

Now down to procedure. As always, dates at the bottom, and I've purposely left out location, but either Alex or my partner has all the details you'll need to know for the just in case stuff, so don't worry and I'll always have my phone on me if you need me. I hate to have to write this, but if something should happen to me, even though it won't, but if something does Alex will be in touch. Now, no matter what happens, please stay out of it, Misty. You're out and I want you to stay that way,

I can't see you get hurt. Stay safe, and don't do anything stupid; that's my department.
Oh, and sis: don't worry. I know what I'm doing.

Love, Damien
12/5/09

I wanted to scream, I was so mad. My fists balled and nearly screwed up the letter in frustration. I couldn't believe he was doing this again! After everything we've already been through. I decided, after a bit of mental protest, that it was best not to rip up the only shred of evidence I had that my brother was alive, so I slammed it down on the table instead. My palm stung and the table shook, but I barely noticed.
Damien, my oh-so-charming brother, had adopted our father's method of letting the family know where the job was taking him. Well, more or less letting me know. Of course, when our father was the active hunter in the family, there were no cell phones, and most times a pay phone was inconvenient. So the letter method worked for him. But in today's world it was just plain impractical. There were thousands of faster ways to get in touch with people nowadays than the post.

Of course, Damien didn't do it for practicality. No, he did it because he knew he'd be long gone by the time I got the letter. Meaning it would be too late for me to stop him from doing whatever crazy thing he was up to this time. When he called, it was always only to see how I was. He would never let me speak to his partner or even tell me where in hell they were, which was more than frustrating. Damien's always been stubborn that way. Once he set his mind to something you couldn't change it, no matter how hard you tried. I re-read the letter carefully for hints but Damien had written it as all good hunters would. He gave the facts, said what he needed and nothing more. My only clue was the date.

Wait a second! May? Did I read that wrong? I knew something was up even before I got the letter, and in my family's line of work that was never good. How did I know this? Well, for a start, it was September. Meaning either the letter was sent three months ago, or it was held until now. Feeling a small surge of panic, I ripped my cell phone from my pocket with little regard to its general well-being and dialled his number. I paced the hardwood floor by the kitchen table as I waited for him to answer.

"Hello." Damien's voice said on the other end of the line. Just hearing it was like lifting the weight of the world off my shoulders. I was so relieved I could have collapsed into the chair behind me. Of course, that being said, he still wasn't on my list of favourite people at the moment. I was still mad as hell!

"Hey, Dee where are you?" I knew I had to keep my voice level, at least let him explain before I ripped him a new one.

"Psych got me messages. Can't talk at the moment busy off kicking ass so leave a message or if its life or death, call 555-361-482, if not, you know the drill."

Shit! "Damien, where are you? I only just got your letter and, by the way, if you don't stop with the letters I'm going to kill you myself. Dee, it's September; I know you said you would try to stop in, but I'm worried. Normally I at least get a phone call. You have to stop this. You're becoming just like Dad and as much as I hate to say it, you're going to end up like him too. I don't want that to happen, Damien; I need you back home. And if that's not possible, you have to take me with you. I'm so sick of this place and I'm not a little kid anymore; I can handle myself. So I'm giving you until tomorrow to call me or I'm coming after you and I mean it. Please, Dee, be careful and don't get yourself killed. I know you're just trying to live up to his expectations, to make Dad proud, but this isn't the way to do it."

I paused for a second; I could feel my anger at him boiling over, clouding the line between loving, worried sister and his worst nightmare, which made what I said next not exactly what I wanted to say. See, what I should have said was *I'm worried about you; please call me back* but of course what blurted out was more fitting to my mood: "Because I'm sure that getting yourself killed would make him real proud. Jerk off."

The phone was the next thing that was being slammed into the table. I knew straight away I was going to regret that when I had to replace it. The mix of emotions racing through me wasn't really that uncommon. This happened more often than I cared to admit. But the messy handwriting on the letter hit a sore spot for me. It made me realise just how much I actually had missed my brother, and how much I hated waiting to hear from him.

Especially since it was supposed to be over. Neither of us was supposed to be doing this anymore. We were done. We got out. So why was I still putting up with this shit? I could feel my anger at him growing with every word that my eyes skimmed. Finally, though I'm not proud to admit it, it got the better of me. I snatched up the letter and tore it in half. Scrunching the pieces in my fists, I screamed. Okay, sure, I knew doing that wasn't going to change anything, but man, did it feel good. Most of all, it worked. I wasn't nearly as mad at him as I had been. In a way, I knew my anger was unfair. But choosing to return to a life that we had both fought so hard to escape made my anger seem less petty, if only to myself.

Damien was only doing what our father had raised us to do. He was taking over the family business, which in theory seemed harmless enough, but our family business has always been stuff of nightmares, literally. Damien and I come from a long line of hunters, but not the conventional type. We deal with the stuff that other people can't. The stuff that doesn't exist and it's our job to make it stay that way. Think of us as the supernatural police, but instead of arresting the alleged bad guy, we hunt it down and kill it.

Hunting was in our blood. It was what we were born to do. And deep down, there was a part of us that knew it was all we would really ever be able to do. We were hunters in our teens. Good ones, in fact, though it didn't take us long to realise that we just didn't want to face the monster under the bed, so we didn't. We did the one thing we were told was impossible to do. We escaped the life. We became normal, but we should have known that sooner or later the life we were running from was going to catch up with us.

Unfortunately for Damien, it was sooner rather than later. In fact, it happened two years ago. I still remember the moment I realised I'd lost my brother, and ever since then it's been a fight to get him back. It was Damien's twenty-third birthday and we were meant to be throwing him a party that night. Instead, that morning we got the phone call that ended my brother's normal life and made him a hunter once again. Dad had been killed in a hunting accident.

Of course the news was hard for both of us, but Damien simply couldn't cope with the news. He blamed himself for not being out there helping and he was convinced it was his fault, that somehow he'd let Dad down. Things changed after that; our lives as we knew them crumbled and Damien threw himself back into hunting lore. Three days after the funeral, Dad's phone rang and Damien answered it. Since then he has been on the road all the time, coming and going as the job took him.

As for me, I was not so willing to fall back into old habits, especially after what happened to our father. It took some adjusting to not having my big brother around but somehow I managed to maintain my semi-normal life. Okay, so maybe I was stuck in this dead-end town, working in a crappy, low-paying job, struggling just to keep the damn house, but I was normal. Misty West, the only non-hunter in the West family. Wouldn't my ancestors be proud?

Opening the sliding-glass door, I walked out to stand on the small deck looking over the backyard. The place was in a bit of a mess without Damien around. Truthfully, I just didn't have the time or the energy lately to do it myself. The yard itself extended into the woods that surrounded most of the house. I think the woods were meant to represent the property line, but when my great-great-grandfather built the house he never bothered to put up a back fence. The lone oak tree that stood in the yard blocked the glare from the setting sun casting its reddish glow across the sky.

I pulled my cardigan tighter around me as the once-warm wind chilled its way into my bones, a good sign that autumn was on its way. My gaze settled on the driveway. Part of me wished that Damien's old black '69 Mustang Fastback would pull up and relieve my worries; I couldn't help but feel somehow letdown when it didn't. Sure, it was stupid to wish for something you knew wasn't going to happen, but I just wanted it so badly, it was all I could do to keep hope.

"Everything alright, my dear? You look troubled," Mrs Patterson, my lovely next-door neighbour, asked as she made her way to the fence between our two properties. Mrs Patterson was our only neighbour, since ours was the last house on our so-called street. The next neighbour was a good mile away through the woods. I had never really seen this as a bad thing, and my father had always said that if Mrs Patterson were to move, he would buy her out for the privacy. Although I rather liked having a neighbour even though sometimes, with my family's line of work, we need a little privacy.

"Yeah, fine." It wasn't hard to tell I was lying, but the way I was feeling at the moment I didn't have it in me to be convincing despite the rules.

"Good to hear, dear. I thought something was wrong. I could have sworn I heard yelling."

"Oh, that. I was just having an argument with Damien over the phone. He isn't home yet," I lied with a small smile. Lying to people's faces was also part of the job description. We were trained to have no tells. Everything we said, lie or otherwise, was to be believable. It was a useful skill in our line of work; also it made for a hell of a poker player. Believe me when I say there is no winning against a hunter with our expert poker faces.

"Ah, how is he? I haven't seen him in ages. Poor lad didn't look too good the last time I saw him. All worn out. No wonder, though, taking over the family business from your father like that. I saw the way your father would come home sometimes; he has pretty big shoes to fill."

Mrs Patterson had been our neighbour long before Damien and I were born. She had known both of my parents well and treated us like we were family, even though she didn't really know what the family business was. Part of me suspected she knew more than she let on but kept it quiet just in case.

"Yeah, well, he's on a hunting trip at the moment." I watched the colour drain from her wrinkled old face. That was another good indicator she knew more than most people did. People in town don't know what a West family hunting trip actually involved. But since most of the time we returned half-torn to shreds or didn't return for months on end, most people figured out they're not normal trips. "He'll be home soon," I said with another fake smile, which she returned and then turned to walk back toward her house. Another good thing about Mrs Patterson was that she didn't pry.

Sighing, I headed back inside my own house, to lock up and get ready for work. I changed into my short-sleeved black tee shirt and grey pinstriped pants. As the bartender I escaped wearing anything skimpy, low-cut or short, like the waitresses had to wear. Not that I couldn't totally pull it off, mind you, but I preferred my uniform. The black tee shirt had "Danny's Bar" written in big brown letters across the chest, and really, that was my only requirement as far as a uniform went.

Despite the freedom, I didn't much like the shirt. I had enough trouble with drunken guys hitting on me without drawing attention to my breasts, which already do a really good job of drawing attention to themselves anyway. Nature had gifted me nicely in the bosom department, and I had been told a few times that I wasn't too bad in the looks department either. Light brown hair darker than Damien's or my father's dirty blonde, and blue-ish eyes, really more of a turquoise than your normal blue if I had to put an exact colour to it. I wasn't overly tall; none of the women in my family were. I was about five-foot-four without heels but that shadowed in comparison to the men in my family, my brother included. They all stood well over six feet, were built like Army tanks and were just as dangerous.

Not to say I couldn't put the men in their place if needed. I wasn't what you would call small-built either, no supermodel figure here; I was a size eight on a good day. Years of hunting had left me with a toned body and thankfully, somehow, I had still maintained my curves. I grabbed my keys from the table as I passed and walked to the door, locking it behind me. I glared at the beat-up Honda Civic parked out front. I hated that car, and had from the moment I had bought it. It was cheap to run, small and, best of all, it was normal; my new life was all about normal.

I blasted the radio as I drove to work, trying to keep my mind busy. The last thing I needed was to start screwing up people's drink orders because I was distracted by my crazy, other life. The parking lot was packed when I pulled in; the traffic had even over flown into the staff parking area. Cursing each and every car parked there, I finally found a space at the back of the lot, luckily, because it was getting dangerously close to the start of my shift. "It's going to be a long night."

Xavier

"Psych." Message bank again.

"Damien, I swear to god dude, I'm so over your bullshit! When I get my hands on you, you're dead, man. I'm going to kill you in ways you cannot even imagine, if you're not already dead, that is. Of course, you should know even then I'll find a way. Remember, just because you're dead, it doesn't mean you can't still die," I snapped and threw the phone. The phone smashed into the wall with so much force, it shattered the phone and the plaster simultaneously. *Great, there goes the security deposit!* Justifying that to sheer frustration would be a damned injustice; I was so beyond the point of that by now. Somehow I knew finding this place wouldn't mean I would find him, but I hadn't expected to find what I had.

I upended his abandoned duffle bag and tipped its contents on the floor. This was the last place he could have been. All his stuff was here, and the hunt left unfinished. Something Damien never did. I was getting tired of chasing him, tired of hearing his stupid voice say the same thirty-two words over and over again every time I tried to reach him. Sure, Damien can be a dick, so not answering my calls was something I was to expect, but running out on a hunt and leaving it for another hunter to clean up wasn't like him.

I rifled through the stuff on the floor. It all looked to be there, from what I could tell. So why would he leave it all behind? I had a very bad feeling about this. I picked up the photograph that was on the top of the pile and looked at it. I had seen this photo a number of times; it was of him and his sister when they were in their teens. From what I could tell, they were really close once. I knew for a fact that she meant more to him than life itself, and I also knew she was my last shot at getting to him. If anyone knew where he was going, it would be her. Removing the sim card from the wreckage of the phone, I headed downstairs. Much to the desk clerk's surprise, I paid the room out for another month and walked outside.

I had to ditch the car I had used to get here. It had most likely been reported stolen by now. So I needed a ride, and at the moment anything would do. It was slim pickings in a cheap motel parking lot. Most of the vehicles were occupied, or I knew they were alarmed and would be too much trouble. I couldn't help but smile as my ticket out of here pulled up. I watched as the young couple got out of the big black Hummer and walked into the reception area. Thanking my lucky stars, I ran to the driver's side and hoped for the best. I looked in the window to see the keys in the ignition still. I was so happy I threw my fist into the air before ripping open the door and jumping in. Quickly starting the thing, I was out of the drive before the owners would have even noticed it was gone.

Yeah okay, so I know as far as rides go it wasn't the most inconspicuous car known to man. And yeah, if you're going to steal something it's usually best to keep a low profile, but I was on a deadline and it would do for now. The inside of the Hummer was every bit as flashy as the outside. I guess they don't call them luxury SUVs for nothing. It had that new feeling to it, even the new car smell. The poor guy I jacked it from must have been loaded, and seeing that was most likely the case, I was teaching him a valuable life lesson. *One should not brag, especially around guys like me.* It was a five-hour drive to the town Damien's family lived in, but I knew that maybe, if I was lucky, I could do it in four.

The old house looked a little run-down compared to last time I'd seen it. The lawns were overgrown, the roof needed re-tiling and the house itself could use a coat of paint. I knew I had no right to judge, seeing how I hadn't seen the place in years, but it really needed a man's touch. I straightened out the wrinkles in the straight-cut black suit I was still wearing from my last con as a federal agent (which, by the way, had gotten me nowhere). I needed information and I was going to get it the only way I knew how. I grabbed the dark sunglasses I'd found in the dash and slipped them on. I knew they were redundant at eleven o'clock at night, but I wanted to look the part. The fact that I could see in the dark helped my decision. I slicked my long dark hair back with my hands and tucked it behind my ears. I had often considered tying it back at the times I'd found it annoying, but there were two problems with that. One, I wasn't sure it was quite long enough to tie back and two, I wasn't really the ponytail type of guy. It was a clear night. I could see the top of an old oak tree behind the house as I pushed open the broken gate and walked toward the front door. I took a deep breath, closed my eyes and just listened. The house was quiet and the only sounds I could hear were creatures scurrying through the forest behind it. I knocked loudly on the door and waited, just in case I was wrong. It wouldn't be the first time I hadn't heard a hunter. Unfortunately, patience was never one of my stronger virtues, so I knocked again, making the door rattle on its hinges, and added, “Police, open up!”

The porch light on their next-door neighbour’s house turned on. After a few seconds, an elderly woman walked out and made her way toward the fence. I did the same. I had met this lady before, but had to pretend I was indeed the police in order to get the information I wanted. I just hoped it was dark enough that she couldn’t make out my features or the fact that the badge said CDC. Despite that, I had to take the chance anyway.

“Can I help you, dear?” she asked as she stopped next to the fence.

I pulled out my badge while flipping it open quickly, just long enough for her to see it was a badge of some sort, then said, “Yes, ma’am, maybe you can. I’m Agent Crow, FBI. I’m looking for Misty West. Can you tell me where she is?” In order to increase the feeling that we had never met, I faked a southern drawl as I spoke and put the badge back in my shirt pocket.

“Oh dear, she’s isn’t in any trouble, is she?” Her aged eyes were full of concern and it wasn’t hard to tell she was fond of these kids. I know Damien had spoken fondly of her.

“I’m not at liberty to supply that information, ma’am, but I’m going to need her whereabouts.” I tried to sound as formal as I could while faking an accent I had really only ever heard on TV.

“Of course, Officer. She’s at work; she works at Danny’s bar in town. They’re good kids, they’ve just had it hard, that’s all, they’re misunderstood.” I gave a slight smile and a nodded before walking back toward the Hummer.

Well, that was the understatement of the century, I thought as I removed the sunglasses and got in the car, placing them where I’d found them inside the dash compartment.

“Danny’s bar,” I repeated to myself as I pulled away from the curb. I knew that bar. It was less than a five-minute drive from their house, on the outskirts of the town centre.

The parking lot was crowded for a small-town bar, which was a good thing because the Hummer might not stick out as much that way. I parked in the back of the lot and cut the engine. Looking up into the rear-view mirror, I caught a glimpse of my own reflection and then looked down at the suit I was wearing. All of it looked a little too formal for a hick town bar. *Can't go in looking like this, can I?* I thought, while climbing over into the back of the Hummer to see what I could find.

CHAPTER TWO

Misty

It was crazy busy all night, but thankfully it went dead about one a.m. I looked around, trying to decide if I should close early. I mean, really, would keeping the bar open for an extra hour make that much of a difference after the night I had already had? The bartender I replaced informed me as soon as I walked in that it was only going to be me and the short-order cook tonight, seeing that Meg had called in just before I walked in the door, sprouting something about a sick kid and it was far too late to try and get anyone since the waitresses and cooks finished at midnight anyway. I started my nightly duties. I figured I may as well take advantage of the sudden slow spell; there were only two patrons still left in their usual seats.

I figured that they couldn't possibly keep me so busy that I couldn't multitask. I was just finishing wiping down the bar when a cool breeze washed over me. At first I didn't bother to look up, thinking it was only old Mac leaving; he usually left around the same time every night. I looked up to check if he had paid his tab and I saw a guy standing the door way. He was looking around the near-empty bar as if he was meant to be meeting someone and they hadn't showed, but instead of walking toward Mac or Doug his gaze focused on me and he smiled. My breath caught in my throat as he took that first step toward me; part of me had an uneasy feeling like I was a lamb set for slaughter, but the rest of me was totally mesmerized. The amazing emerald colour of his eyes seemed to shine as he looked around assessing every inch of the bar as he walked. His walk was cool and confident, like he was completely invincible and – well, to put it bluntly, the man was hot. I'm talking in-my-wildest-dreams kinda hot. His creamy pale skin contrasted with his medium-length wavy black hair, which was messily tucked behind his ears. Soft, pale lips turned up into a sigh-worthy smile as our eyes met. He made it hard to look away and I couldn't help but notice how his smile seemed to light up every feature of his handsome face. I knew a goofy smile was forming on my own face in response. I was totally checking the poor guy out, but I tried not to feel too bad because if he looked that good all the time, then seriously, he should be used to it by now.

I felt my cheeks burn hot, now I was blushing. *How embarrassing,* I thought as I quickly turned away and pretended to adjust the drinks on the shelf behind me. I heard him chuckle to himself as he leant against the bar, my cue to face the man. *Get a grip, girl, he's just a guy, you've dealt with plenty of attractive men in ya time, what makes him any different? Well? Stop being stupid and turn around!* I took a deep breath to compose myself before doing so.

As it turned out, following my own advice was harder than I expected. "Hey…" I paused, speechless; I couldn't even think past the greeting.

"Hi," he replied coolly, with the same confidence that was in his walk in his smile. His voice was rather deep and husky, almost like the poor thing had a sore throat yet, strangely, it was soothing. Now that he was less than a foot away I could see how his hair was messed in a way that almost looked styled, and his amazing emerald eyes were framed by thick black lashes. He was tall; I had noticed that when he first walked in, but even while leaning on the bar it was easy to see this guy was well over six feet tall, I'd say six-four or maybe even six-five. His body was long and lean, but you can see by the way his clothes fit him that there was no shortage of muscle under them. His black button-up shirt, a size too big for him, hung open over a white tank top. The tank, on the other hand, stretched across his chest and hugged his body in a way that left little to the imagination, then came to a stop at a pair of old blue jeans. Strangely, I couldn't shake the feeling that there was something familiar about him, like we had met before, but that was impossible; I sure as hell would have remembered if I had met him, I tell you.

"I'm Xavier." He pronounced his name slowly and pronounced the X: Ex-avier. I just looked at him, unable to process a single thought. What was wrong with me? "And you are?" he asked in an attempt to get me talking.

"Misty," I said automatically, almost dazed by this guy's sheer perfectness. I was actually surprised I knew my own name at the moment. Suddenly, as if that was my cue, my brain ticked over, working a mile a minute, processing everything so fast that it still left me with that same basic effect as before. Under the overwhelming feeling of this guy's presence was that feeling I had before hiding away in the back of my mind, and I couldn't help but try to focus on it. It was almost like an alarm bell ringing in my head, screaming danger, yelling at me, telling me there is something I should notice, warning me, but what about? I gave him the once-over again, just in case, and come up with nothing.

This guy was perfect. Too perfect, maybe? Hell, for all I knew that was probably it. Everything about him seemed so wrong: his amazing good looks, the way he seemed incredibly charming yet he had hardly spoken, and the way he had me totally mesmerized from the moment he walked in. Something in my gut was screaming as that feeling intensified, telling me to run and run fast. This alone told me there was something wrong about this guy but no matter how hard I tried, or how much my better judgement cried out, I couldn't ignore the fact that at the same time, it felt oh-so-right. His smile faltered slightly, then widened to all of its amazing glory as he grabbed my hand and kissed it softly.

"The pleasure's all mine." Tingles coursed up my arm and through my body, leaving me powerless to resist, and silenced that annoying feeling of dread. I sighed, unwillingly of course from this guy's sheer amazingness; what was I worried about again? Snapping out of it briefly, I felt myself blush once more. *Misty, what are you doing? Snap out of it before you drool over the poor guy!*

"What can I get ya?" I chirped in an annoying, way-too-bubbly voice.

"Whiskey would be nice," he said, his hand holding mine a little longer than necessary.

"Comin' right up," I replied quickly, turning my back to him to grab a glass. What had come over me all of a sudden? I poured a glass of our finest whiskey (which, seeing as we were a small-town bar, wasn't all that fancy) and tried to compose myself again before facing him. I sat the drink on the bar in front of him and smiled what I hoped was a sane smile. "On the house."

"Thank you," he said, picking up the glass and raising it to me before taking a drink. *He is so cute*. My mind seemed to have a mind of its own; no matter how hard I tried, I couldn't get over the fact that he was super-hot. His smile widened and he took another sip. *Oh my god, look how you're acting. No wonder the poor guy's laughing; pull yourself together!* I lectured myself but no matter what I thought, my mind wouldn't listen. *I wonder if he's single?*

"So, I haven't seen you in town before; you just passing through?"

"Well, I pass through every now and then, but actually I'm here on business at the moment, and that's what brought me to you. Do have a minute?" he asked. Business with me? Even I found that hard to believe; what possible business could he have with me?

"Well, I can't really leave the bar," I replied. That nagging feeling returned with force but this time I had to agree with it: something was up. Natural instinct told me to run, or better yet fight, but I couldn't very well kick a customer's ass in the bar and I sure as hell wasn't following him outside. He watched my indecision cross my face (I knew it would, I was like my brother in that way), but strangely, it didn't deter him. He nodded in response but leaned forward to catch my gaze. His hand found mine on the bar and he spoke slowly again.

"But this will only take a minute." His voice washed away everything I had just decided, and once again that nagging feeling, the one which only moments ago I had thought was right, was gone and I found myself nodding.

"Sure."

"Excellent," he said as he grabbed the glass and swallowed the rest of his drink. Not breaking my gaze, he stood and walked to the small exit hatch on the bar and held out his hand in an invitation. I followed his every move, fixated like there was nothing more interesting in the world. I pressed the lock on the till as I passed and walked out from behind the bar to take his hand. He led us both to the employee exit, then outside. We walked out into the crisp morning air; he was careful to keep the door ajar, which was smart because I had locked it earlier as I always do when the other staff leaves. He dropped my hand and stepped back from me and the door. It was almost like I was waking up from a dream; I still remembered what had just happened, but suddenly now I knew exactly how dumb of an idea this was. In fact, all of it was one big warning sign; how did I not see it before? I backed up within reach of the door, but he didn't make any attempt to stop me. The crazy alluring air that had been surrounding this guy in the bar was gone, and his face was nothing but serious.

"Okay, well, as I mentioned, I'm Xavier. I'm the next heir to the throne of the western coven..."

I interrupted him. I know it's rude but I couldn't help it; had I heard that right? "Whoa, whoa, stop. Coven?" There was no way I could have stopped that from coming out; of all the things I had expected, supernatural problems were not anywhere on the list.

"Yes," he replied calmly with a small nod. I had to think for a second; there was only one thing I could think of that lives in covens.

"As in witches!" I exclaimed. He paused and gave me a look that questioned my sanity. *Yeah, Misty, sure he's a witch*, I scolded myself.

"No, as in vampires," he said coolly in a tone that suggested that I should have known that already.

It took me a few seconds to realise what he'd just said. "Vampires?" I tried my best not to laugh but it was hard to hide the amusement in my voice; well, *that* was not what I was expecting! "Let me get this straight: you're an immortal creature of the night?"

He looked insulted for a second them nodded. "You were ready to believe witches, but vampires are too big of a stretch for you?" he said, not hiding the annoyance in his voice.

"I'm sorry, but *vampires*? Really? Couldn't you have picked something more original?"

"No, I didn't really get much of a choice in the matter. You don't believe me?" he said in a tired voice. I could see his mind working; apart from being insane, there was something about this guy.

"No, sorry, I'm finding it a little hard to believe…"

He interrupted me this time. "Okay, look, what I am isn't important at the moment. What's important is why I'm here…"

He started to explain but I interrupted him again. I wasn't finished. This was way out of my league; the dude was a full-fledged nutjob and even if he wasn't a nutjob this was a job for an active hunter, not me.

"Okay, look buddy, there is no such thing as vampires. They do not exist, okay? So here is a number." I grabbed a pen from my apron and wrote Damien's number on his hand; maybe this guy could have better luck getting in contact with him. "He knows what he's doing, and he's a great listener, he'll help you with the whole thinking you're a vampire problem, okay?" and with that I walked toward the door.

"Misty, wait! You don't understand" he called after me as I shut the door. I walked back to the bar kinda disappointed. That guy was far too hot to be crazy and even if he wasn't, I really didn't have time for vampire issues at the moment, or ever, really. *Why are the cute ones always taken, weird, supernatural or gay? It's just not fair,* I thought, allowing myself a quick laugh at the situation as I walked back behind the bar to continue cleaning.

The hours until closing dragged on; it felt like each minute was an hour in itself and, truthfully, I would have done just about anything to speed it up. I stood staring at the clock, thinking this night would seriously never end. Mac left about half-past, leaving only me and Doug, who I knew full well wouldn't leave until thrown out. I decided to skip the last call, seeing I had already cut Doug off, and called him a cab instead. I walked up to him, taking the keys that were sitting on the table as the clock ticked over to two.

"It's time. Come on, old boy, you know the drill: you don't have to go home but you can't stay here," I said he looked up at me, then nodded. "I called you a cab; you can come get these tomorrow." I dangled the keys in front of him to show what I was talking about, then walked over a behind the bar to hang them on the hooks we kept for just this kinda thing.

I locked the door after Doug and removed the cloth I had shoved into my apron. It took me longer than usual to close up for the night, which I knew would annoy the hell out of my boss when I handed in my time card but I think I earned it after the night I had. I emptied out the tip jar, which for the first time ever was going solely to me, and chucked the apron on the corner of the bar as I headed for the door, flipping the light switch as I left. I fumbled with the keys on the outside door and set the alarm. The night was slowly fading away and the crisp cold air had warmed. Feeling more than a little relieved, I crossed the now-empty car park. There were still a few cars scattered around but it was hard to make them out, seeing that the car park was only illuminated by a single street lamp near the road. I stopped in my tracks as I noticed someone leaning on my car. I could feel my heart rate quicken, and walking back to the bar and calling the police crossed my mind, but I knew by now whoever it was had seen me, and it would take me longer to disarm the door than it would for them to cross the car park.

Get a grip, girl, you're a hunter. Kind of. You were trained to fight monsters since you were a little girl, taking down an attacker isn't a problem for you, I mentally scolded myself. *Although it has been years since I've had to use that training.* I decided to take the risk and continue. I could defend myself if I had to and, luckily, I always carry mace for situations like this; you never really know who or what's out there. I slowly made my way over to the car while trying to make out the figure in the dark. Why had I parked in the dark part of the lot? The figure lifted its head as I got closer, as if it had heard me coming, and smiled.

I stopped in my tracks once again. "Xavier," I said in a voice that would have put a whisper to shame. I couldn't believe it; it was the weird hot guy from before. To tell you the truth I couldn't say that I hated seeing him again, because just looking at this guy was pure sensory overload, but I wasn't too thrilled that he was still hanging around after I had told him to get lost. He nodded and walked toward me. I thought about ripping out the mace and macing him back to the last century. I mean, come on, the guy thinks he's a vampire, delusions like that could make him dangerous, and if he was in fact a vampire he really was dangerous, so either way I knew I was up a certain creek and there wasn't a paddle in sight.

It took me a whole three seconds of gut-wrenching fear before I was once again lost in his breathtaking emerald eyes. He stood in front of me, staring deep into my eyes as if he was trying to see what was running through my mind. The urge to run was extreme and the urge to scream was greater than that but I couldn't do either; it was almost like I was frozen solid. Warmth washed over me like a blanket on a freezing-cold day, warm, nice and as long as you had it you wouldn't freeze, you knew you were safe … that's what it was like in his eyes; they made you trust him even if you didn't want to. He raised his hand and traced my cheekbone with his finger. His touch was followed by a cold tingle, a feeling I'd felt before but couldn't remember where or when.

"I didn't want to do this," he said, staring deeper into my eyes. His voice entranced me, drawing me deeper with every word. "But you leave me no choice." I tried to break his spell, but with every word I was rendered more and more powerless to resist.

"Now, as I was saying, I'm a vampire, but I'm also your brother's best friend and hunting partner. Damien and I were separated in a hunt and I haven't been able to get in contact with him since. I've had a bad feeling he's out to do something stupid that might end up with him getting killed, and I can't stop that from happening if I don't know where he is. I've been checking up with Alex, but he's disappeared as well. Damien is the head hunter of your family and one of the only hunters in this area. Since his disappearance the supernatural world has gone into a state of shock and finding other hunters in the area willing to help me is proving to be difficult. I can't find your brother if I'm spending all my time hunting whatever decides to go bump in the night and even that I can't do alone; I need your help."

"What can I do? I have no idea where he is and I'm not even a real hunter," I said, still dazed.

"Yes, you are. You're the last West in the line. I need you to help me save Damien and restore order. If they turn on us we're not going to have the men to restore peace, so we need to show them that the head family is still running the show and we still have the upper hand, before we lose total control."

"We?" I whispered.

"The hunters. I'm a hunter." His hand fell from my cheek and he backed up a few steps. Once again it was as if I was waking from a dream and had been thrown back into the harshness of reality, and that reality sunk in pretty quickly. Without another thought I dug through my purse for my phone and chucked the bag to Xavier, not as worried as I should have been about him taking off, but I figured if he was planning to rob me he would have done it by now. I was more worried about what I had just heard; one hunter going missing is bad luck, two hunters is suspicious, especially seeing one was a head council member, so if what he said was true, Damien might be in real trouble, because doing stupid things is what Damien does best.

"Hold this," I ordered after he had hold of the bag, and I dialled Dee's number. I watched curiously as Xavier tossed my bag from hand to hand, an expression of discomfort on his face. His breathing shallowed and he looked to be in pain; all of a sudden he dropped my bag and jumped back. The dial tone switched to Damien's message bank and I hung up, more startled by Xavier's strange reaction than the fact that Damien had again failed to answer my call.

"Are you alright?" I asked.

"What the hell do you have in there?! The entire New Testament?" he cried. Too startled to even contemplate that, I walked over and picked it up before rifling through it.

"Um, my wallet, sunnies, keys, and mace." I pulled out my keys as I said it and Xavier's eyes widened.

"Get that thing away from me," he said, stumbling over himself to get away from me. "Please, I'm begging you, get rid of it." His once-sexy voice now sounded weak and desperate.

I looked at my keychain. *Dad's cross, of course.* It was strange. I had never heard of religious artefacts having such an extreme effect; this was certainly suspicious.

"Okay," I replied in a calm voice as I slowly walked toward the car. He moved from my line of sight as I opened the car door, removed the cross and threw it in. I turned around to see him standing a couple of yards away.

"That cross wouldn't happen to be your father's, would it?" he said. I just stared at him, trying to figure him out. Vampires are burnt by holy objects, sometimes repelled, but it would have to be one hell of an object … well, actually, the exact opposite. *How'd he know that?*

"I thought so," he muttered to himself. I just looked at him. I hadn't confirmed he was right, so how'd he know? I must have nodded, or he read my body language, or something, I guess.

"How'd you know?" I asked, curiosity getting the better of me.

"Let's just say that I met your father and he didn't like me very much," he said, and I got glimpse of a genuine smile as he turned away. He looked to his watch, then to the sky. "I hate to rush, but we should get going."

"Hold up! I don't know you and I never said I was going with you." I wasn't really sure if I should trust the guy; I mean, I've already established he may be insane, and just because he's freaked out by a cross doesn't mean he's a vampire. This guy could be anyone; hell, he's probably not even a real hunter, and saying he knows Damien and Dad doesn't make him a hunter.

"Misty, how would I know that your entire family are hunters? How would I know Alex and know that he is your late father's hunting partner? How would I know as much as I do if I wasn't telling the truth?" he said in a tired voice.

"Well, how do I know you know that stuff?" I realised how stupid that question was only after it left my mouth and quickly tried to make up for it. "You could just be saying that you're really a vampire and that you're my brother's best friend and all that other stuff you could have found out anywhere."

He rolled his eyes and shook his head. "You're a hunter; this shouldn't be so hard to convince you," he said, looking around as if he was looking for something to prove his story. "Must I prove everything?" I nodded; a little proof never hurt. "Fine, if I can prove I'm a vampire or at least that I'm not human, will you believe the rest?"

I had to think that over for a second; that would be impossible to do if he wasn't, but then again, if he could, did I really want to trust a vampire? I nodded; I would for Damien's sake and besides, I reckoned I could take him if I had to.

"Very well." He closed his eyes and took a deep breath as if he were centring himself. When he opened his eyes his irises looked strange, almost like they were flickering, and something was out of place in his smile this time: he had fangs. Not giving me time to process what I had just seen, he took off running, circling me at amazing speeds that weren't humanly possible, and in a blink of an eye he would disappear completely. I watched as he leaped into the air over me, jumping higher than my head could tilt to see. He glided over me as if suspended in the air; it was almost like he was flying, and landed without a thud on the roof of my car. I cringed at the nasty dent he left, but then again I had always hated that car. He jumped down and landed gracefully in a crouch, with one hand on the ground to steady himself. He looked at me and raised an eyebrow with a cocky look on his face. He was enjoying it way too much.

"Still think I'm crazy?" he said as got to his feet and then lifted my car from the ground, holding it with one hand above his head as if it was nothing to him. "Shall I continue? I've got this pretty cool juggling act I could show you." His smile was smug as he stood tossing my car in the air and catching it like a ball. I stared at him in disbelief; even to me that didn't look possible, and I knew better. I wasn't sure what was worse; the fact that he was telling the truth and was able to do that, or the fact that he was standing there doing that in public, where someone who didn't know it was possible could see.

"Okay, okay, put it down before someone sees you," I said, more shell-shocked than anything. I was still trying to process it. It had been a while since I was around something supernatural. He gave me that smug smile and sat the car back on the ground. He dusted his hands off on his jeans, giving me that smug look and, yep, the fangs were still there. "So you're definitely not human," I said, more to myself than anything.

"Nope, definitely not," he confirmed.

"So you're really a vampire?"

He nodded. "Most of my life."

"Either that or you're just a freak that happens to be really strong." He rolled his eyes. I guess he just didn't get that I wasn't actually talking to him anymore; more at him. If anything, it wasn't him that needed the convincing, it was me.

"Really, is that the best you could come up with?" he asked.

"Hey, leave me alone; it's all well and good for you, but I'm still wrapping my head around things."

"Come on! Your, a hunter, for crying out loud! I can't be the first creature you have ever seen and I bet I'm not the first vampire either. You Wests are notorious for hunting vampires. I should know; I work with your brother."

"I'm not a hunter. That's what I tried to tell you. Not anymore. I don't have to deal with monsters, or vampires, or reptilians, or anything! So why would you possibly need me? I can't do any of what you just did. I'm not even sure if I could kill anything anymore. That part of my life ended years ago. I don't even reckon I could tell you the difference between a shape-shifter and a werewolf."

"Well, there is little difference between a shape-shifter and a werewolf; they are both shifters so they… you know what, never mind. The fact that you are a West is enough to keep everyone quiet long enough to find Damien. Misty, the hunting can wait. I want to find Damien and I thought you might want to too but if not, that's fine, I'll find him myself." He said that as if chastising a naughty child throwing a temper tantrum, and turned to walk away.

He had no right to be mad at me; I was only stating facts and of course I wanted to help my brother, I would do anything for Damien. It was just the thought of having to team up with a complete stranger to do it. Really, he should be more understanding; most complete strangers don't have fangs and a thirst for blood. Then there was the fact that he must really enjoy killing things, because he's a hunter, after all, and that's basically the job description. There was also the little fact he was a supernatural creature in a hunter's world; that was just plain suicidal, which brought me right back to the possibly crazy theory.

"Hey, hey wait!" I called after him as I ran to grab his arm and spun him to face me. "Don't you walk away from me. You're the one who stalked me, buddy, you don't get to walk away!"

"I stalked you?! No, I sought you out and requested your assistance, which you're clearly not going to give. I've wasted enough time here as it is thanks to you, so yeah, I do, and I'm leaving right now", he said as he pulled his arm from my grip and walked off once again.

"I never said I wasn't going to help," I yelled after him. He stopped next to a black Hummer but didn't turn around. "I want to find Damien."

He pulled open the door. "Well, what are you waiting for? Get in." Throwing my better judgement to the wind, I ran to the passenger-side door and jumped in. I knew I was going to regret this but, like I said, I would do anything for my brother, anything.

"This is your car?" I asked as I strapped myself in.

He nodded, then followed it with "Well, let's just say it's mine now."

"You stole it?" I exclaimed. I don't know why that surprised me. The guy was already a vampire-hunting vampire who was most likely clinically insane; could it really hurt to tack thieving to the beginning? Besides, he did hang out with my brother after all, and Damien had stolen his fair share of cars over the years.

"Stole is such a horrible way of putting it. I like to think of it as borrowing with no intention of ever returning it; besides, the people I steal from can afford it, most of the time, so really I'm like a modern-day Robin Hood, stealing from the rich and giving to the poor, the poor being myself in this case."

"Uh huh, right," I said, and looked around. He was right, though, not about the Robin Hood thing but whoever he took this from had to be loaded. It had a black and red leather interior, a super-advanced sound system and all the modern luxuries including heated seats. It really was the most expensive car I had ever laid eyes on, let alone been in. Thanks to being raised by a teenage boy, I had somewhat of a thing for cars. The rumble of a muscle car's engine could get me going just as fast as any man could, so this, luxury or not, was truthfully like heaven on wheels.

"Oh, and just one thing," said Xavier as he shifted into gear.

"And what's that?"

"Hold on." He smiled that genuine smile and floored the vehicle. We flew down the highway at speeds well over the limit. I had to restrain the urge to tell him the signs on the road displaying the speed were limits, not challenges, like I had often told Damien, but I figured since Damien never listened, he wouldn't either. He attempted general conversation as we drove, if you could call it that. Talking about bits and pieces – nothing important, just things two strangers would talk about.

I tuned out mostly; I didn't want to be rude but my mind was on other things. Like how my brother could be dead right now, and I was sitting next to a vampire, but what I did manage to catch of what he said took me back to one of the first hunter lessons Dad made us sit through. We were young at the time, and something had happened that day that made Dad think we needed to learn about vampires. Dad's voice played out in my head, as clearly as if it was him sitting next to me, not my brother's vampire friend.

"Okay guys, now I know what I told you sounds glamorous to say the least, but vampires are just another creature, a hunter and a very good one. We are their prey, their weakness, their destroyer; we hold their lives in our hands. Now, vampires can be our best friend or worst enemy and are not to be trusted, no matter how nice they seem. There are two things that a hunter often underestimates. One is their fangs, they may be beautiful and alluring but they're deadly, an inbuilt weapon, and they

will not hesitate to use them. The second thing is their scent, it's like a pheromone a vampire can emit, it hypnotises you until you can no longer think for yourself, it's almost a weak form of compulsion, which some of the more powerful ones also have. A vampire may claim to be your friend, or be on your side, but I promise they will turn on you quicker than you can imagine, and if you ever have the displeasure to work with one keep a wary eye, because the moral to this story, kids, is: none of their kind can be trusted, and they are damned hard to kill." He sighed. *"Okay, on to something more relevant to our hunt: tomorrow we move on to werewolves."*

CHAPTER THREE

Xavier

I looked over at Misty for at least the millionth time since we had entered the car. I couldn't get over how beautiful she was. The picture Damien carried didn't do her justice at all. Her long, light brown hair was pulled back into a tight ponytail at the back of her head. It was perfect and so neat: there were only two strands of fringe, purposely left out, that framed her delicate but structured face. She was thinking back to something her father had told her when she was a kid. A lesson on vampires, if I wasn't mistaken. I could hear his voice in my mind as clearly as if he was saying it right now. Her blue-ish eyes were distant and there was a hint of a smile on her soft, alluring lips. I wanted to look away. I really did, but I couldn't. There was something about her, even in the way she smelled, that sucked me in. Dusky and powerful, like all hunters were.

I took a deep breath and I could almost taste it. I felt my fangs slide into place, and that snapped me out of it. No, what was I doing? I couldn't; she was Damien's sister and I have already been told that she was off-limits. Sex and blood often went together for my kind, so it was easy to get the signals crossed, have lust for one cause lust for the other. That couldn't happen, not now. I needed a distraction; what I needed to do was get her talking so I could fight the sudden attraction I felt toward her, get my mind out of the gutter.

"Misty," I said a little louder than was probably necessary. She snapped out of it with a small jump, looking to me. I couldn't help but smile at how cute she looked when she was startled. Her blue eyes looked dazed, and that faint hint of a happy smile still lingered on her plump, kissable lips. *Will you cut it out already!*

"Off in ya own world, huh?" I asked, kicking myself for sounding so stupid. I watched as those soft lips formed that cute smile and it nearly melted me.

"Kinda, I was thinking…" she said, then stopped. I already knew what she was thinking about. That was the advantage of being a mind reader, but now her mind was fuzzy. Her thoughts were only coming through as white noise. I puzzled for a second as I dug a little deeper, but I still got nothing. Hunter's minds were always hard to get a read on. I wasn't sure why; they just were. But eventfully, if I tried hard enough, I got something. With her I only got snippets, and they were totally out of my control no matter how hard I tried. It was true that some minds were harder to get a read on than others, so it wasn't exactly unexpected. After all, reading minds was harder than it sounded, you'd think I would have gotten the hang of it by now. It frustrated me a little bit, that my access to her mind was out of my control, but that's the way it worked. Damien had taught himself how to block me out because, unlike his sister's, his mind was incredibly easy to crack.

"What?" I asked, antsy because I didn't already know the question. "Did I do something?"

"Well," she said, looking away. I tried again; still nothing. *You have got to be kidding me!* I wanted her to say it already. Just spit it out. I hated not knowing. After a while you get used to knowing things before they are said and, really, it's how I manage to be charmingly articulate; unlike most people, I get planning time. In a normal situation I could use what people were thinking to get my own way. To manipulate the situation, but there was something about Misty that told me even if I could read her thoughts right now, she would make it difficult for me anyway. Of course, I already knew if she was anything like her brother, she would make it very difficult indeed.

"Maybe, did you use your scent on me to get me to come with you?" she asked. *That was it? That was all she was worried about?* I tried not to laugh. Personally, I would have been more worried about compulsion if I was her. That was much more dangerous. Although I didn't know how to compel people, yet, she didn't know that I couldn't, and should be at least wary.

"No!" I said, pretending to be insulted. "I would never." She stared deep into my eyes, as if she was trying to see if I was lying or not, even thought it was pretty evident that I was. "Okay, I did." I had to give in; I knew she wanted me to admit it so I'd play nice, for now.

"Why?' she questioned. I gave a slight laugh; she had to be kidding, right? I remembered the way she reacted when I tried to talk to her without it; she just looked at me like I was crazy and gave me Damien's number. It wasn't like I had a choice. She was really lucky I hadn't figured out how to use compulsion yet, and that's not from lack of trying, I assure you.

"Misty, I think you already know the answer to that," I said as I fixed her with a hard look. "Tell me, would you have listened to me if I hadn't?"

She looked away again. She knew I was right. I didn't need to be a mind reader to know that. Seriously, the girl had been thinking about ripping her mace out on me. Sure, I may be a vampire, but that shit still hurts.

"I never gave him the chance the first time and I wouldn't have again if he hadn't," she thought. The voice that invaded my mind was fuzzy, but it was still a thought. *There we go,* I thought as I tried to catch her gaze for a better read, but got nothing, I drew blanks, which only increased my frustration. She still didn't answer me. Well, not out loud, at least. I took a deep breath, trying not to let my temper get the better of me. But a sweet, alluring smell filled my lungs, and I had to stop. I had grown used to being around humans, but hunters are different. A hunter's blood always had a wildness to it, a distinctive smell that seemed sweeter than most. A familiar smell now, seeing

I had spent the last two years with her brother, but Misty was different. I wanted her blood more than I had ever wanted anyone's before, just for the fact it was hers. She smelled so good, and my willingness to not breathe for the duration of the car ride was testimony to exactly how badly I wanted it. There was something else that was mixed with that want. A want for her of a different kind. A feeling I hadn't let myself experience in many years, and I knew this was the reason I lusted for her blood. I lusted for her blood because I lusted for her. I wanted her, all of her. The way a man wanted a woman. I wanted those soft pink lips caressing mine; I wanted it so bad I could almost taste it. I wanted her toned shapely body intertwined with mine, pressing so close that the warmth from her skin would be agony.

Everything about her was driving me insane with lust: the way her black work shirt hugged her curves, giving a look at what to expect but leaving you longing for more. Or how her slacks hugged the curve of her butt; the thought of that made me ache in a slightly embarrassing kind of way. The creaminess of her naturally tanned skin. The light blue of her alluring eyes. Everything about her called to me, making it so much worse. *Look away,* I warned myself. It was all I could do not to act on those desires. I couldn't think like that. I couldn't get emotionally or physically attached, and I knew it. It was so bad I could almost hear Damien's voice in my head, calling me a chick and telling me I really needed to get laid – on the condition it wasn't with his sister, of course.

It was alright for him. I couldn't use a human like an object like he could, or like I could when I was one of them. There were bigger things at stake now. Worse hungers I have no control over and I wouldn't let myself hurt Misty just to fulfil some selfish need. I felt the anger and disappointment well up inside me. No matter if it killed me I would keep focused on the job at hand, not anything else involving those words.

"That's what I thought," I snapped, turning my disappointment outwards. My outburst was partly due to her lack of response, and partly at myself for getting too carried away. Before she had a chance to speak, and before I had a chance to do something I probably would regret, I got out of the car, slamming the door behind me.

Misty

Can vampires read minds? Dad never covered that in training, I thought as I opened the door and got out of the car. Xavier's sudden mood swing shocked me. It made me wonder if it was the way I had acted toward him that brought it on. I looked around as I closed the door. We were at an old house. Somewhere far out of town. In the middle of nowhere, really. It was light out, early morning at best guess. I hadn't really kept track of how long we were driving. This place had an eerie feel to it, and I couldn't help but feel like I was being watched. Xavier stood at the door of the old rundown house.

The place looked like it should be condemned and no one, no matter how undead and invincible, should be anywhere near it. The roof was old rusted tin filled with holes, and in some places there were entire sheets of tin missing. The deck that Xavier was standing on looked rotten. The boards were cracked and broken, and I was convinced the whole thing was going to give out any second. The three wooden stairs barely looked like stairs anymore and all the windows that I could see were badly boarded up, because they had been smashed. To the side of the house was a long drive that seemed to sink into the ground as it wound behind the house.

The only thing that struck me as odd about the whole place was the yard. Sure, it was overgrown but it wasn't what you would expect, seeing the rest of the house. It almost seemed like it was purposefully messy, staged somehow. It just didn't have that wild feeling to it. In fact, the whole place seemed like a setup, like it was too rundown. I wondered why anyone would want to stay here and figured that this was their so-called base of commands. Really, if it was, I was going to be so mad at Damien for not coming home, because this place made our house look like a mansion. I couldn't see why anyone would even want to look at this place, let alone live in it; it was like an old haunted house. Xavier didn't walk with care as he walked to the door. I half expected him to fall through the deck at any second and, seeing the mood he was in, I couldn't say he wouldn't have deserved it. He shifted from foot to foot, fixing me with annoyed looks of impatience.

"Will you get up here?" His voice had a kinda irritated tone to it and his stare was ice-cold. The combination snapped me out of my head for a second. The coldness of his voice sent shivers down my spine and wondered if I should regret trusting him so easily, but even now I couldn't help but feel like there was something I trusted. Something that, no matter how hard I tried, I would always drop my guard for. Even if I couldn't put my finger on what it was. I walked up the poor excuse for a staircase slowly and carefully. I made my way across the death trap that passed for a porch, to stand just by the railing. I wasn't really game enough to go much further; there was no way this thing would hold the both of us. I kept my distance, not just because I didn't trust the deck. He looked me up and down and I saw a strange look in his eyes. It disappeared as quickly as it came, and even though I only got a glimpse of it, I didn't like it one little bit. To my kinda relief it was quickly replaced by annoyance, which was better than whatever the hell that was; annoyance I could deal with.

"Will you come here? That's if you want to go inside sometime today?" I walked a little closer. *A matter of fact I don't, I would much rather stand out here!* I thought. He fixed me with a glare that could kill, as if he heard what I was thinking, and pointed to the spot next to him on the welcome mat. "I don't bite," he said, his voice filled with as much venom as his look, but it quickly faded when he realised what he said. A small teasing smile tugged at his lips and his voice came out light and playful: "Well, I do, but I'm not hungry." I tried not to laugh; this guy's mood swings were driving me insane. I was really lost as to where I stood with the guy. One second he seemed pissed off at me, the next he was fine; I didn't know how much more of it I could take. *For Damien* I said to myself as I stood next to him. I allowed myself a small laugh at his joke, but it was more of a nervous laugh than anything.

He pulled the door handle down, which I thought was a bad idea. The door looked like it was barely standing, but instead of pushing open the door like I expected, the door handle glowed and a numeric lock slid out of the side of the doorframe. He punched in a seven-digit code that I didn't really catch and grabbed hold of my hand. I tried to pull it from his grip and contemplated yelling at him until I felt the mat shudder beneath me; I suddenly didn't want to anymore. The mat we were standing on started to descend. I felt my balance fail and I nearly fell. Xavier yanked on my hand as I felt myself fall backward into the nothingness behind me. He placed a hand on my shoulder, steadying me so I wouldn't fall again. It was like we were in an empty room; I could feel the largeness of the space around us but couldn't see a damned thing. The one scrap of light from above disappeared as the hole where the mat used to be closed over, leaving us in complete darkness. I felt his arm go from my shoulder to around my waist and pull me into him, so close that I could feel the hardness of his muscles and the coolness of his skin through our clothes. *God, doesn't this guy understand the concept of personal space?* I thought as a rail rose up in front of us and the platform beneath us changed.

I struggled in his grip but he was too strong for me to get loose, which should have been no surprise. He guided my hand to the rail and kept it in place with his own. His grip was so firm it kinda hurt.

"Hold on," he whispered in my ear. I felt his lips brush the curve of my ear as he leant in and I felt his warm breath against my neck as his face lingered close to it. *Okay not good,* I thought as the feeling of panic rose up in my chest. He straightened up as the platform started to move, which happened not a moment too soon. Having a vampire that close to your carotid artery isn't a great feeling. The platform picked up speed as it dropped, getting faster and faster as it went down. I caught glimpses of shapes whizzing past in the darkness, but none of them were clear enough to make out. I latched on to Xavier with my free hand, wound my free arm around his waist and held on for dear life, more frightened of the fall than his fangs. I felt his grip around my waist tighten in response to my action and pull me in closer to him, which, frankly, I didn't think was possible.

"Misty," he said suddenly. His voice made me jump; I guess between the terror and the fearing for my life, I hadn't expected him to speak. "When we stop we have to get a move on; it's really not safe for a human to enter a coven, especially a hunter, so whatever you do, do not stray from my side and you'll be okay."

I nodded, not really grasping what he said. *Wait! What?* We were at the coven; a place filled to the brim with evil night-stalking creatures that want nothing more than to tear me open and drink me to death. Okay, I know that sounded stupid, but essentially that's how they killed. Well, maybe I was being a little judgemental; after all, Xavier was weird but he hadn't yet given me the impression he would hurt me, so maybe I was safe, although he did say himself it wasn't. A small cry escaped my lips as I contemplated my impending doom and buried my head into Xavier's chest, too afraid to even look. The platform stopped falling and I took a deep breath.

I let go and opened my eyes. We were still in complete darkness. Xavier must have felt me let go of him, so he pulled me in closer. Suddenly the platform dropped out from beneath us. In a moment of shock I latched on to him once again, tighter this time, and screamed my lungs out as we fell into the darkness. I kept my eyes clamped nice and shut; there was no way I was watching this. His body jarred and I heard him grunt as we hit the ground, and I was practically in his arms by this point. Finally, it seemed we had stopped falling, but still I didn't let go. There was no way I was trusting that thing again; I knew any second we would fall further into the darkness. He set me to the ground and his grip softened; his free hand that had hold of my mine was now stroking my hair softly. I wanted to say something to him for that, but I was way too busy bracing myself.

"Misty," he said. His voice and touch had a gentleness to it that made me feel all tingly inside. "Although I like your embrace, I must tell you it's over, we're here."

I opened my eyes and lifted my head. People were staring at me with a strange look in their eyes. *Oh my god!* Realising he still hadn't let go, I shoved him away from me with an annoyed huff. A playful smile hinted at his lips as he looked around, obviously pleased with himself.

"She's new," Xavier explained casually. The people who were watching us didn't look the least bit convinced, but they keep on with what they were doing anyway, much to my relief. Suddenly feeling uncomfortable, I straightened myself up and glared at Xavier, who just laughed.

"Follow me," he said, a hint of laughter still on his voice as he stepped off the platform. He led me through what looked like an underground mansion. This place made the place above us look even worse, even though I was sure that wasn't possible, but it did. Or maybe the place above made this place look even better in comparison; either way, it was amazing. I would go as far as calling it breathtaking. Everything was so old, so elegant and so not me, yet I loved every inch of it that I could see. The walls were high and they had those elegant mouldings you see in really fancy old buildings, near the roof. The carpets were soft, incredibly soft, softer than I could have ever imagined carpet to be, and blood-red, making the white on the walls almost glow in comparison. The trimmings were gold, and a slight red smudge on one near the floor made me think that maybe they had chosen the carpet colour for a reason. Paintings of people and places that looked like something straight from the Louvre hung around decorating the spaces. The main hall split off into a number of different corridors, all seemingly endless. *This place must be huge.*

Xavier must have noticed my eyes darting around like crazy, because he said, "Breathtaking, isn't it?" I looked to him to see him looking around himself. "It still overwhelms me, even though I've been here so many times," I looked at him; what he last said sparked so many questions in my head, I wanted nothing more than to bombard him with them, but before I even got the chance to start, he placed a hand on the small of my back and led me toward the middle corridor.

"Come Misty, this way," he said, walking off. I followed, still trying to take everything in. He broke off to the left into a smaller corridor. This one had lines of doors and kinda reminded me of an apartment building, or maybe a five-star hotel. We stopped at a door right near the end. The doors were spaced further apart at this end of the hall, and the key locks I had been noticing on nearly all the doors were replaced with pin code and finger-scan locks. He typed in a code on the key pad next to the door we were standing at. I'm not really sure why but I held my breath, waiting for it to unlock. The key pad beeped, the door clicked and I exhaled. Xavier turned the door knob and pushed it open. He motioned for me to enter with a sweeping gesture so I did, as I couldn't really see the sense in not.

I looked around as I slowly strolled in. The room, which was more like an apartment, was just as amazing (if not more amazing) than what I had already seen. The walls were a light grey in colour, and the plush carpet a royal blue. We walked right into what I would call the living room. There was a big plush leather couch that sat between matching armchairs, and a huge flat-screen TV sat on a black wooden cupboard, with two huge stand-up speakers on either side. The TV was hooked up to a PlayStation, and two controllers lay next to a stack of games and magazines messily chucked on the coffee table. I noticed a few discarded weapons and beer cans on the floor by the couch, and a few pairs of shoes kicked off by the wall. There were a few rooms that led off of this one, but overall, the place had a very bachelor pad kinda feel, a very high-end bachelor pad. When I looked around this place I could see why Damien didn't come home often, and despite the overall guyishness of it I couldn't really blame him. This place was way nicer than our house and I found myself thinking, *can I move in?*

"Ah, sorry about the mess, I didn't really plan on having company," he said, walking over to the couch to kick the beer cans out of sight before sighing and gesturing around the room. "Nevertheless, welcome to my little patch of paradise. Make yourself at home. There is a TV, Wii, Playstation 2 and 3, and Xbox, everything you could ever want,"

I looked at him as he tidied up, and smiled. *Yeah, sure, if you were hyped on testosterone or sixteen; do vampires even* play *video games?* I thought, rolling my eyes. He laughed as he placed the knife he had just picked up on top of the stack of games, then tucked his hands into his pockets and shrugged. "Hey, I am still a guy, you know; of course I like video games." I looked at him again, shocked; *he can read my mind*! "and yes that does answer one of your earlier questions." I stopped and stared at him for a second, wondering what else he is going to answer without me even having to ask. "Okay, well," he said, looking at his watch, "we have to leave again soon, so we should get some rest. Ah, the bed's in there, and that's the bathroom. Like I said before, feel free to make ya self at home and I'll find you some fresh clothes," and with that he left the room.

I walked toward the couch, running my hand along the cold, smooth surface while looking around trying to get a better feel for this place. I was starting to get the feeling I had gotten the wrong impression of this guy. Xavier walked back in, holding a silk nightdress. I raised an eyebrow at him, wondering what he had a silk nightdress in his room for, but decided not to ask.

He handed it to me then left again, almost like he couldn't wait to get away from me.

I found the bathroom and freshened up a bit before changing and walking toward the room he had pointed out for me. This room was really neat and hardly used; I guessed maybe it was the guest bedroom. The bed was huge and the whole thing was black, sheets, pillows, doona … I was kinda tempted to check the mattress, but decided that was just silly. I climbed into the bed and snuggled down. I nearly moaned as I wrapped the sheets around me; they felt so good. I let myself bask in them for a second; they had this expensive feel to them, so soft and nice, the kind of luxury I could never afford. The bedroom itself was smaller than the lounge but it was cosy, making it easy to fall asleep, which after the night I just had was exactly what I needed.

CHAPTER FOUR

After what only felt like a matter of minutes, I found myself slowly waking. My body spread out in the middle of the huge bed. I sat up and felt amazing. I had never slept that well in my life and for a second I wondered if I was actually dead, because surely this was what heaven felt like. But then I remembered and, with a sigh, fell backwards. I laid there for a few more seconds, not ever wanting to get up, then Xavier entered the room in nothing more than a towel.

My breath caught in my throat as he bent over to rifle through the dresser at the side of the room. I tried to stay silent. He hadn't seemed to notice I was awake, and I really didn't want to spoil the show. *Oh my god, this guy is really perfect, it must come with the whole vampire thing, because damn!* Small droplets of water followed the curves of his muscles as he straightened up looking at a tee shirt he had hold of, while his other hand held the towel in place. My eyes darted to the tattoo on the back of his shoulder. It was identical to the one Damien had, same place and everything. I knew it had some kind of hunter meaning, but be damned if I could think of what it was.

Wow! I saw every muscle tense with surprise as he realised I was awake. He spun around to look at me. I had been quite content looking at his naked torso from behind, but seeing the front didn't disappoint. A smooth sculpted chest ran down into rock-hard abs, every long lean muscle was exposed and each was better than the last. Butterflies fluttered around in my tummy, and here I was thinking he looked good with his clothes on!

"Oh," he said, pulling the towel tighter around him and smiled nervously. He seemed to be in a much better mood this morning. "Afternoon, sleep well?" I could feel the tension and surprise rolling off of him and I would be lying if I said I didn't enjoy it, just a little.

"I did, thank you," I replied, trying to repress the sigh as my mind ran wild. His smile widened and I was kinda surprised to see he had his fangs extended. Dad was right. In a weird kind of way they were alluring, and they really did look natural in his mouth enhancing his already perfect smile; it was almost like he should have been born with them. His tongue brushed against one and they retracted like he had only just realised they were extended.

"My apologies, I'm usually good at controlling that," he said, looking almost embarrassed. "Um, oh yeah, I got you something" he said, quickly leaving the room. "Now, don't get ya hopes up, you need these, but it still was quite a challenge getting something you would actually wear," his voice sounded from somewhere in the apartment. He walked back in fully dressed this time (much to my dismay). He was wearing a pair of dark denim jeans and a tight white tank top. He smiled as he sat a set of clothes on the bed, then turned to grab what he was fishing for from the drawer and walked back out.

I dragged myself out of bed and managed to dress, even while my mind still wandered. There was no way you could expect a girl to be able to concentrate on anything after seeing that. I let my little fantasies have free roam as I walked through the apartment back to the central living area, which (might I add) was in pristine condition this time. I sat on the plush leather couch and rubbed my bare feet on the carpet and sighed. *I'm in love; I could sleep on this carpet.* I thought as I squished it between my toes. Like everything else around here the carpet was amazing; I knew this kind of carpet didn't last long before it became matted and run down, so either they spent little time here or it was replaced often. Xavier walked out of another room, buttoning up a white shirt and then slipping a black coat over it. He ruffled his wet hair with the towel, somehow making it sit perfectly. A small confident smile crossed his lips when he noticed that I was starting, Okay, *screw the carpet, that I could go down on any day*. He raised an eyebrow at me and I watched as his gaze run down my body. I couldn't help but shy away from him; it was stupid, I know, but I felt myself blush as I realised he had heard that. Xavier gave a quirk of his lip that was accompanied by a small shrug as he walked toward me and took a seat on the couch next to me. *Note to self: I really have to control my mental outbursts.* He laughed, then nodded, and I wanted to die; I couldn't believe he had heard that.

"Yeah, maybe a good idea."

"Oh my god, I'm sorry," I said, burying my head in my hands.

"No, it's fine; I actually think it might lighten what I have to tell you next."

"What is it?" My whole body froze, thinking the worst; hunters very rarely delivered good news.

"Last night," he paused to correct himself, "this morning rather, after you went to bed, I did some digging. Vampires are great sources of information if you know where to look and I found out a few things." He stopped and gave a humourless laugh. "Now I wish you were the one who could read minds." It was clear he didn't like what he had found out and that meant I would like it even less but I had to hear it, I needed to.

"Why? What's wrong?" My voice was soft and each word felt like a knife as I held back my tears. Panic rolled through me in waves as I sat for what felt like forever waiting for him to continue, but he just sat there not looking at me. "Tell me, Xavier, he's dead, isn't he?" My words were like razor blades cutting deeper than I thought a word could. I feared the worst, and if it was true I needed to hear it. Until that moment I hadn't realised that I might never see my brother again, but the whole time I knew that it was a real possibility. In this business it was stupid not to realise that and of course it was Damien we were talking about; he had enemies and he was really good at what he did and things like that didn't go unnoticed in our world. The thing that scared me the most was the fact that I already knew that, I already knew my brother was a dead man walking, hell, we all are. Xavier placed a hand on my knee, to calm me I guess, but it didn't work.

"No, Misty, as far as I know he's not…" he started. I knew there was a but coming, there always is. "But I know he's being held captive, most people were pretty tight-lipped about it despite my persuasions." His voice had a deadly edge to it on the word "persuasions" and I knew without really knowing that if Xavier wanted you to tell him something you were going to tell him, one way or another; he just struck me as that kinda guy. "The fact that he's still alive means something," he continued. I missed most of the rest of what he said but I think I got the important parts: Damien was alive.

"Captive….?" I couldn't form a sentence. My mind was whirling; how could I not have been worried about this? How?

"Misty, look at me, look," he said, grabbing my chin to turn my head to face him when I refused. I was wrong. I didn't want to hear this. I couldn't but I was frozen with shock; my poor brother. "I don't know much, but I do know Damien, he's strong and resourceful, it would take one hell of a creature to get a jump on him, if anyone can handle it, it would be Damien."

Captured and held alive? I wasn't stupid; I knew how it worked. He would stay that way until his usefulness ran out, but what could they have possibly wanted from him? What would he have that could have possibly warranted this? And, worst of all, I couldn't save him; there was absolutely nothing I could do. It all kinda overwhelmed me; I felt tears stinging my eyes. *This can't be happening, he's all I have left, I can't lose him, I just can't!* I tried to hold it together. I didn't need a stranger to see me break down. I am a West; I have a duty to be strong no matter what. I felt a tear roll down my cheek. I turned my head to hide it.

Softly, Xavier reached up, grabbing my chin, and gently turned my face back toward him. His palm was cool against my cheek and his gaze was gentle and sweet. He gave me an "everything's alright" smile and I found myself pressing my face harder to his palm, reaching to place my own over his. He wiped away the tear with his thumb.

"Never be ashamed of your tears," he said, wiping another away. "You may not have them forever." I sniffed back more; everything about him suddenly seemed so safe and warm. His gentle touch, his sweet soft smile, the way I knew he feared the worst but was putting that aside to reassure me, and knowing that only made it worse. I'm not used to that; why would he care what I felt? It must be hard for him too. Tears spilled from my eyes and I looked away, turning my face to the roof. In the light of probably losing his hunting partner, his best friend, he cared about me. Before I realised what he was doing, he pulled me into his arms to comfort me. I hated that he felt that I needed holding like some sobbing child, but truthfully, it was exactly what I needed. I pressed my face against his chest. My hands were ready to push him away but they never found the strength. I couldn't hold back what I was feeling any longer and I started to sob, ranting incomprehensible gibberish, as I thought through this whole situation again.

"Shhh," he soothed his voice wrapped around me like a warm blanket. How I loved the sound of it. "Come on, it'll be alright; I'll find him, I promise."

"I knew this would happen," I sobbed, my words finally sounding English. "I warned him, you know, I told him it would!"

"Misty…" he started but stopped. I looked up at him, mentally scolding myself for thinking how amazing he looked from this angle with everything else that was going on. Our eyes met as he looked down at me and suddenly everything felt alright. The emerald of his eyes entranced me and his gaze seemed to be staring deep into my soul, soothing me from within. He tilted his face slightly; a look of frustration crossed it before he sighed and gave me a warm smile.

"You have amazing eyes," he said, not looking away, like he had forgotten what he was meant to be saying. I felt myself blush as he pulled away, putting distance between us. I watched as he shifted uncomfortably in his seat.

"I'm sorry," I said, not really sure what I was apologizing for; at the time I just felt I should. I felt so stupid for breaking down on him, but it wasn't irrational. "I don't normally break down like this, but it all just –" I stopped, not knowing how to put it.

"Missy, its okay, you don't have to explain yourself to me, I understand," he said, his voice soothing, but this time he didn't look at me. A twinge of pain shot through my chest at the sound of the pet name but it made me smile; I hadn't been called Missy since last time I saw my brother…

"Sorry about the jacket," I said with a light laugh, looking at the smudge from my makeup.

"Well, really, it's my shirt that got most of it." He laughed, getting to his feet and pulling off the jacket. "But that's okay; I do have others. I'm just glad to have helped you feel better; you are feeling better right? Because I won't change it if you still need a shoulder to cry on," he said, giving a slight laugh before slipping it off and chucking it to the floor. He walked from the room.

I looked down at the shirt. It had a black smudge from what was left of my make up on it. I did it to distract myself; he still hadn't really told me what was going on. What was his plan to save Damien? Did he even have one? I sighed, still on the edge of tears thinking about it. I did my best to focus my attention elsewhere, but really, that only left one thing to focus on.

"Although," called Xavier from the other room, "that was my last white one."

I smiled. *Wow, this guy is too good to be true. I can't believe how sweet he is, and talk about hot!* I thought, not proud of where my thought landed.

"I thought we agreed on controlling our thoughts?" he said walking back into the room with a smartass smile on his handsome face; he loved it and I just wished I could control it. *Smart ass,* I thought, knowing he would hear. He laughed as he walked over; the small glimpse of midriff I caught as he pulled down a grey tee shirt sent chills down my spine. I really wished he would refrain from removing clothing in front of me, especially since I was trying to be on good behaviour.

I looked at the shirt. It looked familiar; my eyes glanced to the printing on it. It had a printed name tag with Mr Right handwritten inside and underneath it said "I've heard you've been looking for me." I laughed; I had seen this tee shirt before. "Nice shirt," I said, giving him the once-over. It was a little too big for him and I knew as soon as his smile faltered who had given it to him. He opened his mouth to say something but stopped mumbling. "Not mine, it's Damien's."

"Oh," I said feeling the dread from before washing over me. So much for my flirty little distraction. "Damien did always have a thing for slogan tees."

"Okay," he said, dropping to the couch next to me. His eyes were closed and I could see the torn expression on his face. Panic shot through me again; he did know something, I knew it! "I can't put it off any longer; I have to tell you the truth." I could feel the colour drain from my face. *No, no, no this is not good, please don't tell me!*

"What is it?" I said, seeing his hesitant expression; as much as I knew it was going to suck, I needed to know.

"I know a little more than I've let on but…" his voice trailed off. "Well, the thing is, I might know what we're up against but…" He stopped again. *Get to the damn point, man!* He nodded and grabbed my hands, which were linked in my lap playing with my fingers. I could see his mind working and I knew he was considering not telling me. He stared down at our hands as he rubbed his fingers along mine. "Why is this so hard?" he said softly, and I got the impression that was more to himself than to me. With a small sigh he looked up at me. "I want to tell you and I don't blame you at all, but I know it'll hurt you, knowing this kind of information doesn't do anyone any good if you can't handle it, and I don't want to hurt you," he said with a humourless laugh.

He looked away again and this time he didn't look up as he continued. I could see this isn't easy for him either, but he had to trust I could handle it, even though I wasn't sure I could. "There's this group of, well, let's say people, who have a price put on the capture of hunters, human and supernatural people alike and, needless to say, they are pretty high on everybody's take list at the moment. Unfortunately they seem to have a list of their own and there is big, big money for the capture of anyone one on it. A few hunters Damien and I ran into a few months back seemed to be on their trail, but within a matter of days following the trail, they disappeared without a trace. There have been rumours about who's on this list and those rumours said that Damien and yours truly were at the top. Personally, that didn't faze me, I mean you're not doing your job right if someone isn't out to kill you, but Damien didn't quite feel the same way. I tried to stop him, but you know how he is; I told him a thousand times that they would come for us, it was stupid to walk right into their arms. Of course Damien has to be the hero so he dug into it, he thought I didn't know exactly what he was doing and I did everything I could to get there first before something bad happened but I drew blanks, turns out you only find out what they let you find out and he found out something first, something big, but he wouldn't tell me. Just before he disappeared he told Alex everything, and days later he was gone too."

He looked up; his once-amazing green eyes seemed somehow lighter. He let go of my hands. "I think that's how they work and lately I've been hearing things, just snippets but enough to know that if history is anything to go on I'm next, and if they can get to me before I can get to Damien, they'll disappear again and there will be no chance of getting him back alive."

I winced on his last word.

"And that's why you need me, in case that happens?" I said, feeling lightheaded.

He nodded. "I'm sorry I have to drag you into this and I really don't want to put you into that kind of danger, but like I said, they have a list, when word gets out you're hunting again you'll be on it and sooner or later…" He didn't finish his sentence but he didn't have to; I knew what he was going to say next. *They'll come for one of us!* I jumped to my feet, my heart racing. I hated the thought of them playing with us like that, using a hunter's need to help people to make them walk right into their trap. Xavier knew this was coming and still he couldn't stop it, and he didn't seem to be the kind of guy who's stopped easy. So I stood no chance, I knew that, but together, maybe, if we stay one step ahead of them we can get there first, and all we could do is pray that they don't see it coming. I felt myself start to panic, but in a weird kinda way I felt pumped, until I started hyperventilating. That was hell; even hunters can have panic attacks.

"Well, we have to go now! We have no time to waste; we have to get there first, we have to find him!" He was on his feet in a blink of an eye and he didn't seem quite as eager I was to get going. He grabbed my shoulders to steady me, which was a good thing; I was starting to feel really lightheaded. I did this from time to time, got worked up and before long I couldn't tell which way was up or which way was down and it normally ended in the same way. Right now I was at the emotional stage; part of me wanted to save my brother and part of me wanted to save myself, another part didn't want to put Xavier in danger but then again, it was better him than me, right? I felt guilty, mad, sad and just plain overwhelmed, and collapsed in a hysterical heap.

"Misty, relax, I can hear your pulse; you need to calm down." He pulled me into his arms before I had a chance to hit the floor. I fought him, I rambled and I cried, but the lightheaded feeling just got worse.

"Let me go! I'm fine!" I screamed into his chest, but he ignored me. I could feel his cold skin through Damien's tee shirt.

His voice soothed me as he refused and told me once again to calm down. I felt the rise and fall of his chest quicken as he held me, stopping me from struggling. My fists pounded his back as I thought of Damien, but he hardly flinched.

"Are you okay?" he asked, his whisper sounding as if it was far off in the distance. I knew what was coming and I wouldn't really call myself a fainter but there were only so many emotions one girl could process at once. "Misty," his voice whispered. I tried to focus my eyes on him, feeling a wave of dizziness wash over me. My vision slowly faded and the faint sound of Xavier calling my name was all I heard as the darkness consumed me, and then nothing.

CHAPTER FIVE

Xavier

'Misty?" I said as she went limp in my arms. "Misty?" She had passed out; at least I hope that was all it was. Damien would kill me if I killed his sister before we even had a chance to save him. I picked her up, gently lifting her fully into my arms to carry her over to the bed. That was not the reaction I was expecting. Sure, I figured there would be some fear, maybe even anger or sorrow, but I hadn't expected that. She had them all rolled into one and it told me nothing more than I already knew: she was one complicated woman. I checked her pulse and looked to the door. *There must be someone who knew something about medicine in the coven.* Weighing my options, I quickly decided that I should get her checked. Locking the door behind me, I walked out into the main hall.

"Coven meeting now!" I yelled, bashing on a few doors as I made my way down the hall toward the centre of the coven where the stage was located. I knew it wouldn't take long for news to travel; in covens, news travelled fast. It isn't uncommon for vampires to have human mistresses or un-coven supplied donors but anyone who knew me knew it was strange for me to have a human "pet," but that being said, it's not quite as strange as me calling a coven meeting, so I hoped one would outweigh the other. Normally I ignored the rest of the coven and frankly, they liked it that way. I'm not what you would call a treasured member of the community, but I was next in line to be their leader so they would listen when I told them to. By the time

I made it to the hall, it was nearly full and I figured that there would be enough members here to find me what I needed.

Vladimir the coven leader grabbed my arm as I went to walk out onto the stage. His grip stopped me in my place. Vladimir is quite a bit older than me and much, much stronger. I knew I would lose my arm before I broke his grip and frankly it pissed me off a little; I don't like being over powered. Vladimir was powerful among our kind, feared and hated; he was so much more than just a coven leader. Rumours say that he was among the first to be created, but of course he will never verify a thing. Not only that, but the guy was kinda creepy as well. I'm talking about full-blown Bram Stoker *Dracula* here. I mean it, the dude just screams vampire. Okay so maybe the views of a stereotypical vampire may have changed a little in the last decade, but I still think most people would see it. Sure, he doesn't wear a cape, and no, he does not sparkle! But he does have the accent, although I think his may be Romanian or something. He always wears his black hair short and slicked back and his eyes are red, the exact colour of blood, but he is the only real vampire I have ever seen like it. Vladimir is a good way shorter than me and in physical appearance older too, late thirties I'd guess if I had to put a rough number to it. He had been coven leader for about four hundred years, I'm told, and was widely feared and respected, neither of which he got from me.

"What do you think you are doing, Xavier?" he snapped. I tried unsuccessfully to yank my arm from his grip and glared at him until he let go. I stepped away from him just in case.

"Don't you dare touch me again," I growled, trying to sound as threatening as possible, but there was a fat lot I could do if he did, other than rip my own limbs off, which is not as fun as it sounds.

"We are sick of your games, Xavier, you do nothing but use us, for protection, for shelter or for money, is this what I am to expect for my coven?" he asked. I had to resist the urge to mimic him, which was really, really immature but you haven't heard this guy's accent; it's hilarious.

"Well, that is all you are good for," I replied coldly, being the ever-mature man I am.

"We are good to you, we house your many cars, we shelter hunters, we even overlook your unnatural obsession with hunting, and you do nothing in return. I pray that one day you will buck up your ideas, hopefully before you take over, but I am unhopeful, so please tell me you have a constructive reason for calling a meeting without coming to me first,."

Huh, it actually hadn't occurred to me to try him first; he was coven leader, after all. Really, it would have been much simpler and a lot less trouble, but then of course that would have involved me having to go see him, something I tried to avoid doing, seeing how I wanted to stake the guy and really I couldn't care less if I caused him any amount of trouble.

"No, I just wanted to say hi," I said with a bright but extremely fake smile. He shook his head.

"Then I will call it off; remember I overpower you, Xavier, and I know there aren't many that can in rank or at all but I do," he reminded me in an almost cocky tone. And he wondered why I hated him.

"I'm sorry, Vladimir, but you just don't scare me and I have authority issues so I'm calling this meeting," I said.

"What is it you need, money, blood, an army?" he asked. I knew this was his way to try and bribe me into going away, and normally it worked but not today. Wait! *He would give me an army?* I snapped myself out of it; as cool as that would be I had more important things to worry about.

"A doctor," I said, finally pushing away the temptation of my own personal army. His bewildered expression told me he was listening.

"That may be so, but what do you need from the coven?" he said, a smile hinted on his lips. I laughed; there may be some life in the old boy yet.

"Very funny, Vlad, but I have a human mistress who needs medical attention," I lied. I couldn't very well tell him she was a hunter, could I?

"Human, I doubt she's your mistress; even lunch is too big of a stretch for you," he said in his judgey tone. *Stupid judgemental old bastard!*

"Are you calling me a liar?" I growled. He shook his head and sighed as if it was too much of an effort to indulge me.

"Of course not, Xavier, I was just working from character. It's unlike you, that's all." This time I shook my head. He didn't know how wrong he was; I would kill to have this girl as a mistress, but of course that would get me killed in the process and I couldn't bear to hurt her, even as much as I wanted to.

"People change, Vladimir; I'm not the patient saint of vampires I'm known to be."

A smile crossed his lips. "No, Xavier, that much I am sure is true. I will get you your doctor, and pray that one day you come around," he said in a defeated tone.

"Be careful; you might burst into flames if you do that too often," I joked, but it fell flat as he didn't even crack a smile.

"Then I will hope, my brother."

"Yeah, doubt it, but you can keep hoping and I'll keep not caring and we'll see where that takes us." I said. He looked at me and shook his head one last time before walking out onto the stage. I followed after him, which felt weird. Truthfully, I felt uneasy standing there looking over the hundreds of vampires gathered. I'm not shy by any meaning of the word but I knew their general opinion of me, and I couldn't really blame them for feeling that way. Some I know enough to consider friends if I had no other option, some I've just hunted, there were even some I wanted to hunt right now but I had no time for that at the moment; there were more pressing matters. I took Vladimir's side, standing tall as hundreds of thoughts flooded my mind, and did my best to look unaffected. I have, after many years of practice, learned how to sort and process many thoughts at once.

The main theme of the thoughts I came across was that Vlad was stepping down, which would explain my presence, and a few were already working through their plan to stage dominance, which is basically a fight to the death for the right of power. Vampire tradition, and they wonder why I refuse to step up. I looked around. One thing I knew for sure was I could never lead this, but I wasn't above abusing the power that came with it. After a short full-of-shit speech Vlad made up, which seemed legit enough, he finally found someone with medical training, a medic from the civil war times. A young bratty-looking boy who barely looked old enough for puberty let alone old enough to be a war vet, not exactly my ideal choice but it was the best I could do without rushing her to a hospital, an option I had also neglected to think of until right now.

I led him back to my room, barely saying a word to the guy. He emanated arrogance and the few things I was actually listening to only made me dislike him more than I already did. Don't get me wrong; I on occasion had been accused of being arrogant myself, but this guy was a total dick.

"So, Lord Xavier, you've turned to the dark side, sick of the bitter taste of animal blood," he said with a smirk.

"I don't believe I called you in for idle chitchat, and unlike others I would never," I said as I led him into the room.

"Well, then, she must be your toy, everyone get an itch or two, sir, it's understandable, humans do seem to enjoy it more." We stopped beside the bed and he looked her over. "But not all of us are this lucky. She is quite a looker, sir, and she smells so good, spicy but sweet. I bet she tastes great," he said in a tone I really didn't like. I growled as his thoughts invaded my mind, so vile, so violent, so like my own that I think jealousy was playing a big part in what was pissing me off about them. I wanted to kill him for even thinking such things; this was Damien's sister Misty, I could never treat her like that. Of course I have no claim over her but the thought of him touching her, of anyone other than myself, sparked a fire within me that I'm not sure I could control.

"No, she is not my toy, she is nothing more than a friend," I growled through gritted teeth. All my rage crammed into those few words. I had no right to get upset, yet the more I heard the worse it got. *Just relax, he won't touch her while you're here, it's too dangerous and he knows it, killing him will solve nothing.*

"Whatever helps you sleep at night, my lord," he mumbled, leaning over her body. *But it would make me feel so much better!*

Misty

"I swear, you even think about putting your lips anywhere on this girl, I'll kill you myself," I heard Xavier growl. His voice was getting louder with every word.

"Never, my lord; do I look stupid enough to touch something that belongs to you? I do quite enjoy living here, well, living at all." Xavier growled, I mean really growled, and the other voice sighed. "I don't see your fascination with humans, they're only good for two things, if you want to dispose of this one I'll…" I heard Xavier growl again but this time it was followed by the slide of a chair and a loud crash.

"How dare you!" Xavier cried. His voice was deep and shaky. The sound of snarling made me sit up. I looked around to see what was going on. My gaze fell on Xavier leaning over another man. His irises flicked like emerald and black flame, and I knew for sure this time I wasn't seeing things. His face was vicious as he pinned the man to the ground in a way that would normally choke someone. His voice came out as a growl through extended fangs. "You speak of her as if she is an object, useless, unwanted; I am appalled by the amount of disrespect you have shown! As your leader it's my job to tell you that she is a guest of our coven, and will be treated as such. But as her friend I'm telling you, you so much as take another breath or even think about making one little sound in the next three seconds, I will tear you to fucking shreds without so much as a second thought. Understand me?" he yelled, his voice still little more than a growl. The threat was followed with a blow that forced the other man so hard into the floor, the tiles beneath him smashed.

"Yes, sir," the man said. His eyes were grey and his boyish face was ripe with fear. Xavier's eyes darted across the man's face. The flickering in his irises stopped and his face relaxed a little. Seemingly happy with the other man's response, he loosened his grip on the guy's throat, just enough for him to turn his head at the sound of my gasp. Their eyes focused on me, both filling with relief, likely for different reasons I was sure.

"Get," growled Xavier, putting more menace and authority into that one little word than I could in a whole speech. As soon as Xavier let the guy up, he was gone. *I swear that was fast even for a vampire!* I thought. I was not sure I really blamed him though; I almost wanted to leave myself. Just as fast, Xavier appeared at my side, all traces of the rage I just witnessed gone as he sat down on the bed next to me. "Misty, you're awake," he said. A charming smile crossed his lips, relaxing all his features back to the sheer perfection I was still getting used to. His eyes were darker in colour than they had been last time I had seen them, but at least they were green again.

I couldn't keep the shock or the fear from my face, as I looked at him. Dad was right; vampires were dangerous, even the nice ones. I couldn't even imagine what could have caused his reaction, but I could only guess that it was bad. Xavier had viciously turned on him, on one of his kind, and it left me thinking how quickly and easily he could've killed him. The scary thing was there was no doubt in my mind that he would have, given the chance. I couldn't quite recall what the conversation I had overheard was about but I knew one thing for sure: this guy was dangerous. I shouldn't have trusted him so easily. *That could very well be me if I push him the wrong way.* He cupped my face in his hands and I winced from his touch, partly because his hands were cold and partly because I was terrified of what those hands could do.

"You're scared," he said softly, his expression worried. "I wasn't going to kill him; well, at least not in front of you. I would have taken it to the hall first." He smiled playfully at his attempt at a joke. Could I have been overreacting? I mean I had seen my brother do stuff like that hundreds of times and I know he's perfectly harmless, to me at least. Fear is a good persuasion technique; it's one of the first things you're taught as a hunter. But still it was hard to believe that this man, the one who was looking at me so gently, had a killer other side, even though I had seen it. Yes, he's a vampire, and yes, he's a hunter, but looking at him now, knowing how caring he had always been towards me, I would never have believed he was capable of tearing someone to shreds, of killing in cold blood as if it was nothing to him, but he was and I saw it; I'm just not sure I wanted to believe it. *Misty, what's wrong with you, girl?* I smiled back cautiously and couldn't help but laugh with him for just a second. I would have to think twice before fully trusting this guy again, that was for sure.

"Well, thank you for that," I said softly, my voice still shaking.

"I'm sorry if I scared you. I have no patience for vampires like him, and a bad temper when rubbed the wrong way," he said; his voice was apologetic. I knew I wasn't meant to see his outburst and wasn't hard to tell he hadn't wanted me to, either.

"Ya think?" I replied, half joking. He smiled and laughed softly.

"Hey," he said softly, knocking my shoulder with his. I couldn't help but notice how hard he had to try to make it soft. I felt my fear of him fading quickly; there was no way I could stay afraid of him, not when he seemed so genuine. But I would have to keep my guard up from now on. As much as I wanted to, I couldn't ignore the little voice in my head screaming at me the rational thing to do, the hunter thing to do. I felt like my head was a war zone, the hunter in me fighting against another feeling. Stronger than the fear I felt toward him, a safe, trusting feeling that drew me to his cheeky smile as if with him is the safest place in the world, *which it very well might be if I keep on his good side,* I thought.

"Trust me, Missy, I would never hurt you." His smile widened. "If you keep on my good side, that is." I laughed out loud; for a second there I had completely forgotten he could read minds, but knowing he had heard my thoughts and all my fears reassured me a bit. For some reason, one I knew I would probably come to regret, I trusted him. Call it instinct but I knew I was safe, as safe as one can be around a vampire, that was. I punched him playfully but doubted if he even felt it. *Then keep out of my head,* I thought as a reply.

"What if I don't want to? I rather liked watching your fantasies while you were out." He smiled a cheeky smile. "I especially enjoyed the one where I was standing shirtless on the beach." He stopped and I felt myself blush. I officially wanted to die right about now. I wasn't sure if he could tap into my dreams and I really couldn't recall if I had any but still, it was kind of embarrassing because, frankly, I couldn't think of a better star for any of my fantasies than him.

"Only you could turn yourself on, that's sad really, but on a more happy note I've got a good idea what ya can suck, vampire," I said with a smirk.

He looked genuinely shocked and mumbled something that sounded like "There's no way she's not related to Damien." Then, louder, he said, "Hostile," looking to me with a smirk on his face. "And I thought I had issues." I couldn't help but smile at that. "How are you feeling? I don't mean to sound like a jerk...."

"Might be a bit late to worry about that," I interrupted with a playful smile; he just looked at me as a smile curled in the corner of his lips, and kept going.

"But, we really should get going."

"Okay," I replied. I was ready to get on with it hours ago, even if it didn't really look like it. He grabbed my hand to pull me off the bed onto my feet, but he didn't let go like I had expected. I gave him a cold warning stare. He really did love overstepping boundaries.

"Shall I remind you we are in a vampire coven, what exactly do we eat again?" he mused. I didn't argue like I knew I should, but secretly I can't say I hated the safe feeling his presence cast over me, and the cool addictive tingle his touch sent up my arm was simply just the icing. It was stupid, yes, but he was hot and no amount of apparent insanity could change that fact. Once again I found myself trying to refrain from sighing; what was it about him that had me hooked? He was annoying, I mean I barely knew the guy and he annoyed me more than anyone else I knew, well almost everyone, but somehow I wished he would. I loved his playful flirty banter and, quite frankly, I loved to give it right back. I guess it had been somewhat of a slow year in the guy department. I just forgot how good it felt to flirt and it was all harmless fun, right? It wasn't like I was fixing to marry the guy; hell, I wasn't even trying to get into his pants, although if the chance arose I don't know if I could turn it down. But this guy was single, *I hoped*, fun, violent and weird, but somehow I found that totally addictive. *What have I gotten myself into?*

"Do you pick up anything else but static?" he said, frustration crossing his face as we walked hand in hand down the hall. Yes, I'll admit it was a little strange and sort of reminded me of the buddy system in preschool, but better safe than sorry, right? The halls seemed deserted and I was staring to be grateful he was with me. This place was like a maze, all hallways and doors.

"What?" I replied, stopping for a second to look at him. He dropped my hand and stepped in front of me, blocking my path.

"Your thoughts," he said, staring into my eyes, which was kinda creepy, random and weird but, sadly, I was starting to expect this kinda thing from him.

"What about them?" I asked, raising an eyebrow at him. *Boy you're lucky you're cute.*

"I can't hear them. All I can hear is static… of sorts, it's frustrating,"

"Good," I said, making a point of stepping around him, but he was at my side again within two steps. He was quiet for a bit, which told me he wasn't going to give up on getting a good read. He stepped in my path again – well, when I say stepped, it was more like appeared. I stopped in my tracks so I didn't walk into him.

"For fu…" I stopped myself before I cursed out loud. I swear, this guy *wanted* me to stake him.

"It must be shock. I mean, I was getting perfect readings before; what changed?" He asked himself, seemingly oblivious to my annoyance, and changed the subject quickly. "I can't believe you told me to suck my own…"

I interrupted him, smiling my most devious smile. "Well, don't push me then, and you won't have to find out just how much like Damien I really am," I warned, hoping he would get the drift, but seeing the look on his face, I wasn't too hopeful. I felt a flirty smile draw across my lips as I stepped around him once again. I walked off trying to make my walk look confident and cocky as I could, just to get my point across, of course. *What am I doing?*

"Ha! God, I love this girl," I heard him say to himself from behind me.

CHAPTER SIX

I was starting to get used to seeing him appear at my side even when I'd left him behind. I looked to him, waiting for him to say something, step into my path again, or grab for my hand, but he just walked next to me, smiling my favourite smile. I could've just melted into a puddle right beside him. *Man, he's gorgeous*. We came to a dead end. *What are we doing?* I wondered still, looking around.

"Being powerful has it perks," he said, punching a code into the electronic lock I hadn't noticed on the wall next to him. "May I present the most impressive thing you'll ever see, well, apart from myself, of course," he said, stepping away from the wall as it opened into a doorway. "Welcome to my hobby, my pride and joy, my garage." The door flew open as he said the last words. I looked around the impossibly big room, which reminded me of a showroom floor. It was filled with the most amazing cars you could ever imagine: Porsche, Ferrari, Bugatti, McLaren, Lamborghini … if it was Italian, sporty, expensive or just plain fast, it was in here. Xavier looked around his collection with pride, and smiled.

"It's only taken forty years, but I've nearly got every car I've ever wanted, well nearly every one," he laughed. "I really used to despise the black mess of a Mustang your brother calls a car, but in the three years I've been working with him, it's grown on me, and I thought I had good taste," he smiled. Good was not the word I would have used; maybe expensive was a better fit. All I could do was wonder: how in the hell did he afford all of these? I happen to know hunting doesn't pay that well (it doesn't pay at all, really), so I guess being whatever he said he was before does have perks. I tried to focus on what he said and answer accordingly; mind you, I was a little awestruck.

"Don't worry ya self, the rumble of that engine grows on everyone just as quickly as the owner does."

"Must be the West family charm, although I've known of few generations of Wests, but none quite like you and your brother," he said, walking into the room looking around, as if trying to decide which one of the amazing cars before him we were going to take. I followed him into the room. Like I said before, I'm a car girl, and this just shot Xavier to the position of god in my eyes.

"You think quite highly of my brother, don't you?" I asked. It sounded like an observation but really it was a guess; I mean he was spending all his time looking for him.

"He's my best friend," he said simply, with a small shrug. "Now, don't take this the wrong way; I have the greatest respect for Damien, but he's not like other hunters. He didn't think of me as just another monster that needed to be beheaded or burnt. He gave me a chance, even when I didn't deserve it. Your brother, despite his faults, is a good man, and yeah, I respect him for that."

"What makes you think you didn't deserve it?" I asked, running my hand along a red Ferrari 911.

"Long story," he said and even though I wasn't looking at him, I could still feel his eyes following my movements as I wandered between the cars.

"I don't have anything better to listen to," I said simply, before stopping to turn to him. He nodded and sighed; I guess he figured I wouldn't let up unless he told me, which was smart because I probably wouldn't have now that he had sparked my interest.

"Damien was only just starting out, I guessed from his sloppy hunting techniques. When we met he found me in an alley." He stopped and looked away, his voice going quiet.

"Covered in blood, I was in the midst of a frenzy. Crazed and out of control, subject to the thirst and my own lust for violence. I was in the middle of what we call blood lust, and this is how I knew he was new because vampires in blood lust are to either be killed or subdued and relinquished to vampire authority if possible, but he approached me. All he had was a small silver cross keychain a lot like yours, and he asked me if I was alright. I of course turned on him, more than willing for dessert. I had been at it all night, killing just for the fun of it. He had the right to kill me where I stood; hell, he should have, it's the rules. He could have treated me like the monster I was, but he didn't. I knew he wasn't going to try and stop me until I calmed down but also he wasn't going to let me leave the alley; that I had pulled from his head. I threw the body of my last victim to the ground and went for the kill. I threw him up against the brick wall, pinning him there so I could see the look in his eyes as he died, as he pleaded for his life." I winced as he said it; his eyes were black and staring off at something I couldn't see. The look of pain and horror on his face was like nothing I've ever seen before; he truly believed he was a monster. You could tell the memory was painful for him, how much he hated himself for it. I looked at him, trying to understand how he felt; what he must have been going through, and wondered why was he telling me this? Why tell me the truth? He could have said anything.

"All he said was 'Look, dude, it's okay, I don't want to hurt you, I can help, you don't have to be a slave to the thirst, together we can fight it, man. This is not what you want, is it? Killing for fun. Let me go and we'll work it out.' His word shocked me; he didn't know me, what if it was what I wanted? And at the time I wanted nothing more, but something in his eyes stopped me. It wasn't something I was used to seeing in the eyes of my victims, and especially in the eyes of a hunter. It was something from the past, although I see it all the time, even in your eyes." He stopped again. I wanted to tell him to stop, it's okay, really,

I don't want to know, but that was a lie. I did, but his pain was unbearable. I couldn't even look at him as he finished.

"I lost it, I was scared, and I didn't understand why he would help me. I set him down but did not let go; I stared into his eyes trying to see fear as I yelled. 'But that is what I want, hunter, I want them all to fear coming out at night, fear me.' I loosened my grip for only a second but it was enough; he wrapped the cross around his knuckles and punched, knocking me to the ground. He pinned me face down with the cross shoved into my shoulder. I remember every word and it still shocks me that they came from a hunter. 'I'm giving you one last chance; let me help you, boy.' I knew the other choice, but I gave up and he kept his promise. I was reluctant at first but he got me back in the game. He let me hunt again; later I helped him in with a job and saved his life in return. Funnily enough, haven't been able to get rid of him since, but he changed my life and I'll always have the little reminder on my shoulder if I ever lose it again." He pulled his collar down over his shoulder, then turned around. I ran my hand over the cross-shaped scar that was barely visible. He cleared his throat; he obviously hadn't meant to get so carried away. "That answer your question?" His eyes slowly faded back to green but the pain from the memory never left his face as he led me thought the cars to a red Porsche parked closest to the garage door.

I ran my hand along the car. "Amazing," I said. "Is this an 09 Porsche Cayman S?" He nodded. "But these aren't even out yet."

"I know," he said with a cheeky smile on his face. "I'm getting good at getting my own way."

I smiled, looking at the car. " I love this car, 3.4 litre engine, six-speed manual, rear wheel drive, nineteen-inch wheels standard, fixed roof coupe." *Oh yeah, I should be the poster girl for this car.*

"Wow, I'm impressed; anything else you want to add?" he said, looking from me to the car, then back to me.

I thought about it for a second. "Well, let's see, 320 horsepower, zero to sixty in 4.9 seconds with a top speed of, I don't know, about 171." I smiled victoriously; I just love beating the boys at their own game. "And don't even get me started on the standard extras." He looked at me for a second. I looked over the car trying to pick out things I could see, in case he wanted more. Sometimes it pays to be Damien's sister; he has more car mags than any one person could ever care to read and I have a lot of free time. Xavier smiled that amazing cocky smile, the one that lit up his whole face, then he sighed, of all things to do.

"I think I'm in love, where ya pick that up? That was so cool! Can you do it again? I mean, wow! Chicks shouldn't know that kind of junk." He stopped. "I'm rambling again." I laughed and smiled. There was no need to read minds when he was like this; it was all in those amazing emerald eyes.

"In order, my brother, I know, yes and I'm not your normal chick," I smiled. "Oh, and I'm driving." He looked at me as if he didn't realise what I said. You could see the moment my words sunk in; it was written all over his face as he tensed up in surprise.

"Huh, what, no, no, no you're not."

I gave him a cheeky smile. "Hey, don't worry, I'll keep it under 170."

"Damn, you can tell you're related to Damien," he said to himself before looking to me. "No, Misty, humans don't have good enough reflexes to drive safely at that speed on busy suburban roads; there's no way I'm letting you get your hands on this kind of horsepower." I looked around. There was plenty of horsepower in this room; the least he could do was share it.

"Lighten up, I'm not really going to do 170," I said, walking up to him. I noticed the keys in his pocket. I wondered when he had gotten them but this guy was fast; it would have been easy for me to have missed it. I smiled flirtatiously, going over my evil plan in my head. He gave me a puzzled look, which told me he couldn't hear it, and silently I thanked god for that.

Xavier

Her mind went fuzzy again and I knew she was planning something, because she had that look in her eye. I had seen it a thousand times before, family trademark, really. They all got it when they were up to no good, but this time it was accompanied by a very flirtatious smile which made me worry. *Look away,* said the voice in my head, I felt myself smile an equally flirtatious smile back. *Damn, why do I never listen to myself?*

"Although you would look sexy behind the wheel of that beast," she said, walking up to me. She used slow and calculated steps. Her body moved in a way designed to entice the imagination and damn, was it doing that. She stopped right in front of me, placing both hands on my hips as she pulled me into her. My rational brain was telling me this was all part of her plan, but sadly, I wasn't listing to that brain at the moment. *What is she doing? What are you doing? Don't lean into it, you're the stronger one, pull away,* I warned myself but I didn't want to pull away; I had been wanting her this close since I first laid my eyes on her in the bar, but I knew I shouldn't. *This doesn't count; she's coming onto you,* said the vampire in me, but I know all too well what he wanted. She bit her bottom lip. Her scent filled my lungs and my mind got the better of me once again. *Would one little kiss hurt?* I stared deep into her blue eyes which didn't help at all; it only made it harder to look away. I wanted her so badly it caused me physical pain to resist her and frankly, I didn't even know that was possible; I could basically melt to putty in her hands.

"Do you really think I'll be that dangerous?" she pouted as she traced the contours of my chest, working her way down. I tensed up. *Oh, this is so not fair.* I knew this wasn't going to end up in a happy ending, or anything equally as happy, but I couldn't stop myself from responding. I needed to distract myself. *Baseball, Fourth of July, Damien's twenty-fifth.* I shuddered at that thought, yep, that did it; truly a night I never wanted to think of again, not even briefly.

"No, I just…" I stopped trying to concentrate on what I was saying; the softness of her touch along with the closeness of her body was making that difficult, almost leaving me breathless as I tried to remain strong. "Don't want to be responsible for injuring both siblings," I felt her fingers trace the waistline of my jeans. My muscles tightened in shock as she fiddled with the button on them. *Oh shit!* Her beautiful blue eyes gazed over my face while I watched as those soft lips formed words that I didn't even think I was capable of registering. *Baseball man, think baseball!*

"But you won't, I'll be driving," she said, reaching up and taking the side of my face in her hand, locking my gaze, inching my face closer to hers. *She smells so good, sweet, oh I bet she tastes even better, just one little…. No! why must she be so tempting!*

"Really," I said, trying to remember what we were talking about to start with, "not that I'll be supplying you with the car or anything." She smiled; her lips were just so inviting, so soft I didn't know how much more of this I could stand before I caved or something even worse happened. I had no idea she could be such a temptress. She leaned up, pulling me down as she did, putting her face next to mine so close I could smell the sweet irresistible fragrance of her skin and the metallic smell I craved constantly, putting me into a daze.

"All I need is the keys," she whispered into my ear. The soft brush of her lips on my ear sent shivers down my spine and an ache through a place she might not want to be up against real soon. I wanted to give it to her, the keys, that was. Hell, I would give her anything she wanted if it meant I could have those sweet, sweet lips. I gave in, pulling her face back away from mine so I could keep control and see those baby blues as I spoke.

"But I would be giving them to you," I said, trying my talk down again, but even my mental images faltered and betrayed me by changing into to what I craved to do to her. She smiled and ran her finger along my cheek softly. I wanted her so bad, *why was I resisting her again? I mean, she is coming at me guns blazing, the least I could do is reciprocate it a little right?*

"Really," she said, leaning up and putting her face so close I could feel her breath on my lips. I wanted to kiss her, no, scratch that, I was going to, but I knew I shouldn't. I tried to fight the urge, but again I wasn't strong enough to resist.

"Yeah," I whispered, so lost in my own desire I totally forgot what we were even talking about. I went to kiss her but she pulled away at the last second.

"Well, I'll just take them, then," she said, taking a couple of steps back and holding up the keys. It took me a few seconds to realise what had just happened. *She didn't,* I thought, patting my pockets. She smiled that sexy, sweet smile as she made her way to the driver's side. The sweet smile turned to one of pride as she shook her head.

"Men," she said, looking me up and down. I stood frozen to my spot as she opened the driver's side door and got in. *I can't believe I fell for that, oldest trick in the book.* She sexed me into it and I caved, crumbled like dirt in a landslide. No one had ever been able to fool me so quickly before; I wasn't normally such a sucker. Was I really that transparent? Against her I was helpless, and all it took was a flirty smile and my head was all too busy fighting itself to think. What was it about her that left me speechless? Trust me, I knew it was a pointless question; the fact of the matter was that I wanted Misty more than I had ever wanted anyone. *Damn forbidden fruit complex!* I was totally hooked and apparently she knew it. I smiled, knowing that was going to make it harder for me to keep my distance, harder than it already was, that is. It took me a few seconds to settle down enough to face her. I made a point of turning my back to her while I did. I looked toward the car over my shoulder; she was watching me out the rear-view mirror. *She's good,* said the voice in my head, and for once I agreed with it.

CHAPTER SEVEN

Misty

Xavier opened the passenger side door and got in. To my surprise, he was smiling. "I underestimated you," he said, shifting uncomfortably in his seat as he sat down.

"Well, I'm good at getting my own way," I said and he laughed quietly and nodded.

"Yes, I noticed. That was a low trick, but well played. It's easy to see you have the evil mind of a hunter; there may be hope for you yet." A smile still lingered on his lips as he said that. I had expected him to be mad, but his look was almost of admiration. I really wouldn't have blamed him if he was upset. I mean, come on, I just played on the most basic male instincts; lesser men have caved under that, but all it did for him was provide a distraction. He should have crumbled; hell, I pulled my best moves, but to him I was just another girl. Seriously, look at the guy! Way out of my league, he could have any girl he wanted, and guys like him do not go for girls like me. I knew I shouldn't flirt, but it did feel really good to have him looking at me like that; it felt good to be wanted, even if it was only a lusty want.

"Well, the supernatural world isn't really for me," I said, even though that was a lie. I have been a hunter my whole life and, truth be told, years ago I was really good at it, too.

"Damn, looks like I have to find somewhere else to spend Christmas," he joked. *No, please don't be so cute. I'm trying to resist you here!*

"Well, it really depends on what you want for dinner, because I'm not available," I said sweetly, looking up from under my lashes. *Yeah, yeah okay I can't help myself;* I had to, if only he knew how big of a lie that was. He can have me anytime wants, oh my god that was really slutty, I wasn't usually like that towards guys, but for some reason he just brought the bad out in me. Maybe it's the whole vampire thing. Rule number seven, hunters' code: never date what you hunt, but surely he must be an exception to that rule, right? He laughed softly and I could see his mind working.

"Again, damn, I guess I'll just have to pack my own." He smiled evilly, and the look on his face only made it funnier. I laughed almost hysterically at the strange mental picture that popped into my head. I know what he was implying should disturb me, but the conversation seemed so natural; I guess I was just desensitised to it. I couldn't help but smile around him; it was almost like I'd known about him for years. I could be myself around him, there was no hiding freaky symbols, stashing my gun when he walked into the room, and I knew he wouldn't judge me if I started to salt the windows and doorways when I felt a little freaked out. There was no explaining with him. I was so sick of explaining stuff that I can't explain; it was refreshing, really. So he wasn't normal, hell, he wasn't even human, but he understood and I loved that, way more than I should have.

"It's funny, really. Damien would drop me at the bar outside of town, when he returned home. He was convinced I would scare you, you know, maybe kill you or worse, which of course I would never do, but ya know Dee, always watching out for his little sis, which is a real bummer, because I really would have liked to have met you before now, seeing if this all goes to hell we'll be dead and all," he said with a laugh.

I smiled, but it quickly faded. *What if Damien isn't going to be around for Christmas this year? What if we can't save him? Do we just sit around and wait to die? Just me and his vampire hunting partner?* I tried to stop thinking like that. I needed to concentrate. Xavier reached over and took my hand in his.

"He'll be there, Missy, and well, of course, so will I. You know Dee's always got your back and he's family to me, like the brother I never wanted to have, so no matter what happens I'll always be there too, right until the end if need be. I promise you won't have to go through it alone," he said, smiling that reassuring smile. I know he was trying to make me feel better, but it wasn't working. Damien was all the family I had left, really all I had left; without him I had nothing.

"Thanks," I replied in a small voice.

"I'm sorry," he said. "I'm not really good at this kind of thing; I don't really get a chance to talk to anyone other than Damien. You know how it is; normal people steer clear of me. I scare them apparently, so when I do get the chance, I tend to overstep boundaries or tell a lot of stories. Also somewhat of a nervous habit, the whole awkward silence thing gets to me, it drives Damien crazy. But the blokes at the bar love my farfetched thick action yarns, when they're drunk enough to believe them, that is."

I gave him a puzzled look; right, change of subject, great idea, I needed to be distracted. I smiled; he was such a nice guy, and all he was trying to do was make me feel better, but I'm making him feel like he'd done something wrong.

"No, it's okay, I don't mind really, I'm just scared and, well, kind of jealous. Damien's out kicking ass with his mates, saving the world one ghoul at a time, while I'm stuck at home bored out of my mind and helping no one."

He smiled but didn't reply. I started the car; the purr of the engine broke the silence that suddenly settled. I knew that connection we just had was gone, and maybe it was for the best. I wasn't here to make new friends but to find my brother and the two of us just happened to be doing the same thing. *It's for the best,* I kept telling myself; funny how I didn't believe it.

The radio pulled me out of my head and back into the car; the sound of soft rock filled the car, some mushy love ballad belted out from the speakers and we both just looked at the radio, which somehow made it a little awkward. Xavier leaned forward and turned it off before giving me directions to our next destination. I floored the car, just a bit along the straights, just for fun; driving this baby after a Honda was a big difference. We flew through traffic but he kept his head down, only speaking when telling me which way to go. I pulled up at the gas station he told me to stop at and I couldn't believe my eyes.

"Okay," he said, "no doubt he went through here and, knowing Dee, this is the first place he would have stopped. Joseph, the guy who owns this place is an ex-hunter, always our first stop for any problems we run into. If anyone would know where he was heading last, it would be him." He got out of the car.

I looked out the window and smiled; it had been so long since I had been out to this old place. Last time would have been when I was a kid. Dad stopped coming here before I was a teenager, so I had completely forgotten how to get here. I jogged to catch up. I knew it was a pointless effort trying to keep up to his lightning pace, but damned if I'm not a determined little thing.

The bell on the door chimed as we entered. An older man looked up from behind the counter. He smiled a friendly smile and I could have just cried. He looked in his late forties, early fifties at the max. He had greying brown hair and blue, aged eyes. I remembered them; it can't be! He's alive? Dad had a falling-out with him when I was a kid and Damien told me he had died in a hunting accident, like Dad.

"Well, well, well," he said as Xavier walked in. I followed. "If it isn't our very own lean, mean, blood-drinking machine; where have you been, boy?" he said, throwing his arms around Xavier and patting him on the back.

I was speechless; it was really him. He looked up at me. "Well, hello there…" he squinted and took a few steps toward me. "Well, I'll be a werewolf's chew toy, is that young Misty West? Come here, girl, and give ya Uncle Joe a hug, come on now," he said arms outstretched. At first I couldn't move; I couldn't believe Damien had lied to me.

"Joe," I sobbed, running to him. I met his hug and held him tight; he returned it just as firmly. "I thought you were dead," I said into his shoulder.

"Not last time I checked, darlin'; who in the world filled you're head with that idea?" he said, stepping back and looking at Xavier.

"It's so good to see you," I said with happy tears rolling down my cheeks.

He looked me over. "I bet I can guess," he said. "Well, I'll be; the last time I saw you, you were knee-high to a leprechaun, and now you're all grown up. I was so happy when I heard you got out of the game, honey, but that leaves me with one question: what are you doing here, with him? Damien would spit stakes if he knew you were involved with this guy."

"Involved? Huh? What do you mean, involved?" asked Xavier, tensing up.

"Huntin' kid, what else would I be talking about?" asked Uncle Joe, raising an eyebrow at Xavier and giving him a warning look; maybe the weirdness I have come to expect wasn't a normal thing after all.

"Oh, right, of course, what I was thinking… Anyway, has Damien been through lately? No one's heard from him or Alex in months," said Xavier quickly.

"Yeah, awhile back, just after I sent you looking for…. well, you know, he just showed up here. I chewed him out for being such an idiot, and then I asked had he met up with you and he said you were busy, but he would look for you."

"What did he want?"

"To know where North Ridge was."

"The coven?" asked Xavier.

"Yeah. I told him I wasn't positive; I'd always had you to deal with that kind of stuff and that you would know better than I would, but he said he'll risk it, and took off. Damn kid! About a month later Alex came through looking for Damien; I told him North Ridge, then he was gone too, haven't heard from either of them since. I just assumed, since I hadn't heard from you either, that he'd found ya," Joe said, giving Xavier a chastising look.

"Yeah, sorry about that," said Xavier, and I looked to where he was standing only to see him at the door. "North Ridge? Right, well, have to run, I'll fill you in on the way back." Then he was gone.

"Xavier, boy, you get back here!" yelled Joe after him. I heard the car start in response. *Man, that boy is fast*! I looked back to Joe, who gave me a loving smile. "Now, looky here Missy, be careful with that one. I've known him for a long time and don't take this the wrong way, Xavier's a hell of a kid and god knows I love him, but just watch ya self around him, he isn't known for his mild temper and self-control, or for his sanity, for that matter. Just promise me you'll keep an eye on him, and watch ya self." I nodded as the car revved, my cue to hurry up, I guess. I headed for the door but before I got there I stopped, turned and ran back for a quick goodbye hug; it might be my last chance after all.

"I'm glad you're not dead," I said and I truly meant it.

He chuckled. "Me too love and keep it that way," he said. I nodded and walked for the door. "Oh, and Misty, when ya find Dee tell him I had nothing to do with you being here and that I'm going to kick his stupid ass."

"Yeah, I will," I said with a wave, and quickly ran out to the car. Xavier was already in the driver's seat. I jumped in as quickly as I could and we sped off before I even had a chance to buckle up. I looked at Xavier. He was gripping the wheel so tightly it looked as if his knuckles would burst through his skin at any moment. His eyes looked darker than usual, and they were so distant. Actually, he looked kinda mad. *What was at North Ridge he hated so much; isn't he like their leader or something?* He looked at me with that thought.

"North Ridge is a vile and immoral coven. They only respect two things, power and money, but even then it is only an imitation of respect. The vampires that roam its walls are the lowest form of scum to have ever roamed the earth, and if I was sure Damien didn't stop here I wouldn't either." He stopped, worry washing out his features as he looked to the clock on the dashboard. "Unfortunately, by the time we get there it'll be late, meaning it'll be best if we spend the night so we can depart by morning when it'll be safest, seeing you're not a person of great power, and the fact that you're a hunter means it'll be very dangerous just getting into the place."

"But you're a hunter," I said, puzzled, but he simply nodded.

"Yes but, as you mentioned, I hold a great deal of power over them, so they'll at least pretend they respect me. I can handle whatever they have to throw at me, but you are an unknown hunter; they won't hesitate for a second to dispatch you."

"Dispatch me?" Oh, I didn't like the sound of that!

"There is a way to get you in safely, something no vampire who wishes to live would ever even think of violating; it is one of the very few understandings we have amongst our kind," he said but he sounded unsure, so I guessed it was somewhat of a long shot.

"What is it?" I asked, willing to do anything to find Damien.

"We will have to pretend you're my mate," he said like I knew what he was talking about.

"Huh? Whoa, your what?"

"Mate, it's uh, sort of like a vampiric arranged marriage, a human that is promised to a vampire for eternity, it's very old-fashioned and it is the most sacred ritual that we have; once a human is pledged there is only one way out."

I tried to swallow the lump forming in my throat. "Do you really have a mate?" I asked slowly.

"Me? No, of course not! Are you serious? It's, ah, well, *disturbing*," he said, much to my relief. "Although I can't say it isn't tempting; the thought of spending eternity alone is kind of daunting but I couldn't condemn someone to this, no matter how daunting it is."

"Okay, but they don't know that, right? I mean, I would hate to be killed because they called your bluff," I said with a nervous laugh. He looked at me; his face was dead serious, no pun intended.

"If they did, I would defend you as if you were, I swear that they would regret the day they touched my mate!"

I just looked at him. He was for real, he meant that and sure I was grateful, you know, knowing that he was on my side, but the way he said it sent chills down my spine. I couldn't reply to that; what was I meant to say, thanks? We drove in silence and the closer we got the tenser Xavier became; he was downright near terrifying when we pulled up. *He's only playing the part,* I reassured myself, but I wasn't so sure. "Misty, it is very important you do exactly as I say in here and under no circumstances are you to let go of my hand or leave my side, unless I say otherwise; this place is dangerous and remember no matter what you see, or how I may act in here, I would never hurt you. I need your full trust, can you do that?" he asked, his eyes darkening again; now they looked closer to black than green.

"Yeah," I whispered. The tension radiating off his every limb was so thick you could cut it with a knife, which made me nervous. He nodded, then ripped off his jacket, tossing it into the back seat before opening the door.

"Stay seated until I let you out, and try and look like you're indebted to me." There was an edge to his voice that frightened me. I was actually afraid to ask, how exactly was I meant to do that? His face was tense as he slammed the door.

CHAPTER EIGHT

It took him less than a second to get round and open my door. I knew he meant for it to be gentle as he helped me from the car, but it was far from it. Keeping hold of my hand as tight as he could without breaking it, he pulled me to his side and angled himself so he was in between me and the driveway that lead to an old-looking mansion. The irises of his eyes went completely black as we watched a young man walk down to meet us. The huge iron gates opened as he approached them. The place looked like it should have lightning striking in the background, or barren trees filled with crows cawing away. Of course it didn't, and really it just was an old manor, but still I thought it should.

"My lord! What brings you all the way out here this fine evening?" he said to Xavier in a posh, slightly cocky voice.

"Markus," Xavier said as a greeting. Markus I'll admit was quite handsome, tall and thin, with boyish good looks, yet there was just something about him, a presence, something I can't place. His spiky black hair contrasted with his pasty skin, making the smile he wore look twice as evil as it already did, but his eyes were entrancing, as blue as the sky itself. He stared at me with a look that could have almost been hunger; god knows I hoped it wasn't. Xavier growled, pulling me closer to him; Markus broke his gaze and looked back to the vampire at my side.

"Business, as usual," Xavier snapped, and Markus's smile widened it truly was evil.

"Human, my lord? They always have been your weak spot," he said in a tone I really didn't like. Xavier growled again, louder this time, causing Markus to flinch.

"She is no normal human, she is my mate. She will soon be mine forever," he said, his voice emotionless.

"Your mate?" he said in a shocked voice, "I am surprised, but humbled that you are finally coming around; you can be assured, my lord, she will not be touched."

"Good, you will be held personally responsible if she is," Xavier said, his voice so cold it froze me to the core, but Markus merely nodded.

"Of course, I would have it no other way. Now, my lord, my lady," he nodded at each of us as he addressed us. "Please, follow me."

We walked toward the huge manor house. I hadn't seen a single house on the way in, but of course it was kinda hard to see anything but blurs at the speed we were travelling. We climbed the stairs toward the huge gothic front door. Xavier squeezed my hand and flashed me a quick smile, as if to tell me everything was fine. It warmed my insides, leaving me feeling as if we were climbing the stairway to heaven, not hell. I still couldn't see any green in his eyes, meaning we weren't out of the woods yet. I wanted to leave. Surely, someone else had to know where Damien was.

"Markus, take us to Jamie now," barked Xavier as we entered. Markus nodded and led the way down the hall. I could see the other vampires watching me with hungry eyes. This was nothing like the other coven; this one felt wild, more dangerous. I felt unsafe here, even with Xavier's presence, where I didn't at the other one. Rows and rows of doors lined the long dark hallway. I couldn't help but imagine the horrors behind them. I walked as close to Xavier as I could without him having to hold me. Xavier's lips were curled into somewhat of a snarl, and the low rumble of a growl echoed in his chest as if to warn the owners of every set of cold, hungry eyes to back off.

Between silently praying and fearing for my life I hadn't got a good look at the place, but really, that didn't worry me at all (unless of course I had to escape in a hurry, then it might).

We stopped at a giant door at end of the hall. I didn't think it was possible but the door itself looked menacing; it was old, heavy looking, thick and impossibly big. The details and decorations on the doors were made out of gold. Xavier watched as I took in my surroundings and studied the gold patterns.

"Some vampires are more sensitive to silver and light than others. That's why covens are always kept dark, and you'll never see any amount of silver," he whispered in my ear as if I didn't already know that.

"Here we are, my lord, if there is anything else I can assist you with just yell," Markus said.

I turned to thank him but he was gone. Xavier pushed open the door with one hand and dragged me in, letting go of my hand as we entered.

"It's okay," he whispered as he shut the door behind us.

"Ah, Xavier my friend what can I do for you?" said a vampire I could only assume was Jamie from behind the desk. Jamie had long dark brown hair which he had tied back at the nape of his neck. His eyes were strange, almost orange in colour, and his face was as tense as Xavier's.

"I am not your friend, Jamie; all I need from you is for you to tell me where the hunter Damien West was heading and don't lie to me, Jamie, I know he was here," Xavier said coldly.

"Now, why would I tell you? After all, you are a hunter yourself. For all I know, this is a trap. I tell you the wrong answer, you prosecute me under hunters' law, which give you the barbaric right to murder me and anyone else who gets in your way with only your word to go on, so what shall I say, Xavier? " he said with a smug smile on his face.

"Kill, murder doesn't apply; that would suggest you were completely innocent, and I happen to know for a fact that you're not, so save the pity party and stop trying to play me. I have no time for games," Xavier replied, his voice just as smug. Jamie looked at him and shook his head as if debating what to do. "I'll call it vampire business, then, and call in rank. Don't make me command you to tell me what you know."

"NO!" Jamie snapped, suddenly slamming his fist down on the desk, "you will never be mine or anyone in this coven's ruler. We have been true to Vladimir, and you are unfit and unworthy to follow his reign. You're weak and you betray your own kind by helping those hunters," he said, looking over to me in disgust. "They are nothing more than humans who know more than they should; they need to learn their place in the grand scheme of things, but you, you are worse than they are, you know yours and you exploit it. I will never bow to you Xavier, never!" he growled.

Xavier snarled in return and before I could even blink Jamie had fled from behind the desk. He grabbed me, turning my head to expose my neck. "Look at them, they are not strong enough, fast enough or smart enough to match us. They are evolutionarily pre-positioned to be prey, to be weak and, like all other mammals, they are meant to be nothing more than food to us. They cannot be our killers, they cannot be our friends, they are nothing to us. When will you learn that as long as you have this weakness, that compassion for these creatures, you will always be thrown from power, huh? And when that happens I will be the first in line to try!"

"Let her go, Jamie," warned Xavier, his eyes starting to flicker like green and black flame again, which they did when he was really mad and, judging from the murderous look on his face and the way every muscle in his body was tensed to fight, I would say he was really mad.

"You are fond of this hunter?" Jamie said. His tone implied more of a question than a statement. "She and the others will only be used against you; you cannot live a human life, Xavier, because you are not a human, not any more."

Xavier watched his every move. Jamie sighed when Xavier didn't respond. "You will never learn… so think of this as a favour." I cringed as I realised what he meant by that and even though I couldn't really see what he was doing, it wasn't hard to figure out that this was not good. I closed my eyes waiting for the bite; *he's going to kill me, I'm going to die, shit*. I waited for it but nothing happened, at least not for a second or two, both seconds feeling like eternity but within another, Jamie's steel grip released and I fell to the ground.

I opened my eyes, unable to move. Shock and relief coursed through me as I realised I was still alive. I knew that sounded stupid, but when you are sure you are going to die, knowing you're not dead is a great feeling. I watched my relief turn to fear again as I saw Xavier throw Jamie against the wall. Jamie crumbled to the ground, a hole in the plaster where he hit. He got to his feet within a blink and launched himself at Xavier, who met his attack with vicious force. I watched in horror as they fought. They were moving too fast to see who was winning, and watching a fight you couldn't see was every bit as nerve-wracking, but what was worse was not knowing whether Xavier was okay or not. That feeling was horrifying, especially because he was only in this situation because of me. He may not have admitted to being fond of me but I was fond of him, very fond, so seeing him get hurt on my account was horrible.

Okay, so I'd only known him for a short time, barely forty-eight hours, but I cared for him. Hunters always protect their own, it was rule number eight, but even so, this guy was risking his life to save me and to top that off he's the only other person in the world who cared if Damien lived or died, to the point that he would put himself in this position, even when he knew what was going to happen when we came here.

I respected that and wanted to help but I was unarmed, unprepared and just plain scared, and there wasn't a thing I could do. I got flashes as one or the other would go down in the fight, and it was killing me not knowing. I watched as Jamie went flying through the air across the room as if in slow motion, but really, it all happened so fast I'm not even positive how I saw it. Somehow, it was like Xavier appeared out of thin air over him. I'm sure he jumped or something, but they moved so fast it was hard to tell. He wrapped his hand around the man's throat (a move I was learning he was fond of) and as if suddenly yanked from the air, they fell straight down through Jamie's desk. Paper and junk piled on the desk exploded all over the place on impact. Timber wreckage littered the floor and, looking at it, it was extremely hard to believe the mess had once been a desk even though I saw it happen.

Xavier's eyes were black, but no longer flickering. His expression was evil and he was snarling, baring his fangs, pinning Jamie to the ground by the throat. It reminded me of the instant at the other coven and for a second I feared him all over again. I could hardly process what I was seeing; he looked nothing like the vampire I knew. Somehow in that moment he wasn't the funny, slightly quirky guy who talked too much when he felt uncomfortable and had a passion for collecting cars. This one was crazed, maybe even evil. I wonder if this was how he looked the night Damien found him; that was the exact explanation he had given. Seeing this side of him made me wonder how Damien, who was a stranger at the time, saw the side I was only just starting to see, how through this he saw more than a monster, because I couldn't. I watched in horror as he grabbed the scruff of his shirt, lifting him slightly off the ground only to slam him back down, breaking the polished wooden floorboard under his head. I heard the bones in Jamie's ribs crack and a small amount of blood seeped from his head, where the skin split, and started to pool on the floor in the cracked boards.

"One! You will bow to me; even if I have to cut you off at knee level to achieve it, you will bow. Two! You will tell me where the hunter was going and what he wanted. Or I'll make it higher. And three! You will NEVER! And I mean *never* touch her again. We will be staying the night, much to my displeasure but, as you pointed out, my companion is human. So I'll make it clear now: I do not want to be disturbed and she will not be touched. Anyone so much as thinks about touching her, I'll know and I'll make sure my sword strikes below the neck of you and the entire population of your pathetic little coven. Do I make myself clear?"

Jamie's eyes were practically colourless. His face was no longer tense but riddled with fear; Xavier had him where he wanted him, at least for now. Xavier shook his head out of impatience as Jamie didn't answer. "I said, do I make myself clear?!"

"Yes, my lord," Jamie choked under Xavier's grip. I was under the impression it was extremely hard to hurt a vampire, but maybe not if you're a vampire yourself.

"Good, now the hunter," he said his voice suddenly having an edge of – well, I would say sanity, but I can't be sure if that was true though it did sound more reasonable.

"He was looking for Lincoln, my lord. I told him the last I heard he was in Florida and that we didn't have contact with criminals, so we were unsure of how reliable that was."

"What else?" he growled. Jamie went to say something but stopped; I'm guessing Xavier saw that as well because he growled and pulled a knife from his boot, placing the tip over the man's windpipe. "Tell me!"

"That's all I know, please, that's it, have mercy," Jamie pleaded, his eyes fixed on the knife with horror.

"Why Lincoln?" yelled Xavier. "Come on, Jamie you know as well as I do that it's going to hurt very much, and it's going to be a real bitch to heal." His tone was almost sympathetic but it was easy to tell he didn't care in the slightest.

"I don't know. His visit was brief. That was all he wanted, I swear. Please don't kill me." His voice was weak but you could hear the truth in it. Jamie's plea seemed to snap Xavier out of it; he loosened his grip.

"You'll live, for now, but that is assuming that you don't cross me again, Jamie," Xavier said, getting up. His face was expressionless and his eyes still black as he made his way over to take my hand once again. He opened the door and looked back to the other man, who was struggling to pick himself up. "Our room, if you please," Xavier said coldly.

"Of course," said Jamie, pulling himself to his knees, touching the healing cut on his head and calling for Markus. Within a blink of an eye Markus appeared next to Xavier, who pulled me away from him slightly. "A room for the lord and his mistress," said Jamie, his voice hoarse from where Xavier had crushed his throat. Markus nodded, looking in at the mess in his leader's office and at the state his leader was in. A look flashed in his eyes, something I couldn't place, but in no way did I like it.

"Follow me," he said, disappearing again; this guy was fast even for a vampire. We stood in the door way; I wasn't even sure if Xavier had seen which way he went. He reappeared after he realised we weren't following. "Sorry, my lord, I forgot the girl was human."

Xavier turned to me with an almost apologetic smile. "May I?" he asked, letting go of my hand and holding out his arms in a gesture I didn't really get. His eyes were still black, and even toward me his voice had coldness to it. It was clear to see he was still very on edge. I nodded, not really wanting to piss him off anymore, and after what I saw in there I wasn't game enough to argue so I didn't ask. He placed a hand on my back and reached down and took my legs out from under me, lifting me into his arms with an ease that seemed unnatural. *That's the thing, Misty; it* is *unnatural.*

"Put your arms around my neck and hold on," he whispered in my ear, and I secretly hoped he couldn't hear what I was thinking. I laced my arms around his neck and held on tight.

Something in me was terrified that he was going to drop me. while something else was laughing, saying that's the least of your worries, and it was right. Markus took off running, and this time Xavier followed. For creatures that have eternity to waste, they sure don't like to take their time. Xavier pulled me in closer as I tightened my grip and closed my eyes. I could feel the coolness of his skin through our clothes, and the coolness from the air that was moving so fast it was hard to breathe. Strangely, even after everything, or maybe even because of it, I felt safe in his arms even though at the same time I was completely terrified; funny that. I shivered, not from the cold but the strange tingle his touch always brought. I rested my head on his shoulder.

"Sorry," he muttered. I wasn't quite sure what he was apologizing about but I accepted anyway.

"It's alright," I whispered into his ear. We slowed; the first thing I noticed was that this place seemed a lot bigger than the other and, although it was hard not to like the expensive feel of the place, I would much rather stay in one of those pay by the hour motels any day. Xavier came to a stop and set me on my feet.

"Your room and your key, the only one we own, so no one's getting in or out." Markus paused and looked at me; that look flickered in his eyes again before he continued. "Unless you wish. I hope it's to your liking, and have a pleasant night, my lord." He pushed open the door and held it as we entered. *Yeah right, buddy, like I would want to leave with the likes of you roaming the halls.* I thought as I walked in. As soon as the door was shut and locked, Xavier relaxed. He turned to me and bent down to look deep in my eyes; concern was evident on his face.

"Are you okay?" he asked. I watched as his eyes dissolved back to green. "I mean, did I scare you?" He turned away. "I didn't mean to lose control like that, but when I saw him grab you I didn't know what to do. I have a wild temper sometimes."

"No," I said, my voice thick with sarcasm. "Why did he ask you not to kill him?"

He laughed a humourless laugh. "I'm worried you might be in a state of shock and you're worried why someone I was threatening to kill asked me not to kill them," he said, straightening up.

"I mean, you couldn't have even if you wanted to, could you?"

"Of course I could have, a number of ways in fact, the quickest of which would have been with my knife, which of course he was thinking," he said with a small laugh, I think directed at me. *Okay, I get it, my hunting lore's a little rusty.*

"But it would just break, wouldn't it?"

"Blessed silver. I am a hunter, remember. Sure it's a bit dull for the job, but it wouldn't be the worst thing I've hacked someone's head off with."

"Decapitation!? You were going to decapitate him."

"No I wasn't… well, not really, but he didn't need to know that. I was just using a common hunting technique; fear is a powerful persuasive, but I guess I would have if the situation called for it. Let's just say I didn't intend to but who knows, right? Sometimes heads just have to roll."

"Wow, that just confirmed my crazy theory," I blurted before I could stop. His lips turned up in a smirk at first, then he laughed. I couldn't help but smile; I think that's the first genuine laugh I ever heard from him.

"Well, I'm glad that's finally put to rest, but you are okay, right?"

"I'm fine, it just surprised me." I stopped and looked at him. "Never mind, I'm fine really, just a bit shaken if anything."

"I'm sorry about that, Misty. None of that should have happened. I feel terrible. I knew it was dangerous but I was careless. I underestimated him; it's all my fault. Really, I should have never left your side, I knew what he was like and I should have heard what he was thinking. You could have been killed or worse. God, I'm an idiot, what was I thinking, I'm so stupid," he rambled. He stopped talking to me about halfway through, when he started pacing. He hit his forehead with his palm and kept going on about all the things he should have known or done.

"Xavier," I said, grabbing his arms to stop him, "you're rambling; it wasn't your fault."

"I'm sorry," he said, not looking at me.

"Stop apologizing. You're not the fault of everything," I exclaimed, losing my temper a bit. I didn't blame him for what happened; he had to know that. He gave a half-hearted smile which told me he thought I was saying that to be nice. He did truly blame himself for how things went down. I'd seen Dad and Damien do it enough times to know the look, and he had it. It was a hunter thing, to think they can save everyone, but the truth of the matter was there was no possible way he could have known Jamie was going to try and kill me. I wanted to give him the same speech I gave Damien, but something told me it wouldn't help even if I did. There was an awkward silence and my stomach growled, breaking it. Xavier laughed softly.

"After living with a human for three years you'd think I'd learn, especially after the mood your brother gets in when he's hungry. You must be starving; you haven't eaten all day. I'll go get you something." He turned to leave.

"Um, wait," I said softly, so softly I wasn't sure it came out. I felt stupid for even thinking about saying what I was thinking but I didn't want to be left here alone; was that even safe? He stopped reached behind him lifting the back of his shirt. He passed me a gun, and I just stood looking at it.

"Holy water bullets, these should keep anyone back, it won't kill them but it will keep them down long enough for you to subdue them until I get back. No one will try, but if they do don't even hesitate. Head or heart are best; you can always apologise later," he said, putting it in my hand.

"Okay," I said, wondering why in the world I would want to apologise to someone I just shot. Well, I guess I would if they didn't deserve it, maybe.

"There are clothes in the cupboard, both sexes normally, you should be able to find something to fit, bathroom through there, but sadly this place is not well-equipped with gameage, but you should be able to entertain yourself until I get back," he said. I nodded, flipping the gun between my hands. "You do know how to use one, right? Because I just assumed…"

"Well…" I started. Yes, of course I knew how to use a gun and when I was younger I used them quite well, but I hadn't even held one in years, not with the intention of using it. Dad used to say it was like riding a bike, and maybe it was, but looking at the heavy silver gun in my hand, I didn't know if I could use it even if I wanted to. He laughed another genuine laugh; it was so amazingly adorable, it just seemed out of place. I knew there was a side to this man I might never see, a happy carefree side, and that really sucked because from the glimpses I did see it was amazing.

"Come here," he said, not even trying to hide the amusement in his voice as he stood behind me. "You hold it like this, that I guess you know." He put his hands over mine, moving them into position. "Safety's on, make sure you turn it off before you fire, that's that switch there." He ran my finger over it. "You cock it by pulling that back." He used my hand to slide the barrel back, and the strange tingle shot through me. I was actually starting to be grateful this guy didn't know the meaning of personal space.

"Of course, that's merely for show and you pull that to shoot, which I hope you know as well; aim, fire and bob's ya uncle, got that?"

"I have used one before, I was just thinking," I said, kinda pouty.

"Humour me anyway."

"Okay," I said, flicking the safety off and checking that it was indeed loaded. I stepped back and aimed it at him in a split second, holding it in one hand like an old pro. *It really is like riding a bike.*

He smiled; trust Xavier to smile when someone pointed a gun at him. "Good," he said, reaching around me to flick the safety back on, "Let's keep that on for now, okay?" he said in a playful tone. I couldn't help but notice how his touch lingered and he seemed to take his time stepping back despite the fact I had a gun to his chest. "I won't be any longer than an half an hour, have fun." He took off before I even get a chance to reply.

CHAPTER NINE

Xavier

What are you doing!? I snapped at myself as I leaned on the back of the closed door. Hundreds of voices invaded my mind all at once, and I tried to push them away long enough to think. *You happen to know for sure that girl knows her way around a gun. Off limits.* Damien would kill me if he heard half the things I had been thinking, and after that scene in the garage, I may as well have painted *I want you so bad* on my forehead and asked her if she could read. I was done. There was no way I was going to last however many days it was going to take to find Damien; hell, I wasn't even going to make it through the night at the rate I was going.

I either had to man up and deal with the consequences, or stay as far away from her as possible. Misty was smart, beautiful, funny and unbelievably sexy. Nothing was stopping me from living some of those wild thoughts and I was going to even if it killed me, which it most likely would in the long run. The semi-uncontrollable buzz of voices broke down my mental defences in small waves, making it hard to sort my own thoughts from thoughts of others, to the point that I thought my head would explode as I finally set off to get what I was going to get in the first place.

I resisted the urge to scream "shut up" at the top of my lungs and did my best to block them back out, but I knew it was all in vain. That required an intense amount of concentration, concentration I really didn't have to give. Besides, I already knew what they were saying. It was the same old things and really it wasn't unusual for me to be the buzz of the Coven. Ninety precent of the time I had Damien with me and he's got somewhat of a bad reputation; many don't sleep thinking the big bad hunters were coming to get them, especially the Night-timers. Night-timers are vampires that can't go out into the sun, so many of them live their lives cooped up in covens, and they are the reason most covens run on a night schedule. Because of that, they don't have the exposure to hunters and other supernatural creatures that Day-walkers like myself have. I'd like to say I felt sorry for those poor guys stuck in the dark, but not all Night-timers are "born" that way. It is true that sometimes unlucky vampires, when they are turned, cannot venture into the sun, but the so-called allergy to the sun can become worse over time, especially if you do not have constant exposure to it. It's really a use it or lose it situation; those who choose to be a true creature of the night will be forced to live with that choice for eternity.

Frankly, I was lucky in most departments; I had been a hunter most of my life and was exposed to the things that most vampires hate. I like to think it helped me build up a tolerance, which is good, because hunting would be a real bitch if a little bit of silver or a holy object could kill me. Don't get me wrong, they are anything but pleasant, but I manage.

I walked through the hall at a very human pace; I wasn't too eager to get back to the room and face Misty, well, I was, but that's the reason I shouldn't, and there was also the little fact that I myself was starving and she was a temptation too good to resist. I stopped and considered my options: there was no time to hunt, not at least while I was here. It would take too long and I couldn't leave Misty alone for that long; if word got out she was a hunter the temptation would be too great for some to resist. On the other hand I was at a coven, a place where there was no shortage of blood, donors, banks and vintages. Hell, if you were in the mood there was even different flavours, but it was all human and I didn't do that anymore. I started to walk down the hall toward the entrance of the coven, I knew the longer I took the longer I would have to think over my situation, even if it was just to clear my head.

"Traitor," hissed a voice form the shadows. I stopped; this was not what I needed right now.

"Murderer." "Liar."

Don't get me wrong. I was used to that; it was the price I paid for re-joining the coven lifestyle, no matter how temporary it was. Before, yeah, it used to bother me, but now I just shrugged it off. Well… normally I just shrugged it off, but right now I was hardly in the mood to do that.

"I bet none of you have the nerve to say that to my face," I snapped, looking around the open space for the owners of the voices. The whispers stopped and I felt all alone in the hall, but I knew better. I was in the company of the dead, and they don't call it dead silent for nothing. I made my way outside to my car, now parked neatly next to the mansion in the guest parking area. I hadn't recalled giving them my keys, but I wasn't the only one around here with tricks up my sleeves. It was about a twenty-minute drive to the nearest town if I intended to stick to the speed limit, but it was a rare day that I felt the need to abide by the law.

My belt felt bare without my gun and I hated being unarmed, but I knew it would do Misty far more good than it would do me at the moment. I couldn't help but smile at the clueless way she looked at the gun when I gave it to her. I loved how warm her skin felt against my hands, and how it made my breath catch in my throat like it used to do when I was still alive. It was almost like my lungs were going to burst if I didn't take that breath, if I couldn't breathe her in one last time. It was stupid, really, just a feeling, because breathing was really just a habit, not a necessity, but she made it feel as though it was. Even holding her like that sent my world crashing in around me. Just having her close, seeing that smile, even the annoying white noise of her thoughts, was worth every moment of self-loathing it brought, and just for a moment with her I felt human again.

I knew Damien would make me pay for even thinking that way; he was very protective of his little sister. Family meant the world to him, he was like his father in that way, but every cell in my body, living or not, craved Misty as if she was the key to life itself, and there was no way I was ready to give up on her. I would kill just to have her around, and with me that was never a good thing. I never felt that way toward someone before, not even my ex-wife Mary, god rest her soul. Sure, I loved her with everything I had, but I couldn't recall ever feeling like this; this was something else entirely. I was falling for my best friend's sister, one of the most feared hunters of his generation, and there was nothing I could do about it. I pulled up at a takeaway store Damien was fond of. I had come to memorise most of these places to avoid conflict. Normally Damien preferred dinners, and seeing how I couldn't care less I didn't argue, but whenever we would pass through he would always stop here. I walked up to the counter and was greeted with friendly smiles, even though I knew my presence was making them uncomfortable. The young girl serving me smiled and looked behind me, waiting for Damien. The last time we were in here, he flirted his arse off with her and scored her number, even though she would have to be a good seven years younger than him.

"Hey, stranger, long time no see; where's your friend this afternoon?" she said, her smile still pleasant even thought I knew she was mad that Damien had never called her. Her thoughts told me more than I needed to know and I tried to keep my smile pleasant as I smiled back, but apparently I only managed to creep her out (oh, the joys of being a vampire).

"The usual," I said, deciding to cover all the bases. Surely, seeing they were siblings, their tastes couldn't be that different, right?

"Sure!" she said, setting to work, and I tried not to take offence that she was relieved she didn't have to talk to me for a while. I looked around, picking up a different thought process, and smiled at the other woman staring at me from across the shop. She was older, closer to my age (my physical age, anyway) and kinda pretty, in a "she didn't know she was staring at a monster" kind of way. She didn't seem at all freaked out by me; quite the opposite. I had contemplated going over to get Misty a drink and was starting to think that may be a bad idea, but since I was sure Misty wouldn't fancy anything the coven had to offer, it was probably best. I slowly walked over to the fridge, looking over all the different types of soda pop and other drinks. I distinctly don't remember there being this many different types when I was human. Damien liked Red Bull but he also drank that with whatever hard liquor he had in his flask at the time, and it mostly ended up being more alcohol than soda, so I thought I would pass on that. I wished I had thought to ask her what she would like before I had left.

"You alright, hun?" said the girl who was checking me out from across the shop; her name badge said Wendy but her smile said "come get me."

"Yeah, I uh, just can't decide," I said, turning on the charm. She smiled a flirty smile and leaned across from me, pulling a fruity-looking drink out of the fridge. I took a deep breath as I caught her scent, and my jaw ached as my fangs tried to extend. I did my best to stop them.

"Try this, I know it looks like a girly drink, but trust me it's to die for," she said, looking up from under her lashes.

"Is that so?" I said with a flirty smile, turning on all my predatory skills before I could stop myself. I watched the dazed look cross her face, and her thoughts were on nothing but me. My throat ran dry as I stared at the stretch of skin covering her neck. I could hear her heart beating and I was just so hungry. "Do you have a break coming up?"

"I finish in five minutes," she said, smiling seductively.

"Is any one picking you up?" I said, trying to ignore the burn in my throat or the ache in my jaw.

"I brought my own car, it's out back," she said.

"Perfect," I whispered, standing closer and bending to whisper in her ear, allowing her to get the full power of my scent. "Do you want to get out of here?" I pulled away and smiled.

"Sir! Your order's ready," called the other girl from across the shop. I did my best to try and snap out of it, but I couldn't.

"I'll be right back," said Wendy, running out back.

"I'll be waiting," I said, winking at her as she left. I walked toward the counter teetering on the verge of blood lust. I knew better than anyone what I was doing was wrong, but I couldn't help myself. The younger girl smiled a much different smile as I passed her one of the fraudulent credit cards Damien and I had collected on our travels. I gave her my best charming smile as I thanked her and took the food. It smelt repulsive but I knew that was only because I was on the verge of blood lust; anything other than that sweet metallic liquid would stink at the moment.

Wendy met me as I made my way to the door; the other girl watched us as we went. My jaw was killing me as I walked her to her car. She leaned on the door and smiled. The smell was driving me insane and I couldn't wait any longer. I placed my bag on the bonnet, pulled the girl into my arms and moulded my mouth to hers. Her pulse raced and her nails dug into my back, pulling me in closer. I rammed her hard against the door of the car to avoid escape as my fangs slid into my mouth. I kissed her again, this time letting them trail downwards. My breath quickened as she moaned and I stared at the soft stretch of skin. I could see it pulsing as her pulse quickened. I lowered my head and let my fangs graze the surface as I breathed her in. Tightening my hold, I went for it.

Wait, what was I doing!? I stopped myself and threw myself backwards, my breath still rapid and my fangs still extended. I could have killed that girl and, worst of all, I was just about to do the very thing I would kill another vampire for. I wasn't that guy; I didn't prey on pretty women because I was feeling peckish, and I don't hunt humans.

"I'm sorry," I said, quickly grabbing the bag and walking off before I changed my mind again.

"Wait! Where are you going?" she yelled after me, her thoughts mentally cursing me. If only she knew how close she had just come to dying, and how easy it would be for me to change my mind and go back, she wouldn't be protesting so much. As soon as I was out of sight I ran to the car and hopped in. I tore out of that car park as fast as the car would let me, and didn't look back. I drove more slowly back to the coven, to let the blood lust pass; my jaw had stopped aching and my throat was still dry, but I was in control and that was a good thing. I parked the car back where I had found it before heading inside. I stopped in my tracks as someone stepped out, blocking my path.

"Xavier," said a voice I hadn't heard in years.

"Hey," I said slowly as a girl walked toward me. I tried to recall her name. I remembered we had a fling about twenty years ago, but what was her name?

"Wow, you look amazing, you've grown you hair out, right? Suits you," she said. I could vaguely remember the details of how we met; she was newly turned and I was doing a recruitment drive for the rouge army. I flirted to prove to the guys I could land a babe like that and she fell for it because I was dark and mysterious; for a while there I had this whole broody thing going on, but it worked. The reason we dated was more lust than love, and looking at her now I remembered why. She was very beautiful, but almost in a manufactured kinda way, a vampire Playboy bunny. She was tall, closer to my height, taller than most girls. She had never told me, but I suspected she was a model before she was turned; we never did do much talking. Her golden-blonde hair sat to her shoulders and was neatly styled, not a strand out of place. Her long body was toned and curved just right. Really, she had an amazing body. She was real arm candy; shame I only dated her for bragging rights. She had strange eyes, not strange as in they looked funny, but the colour was hard not to notice. Hot pink, the only vampire I have seen with that colour eyes, and they were big, bright and framed by long black lashes that she knew how to use to get her own way; this girl was the queen of puppy-dog eyes. She was beautiful even according to vampire standards, which made it funny because me, well, I'm kinda plain according to those same standards, and really, this girl was way out of my league. Thinking about it now, maybe I was only a novelty to her as well. At the time I was the only rogue she had ever met and I was a soldier; chicks dig that kinda thing, even dead ones. I can't say my motives for wanting her were any better than hers, that fling was all about the sex; still, her name escaped me.

"You don't remember me, do you?" she said. That wasn't entirely true; it was just her name I had forgotten. It is hard to forget some of the other stuff. I shook my head. Still, I felt pretty bad.

"I'm sorry," I said.

"Let me spark your memory," she said, walking up to me, and before I had time to realise what she was doing she kissed me.

It was fixing to be my lucky night. I was shocked at first but found myself kissing her back. Coming to my senses, I pushed her away. My mind kicked into action. *What do you know that really worked?*

"Stella," I said as it popped into my mind. She smiled a big bright smile.

"That was as good as I remember too," she said, and I had to agree with that one.

"So how have you been?" I said, making small talk.

"Okay, forever's a really long time, do you even find yourself feeling all alone?" she said, stepping close to me and running her hand down my chest. The edge to her voice was so hot it would have melted asphalt. I grabbed her hand and pulled it away.

"It gets like that," I said, trying my best not to fold to her will. Even to other vampires, pheromones were dangerous tools.

"So you're a full-time hunter now?" she said, biting her bottom lip. Here we go again; sadly, I wasn't the same guy she'd hooked up with, I didn't do novelty, not any more.

"Yeah, I'm sorry, Stella, but I should be going, I have business to attend to," I said, wanting to get away from her. Don't get me wrong; she was still hot, but why climb Everest twice? If it was any other girl I could just say I was married. You know, plaster that big not-available sign on my head, but I was sure even if I was, it wouldn't deter her. I went to walk off when she didn't respond, but she stopped me.

"I miss you, Xavier. Don't you ever think about what might have happened if we had stayed together?" she said. *No, in fact I hadn't, not even for a second, and if you weren't such a power-hungry bimbo and I was just any other guy you wouldn't have either!* I wished I was heartless enough to say it because she was starting to get on my nerves; now I remembered why I dumped her in the first place.

"Not really, that was twenty years ago," I said with an edge to my voice that I couldn't stop emerging. I wanted to be polite but she always had a way of getting on my nerves.

"I do," she said softly.

"Look Stella, I'm seeing someone, besides I gave up coven life long ago as you know, we could never work, and even in a thousand years if I'm still single, I still can't, I'm sorry," I said and she smiled. I said that to be mean and I thought that was kinda hurtful, but apparently she didn't.

"You can't hate something you rule, you know. Besides, it'll get lonely up there on the throne and I have forever, I can wait," she said, running her hand down my face before walking past me. I shook my head. I knew exactly what Damien would say if he saw me pass that up and for once it was a good thing he wasn't here because I wasn't in the mood; just thinking about it was pissing me off. I composed myself again and headed inside back to the room.

CHAPTER TEN

Misty

I wandered around the room for a bit after Xavier left. It sure was flash but, like I said before, no amount of luxury could remove the creepiness from this place. I had a quick shower before heading to the bedroom and looked around trying to find some pyjamas, except the only ones I could find looked more like lingerie. I found a lace strip that was meant to be panties; there was no way in hell you would ever catch me walking around in something like that, at least not normally, but since I needed my clothes what other choice did I have? I grabbed the least-revealing set and a bathrobe, then put them on. I put the gun in the pocket of the robe and relaxed back on the bed, turning on the TV.

I flicked through the channels; all this damn money and they didn't even have cable! I settled for some crap show about criminal profiling. It was low-budget and cheesy but it was either this or a documentary about spiders, and I hate spiders!

"Madmen, murders, America has had its fair share of these over the years but none compare to the two from our next story. The Deranged Pair were born and raised in Ashfield, Connecticut, known culprits of the Massachusetts massacre, four murders in Washington, and ten still pending investigation. The brothers are among the most wanted men in the United States. When it comes to these boys, it turns out evil does have a name, and it goes by Damien and Xavier West." A mugshot photo of them appeared on the screen, and it was lucky I wasn't drinking anything because I would have spat it back out. "The pair have evaded three statewide manhunts, escaped countless captures and have even managed to get a presidential pardon, but when asked for that knowledge and the reason that these two men never seem to stay in custody, the police refused to give a statement on the pair, only saying the two are armed and dangerous. If seen they should be reported to your local authority and not approached, because they have been known to be hostile. Coming up next on America's most wanted criminals, Damien saved my baby, an interview with real-life people saying we have it wrong."

I turned off the TV and just looked at the black screen, shocked. What if the cops got Damien; could it be that simple? That would explain why he had suddenly gone off radar. No, they would have said, and surely someone would have heard if he had been arrested. This was serious; how come he never mentioned he just happened to be one of America's most wanted? I knew he was in some trouble, but that – wow. *Wait!* They got it wrong; Xavier's not a West. I think I would know if he was related to me; besides, I'm sure he said his last name was Connor, unless he's like some kind of uncle I don't know about.

No way was that right, I mean, come on, he's not related to me, at least I didn't think he was. He's definitely not my brother, not that that made me feel a whole lot better. I heard the door open and every muscle in my body tensed. I wasn't sure who I would rather it be, Xavier the homicidal manic and possible relative, or a murderous bloodthirsty vampire hell-bent on killing me; yep, that's a hard one, alright.

"Zay, is that you?" I yelled and then laughed at my own stupidly; if it wasn't Xavier, not only would they not answer me, but I just told them where to start looking. *Stupid.* I put my hand in the pocket of the robe and grabbed the gun, ready to use it if I had to.

"Yep," he called back, much to my relief, and it felt like a weight had been lifted off of me. I sighed and collapsed back on the bed.

"Come here for a sec," I said, just louder than a whisper. Part of me wished he hadn't heard it, but part of me knew he had and another small part of me was telling me how stupid I was for asking him to in the first place. Yeah, thinking is complicated. He appeared at the door holding a bag full of various takeaways and I secretly hoped he couldn't hear what I was thinking.

"I wasn't sure what ya would like but I got you some of the stuff Damien normally has," he said as he passed me the bag and sat down on the edge of the bed. My heart did a back flip as the mattress sank and my mind whirled with the thought that we were on the same bed together, alone, in a sealed room. *No, stop it! He might be related to you.* I dragged my thoughts away and asked him what I had intended to ask him.

"You're a West?" I said. *Straight to the point, Misty, don't ease into it or anything.*

He laughed and relaxed a little; what had he expected me to ask? "We were on the news again, weren't we?" he said. His voice indicated that it annoyed him, but his smile said something completely different.

"No, *America's Most Wanted* was doing a profile on you two, and why didn't you feel the need to let me know that you and Damien are wanted men? It said you've evaded three state-wide manhunts, that's not good. Xavier what they have you pinned for, you two are facing the death penalty if they get their hands on you! And if they can't it's going to go fully ye olde Wild West, with DOA posters and everything." He laughed as if what I was said was funny. "It's not funny!" I snapped. "And why are you using my family's last name to commit your felonies?"

"We're hunters; it's not a felony to knife a shifter, or exorcise a demon. It's part of the job description. We kill things, well, we kill creatures that don't belong mingling with the human race; unluckily for us, many have a human cover. Hunters have their own rules, we have our ways to deal with things and the rest of the world has theirs. Me and Dee are about due for a hunter's escape," he said as if he just expected me to know what he was talking about, and I was really starting to get sick of that. I was a real hunter, damn it, so why didn't I know this stuff! I looked at him, waiting for him to explain; I didn't want to rip him a new one for making me see how incompetent I had become, *Okay, I give up.*

"Which is?" I asked, hoping for an actual answer.

"Faking our own death," he said in a matter of fact tone accompanied by a look that said *Duh. Well, FYI Mr Vampire, I suck at hunting, don't judge me!* He continued and part of me hoped he didn't hear my mental outburst. "Which is a lot harder to do when you're not dead already, all I have to do is go to a public place and collapse, arrgh, this man's dead." He said the last part in a high-pitched voice while waving his arms slightly for dramatic effect, and I couldn't help but laugh. It was true, wouldn't take much more than that; he had no pulse and he was already ice cold. If he laid still and didn't breathe it would be hard to prove otherwise. "And I can just dig myself out later. Total pain in the arse but I've done it before, but with Damien things just aren't that simple, although I have heard of a toxin that paralyses the body and slows the heart rate so much that it's impossible to tell the person's still alive, but unfortunately I also found out that it is fatal to humans, so not a really good idea and therefore not helpful at all, so we're working on it." I looked at him, sorting out the useful parts of that story and still not really getting the point.

"What? Making him undead?" I said, shocked. *Hell no, no one was sending my brother into un-life.*

"No, of course not, killing him is the obvious choice," he said a little too seriously. My jaw dropped; *was he joking?* He cracked up laughing and shook his head as if he couldn't believe I would believe him. *Well, news flash, dude, you're one hell of an actor.* "I'm kidding, Misty, relax. I couldn't kill Damien, even though sometimes I really want to. I just meant it takes quite a bit to fake a death of someone who is still alive, so that's why we haven't yet; too time consuming, and I have better things to do."

"But you have before, right?" I said

"Well, it's different for me, like I said, it's a lot easier. I was born Xavier Charles Connor and he died from a gunshot wound to the chest forty years ago at age twenty-five."

"So you're sixty-five!" I said, choosing to take that from his story. He nodded.

"Not the world's oldest vampire but I'm looking pretty good for my age, if I do say so myself," he said, giving me a charming smile. *Oh yes indeed you do.* I nodded before I could stop myself, then blushed. "Anyway, after I was turned I faked my own death so I could continue hunting without this sort of problem. When I started hunting with your family I used your name for convenience, seeing the Wests are the most widely known hunting family." I nodded again; finally, an answer.

"Right, so you guys aren't murderers, you're only doing your job?" I grabbed some chips out of the bag he sat next to me.

"Well, that I thought would be pretty obvious, Misty, I mean at the very least you know your brother," he said.

I nodded. "Yeah, I do, and I know exactly what's he capable of; if he thought killing someone was the right thing to do he'd do it, I have no doubts about that," I said in a matter of fact tone.

He looked shocked and shook his head. "I'm not so sure about that. Now me, on the other hand, cold blood isn't too far out of my range," he said.

"I've noticed."

"Gee, thanks for the vote of confidence, you were meant to disagree" he said with a laugh.

"You welcome," I replied, overly cheerily.

"But really, hunting isn't really your garden-variety job, the things we hunt use humans and all the police see is two guys killing people, even though they might have really been demons, the guys holding the guns get the blame and telling the truth doesn't really cut it anymore, no one believes in monsters except the people who already know better. Everything would be so much easier if everyone believed again; what happened to all the good old God-fearing folks?"

"Well, if it's so hard, why do it? You make it sound like it's not even worth it," I said, and I could see how. The pay was nonexistent, the job was dangerous and you could save the damn world and they would still arrest you the next day; yep, hunting was a sucky job.

"It's worth it; you have no idea how many lives we have saved. I do it to save people; without hunters, people would die. And in the long run it's worth it to see the look on people's faces after we burst in the room, guns blazing, and save their asses. I do it for their thanks, but when you think about it, the truth is hunting has no rewards, only punishments."

I laughed at that. "You're so corny," I said.

"Just ruin my great speech," he said. "I spent a little time on that in my head, thank you very much."

"Oh, it was lovely," I said, giving him a sweet smile. He grabbed the pillow next to him and threw it at me playfully.

"Well, I'm going to get some shut eye. We have a very early start in the morning, you done with that?" he asked, picking up the food. I removed my chips from the bag and sat them on the dresser. He grabbed the bag and fled the room. Thinking it was probably best if I hit the hay as well, I got up and hung the bathrobe on its hook near the door. I placed the gun next to the half-empty bag of chips for easy accessibility, then pulled back the sheets. I fiddled with the covers and adjusted my PJ's trying to get ready for bed. Out of the corner of my eye I saw Xavier standing in the doorway. I turned quickly to face him, as if he had just caught me in the middle of a criminal act. I crossed my arms over my chest, suddenly feeling self-conscious at my choice of pyjamas, or lack thereof. Really, all I was wearing was a pink bra that had lace instead of a body and almost see-through lace panties, and yes, they were the least revealing set.

My cheeks burned hot; I hadn't expected him to come back in. I looked up to meet his eyes, only his weren't on my face, far from it, actually. *Oh my god, he's checking me out!* I had to admit it was a good boost for my confidence, but that didn't mean he could ogle me and get away with it. I put my hands on my hips and cleared my throat; he looked up to eye level.

"Um, well." He stopped and looked away, totally caught in the act. "Oh right, that was it, there's only one bed and I couldn't find a couch," he said. I raised an eyebrow. *I bet*, I thought, and he laughed but still didn't meet my eyes. "No, really, so you can have that if you want and I'll sleep on the floor."

I looked at him; this was a trick if I had ever seen one! He so knew I wouldn't make him sleep on the floor; the guilt would kill me. *Very clever, Mr Connor, bravo.*

"No, it's cool, you can share this one; you don't have to sleep on the floor," I said, only half-scolding myself for being so polite.

"You sure it won't be too uncomfortable for you," he said, trying to be polite as well, but I knew full well inside he was screaming yes; hell, I know I was.

"I'm sure, now hurry up before I change my mind," I said with a laugh, getting into bed to stop his roaming eyes.

"Those are some great PJ's, by the way," he said as he entered the room. I stopped, still half out of bed, and give him the look.

"Don't push your luck, mister," I warned. Sure, he was hot, but not so hot that I wouldn't consider making him sleep on the floor. He laughed and that devilish smirk that melted me to the core crossed his face.

"I'm sorry, I can't help it. I just assumed that since you chose to wear them you wouldn't mind a compliment, besides, if they didn't look so good on I wouldn't have to." There was a glint in his eye that was making me wish I was the one who could read minds.

"Oh, my god, I'm going to have to kill you," I said, pretending to be mortified, but really I was doing a little happy dance in my head. *He thinks I'm hot!* He laughed again; bad choice on my part.

"Don't lie, you love it, besides, I never said you couldn't look," he said, slipping his shirt off and throwing it to the floor. He quickly covered the totally purposeful action by walking to the cupboard to look for PJ's, but I knew better. He grabbed a pair of what looked like track pants out, and even though I was only looking at him from the back I was starting to think there was no way I could kick that out of bed, ever.

"I never said I haven't," I said slyly with a big smile on my face.

"What?" he said, turning around to look at me. I couldn't help but check him out: long lean muscles, so perfectly sculpted it was as if God himself created this man. Every ripple and curve of his amazing torso was better than the last. I found myself praying that he never put a shirt back on; hell, it should be a damn crime for him to be wearing one at all. I had no intention of hiding the fact I was checking him out. Really, I didn't think I could even if I wanted to, which I didn't. He smiled and walked out of the room. *Misty, what are you doing? I can't believe you're flirting with him! This is not just some hot guy, he's your brother's best friend! And he also happens to be a vampire; you're probably just lunch to him, besides you don't want to give him the wrong idea, seeing you are sharing a bed tonight!* I stopped myself there. *Or did I?*

He walked back in wearing only the track pants, and turned the light off before getting into bed. I rolled over to face him and propped my head up on my hands; suddenly the idea of sleep just didn't seem as appealing. He stared at the ceiling for a second before doing the same. I stared into his emerald eyes even thought I could barely see them in the dark, but they were not something you could easily forget. I wanted to kiss him so bad, but that wasn't the only thing I wanted. The electricity I felt between us was so strong I was surprised things weren't short-circuiting. I wondered if he felt it too, if he wanted me as badly as I wanted him. I knew it was easy to get carried away and I didn't need that right now, but boy, did I want it. If only the timing was better. I sighed, distraction time.

"Okay, time for a bedtime story," I said quickly. I couldn't quite make out his expression in the dark. I only knew his eyes were on my face. His gaze, intense and hot, made me wonder if I had annoyed him by talking. A small smile pulled at his lips and he let out an almost humourless laugh.

"Okay, what one? I know Little Red Riding Hood or Hansel and Gretel, Grimm brothers versions only," he said in a teasing tone, but I wasn't joking about the story; I just had a different one in mind. I doubted he even planned on sleeping and I wasn't sure if a vampire could but I just wanted to enjoy his presence, because after all, at the moment it was all I was going to get.

"No, you said you loved to tell stories, so tell me one." He was deadly quiet for a second while he looked back up at the ceiling.

"Okay, what about?" he asked finally.

"I don't know, um, what was your life like before you got turned?" I asked, hoping I wasn't overstepping any boundaries.

"Um, good question, I don't remember much, really. Most of what I had done I found out from others, or old journals. I used to keep journals religiously, like most hunters of my time it was a necessity, because back then we didn't have the internet or cell phones and I couldn't just Google something whenever I needed to. So we got our info the old-fashioned way. My parents died when I was young. I was sent halfway across the world to live with a hunter. I grew up in a small town. Married my… well, it would have been high school sweetheart except apparently I never went to high school. I married young; I was about nineteen at the time. I spent six lovely years doing much of the same stuff as I always did, then I was turned; nothing special, really," he said. I nodded; it didn't take a rocket scientist to tell that wasn't the whole story and I understood why he wouldn't tell a stranger, but I knew there was more and I would find out, sooner or later.

"You're married?" I said, trying to get him talking again.

"Was married, I'm a widower," he corrected, and I felt kinda bad for prying.

"I'm so sorry, do you mind if I ask how she died," I asked, watching what I said so I didn't spark bad memories.

"No, not at all. I didn't even know actually. I read it in the newspaper. I later found out it was cancer, taken at sixty-three, of course I was upset, but they told me she was happy, that's all I could ask for, right?" I gave him a sympathetic look.

"If she was alive all those years how come you never saw her?" I asked. He went silent again. Maybe I had gone too far this time?

"Well, it was complicated back then. If you were turned into anything you were as good as dead. Hunters didn't want monsters with the abilities of hunters and I proved I was no different than any other creature out there when I killed my hunting partner whilst I was adjusting. He was the only one who still trusted me, and I betrayed him. The incident made me realise it wasn't safe for me to be around her any more. So I left, but selfishly I didn't want to die so later that year I faked my own death, leaving only a love note to say why I had left and good bye, I don't even know if she got it." The hurt in his voice was heartbreaking, but again, I knew the events were more dramatized than he had said and the stories were full of details he would never share.

"What was she like?" I asked, trying to move to a less painful subject. He rolled onto his back and laced his fingers in his hair behind his head. I saw a smile cross his lips as he remembered her.

"Amazing. I never deserved a girl like her, she was so beautiful. When we were younger I loved lying there twisting her dark ringlets around my fingers, whilst we talked for hours on end. Oh and she had the prettiest brown eyes I'd ever seen. She was kind, loving, smart and she didn't deserve the heartache I caused her. She was my world when we were kids and in a way she always was, but we married too young and I was a total arsehole in my youth. Neither of us could see that, like most young couples, we were doomed to fail, but that being said, I certainly did my fair share to speed the process up. I don't remember much but from what I was told I was horrible. I drank, I cheated, I never once told her what she meant to me, when I think about it now I see how lucky I was to have her, to have anyone really, anyone else would have left me, but not my Mary." He smiled and even in the dark I could see the pain in his eyes. "I was a horrible person, it really was for the best she remarried and that she and Roseanna got the life they deserved."

"Roseanna?" I asked.

"My daughter. I only found out about her nearly forty years after she was born. Mary was pregnant; she had been planning on telling me when I returned from my hunt, but I never did."

"How'd you find out about her, then?"

"She was the girl crying by Mary's coffin at her funeral. It didn't take me long to figure out she was Mary's daughter because at first glance I could have sworn it was Mary, but as I looked closer I could see that the two of us had more in common than I cared to admit. She had long dark hair and Mary's smile but her eyes were green and I just knew. I was so stupid, I could have had it all, but I threw it away and seeing her made me realise that. Part of me knew it was wrong to walk up to her but I just had to meet her, you know, just once, it was selfish and the look in her eyes as she recognised me was so painful. Of course she could never know I actually was her father, so when she asked who I was, I told her I was her half-brother and that her father loved her very much, and that he was proud of her until the day he died. I felt terrible that I had missed all those years of her life, and I got to thinking what else I had missed and what was to come. I realised all too suddenly that one day it would be her funeral I would be attending, and as it would any father, absent or not, that scared me. No parent should outlive their children. It was one of the few times the prospect of eternity was terrifying, and the fact that everything that had been keeping me human had died and the life I was still so desperately clinging to was now gone. It was one hell of a wake-up call and I wanted it all to end. Being an ex-hunter I knew it was easier said than done, and the quickest way to do it was attract attention to myself. Which was an easy task at the time; grief for Mary and for the life I missed put me in a dark place and for a while with her my humanity died. I lived fast and had no remorse for my actions; even to this day part of me still can't see the bad in them, a fact that I'm really not proud of. After the high wore off, after I could no longer numb my pain with sin, after I could no longer even look at myself in the mirror, I got the attention I was looking for in the form of a rookie hunter who for some strange reason took pity on me," he stopped.

"Damien?" I said, finally figuring out where he was going with his story, and he nodded.

"And that story you know," he said in a broken voice. I gave him a small smile. I could tell how hard it was for him to tell me that but I could also tell that tale was about the only truthful thing he had told me all night. The rest was a lie, subtle, but still lies. You can't be a hunter without being able to tell when someone's lying, yet so much of it was laced with truth and it seemed unfair to call him out on the rest. Why would he tell me he didn't remember his human life? From what he said it was easy to tell that wasn't someone else's recount, if for no other reason than no one else would be that brutally honest, no matter how horrible that person was, but I couldn't find it in me to call him on it so I didn't.

"So what happened with your old partner?" I asked as he rolled over to face me again.

"I think that's enough boring history for one night, you must be tired." I yawned. He was right, I was, but the room was like a million degrees and I just didn't feel like kicking off the covers with my PJ situation and all. These guys really need to invest in some ventilation. It was all well and good for those who had air conditioning.

"Yeah, I am, but it's just too hot to sleep," I said.

"Come here," he said and held out his arms. I just looked at him; am I dreaming? Oh no, I'd fallen asleep on him, because there is no way that he was holding his arms out for me. It took me a second to realise that I was awake, and as much as I wanted him, I knew it wouldn't be right.

"I don't think so," I replied, and he rolled his eyes.

"Misty, I'm not being sleazy and for once I'm not trying to get into your pants, just come here, trust me." I thought about that for a second and just before I was about to comment about not trying to get into my pants, he pulled me to him. I could feel every long lean muscle of his torso against my back, and heat filled my belly as icy relief travelled across my skin. Shifting us both, he put one of his arms under my pillow, the other across me, and I couldn't help but relax into his embrace. It just felt so natural. "Better?" he asked.

I nodded. "You have no idea."

"Now sleep, and don't worry; you can trust me." I smiled, and you know what? I believed him; I could trust him. I closed my eyes as the coolness from his skin washed over me. He rested his chin on the top of my head; he started humming a familiar tune I remembered from my childhood. I almost told him to quit it, but I found his voice was so soothing it helped my lack of sleep catch up with me, and I drifted off into a deep dream-filled slumber.

"Misty," Xavier whispered.

"Mmmm," I muttered, still very nearly asleep.

"Misty, wake up," he whispered again. I opened my eyes and couldn't believe it; I had my face nestled into his chest and one arm over him. "Can I have my arm back?" I quickly moved, doing my best to make it look like I was still asleep and just rolled over because he stirred me, *How embarrassing*! "It's still early, go back to sleep, I'll get you up later."

"Mmmm," I answered, and he laughed.

"Good girl." He leaned over and kissed me on the top of my head, then whispered something I didn't quite catch but it almost sounded like, "What have I gotten myself into." I mulled over the many different meanings those words could have until I drifted back off to sleep once again.

CHAPTER ELEVEN

The most delicious smell filled my lungs as I woke.

"Morning," said Xavier in an extremely cheerful tone. "Up you get."

"Five minutes," I groaned; it was still way too early.

"Hmm, we'll do this the hard way then," he said and grabbed the side of the mattress, literally tipping me out of bed. I fell to the floor with a thud.

"Owww," I groaned, sitting up and shooting him a look that was pure death.

"Oh, good, you're up," he said with that cheeky smile on his face. "I cooked breakfast, come on, chop, chop, don't make me dress you too," he said with a laugh and an evil smirk, the kind that made me think he would if I didn't.

"No, okay, I'm up, jerk," I said coldly. He smiled one of those genuine smiles. It was a smile that told so much, yet I had no idea what it was telling me. I secretly wished I could dig in his mind, although I'm not sure if that was a very good idea, not even in theory. He left the room with a happy sort of spring to his step. *Someone's in an annoying mood today,* I thought as I picked myself up. I heard the radio blast to life in the other room and groaned, *god he's so much like Dee except not even he's this much of a morning person.* I looked around for my clothes but after it became evident that they were gone, I looked in the cupboard for more. I managed to find something more my style after at least ten minutes of searching through ball gowns and Daisy Dukes. I found a pair of jeans stashed at the back, low cut and not at all practical for the field but jeans nonetheless.

Frankly, the choice of tops was worse than the bottoms and I settled for a plain pink button-up shirt. I was starting to wonder what vampires had against normal clothing. I walked out into the kitchen when I was all cleaned up and the music got louder with every step. *One in every crowd* by Montgomery Gentry started as I walked into the room.

"Love this song!" Xavier exclaimed, turning it up even more, not that it wasn't already loud enough, and started mouthing the words. I looked at him unimpressed. If you haven't already guessed, I'm not a morning person.

"Seriously? I didn't take you as a country kinda guy," I said, smiling because I knew even before he answered where it came from. Montgomery Gentry was Damien's favourite band and this was one of his favourite songs, meaning Xavier probably had listened to it a million times by now. I had brought Damien the *Back When I Knew It All* album the week it was released earlier that year. He shrugged.

"Yeah, you can take the boy from the country but you can never take the country from the boy," he said, looking over at me. I laughed at that.

"Country, when did you live in the country?" I asked, smirking as I pictured him in Wrangler jeans and a Stetson. Like I said before, it should be illegal for this boy to wear a shirt, and I was at least going to live that out in my head.

"I lived in the Australian outback until I was ten, not exactly the type of country you guys are used to but country nonetheless," he said in a matter of fact tone. I smiled. He didn't have the slightest hint of an Australian accent; I would have never guessed. He looked toward the small two-seater table. "It's getting cold," he said, nodding his head to the beat. I gave a small smile at that and made my way to the table to sit down at the only place set with food. I looked at the plate in front of me and will admit I was impressed; it looked delicious. For someone who didn't eat, he sure did know how to cook.

"Let me guess, poison," I joked, grabbing the fork. He laughed and shook his head.

"No, don't be silly, too obvious, flesh-eating bacteria is more my kinda thing." I couldn't get over the cheery mood he was in. It was like a totally different person. "Well, you going to just sit there and stare at your plate all morning? We have things to kill, places to be, you know," he said before he started singing along with the song whilst washing the mess that was left from cooking. I watched him, almost shocked. *Singing, cleaning, who was this guy and where has he been this whole time?*

"Okay, I give, what is up with you, suddenly become a housewife?" I asked. He laughed at that and shrugged.

"What, can't a guy be happy around here anymore?" he said, not turning to look at me.

"No, not unless I know why," I replied. He stopped and turned to face me, drying his hands on a dishcloth.

"Don't worry; you were heavily sedated," he said with the single most evil smirk I have ever seen.

"What?!" I cried out, nearly choking on the bite of pancake I had just put in my mouth.

"Got ya, payback's a bitch, huh."

I wanted to throw something at him; god, he's annoying. "Jerk," I said, unable to stop smiling.

"Really though, I just get in to these hyper moods, a little quirk of mine," he said.

I nodded. "So you're a bipolar vampire? Okay, I'll go for that," I joked. The song on the radio changed to the *Impossible* by Joe Nichols and he twirled around, then bowed and held out his hand for me.

"Dance with me," he said and grabbed my hand.

"Do I really have a choice," I asked, already knowing the answer.

"Well, I'm stronger, faster, and smarter, so, no you don't." He pulled me out of the chair and spun me into him. "Because I can just make you," he said, staring into my eyes before spinning me away from him. We danced around the kitchen until the song ended, and he sat down in the chair opposite mine and I continued my breakfast. "Well, you're a lot more fun than Damien, he never dances with me," he said with a smirk.

I laughed so hard I nearly choked on my food again. *I think he's trying to kill me*. "Really? I wonder why."

"Anytime I would get like this he would normally just shoot me, which is a real bring down, you know; you ever been shot?" he asked, and I shook my head. "It sucks, but I have gotten him out of bed the same way before, except I flipped the mattress while he was on it because he pissed me off the night before," he said with a laugh.

"That would have ended well," I stated, knowing how much my brother disliked being woken.

"Oh yeah, let's just say as usual it involved his gun." I smiled. I tried to join his good mood, because I knew it would be short-lived and frankly it was almost addictive, but I couldn't because I knew soon we would be back to reality and in our reality, happiness is a true gift. *Stupid logical brain.*

"I'm going to miss having you around," he said suddenly. I gave him a weird look and a small amount of fear rose into my stomach; suddenly I wasn't very hungry anymore.

"Why? I'm not going anywhere," I said, trying to imply a question. Was I going somewhere? Or was he planning to get rid of me? I wouldn't put it past this guy to tell me how much he wished he didn't have to kill me.

"No, I mean when we find Dee, he'll send you home and we'll go back to normal." I looked at him and smiled as a wave of relief washed over me.

"Is anything that involves you normal?" I asked, picking up the mood again.

"Good point; anyway, some moron slashed the Porsche's tires," he replied, rapidly changing the subject.

"Shit, really?"

"Don't worry, they'll get it back, I'll just have to borrow one of the coven's cars, and I tell ya now they're not getting it back in one piece, if at all."

"Now I see why you're so happy, you're plotting revenge," I said and he smiled evilly. It wouldn't surprise me if that really was the source of his good mood, because who wouldn't like some good old-fashioned revenge to kick-start the day? His phone started to vibrate on the counter behind me.

"You get that?" he asked, looking over to it. I nodded and grabbed the phone from the bench, answering it.

"Hello?" I said, not even thinking to check caller ID.

"Hey, who's this?" The voice on the end of the line froze me solid. *It couldn't be.*

"Damien?" I barely managed to get out. Shock froze me and I was unable to even answer his next question.

"Yeah, who's this?" he asked. Xavier's face was expressionless as he took the phone out of my hand.

"Damien," he said in a no-bullshit kinda tone, "who do you reckon it was? No, dude! It's Misty. What do you mean, what's she doing here? She's looking for you, and while we're on that subject, where the hell have you been! Don't give me that crap! What? Dude, how in hell would I know where Lincoln is, huh? So, and that means I'm his keeper? What? Where? Okay, but I need a time, Damien. Later tonight? I don't know, man, we'd be pushing it. Yeah, yeah, fine, we'll be there." He hung up the phone. "We got to go." I just looked at him. That was Damien, really; after all the worry we went through, he just calls?

"No, I'm not going anywhere until you tell me what's going on."

He sighed. "Damien got a lead on Lincoln, thinks he might be behind all this, and he wants us to meet up with him, but if we're going to make it we have to go now." He ran to the door and pulled it open. "Markus," he yelled, and within a blink Markus appeared at the door.

"Yes my lord," he said, his voice anything but friendly. Xavier scuffed him; I guess he didn't like his tone either.

"What happened to my tires?" he asked calmly.

"Kids, my lord," Xavier growled,

"Kids my arse," he yelled, then quickly calmed down. "I need a car, a fast car, and I need it now."

"Well, my lord, the only thing we have to your liking is Jamie's Lamborghini," he said with a nervous laugh.

"Where is it?" Xavier asked. Markus didn't answer. "Fine, I'll find it myself then," he said, and put him down. Turning to me, he gave me a small smile and threw me over his shoulder, then rushed out of the room. Normally I would protest such behaviour, but we were on a deadline. He kicked in door after door until he found what he was looking for.

As he put me down I looked at the big yellow Lamborghini parked directly in the centre of the room. "Get in," he demanded, as he opened the door.

"No wait!" I said and he stopped, looking over to me. "After everything he calls and tells you to come running, did he says where he's been all this time? I know my brother, Xavier, this doesn't sound right," I said.

"Look, Misty, at the moment I don't know or care where he's been, all I know is he wants our help, he's my partner, I have to go." I wanted to argue but he was right, and if it was Damien I didn't want to leave him helpless. Even though that was rarely a term you could use to describe my brother. I nodded and got in the car. Really, what did we have to lose?

He sped over to the garage door and ripped it up, the motor crunching as he did. In another move he was leaning in, looking at the finger scan ignition. "Great," he said, popping the hood and disappearing again. He fiddled around for a bit and, as if it was magic, the car started. He laughed cockily to himself as he got in, flooring the car and speeding off. The entire process happened in under a minute, barely enough time for me to process it, and I still couldn't figure out how in hell he got the damn thing started.

"How'd you that?" I asked, trying to catch up.

"With the greatest of difficulty," he said with a laugh and left it at that, but of course I wasn't having it; I needed to know.

"It didn't look that difficult," I stated.

"Looks can be deceiving, you know that," he said. I knew that he wasn't going to tell me and so, like I seemed to have to do with most things, I dropped the subject.

"Well, now you can add a count of grand theft auto to your rap sheet," I said simply.

"Another count, don't you mean," he replied.

"You are a very bad influence," I said and he laughed.

"Comes with the territory, and you're in the car so you have one count too."

"Like I said, bad influence." I looked at the speedometer and suddenly wish I hadn't. A million things ran through my head when I saw the speed, many of which involved me dying in a burning, twisted heap of metal. I guess my thoughts were pretty clear because he turned to me.

"Missy, what's the good of horsepower if you can't open her up." He laughed and put his foot down, sending me flying back in the seat. He rolled the windows down and cranked the music as we weaved in and out of traffic; I guess his good mood hadn't worn off after all. We drove for I have no idea how long, and I watched as the sky darkened; really, it was the only thing I could get a good look at.

"I love twilight," I said, looking at that the reddish glow in the sky.

"Me too," he said with a smile, his eyes meeting mine.

"Xavier," I said.

"Yeah," he replied, not breaking his gaze and as much as I loved his eyes, I wished he would.

"Maybe you should watch the road." He smiled, weaving around a car without even looking; I turned away and decided not to even watch at all. Maybe I should close my eyes altogether.

"Don't worry, we have a thousand times better senses than humans, you're in good hands and besides, if I look away I'll miss that look." I raised an eyebrow at him.

"What look?" I asked.

"The one where you screw your nose up and turn away and you have the cutest worried smile on your face," he said. I laughed dryly; of course he would love that look.

"That would be sheer terror from the driver not even looking at the road!" My voice got high-pitched and I cringed as he weaved around cars at a stupid speed without even looking.

"I like it." He said something else under his breath but I missed it over sheer terror and all.

"You truly are weird," I said.

"I know," he agreed and that made me smile.

"But I wouldn't have it any other way, how boring would that be?"

"Hmm, about as boring as you," he joked. I slapped him playfully, knowing full well he probably never felt it, but he pretended at least.

"Jerk," I watch as he stared past me into the thick woodlands that surrounded us.

"Right," he said, suddenly slamming the brakes and pulling off the road. My heart jumped into my throat and I gripped the dash for dear life.

"What the hell!" I screamed when my breath finally returned, but he didn't break gaze with whatever it was he was looking at, something I couldn't see.

"Look, Misty, I have something I need to deal with, I'll meet you at the bar," he said and then he was gone, no explanation whatsoever. I sat there waiting for my heart to stop racing. Not really having much of a choice, I climbed over into the driver's seat and pulled his door shut before putting it back in gear.

He's lucky I know where I am, I though as I indicated and pulled back onto the road. I was actually a little nervous driving this thing, but I would be lying if I didn't say I was totally stoked. I drove at only a quarter of the speed he was going, and kept below the speed limits. I looked at the time on the radio in the dash and notice his phone sitting there. I grabbed it, looking at the received calls. *Weird,* I thought as I went through them; Damien's number wasn't there at all. I looked at the last number in the received list; it looked familiar, like I'd seen it before, maybe one of his pre-paid ones? I dialled Damien's number from Xavier's phone; couldn't hurt to try.

"Hello…. psych." I got his message bank again. Why won't he answer his phone? He had only called us that morning; why go off radar again? This was all too suss; something was up and I didn't like it. I sped up; it wasn't like it was going to hurt to get a ticket in a stolen car, right? The sky turned dark as I drove along the highway and it was almost nine o'clock as I pulled into the bar. The Lamborghini looked out of place amongst the beat-up pickups and rundown cars that filled the lot. I saw Xavier leaning against the balcony of the old-fashioned bar. His stance suggested that he had been there a while, but I wondered if that was really true. I cut the engine and opened the door. I looked up to see Xavier holding the door. I hadn't even seen him move, although I should be used to that by now.

"What kept you?" he joked with a playful smile. *Well, I dunno, how about we talk about where you went, or is that something I'm just meant to know!* I thought, glaring at him; he really didn't think he could get away with ditching me by the side of the road on the stretch of highway in the middle of nowhere. Part of me hoped he heard it because I wasn't sure I would say it aloud.

"I'm sorry, but some of us are only human, with inferior senses and reflexes," I said coldly, and shoved his phone into his hand.

"Yeah, what was I thinking…" he said and, judging from the change in his tone, he'd heard what I was thinking. "Anyway, we're a little early; he's not here yet. Do you want to get a drink while we wait?" he asked.

"As long as it alcohol. I know you're supposed to try everything once, but..." I stopped and he got where I was going with that, and pushed me playfully.

"Of course I mean alcohol, what else would I mean," he smiled evilly.

"Can vampires even drink alcohol? I mean, it would be pointless, right?" I asked.

"Well, yeah, of course, but it only effects about one precent of our kind, and that's normally the percentage that was drunk when they were turned, although the amount of alcohol needed to get us drunk would be about the same amount as a glass of pure one hundred precent alcohol, so the answer is yes, but it doesn't easily take effect," he said.

"I see, you just made that up, didn't you?" I asked. He laughed and smiled that playful smile.

"Yeah, of course I did, how would I know? All I know is you have enough, you get drunk and that's good enough for me." he said.

"A Cosmo would be nice," I said.

"Well, in that case," he said, putting his arm across my shoulder and turning me toward the bar, "I know just the place." I had been to this bar before with Damien, a couple of times actually; in a small town bars weren't that common, so there wasn't really much of a choice. This one was like most small-town bars, similar to the one I work in. It was old, really; it almost looked like it was built hundreds of years ago, and could have passed as a saloon and I think that's what Damien liked most about it. There were wooden tables with uncomfortable barstools scattered around, and a clear space in the centre that was used for dancing. The colour scheme was mostly black and brown and there were old posters scattered on the walls, mostly old beer or whiskey ones. The bar was at the back and it had Pit Stop in neon above it.

We made our way to the bar. It was pretty crowded tonight; seeing it was on the highway you got all types in here and the crowd was always different. There was a menu that offered the three meals they prepared, and a range of alcohols. We found a clear space near the end and Xavier flagged the bartender.

"A Cosmo and scotch on the rocks," he said and the bartender laughed.

"Xavier, I'm not going to waste a glass," he said as he made my drink and sat a bottle in front of Xavier.

"Thanks, Max, put it on the tab," said Xavier with a laugh as his phone started to ring.

CHAPTER TWELVE

"Hello." A pause. I tried to hear what he was saying but he was a bit too far away. I watched him pace and his frustrated "You have fucking *got* to be kidding me!" rang over even the loud music and chatter. Clearly frustrated, he snapped the phone shut and stormed over. "Damien's not coming tonight, something came up, he said he'll meet us here in the morning." He sighed and grabbed the bottle. "While we're here we may as well enjoy it," he said, lifting the bottle to his lips, and he threw back half the bottle straight out. *Okay, that can't be healthy,* I thought as I watched him. He looked royally pissed but I was too concerned with the feeling of wrongness I was getting. Something was up; I knew my brother and he wouldn't just call and cancel at the last minute if it really was as important as he made it seem.

"Yeah," I started, but cut myself off with a "wow!" as I watched him skull down the rest of the bottle. I wasn't quite sure what his idea of enjoying himself was but I guess it was wild and totally different from mine; frankly, I wasn't sure I could handle that.

"Don't worry, Missy, like I said before it'll take more than this to get me drunk," he said, sitting the bottle back on the bar. The bartender replaced it, as if it was as normal as refilling a glass. The weirdness of that distracted me from my thoughts and before I could pick them up Xavier said, "We should dance."

I finished my Cosmo in a mouthful; man, I was going to need it. "No, we shouldn't," I said, placing the glass on the bar.

"Come on, you know I can make you," he said it as if it was a plea. I rolled my eyes and followed him onto the floor. I already knew he was a good dancer, but me on the other hand … well, I was the kind that gave white people a bad rep. I just stood there to the edge as he tried to coax me out to him. He rolled his eyes, turned and pointed at a pretty little thing who was dancing up a storm by herself. She smiled at him and pointed to herself. He nodded, grabbing her and spinning her into him, tipping her over his arm. She smiled like he had just made her night; of course if a guy that hot pulls you into his arms a girl can't help but feel lucky. I watched her and Xavier take control of the dance floor; the moves he was pulling looked like something straight from *Dirty Dancing*, but the way he pulled them would melt hearts faster than if Patrick Swayze were doing them himself. *Hell, even Patrick Swayze has nothing on Xavier.* There was no way I was even going to attempt that, at least not sober. I walked from the dance floor and sat at the corner of the bar. The song finished and he kissed the girl on the cheek, thanked her for the dance and walked back over to me. He had the biggest smartass smile on his face as he stopped in front of me.

"No one put's baby in the corner," he said, grabbing my hand and pulling me off the stool. I laughed as he dragged me back to the dance floor.

"You're an idiot," I said as he pulled me into his arms.

"I've never been compared to Patrick Swayze before," he said, spinning me away from him. I give a half-hearted effort to try and keep up but, like I said, dancing isn't my strong point.

"Well then, take that as your greatest compliment," I said as he took one hand in his own and I put the other on his waist.

"Come on, I've seen snails with more movement than you, what's up?" he asked. I just looked up at him and shrugged. "Come on, Missy, it can't be that bad; do you realise that the best thing that has happened to me in a long time is you? Uh, I meant because I have such a good time with you. If after everything I've dealt with this year I can still find something to smile at, you can too." I felt myself blush and I looked away.

"No, really, it's nothing, I just can't dance," I said.

"That's all? Look, it's easy, all in the hips, just move to the music, sway with the beat … everyone can dance, they just don't know it."

I looked at him. "Yeah, not me, I'm the only exception to that, trust me," I said with a laugh.

"Come here." He pulled me into him close enough that he could move me himself. Once again he proved that personal space is not one of the things he cares about, but this time I really didn't mind. "You know what your problem is? You need to loosen up, have fun, have another drink." He grabbed his bottle and handed it to me. "One mouthful of this and you'll loosen right up."

I just looked at him and broke away. "Xavier, I don't know, as much fun as getting wasted might sound, I'm not really in the mood." I didn't mean to crash the party, but how could I party when Damien was in trouble? I knew he meant to be here tomorrow, but something didn't feel right. I walked off the floor again and sat down. Xavier sighed and followed.

"Look, Misty, I understand your concern; we'll see him tomorrow and it'll all work out. Besides, you deserve a little fun after the last few days, what harm could one little drink do?" He waved the bottle in front of my face. I looked up at him; I guess he was right. I did need a little fun.

"I suppose…" I started.

"If it's any consolation, tonight I plan on drinking my own weight in alcohol, getting absolutely hammered, gracefully stumbling back to your place and passing out on the couch," he said with a smile, "and I'm planning to do it with or without you so what will it be, have some fun, or spend your night watching a very socially lubricated guy have the time of his life?"

I thought about it for a second; what the hell could one little drink hurt? "Cheers," I replied, taking a big mouthful, and passed it back.

"Cheers," he replied, knocking back the rest of the bottle before he slammed it down on the bar and flagged the bartender again. "Max, I'm out to break a record, keep 'em coming." He pulled out his wallet and passed him what looked like a credit card.

I hate to admit it but Xavier was right; a few drinks later I was having the time of my life. *It's My Life* by Bon Jovi started; Xavier, who I believe had reached the point of tipsy by that point, jumped on a table and was totally rocking out.

"This ain't a song for the broken hearted," he screamed at the top of his lungs. A crowd gathered around the table and, after the third time the song had been repeated, Xavier was standing on the bar and the whole place was rocking along with him. He held out his hand to me after the first chorus. I shook my head and laughed; there was no way in hell I was getting up there. I jumped in surprise as a group of guys standing behind me lifted me off the ground and carried me to the bar. Xavier grabbed my hand and pulled me the rest of the way up. The alcohol did a lot to improve my dance moves and the pair of us really put on a show; between the two of us we had all bases covered and I have to admit Xavier did mean air guitar.

"It's, my, life," we yelled along with the rest of the bar. With that last line Xavier jumped into the crowd and they caught him and set him on his feet. He took a bow; everyone in the bar was cheering and clapping at our little rock show and finally the jukebox had changed songs. A few guys patted Xavier on the back; another pulled him into a one-arm hug as he made his way back to the bar. Xavier looked up at me with a smile like I had never seen on his face; it was truly happy and pure, and I loved it! He held out his arms as if meaning for me to jump and I shook my head. *Was he serious?* I thought as a couple of guys coaxed me to jump.

Xavier nodded as I jumped into his arms and he spun us both around before setting me to my feet. I cracked up laughing. After everything, I was having the best night ever; I wasn't sure if it was the liquor or not but I couldn't remember a single time I had had more fun.

"That, that was amazing, I've never done anything like that before!" I exclaimed. He held out his hand to Max, who passed him a glass this time, and he took a drink. I had given up on keeping track of what he was drinking about the time I had done my third shot of vodka. *Love Me* by Collin Raye poured from the jukebox. I smiled as I remembered my father singing the chorus to me when I was a little girl, before he would leave for a hunt. It only took me a few seconds to realise I had heard it recently; it was the song Xavier was humming the night before.

"Can I have this dance?" asked Xavier, his emerald eyes sparking in the dim lights. He held out his hand to me and there was no way in the world I could have refused. His messy black hair had fallen across his face to one side and his smile, although a bit lopsided, lit up his whole face. I don't think I'll ever get over how beautiful he really was. I took his hand; he managed to be graceful even when he was clearly wasted, and pulled me in close. I draped my arms around his shoulders and he leaned into me. I rested my head on his shoulder and was trying hard not to trip on my own feet, which was proving to be harder than I first expected in my near-intoxicated state but, thankfully, he could dance well enough for the both of us.

The song finished but I didn't want to let go; I couldn't bear the thought of this moment ever ending. It felt so natural in his arms and I tried so hard to deny it but I had fallen for him, in only a matter of days. I looked back up and our eyes met. The room around us seemed to fade away and all that was left was the two of us. I couldn't believe it as he turned away and walked from the dance floor. Strangely, it felt like something from a dream. I stood there trying to clear my head and snap myself out of it. I looked around to find him at the bar finishing off another drink. He looked up at the clock on the wall, then pulled his jacket off the back of the chair.

"Come on, we better get you home before that last bit goes to my head and neither of us are able to properly think straight," he said. I nodded and followed him from the bar. My world was spinning as I walked toward the car. I really didn't think I'd had that much to drink.

Xavier grabbed my arm and steered me toward the highway back into town. "Come on, you, we're walking." The cool night air felt good against my skin and I was so buzzed I couldn't care less.

"Who would have ever thought I would be strolling down the highway, at just past midnight, with a very intoxicated vampire," I said loudly, my words slurring a bit, and he just laughed.

"Alright, keep your voice down now," he said, looking back at me. I watched him as he walked a few paces ahead of me and I couldn't help but notice he looked less graceful than usual, more human than I'd ever seen him.

"Why, who's going to hear me, Bambi?" I said, pointing into the woods. He stopped and laughed, waiting for me to catch up.

"There are a lot worse things out there than Bambi," he said, and I laughed.

"Oh, are the scary monsters coming to get you Xavier?" I said in a baby voice.

"I was more worried about them getting you," he replied, grabbing me and tickling my ribs. I screamed and laughed as we kept walking.

"Well, don't worry, I will just have to protect you since you're drunk and all," I slurred.

"Me? Ha! Look who's talking. At least I can walk in a straight line," he said, doing a very poor job of it. I tripped on my own feet and crumbled, unable to stop myself. Xavier caught me, lifting me into his arms with an ease that still shocked me.

"See, not only can I walk, I can carry you, who obviously can't," he said, smugly tripping a bit himself and causing us both to crack up laughing. "Don't worry, I'm good on my feet," he reassured me and started to jog; it was faster than any human could jog at a steady pace but he had long legs so I guess it wouldn't look that unnatural to any passers-by. He ran down my street with me in his arms and amazed me with the ease he had found it. He had obviously staggered this trip a few times. He bounded up the stairs but tripped on the last step, sending us both crashing to the porch. I landed on him top of him with a thud, looked down at him in my drunken haze and, as soon as our eyes met, we both cracked up once again.

"Good on your feet, hey?" I said with a big smile on my face.

"Well, pretty good." He laughed as we both laid on the deck, his arm around me. Mrs Patterson's porch light came on and I watched as she walked out. The deck where we were laying was dark and I knew she hadn't seen us, but with all the noise we were making I didn't want my elderly neighbour to worry. The fact that she might see me lying practically on top of a guy on my front steps didn't really bother me much.

"Misty, dear, is that you?" she called. I covered my mouth to stop my laughter and picked myself up. Xavier stayed where he was.

"Yeah, it's me, sorry about the noise," I called back, trying to sound as sober as possible while stepping into the light, but I had to cover my eyes when I did. I could see her standing in the doorway of her house looking over at me. I screamed and laughed as Xavier scooped me back up in his arms; so much for not startling my elderly neighbour.

"Sorry; we'll try and keep it down, ma'am," said Xavier, kicking the door open and dragging me inside. He pushed the door closed after he set me down, and I could have sworn I locked that door before I went to work. I leaned against the wall just inside the door. The room was so dark; the only light was the moonlight coming through the window. It cast a white glow across the table next to me, and half of Xavier face.

"Thank you," I said, my world spinning again.

"It was nothing; what's the use of having super strength if you don't get to carry your fair share of drunken damsels home?" he said, leaning one hand on the wall above my head to steady himself. He was so cute, I couldn't help but stare. He was made to be seen in the moonlight, which was ironic, really.

His emerald eyes seemed to be alive with the glow of the moon, and his pale skin was washed with an unearthly glow. I reached up and twisted my fingers in his hair, moving him closer to me. His emerald green eyes studied my face hungrily; my gaze fell to his soft, kissable lips, pink, full and inviting. I wanted them on mine more than I ever had before. My mind yelled at me to kiss him, but my body wouldn't act; I was frozen to the wall lost in those eyes.

"I guess that makes you my knight in dark denim," I said, looking into his amazing eyes.

"I guess so," he said, his voice coming out as a whisper. I wanted nothing more than to kiss him, but I couldn't muster the nerve, even while drunk. *Just kiss me!* my mind demanded, and he obeyed. Heat coursed through my body as I pushed myself off the wall into his arms. He reacted by lifting me up, my legs wrapping around his waist while we crashed back into the wall, our lips never parting for a second. He broke away long enough to run his hands up my waist. Lifting my arms and pulling off my shirt, he threw it to the ground. I dropped my feet to the ground as our lips locked once again. I slipped my hands under the collar of his jacket, peeling it off his shoulders. He shrugged it off as we backed up. My fingers fiddled with the buttons of his shirt and his hand cupped my arse and roamed my body and his lips caressed my shoulder, stumbling, tripping and knocking just about everything over as we made our way to the bedroom. I struggled with the last couple of buttons on his shirt in my drunken state and he stepped back, ripping the thing off completely. I pulled him back into me, my fingers twisting in his hair and digging into his shoulders. He stepped back again, his legs hitting the edge of my bed.

"Are you sure you want to do this?" I asked, watching him sway slightly on the spot, and even I knew that maybe this wasn't a very good idea.

"Come to Daddy," he said just before his eyes rolled back and he collapsed back on the bed.

"Xavier?" I asked, climbing on the bed to shake him. I couldn't believe this! I tapped his cheek. "Xavier!" He was out cold. *Just my luck!*

"Urgh, men!" I cried and climbed over to the other side of the bed. I contemplated pushing him onto the floor but pretty much as soon as my head hit the pillow, I was out too.

CHAPTER THIRTEEN

I rolled over; the light blinded me, my head was pounding and worst of all, I couldn't remember a thing from last night. That meant we must have had a good time, right? I sat up and looked around the room. It looked like a hurricane had hit while I was out. Stuff was knocked over, clothes were strewn everywhere. *What happened here?* I thought, looking back to the bed to see Xavier laying shirtless, half-sprawled out on my bed. His jeans hung open and his shirt was in shreds on the floor. He looked so peaceful in his sleep; too bad. I wanted to know what happened. I nudged him with my foot; he groaned and rolled over, rolling straight off the bed. He jumped up quickly, braced and ready for a fight, and when he realised there was nothing to be ready for he groaned.

"Urgh," he moaned as he collapsed on my bed again. "My head. Man, I must have been hammered last night." He sat up and looked at the remains of his shirt and then to me; it was clear we were thinking the same thing.

"You don't think we?" he said, trailing off on the last word as if trying to remember. Since we were partially clothed I thought it was unlikely, but we got up to something.

"Nah," we both said, but I wasn't entirely sure that our night was an innocent one. I got up and walked toward the kitchen.

"How'd we get home," he asked from another room as I walked into the kitchen and looked at the door. The locks were all still latched but completely ripped from the wall, and the door itself was half-hanging from its hinges.

"Well, I don't know but by the looks of it, you let us in," I said, staring at my poor front door.

"Why?" he asked, taking my side and looking toward the door. "I can fix that."

"You bet you can," I replied, walking to the cupboard to make breakfast. Xavier examined the door's damage, wincing every now and then from the morning light. He was sure a lot more helpful than Damien.

After he had straightened it up, he turned and said, "You get the paper delivered here?" I nodded as he turned back to the door, breaking it completely from its hinges and sitting it to the side.

"Mail box," I said. He nodded and dusted off his hands before strolling outside, in nothing but his jeans. As the sun touched his pale skin it darkened almost like it was tanning, but it had more of a glow to it. It kinda looked like a bad fake tan. I just stared at him from the window. He looked so amazing shirtless but I couldn't help but wonder at the weird way his skin reacted to the sun. Somehow, parts of his torso seemed less affected, like his collar, neck, face and arms, like reverse tan lines. He looked toward the fence and a charming smile crossed his face and he gave a small wave.

"Morning Mrs Patterson," he said, making his way over to the fence. This can't be good, right? I ran to the door.

"Morning dear," she said, giving him the once-over with a curious look. Thank god it was partially shady by the fence or we might have had some explaining to do. He held out his hand.

"Xavier Connor," he introduced himself.

"Amelia Patterson," she greeted with a smile, taking his hand.

"Sorry if we woke you last night, you know how us young ones get when we had a bit much. I already owe Misty a new door," he said with a laugh. She chuckled.

"No, it's fine dear, it just nice to see a polite young man in Misty's life. She needs a stable male influence in her life, the poor dear. It would just break this old girl's heart to see her get hurt again." I smiled at that. *Bless her heart,* I thought, leaning on the door frame.

"Well, ma'am, call me old-fashioned but I treat my women with the respect they deserve and have no intentions of ever hurting her," he said in a tone that made him sound much older than he looked. Mrs Patterson smiled.

"Well, Xavier, I must say you look awfully familiar."

"I'm a friend of the family's," he said quickly. "Been around as long as they have," he added when she gave him a curious look.

"Precious boy, you can't be older than twenty five," she said. Xavier smiled and got that knowing look on his face. *No, he isn't just about to tell my elderly neighbour he's a vampire*!

"Yes ma'am, but I've been around long enough to learn how to keep this lot out of trouble, they're in good hands," he said as realisation lit up her eyes.

"FBI, oh bless you child," she said, giving him an adoring smile like it was the one thing in the world she wanted to hear. "I'll let you get back to your paper and hope you stick around," she said.

"Bye ma'am," he said, strolling to the door. I quickly headed back inside and acted natural, pouring the cereal into a bowl. *Was so not eavesdropping,* but I couldn't hide the smile from my face no matter how hard I tried; that was one of the sweetest things I had ever seen.

"What you have to print it ya self?" I asked as he reached the door, his skin instantly going pale once again as soon as he stepped inside.

"Nah, I was just talking to your neighbour, she seems nice," he said, sitting at the table.

"Does your skin do that every time light hits it, or just intense light? Because I've never seen that before."

He looked up, almost shocked. "Shit, I forgot, photosensitivity. Well, I guess it's lucky for me it's not that sunny or that might have been hard to explain," he said with a laugh.

"Why?" I asked. "It didn't look that bad, not natural but not bad."

He smiled. "Nah, that was only just morning light. At times our skin will burn, even blister, and of course some of us actually do burst into flames, but that's rare. If that was all it was. I would be spending days at the beach," he said, shaking his head. "No, Misty, that was nothing, the sun can be a very dangerous thing," he said, getting up and leaving the room.

I glanced around at the state the house was in; we'd sure done a number on it. I couldn't help but wonder what happened last night. I finished up my breakfast and headed for the shower. I started to get undressed and there was a knock at the door.

"Missy, ya think Damien would mind if I pinched some clothes?" Xavier asked though the door.

"I guess not," I said, turning on the shower. I got in and let the cold water run over my body before turning on the heat. I had a slight headache and the sun was just a bit too bright but apart from that I was feeling fine, considering the amount I must have drunk last night. One of the few West traits I'm glad I inherited was the ability to handle alcohol while drinking it and the morning after. I got out, wrapping my towel around me, and made my way back to my room. Xavier was lying on my bed, still only in his jeans. He was staring at the ceiling with Damien's clothes in one hand and his phone in the other. I walked over to my dresser to find some clothes. I couldn't even imagine how good it was going to feel to be back in my own clothes again.

"Having fun?" I said as I chucked my clothes on the bed, and he nodded.

"Mmhmmm," he mumbled, not opening his eyes. I couldn't help but stare; he really was perfect. I remembered back to the first time I had seen this amazing creature. It shocked me to think that was only a few days ago. We had barely known each other for a few days and it felt like a lifetime, like somehow he had always been around. I couldn't get over the effect he had on me. Like the trance his voice sent me into, that cold tingle I got when his skin so much as touched mine, or that strange safe feeling I got when he was around … they were all so familiar. He sat up.

"You mind if I use the shower?" he asked.

"Of course not. This place may not be as fancy as your covens, but what's mine is yours," I said, smiling in his direction. He left the room and I got dressed then, laid down on my bed. I closed my eyes and flashes almost like memories played out in my head like a silent movie. The feel of my fingers twisting in his hair, that cheeky smile, my lips tingling as his luscious lips caressed mine, our bodies intertwined.

"The best thing that has happened to me in a long time is you," his voice echoed in my head. Was that real or some kind of fantasy? I was sure it was a memory but I couldn't believe it, no matter how real it felt and, damn, it felt so real. I laid there confused by the strange feelings that overwhelmed me as I thought about him. Never before have I hated someone but craved or needed them to be around, close to me, just because I wanted them there. I hated, loathed, needed, wanted, and craved him. *Get a grip, girl*, I thought, *he's just like any other guy you know, who are you kidding, every other guy you know isn't a drop-dead sexy vampire, look what you've gone and done, you've fallen for him*. The same sentence echoed in my head over and over, as if I couldn't believe it was real. Why did I have to torture myself with a drunken mistake? It may have been real but we were both wasted; it wouldn't have happened if we weren't. His sentence repeated in my head and I sighed.

"And I did mean that," said Xavier from the door. I hadn't even realised he was there, and I snapped myself out of it. I looked at him and, to make this just that much better, he was wearing nothing more than a towel. His eyes roamed the length of my body before he averted his gaze and smiled. I blushed. I was finding it hard to concentrate, knowing there was nothing under that towel. Within a blink of an eye he was gone. For a second I was devastated but maybe it was for the best; he didn't try and talk to me about what happened last night while practically naked. I was head over heels for a guy I barely knew, not exactly the kind of thing normal girls do. *Normal, ha, you're a hunter, he's a vampire, normal doesn't apply to this situation; anyway, normal was overrated, right?* He reappeared in the doorway, this time dressed in Damien's clothes.

To tell you the truth, they looked kinda silly on him. They were slightly too big for him and really not his style at all. Damien was your typical broad-shouldered all-American boy, where Xavier was tall, muscular but still slender.

"I've been thinking a lot and really, all I've been able to work out is nothing's ever going to be the same again after this, and I'm not sure if we can be friends." He paused and I could have nearly cried; what was he saying? My heart sunk to my feet at that and it hurt, oh yeah it hurt. "I think I'm falling for you, Misty, and if I have to spend one more second lying to the both of us, it's going to kill me. I want you and I have wanted you from the moment we met."

I looked away this whole time; I had wanted nothing more than for him to say that but now he had I couldn't reply, couldn't move and couldn't think. He stepped closer, taking one of my hands into his. "I know I come on kinda strong but I need you, it's all or nothing and I just have to know: do you want me too?"

I went to answer but I drew a blank. It was really a no brainer, of course I wanted him and the thought of being friends with this guy would kill me as well, so all or nothing sounded perfect. So why couldn't I say that? Could I risk losing him if it didn't work? His eyes roamed my face waiting for a sign, a word, anything, to let him know he hadn't been flat out rejected. An emotion crossed his face but was gone before I could see what it was and he turned away. *What are you doing?* I yelled at myself, letting impulse take over.

"Xavier!" I said, stepping forward to grab his shoulder and turn him back around. Without a second thought I draped my arms around his shoulders and kissed him. I felt his relief as his lips formed a smile before he kissed me back.

Was that the answer you were looking for? I thought. He nodded and stepped forward, pushing the door shut behind him.

His eyes flicked toward the bed, and I smiled and pulled him to me once again.

Xavier

I looked at my watch as I fixed the door I had managed to break last night. It wasn't too hard to fix; I had been a hunter my whole life but I was also an ex-husband so I was good at fixing things and when I was married that was what was expected from the husband, as cooking and cleaning was expected from the wife.

"We should get going, Damien might already be there," I said, holding the piece of wood in place so the glue would dry. I knew this whole frame would have to be replaced and I would do it, I promised I would, but right now some glue and a few screws was the best I could do. I aligned the door and screwed the hinges back I place. Stepping back, I hoped the glue would hold. I smiled as I realised the door was crooked and really, I didn't have time to work out why, so I adjusted the door just enough that it would close as I waited for Misty. The door sat loosely in its frame and I knew it wouldn't take more than a little force to open it back up, so I did the only thing I could think of. I warped the wood so it jammed in place, and smirked.

There was no way anything was getting in that unless they broke it back down again. I smiled as I saw Misty watching me out of the corner of my eye. She had a disapproving look on her face and I didn't even have to read her mind to know what she was thinking. She was so cute when she was annoyed, and I knew it's the whole forbidden fruit thing, but I didn't think there was enough holy water and silver in the world to make me give her up, not after this morning. I knew it was useless to fight it any more, probably useless to have tried in the first place, and the only thing I knew for sure now was that she was worth anything Damien could throw at me. The sun glinted a little too brightly off of her hair but really, it was glinting a little too brightly off of everything. Normally, if I didn't have my head hanging in the toilet, I would down coffee by the gallon until my hangover subsided. Of course, it was really to give me something to bring back up because it had no real effect, it still just felt right. Old habits die hard I guess, but not this morning; a quick hunt and a little hair of the dog was all I needed to get going and give me the Dutch courage I was looking for. I turned around so I could look at her properly. She was amazing. The sun lit up her hair, making it look like she had a halo; I knew it was just the glare from the sun effecting my eyes, but you never know, maybe it was a halo. Who was I to judge. Her blue eyes looked at me in a way I wish they always had. I couldn't help but smile as I walked down the path to meet her. She smiled as I stopped next to her; we both knew that we were going to have to walk to the bar but frankly, I didn't mind. I slipped my hand into hers and she twisted our fingers together and gave my hand a light squeeze.

The warmth of her skin was refreshing; it was usually something I associate with pain but for the first time in a long time my hands were warm, in a good way. Her thoughts were static but the flush of pink in her cheeks told me all I needed to know. Despite a killer hangover and the fact that from now on everything was going to be more complicated, life for once just seemed right. We walked toward the bar. It took about twenty minutes at her pace but with the way I felt this morning I wouldn't have cared if it took days, as long as I was with her.

I looked around the practically empty lot for Damien's Mustang as we entered, but it wasn't there. I looked at my watch; it was a bit after eleven. At least we beat him here I guess. My gaze fell on the Lamborghini I had stolen and I was kinda disappointed it was still there.

"Hmmm," I said, thinking out loud, "remind me to destroy that later." Misty's eyes fell on the car and she frowned.

"What? No, you can't," she said. I knew why she was protesting and normally I wouldn't even think of harming a car like that, but this one was not mine and I had a score to settle.

After all, I loved my Porsche and I knew I was never getting her back.

"I can and I am, they should have thought of the consequences when they slashed my tires," I said, walking toward the bar. She looked over it once more before following me into the bar.

"Well, well, the boy lives yet again, call off that hearse, boys, the dead walks," joked the bartender as we entered. Damien and I went to this bar all the time. Of course they didn't know what I was, but they were still impressed by my amazing drinking skills.

"Yeah, as always, I'm alive," I said, trying desperately to hold back the smirk I could feel moving to my lips. If they only knew how true their previous statement had been.

"And the young lady is more than a dance partner I see," he said, looking toward Misty.

"This is Misty," I said and I knew he would know her once he heard her name. There were many drunken nights Damien had told us all about his little sister Misty, who he loved so much.

"Damien's Misty?" the bartender said. I nodded "Hold on, Max! Call them back' we're going to need that hearse after all. Are you mad, kid?" the bartender said with a laugh. Yeah, maybe I was. I nodded before dragging Misty across the room. I watched as she slumped against the wall. I couldn't help but stare at her. Why does she do this to me? I walked over to her, leaning over her with one hand on the wall. I smiled as I took her hand with my other. I wanted her so badly, but I didn't know how far I could push this before I lost control. Biting and sex comes hand in hand with my kind and there was no way I could do that to her; we got lucky this morning but I wasn't stupid enough to push my luck too far.

"You trust me?" I asked. Her beautiful blue eyes roamed my face with the same kind of desire that I felt. She nodded, a smile forming on her soft lips. I leant, down finding those lips with my own. I traced my lips across her cheekbone, leaving small soft kisses. I slowly moved down; I knew I had control.

I stopped looking at her for a second. She had closed her eyes and was biting her bottom lip; I smiled and continued way down her neck and across her collar bone. I stopped, leaving my lips inches from her skin; her scent filled my lungs and she smelt so good, mouth-watering even. Her creamy soft skin was warm and inviting. I wanted to keep going, pull her in close, feel our lips meet, our bodies touch. Just the thought excited me, in more than just a sexual way, and that worried me. I had tempted fate; I knew I could stop with this but I wouldn't want to. I kiss her neck again.

I felt someone grab my shirt and I was suddenly ripped off of her and sent flying across the room, crashing right through a table. I feel a piece of wood drive through my back dangerously close to my heart, but seeing I had stayed conscious, it had missed. I couldn't pick myself back up before Alex was on me. He pulled a cross from his jacket. I winced as all my energy drained when he pressed it into the side of neck and put a gun to my head. *This is going to hurt,* I thought, closing my eyes, but he didn't shoot. I knew I had a chance to explain myself.

"Alex, look, that wasn't what it looked like," said my voice barely coming out. My chest was tight and I couldn't breathe, not that I really needed to, but I still needed air to talk and it was still uncomfortable as hell; my best guess was I had punctured a lung.

"Alex, get off him!" screamed Misty, coming to my rescue.

"Misty, you're alright? But I thought…" he said, getting off of me, and I slowly picked myself up, reaching around to pull the shard of wood out. I felt the pressure release in my chest as I started to heal. "Wait a minute! You mean he was… the two of you are together! Man, Damien's not going to like that," he said, brushing himself off, and it wasn't hard to see he wasn't too fond of the idea either. I realised what that must have looked like when he walked in and if I had seen a vampire with a girl pressed to the wall, his head to her neck, I would have acted the same way, so I couldn't really get pissy even though he did nearly stake me in the process.

"What are you doing here?" I asked.

"Damien called me and told me to meet him here," Alex replied, but there was just something off about that. His face said he was telling the truth, but his eyes were lying. I gave Alex the once-over. He was dressed in his usual cargo pants and polo shirt with the big canvas jacket he used to hide his weapons. He looked the same, even smelled the same, but something wasn't right.

"I'm going to call him and see where he is," I said, carefully hoping not to let him know I knew something was up. I tried to read his mind but, like Misty's, it was almost impossible; he was a hunter after all, and most of the older hunters had taught themselves how to block out invaders. Even I knew how to when I was still human. He gave me a curious look as I grabbed my phone. I looked through the recent calls and decided I would try the number Damien had called from yesterday.

I turned away and walked a few paces while I waited for it to connect. I looked around the bar as I did and, as if they were huge warning signs, a few things jumped out at me all at once. The door was closed and looked to be locked and the bar itself was messed up, with bottles tipped over and glasses knocked off. I was puzzled; I hadn't heard that happen but finally, the most important thing was that the bartenders were nowhere to be found. The phone connected and started to ring but the noise wasn't coming for the hand set, it was coming from behind me.

"Hello," said Alex, smiling evilly as he pulled a gun and pointed it at Misty. I let the phone drop from my hand and ran for Alex.

"Look out," I yelled to Misty, who wasn't facing the other hunter. She spun around at the sound of my warning and her eyes widened as I dived for Alex, but the gun fired. My mind slowed things down as it normally did in these situations, and I saw the bullet leave the barrel just as I collided with Alex, knocking the gun from his hand. I was too late! Alex crumbled to the ground and I launched myself in the other direction, attempting to do the impossible; I had to outrun that bullet. The bullet hadn't quite made it yet as I dived, putting everything I had into it for that extra speed.

I thought maybe there was still time. I knew I wasn't fast enough even before I attempted to outrun a speeding bullet, but I had to try anyway. I skidded to a stop as the bullet pierced Misty's chest and I watched as she was thrown backward to the floor. My world crashed around me as the smell of blood filled the air. I could feel my rage boil up inside of me and feel the tell-tale signs of my control slipping from my grasp. I would kill Alex for this. I felt my fangs extend as I saw Alex pull himself to his feet; hunter or not, he was going to die. I tackled him to the ground before he even knew what had hit him. Even wounded, I had better reflexes than he ever would. I pulled my fist back and punched him, not even attempting to hold back. I felt his cheekbone shatter under my fist and his body went limp for a second. I didn't check to see if he was already dead or not because I was going to tear him to pieces either way. I lowered my head to rip into his throat but I was too cocky and let rage overtake me, because a sharp pain shot through the side of my face and I was knocked backwards, my skin burning like it had been touched by acid. I knew what he had done. He was a hunter; he knew how to fight me and I hadn't counted on him still being conscious. My energy drained from me with the new wound. I knew it was made from something holy because my body was drawing all its energy trying to heal.

I jumped up with the greatest amount of effort, but it just wasn't fast enough. He had recovered his gun and this time, it was pointed at me. I growled, not scared to be shot, and charged for him. I heard the gun go off before I felt it, and I stopped. A sharp pain coursed through my chest and forced me to my knees. This wasn't right. I wasn't expecting this, what was happening? The room started to shake, then spin, and my eyes were going in and out of focus. What was in that bullet? I clutched my chest, fighting to stay conscious.

"V-tox, vampire, surprised you didn't smell it," he said, coming to stand over me. I felt my body give out and I crashed to the floor. I wanted to pick myself up, I wanted to yell and to scream at him, I wanted him dead, but as the light faded around me I knew that wasn't going to happen, and I managed to get out the remnants of a threat before I passed out.

CHAPTER FOURTEEN

Misty

I slowly came to.

"Alex! Alex, get back here! You're dead, you hear me? Dead!" I heard Xavier yelling from somewhere beside me. I looked around the small cement room as I woke up properly. It reminded me of some kind of basement ,or maybe a wine cellar. It was dark, cold, damp and altogether creepy. My shoulder was killing me but I was thankful to be alive. I knew better than anyone, being shot was an occupational hazard and right now I had more important things to worry about than the enormous amount of pain I was in. I struggled to try and free myself from the chains that were holding me in place. I couldn't move my arms or my legs, and they were just so tight I had no chance of wriggling out of them. I looked over at Xavier; he was restrained in a similar fashion as me except he was restrained a lot more thoroughly and looked to be tied in place with a mixture of what looked like silver chains and rosary beads.

"Xavier?" I said, still feeling groggy from pain but I had to pull it together.

"Misty, thank god…" he sighed, looking over at me, "you had me so worried, I'm so glad you're okay," and the relief in his voice warmed me; he really did care about me.

"Yeah, I'll live, if we get out of this, that is," I said, looking around again.

"Don't worry, I'll get us out of here somehow and when I've done that I'm going to kill Alex, just for the fun of it and trust me,

I'll enjoy every second of it too," he yelled, I guess to make sure Alex heard him. I wanted to tell him how crazy he sounded but I did agree with that plan. The man just shot me; I couldn't say I wanted him dead but at this moment I wouldn't care if he was.

"Where are we?" I asked, trying to pull an arm free.

"I'll answer that one," said Alex, as he walked into the room and stopped my escape plan.

"You wait until I break these, Alex," threatened Xavier. I could see his eyes were black and that was never a good sign.

"Now, Xavier, I've heard what you're going to do, but sadly you're all tied up, so I'll just have to wait," he said as he walked further into the room and stopped in front of Xavier. "Frankly, I expected much more from you, Xavier. The way Damien talked you up, it almost had me worried for a second."

"Where is he? What have you done with him?" snapped Xavier. Alex was behind this, a man I had called uncle most my life, someone who was supposed to be the good guy. It didn't make sense. He was our friend; why would he do this?

"Don't worry, he's alive and… well, he's alive, but I must say he has been rather useful and unlike the two of you, he still had some fight left in him," he said, turning to look at me. I cringed; he looked nothing the man I knew and no matter how hard a tried, I couldn't wrap my head around that fact that Alex would do this to us. He walked toward me next and ran the back of his hand down my face. I pulled my head away; how dare he touch me! "Like his daddy." How could he do this? The man I was seeing wasn't the guy who I loved like an uncle; how could he be? The Alex I knew would never hurt Damien and would never look at me like that.

"They fight the same way too, you know. Oh, Greg would be proud of that boy, grew up to be great, we always knew he would, although I had my worries. Oh, it only seems like yesterday when I shot poor Greg in the back and left him for the wolves, such a waste of a good hunter and a good friend. Shame, really, that the same fate has to befall you and your brother."

Xavier growled, thrashing around like a madman. There was steam or maybe smoke rising from his skin as the beads burnt into him. I couldn't breathe and it felt as if he had just ripped my heart right out from my chest and stomped on it.

"You killed my father! He was your hunting partner!" I yelled, tears stinging my eyes at the thought; I could almost picture betrayal in my father's eyes as he died. "You bastard, he was your friend!" I couldn't believe it. I trusted Alex, I turned to him when Dad died, and he stood by his grave and talked of the bravery my dad showed as he tried to save him and all this time, he was the one that killed him!

"You son of a bitch," growled Xavier. There was a pain in his voice I could tell wasn't physical. "Why?"

"Because he let you live!" yelled Alex, turning back to Xavier.

"He was your brother, he looked up to you, he loved you and I took it away! Tell me how you felt the day you found out he died. Do you remember that feeling? Huh? Well, I get that every day because of you! You left my brother for dead! And now he is the very thing I hunt, I have to face him every single day and remember you were the one that made him that way. He was outcasted! He was hunted and I had to stand back and watch it happen all while the real monster, the one that killed him, was welcomed home with open arms right back into the hunting family. They should have killed you like they were meant to, but now instead it's your turn. You, him and her, their entire family, deserve to die!" yelled Alex, pointing the gun at me with a shaking hand.

"I never killed your brother," said Xavier in an even voice, "and I have never turned anyone."

"Oh now, think hard, vampire, who am I?" he asked. Xavier went quiet for a bit. I could see he was trying to think who it could be, then he said, "Laurence, Alex Laurence.... Lincoln."

"Now you're catching on. Lincoln Laurence, your hunting partner, your friend, my brother! You took everything from me, now I'm going to return the favour starting with her," he yelled, walking over to me.

"Alex… no please," I begged as he untied me and took me in his arms. The gun pointed to my head.

"Any last words, beautiful," he said, and all I could do was cry. I was still trying to get my head around it. I had grown up around this guy, I had so many happy memories with him and they were all a lie, just some part in his deluded plot for revenge, on a man that wasn't even my family. Xavier wasn't my Dad's brother; they may have known each other, hell maybe they were once even friends, but he was not his brother. There was no way to look at this that didn't rewrite my entire life. This man killed my father, kidnapped my brother and was about to kill me, all to hurt the man I think I'm in love with. Never before in my life had I wished someone dead, but right at that moment it was all I wanted.

"You perverted old bastard, I swear you hurt her and I will kill you and I mean it, no amount of chains will be able to stop me!" Xavier threatened again. There was an edge to his voice I didn't like; I believed he meant it, but it fell on deaf ears.

"I don't know what is more satisfying, finally getting my revenge or watching you squirm because you're about to lose the woman you love," he said and laughed a truly evil laugh. I struggled in his grip and he rammed the gun under my jaw, pulling the hammer back.

"I will make you suffer for this, Alex, and I'll make sure you see it too!"

"Oh, and how exactly will you do that?" he said smugly.

"I'll tear your eyes out, making sure they sit somewhere to give you the perfect view and then very slowly rip you to shreds, piece by piece, starting with your skin to make sure every drop of that sweet-smelling blood of yours runs down that drain. I'll work my way to the bone and I'll make sure you live through every painful second of it even if I have to turn you to ensure it. You will suffer," Xavier growled, and he let out a quiet chuckle.

His fangs extended and his eyes were black. I hated to say it, but there wasn't a shred of humanity left to be seen. My heart raced and a part of me didn't want him to get loose if he was actually capable of something like that, and with the way he said it there was no doubt in my mind that he meant every word, and I guess there wasn't in Alex's either because his face was riddled with fear. I watched as Xavier struggled; the pain was evident on his face but it wasn't enough to stop him.

"You really are disturbed, everyone always said you were crazy, Connor," said Alex as he watched Xavier struggle, I guess praying he wouldn't get free. As disturbing as it was, I thanked Xavier for that little distraction because while he was busy watching Xavier try and break free he had loosened his grip, just a little, but it was enough for me to break free and knee him in the shins before diving to the floor in case he fired. I watched the rosary beads go flying as Xavier did just what he said he would do: broke free. He grabbed silver chains that were wrapped around him and snapped them as if they were string. Xavier dropped to his feet and Alex stood frozen, staring at him. He looked pure evil as he smiled at Alex, and within a blink of the eyes Alex was propelled across the room, crashing into a cupboard full of big glass jars. A jar full of what looked like water tipped over him, drenching him and pooling on the floor. The other jars fell and smashed, adding to the mess. Alex laughed as he got to his feet, grabbed another glass jar and tipped it over his head. Xavier stopped in his tracks and stepped back his eyes wide as Alex emptied the jar on the flood in front of him and the doorway.

"Like it, vampire? Hmmm? Oh, I guess you weren't expecting that, huh? But be my guest and try ripping me to pieces now. What, you're not going to try?" he laughed out loud and I looked to Xavier, who was glaring at him but still stepping back. "Can you feel that? I made it special, my half and half mix, and it's no backyard do-it-yourself stuff either. No, Xavier, half of it's blessed by the pope himself and the other half is specifically blessed against you. You remember that trick? Greg showed me that one. I went to a lot of effort to make it special just for you and it was hard as hell to get my hand on but worth every penny because now, and you'll love this, you can't touch me, and you'll be stuck down here for hours if not days, giving me all the time I need to disappear again" he turned to look at me, "and take your big brother with me."

He looked back at Xavier. "So as much as I would love to take you up on your little offer Xavier, I can't, must be getting going, until next time." He waved and ran out the door. I ran to the doorway stopping to see what was keeping Xavier. Xavier looked down at the puddle, then to the door. A look of resolve crossed his face and he ran. His left foot landed in the puddle, and the water splashed up over his shoe and drenched it. He jumped back and screamed in pain, ripping off the shoe. His foot looked like it had been burnt. He fell to the ground with a sickening crunch as he hit the cement.

"Holy water," he said in a weak voice. I looked around the room. It was filled with those jars; he had booby-trapped the whole place just in case. As much as I hated it, he had planned this well. I looked at Xavier who sat cursing on the floor, inching back from the water.

"Fucking holy water, Xavier! What part of that did you not get? But no, you try anyway," he yelled, telling himself off. "You are a moron!"

"Xavier, it's not your fault," I said. He looked up at me; his stare was cold and my breath caught in my throat.

"Not my fault?! Of course it's my fault! I'm the one who threw him across the room. I'm the one who can't touch holy water and I'm the one who let him get away! How is it not my fault?!" he snapped at me. Fear shot through me. I couldn't think enough to breathe and I sure as hell couldn't move. After his violent yet creative threat, that I was now totally sure he was capable of, I didn't want to piss him off. Part of me knew he would never hurt me, but I didn't want to risk it. Could I be with a guy I was terrified of? His face softened as he looked at me. It was almost like he was slowly regaining his sanity. Suddenly he looked horrified and looked away. “I’m so sorry, Misty. It’s not your fault either. I shouldn’t have taken that out on you,” he said, his voice so weak, so helpless, it snapped me from my fear-induced paralysation.

I looked down at the burns on his foot that didn’t seem to be healing. It looked as if someone had poured acid on it, not water. With shaking hands and against my better judgement I knelt down next to him and put a gentle but still kinda shaking hand on his shoulder.

“It’s okay?” I said, my voice sounding unsure and a little bit frightened despite me trying my best to hide it.

“It’s not okay, Misty, I don’t want you to see me like that and I don’t want you to be afraid of me. I can’t control myself; outbursts like that for me aren’t rare and if something were to go wrong and I turned on you, I could never forgive myself.” He looked up to meet my eyes. I didn’t have a response to that. True, he scared me, but I wasn’t scared he would hurt me and no matter how much he proved otherwise, I couldn’t be.

There was some part of me that still clung to that safe feeling he normally brought. Sure, I knew he was dangerous but I couldn’t believe I was in danger and, despite everything, there was a part of me that liked that. Part of my ever-so-complicated mind liked the high of it, the thrill of danger because, truthfully, I had never really been safe, I was a hunter and danger was a part of this hunter’s life and now, so was he.

“So what now?” I asked weakly, looking at his foot and then at the water in front of the door. I hated seeing that side of Xavier, but I would do anything in my power to ensure that Alex got what he deserved and he deserved every single thing that threat entailed. Hell, maybe I would even do it myself, but before I could make him pay we had to get out of here first. I knew there was no way Xavier could get past that holy water and I was starting to think that he might not even be able to walk on his foot, seeing the shape it was in, so we needed a plan.

"Well, I can't go anywhere until that water dries up, and even then I might not be able to cross it. So, assuming I can ever get out of this room, we find out where in hell we are, then we find Lincoln," he said.

"What about Alex?" I asked, letting him lean on me as he tried to put pressure on his burnt-up foot. The look of pain on his face and the speed in which he lifted it again told me he wasn't going to be able to, at least not yet.

"Alex can wait; besides, Alex isn't smart enough to come up with something like this on his own. He had help and I think we both know who. So if we find Lincoln like first planned, we find Damien and hopefully Alex," he said. I nodded and dashed upstairs. We were in an old rundown shack that looked like it hadn't seen a visitor in years. There was barely anything left that wasn't broken or burnt. I looked around and managed to find some old clothes and a walking stick (well, actually, I think it was a broken pool cue). I passed the walking stick to Xavier to steady himself, and mopped up what I could of the water with the clothes. Most of puddle was gone but the area was still wet and seeing that Xavier was still standing as far from it as the room would allow him, I knew it had to dry.

It made me wonder if that technically made that spot hallowed ground? Xavier barely said a word while I was doing this, and I could tell he was disappointed that for once he couldn't win. I knew all about feeling like a loser but, judging from his broodiness, Xavier didn't and I felt for him, I really did, that feeling of weakness must have been killing him even more now with an injury, seeing how he was used to being so in control of everything, but there was no need to mope. After about ten minutes, the floor was dry and I managed after a lot of effort to drag what was left of a broken table down to act like a bridge. Of course he laughed at my awesome idea, but I didn't see him laughing when it worked. Thanks to me, we slowly made it outside. We both knew Alex was long gone by now, and with the fastest thing we had wounded, there was no way we were going to catch him.

We walked at a very human pace until we reached the highway. The sun was making every step harder than it should have been and there were no trees, no shade, nothing we could see for miles, nothing but the melting black tar on a long stretch of highway. The heat was killing me and I couldn't imagine the toll it was taking on Xavier. Weakened from holy water only to get stuck out in midday sun, I was surprised the poor thing hadn't burst into flames but really hoped he wouldn't. We walked for what seemed like forever, the sun taking finally its toll on me as well. I collapsed down on the edge of the road. Xavier rushed to my side, well, he hobbled fast, and pulled me into the coolness of his skin. Truthfully, it felt amazing for a little while, then we kinda just sat there praying for nightfall. Not a single car had passed us and Xavier still hadn't said a word since we left the house despite all my coaxing. I just gazed up at him. His skin looked slightly sunburnt and his breathing was laboured, and I was kinda worried he wouldn't make it to nightfall.

"Talk to me," I said, my voice expressing all my worry into those little words. He looked down at me. His skin looked more like granite than flesh and his emerald eyes had lost their shine.

"No," he said quietly, looking away again, 'cause that was super mature and all.

"Why?' I asked, puzzled and slightly hurt.

"I don't know. I'll probably just stuff it up; I'm good at that," he said. I shook my head; yep, super mature. I couldn't believe he was still beating himself up over that and, to make it worse, he was totally sulking. Here I was worried he was about to die, and he was sulking.

"Well, you will stuff it up if you don't talk to me because I'm not too nice to dump your ass while you're hurt and stranded by the side of the road," I said. He just looked down at me and I could have sworn he smirked, but he looked away again and didn't reply. "Oh for fu…" I started again but caught it; good girls don't curse unless we have to. "God's sake, Xavier! What are you, six or sixty-five? Grow up, if you haven't noticed we're in the middle of nowhere and you look like you are about to die, but on top of all that you're being an annoying prick and chucking a sulk, you big girl," I said, a little harsher than I intended, and this time he did smile.

"I'm twenty-five actually, if you want to be technical, and I'm not going to die," he said, wincing as he moved his foot. I huffed. I knew it wasn't mature, but I kinda felt like not talking to him to see how he liked it but, luckily for him, I was very mature and I couldn't really have a sulk after I had yelled at him for it.

"How long will that take to heal?" I asked, looking down at his foot. All things considered that had to be painful, even to a vampire.

"Maybe a day, maybe a week, you can never tell with holy objects. The one thing Hollywood gets right just proves we're evil," he said.

"You're not evil, I'm sure of that," I said. "Well, maybe just a little." He gave me a half-hearted smile. "What are we going to do?"

"I need blood. Without it I'm useless; the sun is going to drain me," he said.

"You can have mine," I said softly. That sentence left my mouth before I could stop it. I regretted it instantly. I hated the thought of him drinking my blood and I kinda figured it would hurt, but I guess if it would save his life, he could have the lot. He looked down, his eyes lingering on my neck; he swallowed hard, then looked away.

"No," he said simply, not explaining why or giving any kind of excuse. I was relieved but at the same time, the way he was looking had me worried.

"Please, I'm kinda worried you'll burst into flames or something," I said. He laughed at that and smiled.

"You and me both," he said, pulling up the collar of his shirt. Was that meant to inspire confidence? "As much as it pains me to say it, we should avoid moving. We sit here until someone comes or night falls, because at the moment the only thing that is stopping you from getting heatstroke is the coolness of my skin, and you are the only thing that is keeping me upright. We'll discuss the blood thing when it becomes a necessity."

I nodded. "Who is this Lincoln?" I asked; it had been bugging me ever since I first heard his name, and even more so now.

"He's Alex's brother and my first hunting partner."

"Okay?" I pried.

"It's complicated," he said, trying to avoid the subject, but I wasn't going to let him this time.

"We have time," I said and there was no way he could argue with that.

"For the basics, I guess." I removed my jacket and put the hood over Xavier's head, giving him the shade. I could see small burns developing on his skin and I couldn't stand to see him suffer any more. "Thank you," he said, pulling it down further to shade himself. "Well, I guess it all started after I was turned, there is a lot I can't tell you but basically, after I was turned I wanted to go back to hunting like nothing had even happened. Of course, the hunting community wasn't too happy about that and wanted me dead. Luckily I had a few people on my side, some of your family and Lincoln being a few, and somehow the few I had managed to stop them from killing me and got them to let me hunt again – with conditions, of course. Lincoln was more than happy to take me back, so they gave us a trial mission with your teenage father as my chaperone but your father had to bail…I don't really," he started trying to remember why, "oh yeah, I do, he had to bail because he just found out his girlfriend was pregnant, so me and Lincoln went alone. We had travelled for weeks working on this case and had pretty much figured it out, simple really, it was werewolves, one of the biggest problems at that time, and I did the best I could to hold it together. The smell of food repulsed me and I ignored the part of me lusted for blood, telling myself I would rather die than take life from another. Sadly, what I didn't know then was that new vampires aren't known for their self-control but, more importantly, they also need blood at least once a day for their body to even function, and it had been weeks. I was barely able to think straight. So by that point I was far past crazy and one night, as we sat there in the bushes staking out the den, I watched him watching the pack, all while thinking how he wouldn't even mind if I just borrowed some blood from him, and all sorts of other disturbing things you can't really understand until you've been through it. Something caught his attention and he leaned deep into the bushes, scratching himself, and that's all it took. The smell of blood consumed me, and I lost the inner war I was fighting and attacked him. After the lust had worn off I dropped his body, terrified that I had killed him, and ran off, leaving him for dead. At that time I didn't even know about venom or how to control it, so I must have infected him. Close to death, he had to lay there through the changing, at least a week of total agony. I found out shortly after that he was still alive when I heard the news that he had killed his wife and kids in a blood lust, which was the thing that sparked my decision to leave. I tried to find him after I came out of hiding but I couldn't, no matter where I looked. I had no idea he blamed me and that he would hate me so much he would try and cause me the same pain he felt. Your father died because he stuck up for me; he took my side when no one else would and took me in as if I was family and now Lincoln is going after your family because of me," he said as he looked away.

"It's not your fault," I said. I could never blame him for what had happened to my father. No, I blamed the man who pulled the trigger. There were a few inconsistencies in his story, like the fact that in the year he was turned my Dad would have been two and he recalled the day Dad found out he was having Damien, which was fifteen year later. My best guess was it wasn't the only time he had crawled back to the families for help, because Alex would have been a year old when Xavier was turned so there was no way he could have remembered my family sheltering Xavier; there must have been another time.

"The road ahead is going to be really dangerous, Missy, and whoever we turn to for help will be in danger so we're going to have to do it alone, but first we need to get you properly trained," he said, looking down the road and quickly standing up, extending his thumb toward the road.

Trained? I spent most of my life training, I thought and nearly said that but I heard the sound of what was possibly better than anything I could have hoped for: the soft rumble of a motor in the distance as an old truck came into view. The truck was blurry from the heat waves but that sweet, sweet rumble told me it was no mirage.

I ran to the driver's side window as the truck pulled up. We're saved!

"Where you heading, sweetie?" said the lady behind the wheel.

"As close to Ashford as we can get," I said.

"Well, you're in luck, love, hop in," she said as she watched Xavier limp up to the truck. "Do you want me to stop at the hospital? Your boyfriend's foot looks pretty bad," she asked.

Xavier shook his head, careful to keep all other burnt skin covered. "That's alright, I'll be fine," he said as I jumped up into the tray and pulled him up. We sat down and the truck took off. The wind was warm as it whipped through my hair. Xavier pulled me into his arms once again and kissed me on the top of my head. The ride was long. I couldn't believe how far out of town we were. I must have been out of it for a while. The lady pulled up outside of town.

"Thanks for that," I said as I walked to the driver's side window.

"You're welcome, honey, enjoy your stay now," she said with a bright smile.

“We will,” said Xavier, taking my side. She gave him a curious look and I giggled. I didn’t blame her; really, he did look kinda strange with my hood still pulled down over his face, but she smiled again and waved as she pulled out on to the road. We walked toward my house and I thanked god we lived on the edge of town. It was a five-minute walk from the highway but every step was a challenge and I figured as soon as I got home I’d drown myself in water.

“I’m going to go hunt, then I need your phone,” said Xavier as we climbed the steps to the front door. He knocked the broken door from its hinges as we entered. I sighed and followed.

CHAPTER FIFTEEN

I headed straight for the fridge as he limped out back and disappeared into the woods. He returned almost half an hour later, looking a thousand times better. I smiled as he walked back into the house. His foot was healed and his skin no longer resembled Freddy Krueger's, which was nice. I, on the other hand, was rapidly changing a lovely purplish-blue colour and had a hole in my shoulder that was most likely going to become infected and kill me. Yay! He leaned down to give me a quick kiss as he passed, and grabbed the phone from its holder on the wall.

"Yeah, it's me, I need you to teach someone to fight. Just in case, that's why, today would be good, yeah, cool, okay then bye." He hung up the phone and dialled another number. He was talking a lot longer this time, and the majority of the conversation was about Lincoln. I got myself another drink and sat back down, waiting for the verdict. After another five minutes he hung up and come to sit across from me.

"I need to ask you something. And know this sounds strange, but have you ever propelled your thoughts or read someone's mind?" he asked, and I just looked at him.

"No, can't say I have," I said, giving him an unsure look. Where was he going with this?

"Okay, well, there is a reason I asked that. Um, right, in your family they're called the West family abilities, but overall they're referred to as hunting powers. Back in the day when the organisation first started, everyone that joined need this ability to be considered a hunter. All humans are capable of it in theory, but only a small amount have any control over it. I think it's kinda like telekinesis, but being able to use it makes you immune to nearly all mind-probing magic you can think of. It seems to be genetic. It is only still found in certain families, five to be exact. Like I said, it's more of a genetic trait than ability, and it manifests itself in different ways, one being what I just asked."

"The lead families?" I asked, but I was pretty sure that's who he would be talking about since he was talking to me. I knew all the history about the lead families and how originally you needed to be in one to be a proper hunter. I got the full spiel on the family history when I was a kid.

"Right, and normally the children who received these gifts almost always had a birthmark, another original family trait only found on people with original family bloodlines nowadays. Every family's different but," he leaned down and lifted the back of his hair and there was a birthmark which kinda looked like a bullet. "The out of families get them too," he said, looking back up to me. "They traced mine back to Flynn on my mother's side, generations back. I was the only one in my family with it and the only one that had the ability, it's the only reason I'm a hunter and if you're anything like Damien and your father yours should be," he slid down the shoulder of my shirt, "and there it is." He looked at the little half-moon shaped birthmark on the back of my shoulder. "So chances are you have them too, so we will need to work on that."

I had heard Dad or Damien mention family abilities every now and then, but I always just assumed they were talking about hunting. I rubbed my shoulder; it really hurt, like there was a gaping wound, but it was really only a graze and it looked worse than it actually was. Xavier reached over and inspected my shoulder.

"Lucky you," said Xavier, lifting up his shirt. I gazed over his torso. He had rows of little circle burns probably from the rosary beads; some looked blistered and others just looked sore. He removed his shirt completely and I saw a bloodless wound in his chest. It looked like a healing bullet wound; shouldn't it be healed by now? I reached across the table and traced my hand along one of the rows. They looked painful. And to think, my brother and him have to deal with this on a daily basis.

"It's not that bad," he said, meeting my gaze. "I mean, I'll live."

I felt a smirk cross my face and I laughed softly. "No, you won't," I joked and he laughed quietly, like he was expecting it. Well, he did spend most of his time with my brother so, hell, maybe he was. He seemed to lose himself in thought for a second, so I took that time to let my mind wonder, all the while never taking my gaze off of him. He was truly amazing, but I wasn't really quite sure exactly where we stood. Sure, I had joked about breaking up, but technically we weren't even really together. So what, we kissed and we slept together but what's to say I wasn't a booty call. I mean, I was the only one around. I wanted to sort my feelings out before this went too far and there was no turning back. I wasn't going to get hurt over this. All I could think was, what if he turned out to be like every other guy I've dated? I still came back to the same conclusion. We had only known each other for a few days. I shouldn't be feeling like this and it scared me that I was. I was hard pressed to even admit I was in love with a guy I had been dating for a year, and then Xavier walked into my life and three days later I'm in love! And he didn't help the situation any, with his cuteness and his big romantic speeches. I needed to sort this out myself, I really had to.

"Misty, how could you think that?" he said, looking over to me.

"Because it's the truth, this is all moving way too fast and I don't want to get hurt."

"I would never hurt you, Misty, and I don't care how crazy it is but I love you," he said and his voice was genuine, but it wasn't what I wanted to hear.

"Don't," I said, a little frustrated.

"Why?" he asked.

"Just don't," I replied and stormed off. I stopped in my tracks, looking up at him. I hated when he did that.

"Be my girlfriend?" he said, and frankly it didn't sound like he was asking.

"I can't," I said. I even surprised myself with that one.

"Why? Is it because of the whole just-meeting situation? Because that'll go away with time," he joked.

"Xavier. I…"

"Do you love me?" he said suddenly. "Well, do you?"

"Well, uh…"

"Yes or no, Misty, it's that simple."

"Yes."

"Then be my girl, either that or I just pretend you are anyway," he said, and that made me laugh.

"Okay, fine, you win, I love you, Xavier Connor, and it would be an honour to be your girl," I said.

"Damn right," he said, pulling me into him and kissing me. There was a knock at the door but neither of us broke apart. Someone cleared their throat and I remembered there was no door.

"Well now, I see why she would need protecting," said a female voice and we both spun around.

"Magenta?" said Xavier, releasing me from his hold. "What are you doing here?

Xavier

I couldn't believe it; of all people they had to send her. She was just as I remembered, and that made it harder to even look at her. Her dark chocolate-brown hair sat neatly to her shoulders and her eyes gleamed like amethyst crystals. Her skin was pale and flawless and her features were expressionless. Ha! Some things never change. In a way she was beautiful, but that was purely physical; she was cold and dead inside and that was something you couldn't hide.

"Can I come in?" she said, ignoring my question, her gaze never moving from Misty.

"No, why are you here?" I asked. I could hear the frustration creeping into my voice but I had no wish to stop it.

"I heard a few rumours and I just came to see if you were really that stupid, and turns out you are. Are you brain dead?! She's a hunter, a West hunter and, worst of all, she's that psycho Damien's sister! Are you planning on turning her? Because she wouldn't last ten seconds in a coven," she said. I growled, my fangs extending in my mouth. How dare she come around here acting like she knows me best! She knows nothing about me, not anymore. "We didn't think that far, did we, god you're a typical guy, always thinking with the wrong head. Damien will kill you if you hurt her and we can't afford a war with the hunters, not now!" she snapped.

"Okay, who the hell are you?!" snapped Misty.

"Not now, honey, the grown-ups are talking," she replied, still glaring at me.

"Why are you here, Magenta?" I growled again.

"To help. Luke called me," she said simply.

"Fine, be back here by sunset and you're not welcome in this house," I said, glaring at her. She went to take a step forward but couldn't, and looked to Misty.

"Be ready, human," she said, then she was gone.

"Who was that?" asked Misty but I didn't have the time to answer; I had to get her ready and keep her safe the only way I knew how. I ran to Damien's room, looking for his rosary beads. Over the years I've known Damien, he had come up with some pretty creative ways to get on my nerves. One of my favourites was when he washed his car in holy water so every time I touched it, it would burn me. Of course it wore off, but he still found it hilarious. The beads burnt my hand as I pulled them out of the trunk, but at the moment I couldn't care less. I winced at the pain as I rushed outside and blessed the pipes, fitting the beads into the water main. There was only one way to see if it worked.

I walked into the bathroom and turned on the shower. I took a deep breath as stuck my arm under the running water. I pulled it back out instantly; my skin started burning as if the water had turned to acid. *Perfect,* I thought as I walked back out to Misty. I knew she was mad because I hadn't answered her question and really, she didn't have a clue what was going on, but I wasn't lying when I said I loved this girl and I couldn't let Magenta hurt her to prove a point.

"Look, I need you to have a shower," I said, taking her by the shoulders. She opened her mouth to say something but closed it and gave me an unsure look; I guess she wasn't expecting that.

"What? Why?" she said, grabbing my hand. She looked at the fresh burn with concern.

"They're fine," I said, really needing to explain myself, or there was no way she was going to do a thing I said. "Look, really long and complicated story short, Magenta is an evil, heartless bitch with an extremely cold and cruel personality, but she is one of the best vampire combat teachers there is and, seeing you're going to be fighting them, I thought a few lessons couldn't hurt."

"I already know how to fight, Xavier," she said stubbornly.

"Yes, and I'm sure you do too, but can you fight someone five times as strong and six times as fast?" I asked.

"Okay, but why do…." I cut her off there; I knew what she was going to ask.

"I rigged the pipes so they spurt holy water," I said seriously.

"Okay, but what will the holy water stop? I'm sure that holy water doesn't deflect knifes or stop bullets," she said and yes, she had a point, but it stopped a vampire from getting too close and I was more worried about that than weapons.

"No, Misty, Magenta's not like me and if she's in close contact she may…"

"Bite me?" she finished with slight amusement in her voice.

"Yes, that's why I actually called Luke but looks like we have to settle for her, now please, Misty, do this for me?" I pleaded. Her eyes read my face and she nodded.

"Okay," she said and I pulled her onto me. This was probably the last chance I would get to hold her for a while.

"Just give me a second. It will be a while before I, or any other evil creature repelled by holy objects, can touch you," I said, leaning down to kiss her, but it was going to hurt not being able to do that now that I was actually allowed to. She headed toward the shower.

"Misty," I called after her and she looked back at me. "Be sure to drink some."

I paced in front of the door while she had a shower which, while rather creepy, made me feel like at least she was safe, just for a second. Although no vampire could get inside the house without her invitation, I still worried that she would try and I didn't want to worry, not about that. I looked outside. The sun was setting. I knew we didn't have much time. I should have said for her to come back tomorrow, but the faster we got this over with the faster we could find Lincoln. I fiddled with the hilt of my gun; it was full of the same silver, holy-water-filled bullets most of my guns were. Originally designed by William West, hollow silver bullets were filled with holy water and engraved with various symbols. The tip of the bullet had a cross indented into it which caused the bullet to shatter on impact, releasing the holy water. They were the only thing that could hurt almost everything; a marvellous invention really, and I'm not just saying that because I had my hand in creating them.

She met me in the hall a good ten minutes later. She had changed into loose-fitting track pants and an old polo shirt. I lifted my hand to place it on her shoulder, and I felt it. The feeling we got when something was anointed in holy water was hard to explain. It was almost like a thousand voices in your head screaming threats and warnings. Like the sound of it could make your head explode and your lungs collapse simultaneously, and I hadn't even touched her yet. The objects I hunted with gave off the same kind of feeling except not that extreme, but it wasn't pleasant and it took some getting used to. Despite the unnerving feeling I was getting, I had to know would it be enough. If I could push past the feeling and touch her so could Magenta, because she was the one who taught me how to in the first place.

I placed my palm on her shoulder but instantly removed it; she looked back at me and I knew that it would be enough. I gave her a reassuring smile because I could tell she was nervous.

"Let's go," I said, looking toward the back door, and she nodded as she headed outside. Every muscle in my body was tense as we stood on the small porch that stretched across the back of the house. Misty walked toward the steps and I reached out to stop her. My slowly healing hand heated up like it had touched fire when it fell onto her shoulder, and she stopped, turning to look back at me. I pulled the gun from my belt and placed it in her hand, careful not to touch her.

"If she tries, anything use it," I warned, looking up as I heard a noise from deep in the woods. I stepped in front of Misty as Magenta entered the backyard, licking her fingers clean. The smell of fresh blood was overwhelming, but it wasn't human. She stopped in the centre of the yard and looked up to us as Misty stepped down from behind me and walked toward her. I watched as she tucked the weapon into the track pants and nodded in greeting to Magenta, which of course she completely ignored; her eyes were still fixed on me.

"I really do not know how your boyfriend lives off of that vile stuff, but in desperate times," she said, rolling her eyes and finally looking to Misty. "We haven't been formally introduced. I'm Magenta, combat trainer for the Western Worlds Coven Army and Special Forces, and you are Misty West, youngest hunter in the West family and the only female to be born to the West name in over a hundred years."

"You sure we haven't met?" said Misty, and I couldn't help but smirk at that. Magenta gave her an unfriendly smile and gestured to the spot in front of her. I took a seat on the seat swing in the corner of the deck. There was nothing left for me to do but watch and wait.

Misty

"This is not going to be easy, hunter, and depending on how much combat experience you have had with vampires, it will most likely take you all night to grasp the basics. I'm going to teach you how to protect yourself against attackers that possess superhuman abilities and, seeing you're with Xavier, you will need these skills to make it out alive." She said this in a voice like ice. It was clear she didn't like me, and I wasn't sure what her feelings toward Xavier were but it was clear he didn't like her.

I was sort of on neutral ground. I couldn't see us being friends but she hadn't done anything, really, to make me dislike her. My Dad had always taught me that you have to hate people for a reason and she had yet to give me a reason; stupid, I know, but in a world where someone you dislike could very well save your life, you don't go hating everybody you meet even if they were rude. It was the hunter way.

She rambled on a bit about what we were going to cover and what she hoped I was capable of learning. Then she talked me through the first combat exercise we were going to run through. She winced when she grabbed my arm and shot a deadly look toward the porch, and I apologised for having to put her through that, but she said she understood. She walked me through every scenario, first having me attack her in a certain way which always ended up with me on the ground. After that we would switch and she would attack me, slowly at first until I grasped what she showed me, and then she would speed up until I was able to deflect her attacks at full speed.

Luckily it all came really naturally to me, seeing I had been taught most of it before, but really, it just enforced my father's training and maybe took it up a level or two. It wasn't easy, that's for sure, and we took hourly breaks so I could catch my breath. Training was a lot harder than I remembered, and maybe I should have kept at it even while I wasn't actually hunting.

Afternoon turned into night and the night slowly faded into dawn. I collapsed on the ground after managing to avoid most of her attacks, but I hadn't yet managed to get it over her.

She reached down and offered me her hand with an almost friendly smile. I guess my Dad had the right idea after all because, the bad blood (no pun intended) between her and Xavier aside, she was pretty nice. I took her hand and she pulled me to my feet; I guess the holy water had worn off because it didn't even seem to be bothering her any more. I rested my hands on my knees as I caught my breath. Every inch of me was sore, I was using muscles I didn't even know I had, and I knew that, come later in the day, I would be covered in bruises. As soon as my breath was back she came at me again, at full speed. There were times I couldn't even see where she had come from, but somehow I managed to avoid the hits. Ducking, jumping and rolling, I managed to finally get the upper hand. I pulled the gun from my jeans and raised it, pressing it up under her chin as she went in for another attack.

"Bang," I said, and lowered the gun, and she just laughed.

"Very good, Misty, I'm impressed; you are a very quick learner. None of my students have ever gotten one over me in the first lesson; you are truly a natural-born hunter."

I nodded and tried to catch my breath again. I wasn't sure it was such a big thing. I was about ready to collapse, I was so buggered. "Thanks," I said, barely able to get the word out.

"But don't get cocky. Keep on the move, watch your back and never let your guard down for anyone," she said. Looking toward the porch, she took a few steps forward. "I like you. You're kinda decent for a hunter, so I want to give you some friendly advice: he's not worth it. Don't let yourself get hurt for him; many a girl has made that mistake in the past and if I was you I would get out while you still can. Good luck, hunter, and I'll see you around."

She took off before I could ask what she meant by that. I looked to the porch; Xavier was asleep in one of the deck chairs.

I tried not to laugh, because he didn't look at all comfortable. He was kinda curled up and his head was resting on the top of the chair, which he was way too tall for in the first place. As uncomfortable as it looked, he looked peaceful and even had a small smile on his face. The sun was breaking the horizon and the sky had lightened as I curled up on the seat swing. I was too sore and too pumped to sleep and besides, I wasn't sure I would ever see that look on Xavier's face again: no anger, no worry, just peace. As hyped as I was, I found my eyes closing and I fell asleep without even realising I had.

The next thing I knew I was rolling over in bed and couldn't recall for the life of me how I had gotten there. I sat up and looked around the room. The house was really quiet and I looked at the time. It was almost three o'clock in the afternoon; I had nearly slept the day away. Getting up and slipping on a set of old comfortable clothes that I didn't mind getting dirty, I walked out into the kitchen to see if I could find Xavier. The place looked amazing; every surface was cleaned and the door was fixed. I mean, properly fixed, new door and all. I guess I was kinda shell-shocked; I hadn't really expected this. *Wow,* I thought as I called his name. I heard footsteps coming up the stairs and toward the door, and I smiled as he walked in.

"Yeah?" he asked, wiping what looked like grease off his hands with an old rag.

"What were you doing?" I replied.

"I was fixing the gate; I remember Damien saying once before that I had broken the latch on it and that's why you never keep it shut, so I thought while I was here I would fix it," he said with a small shrug.

"You fixed our gate?" I asked slowly, still trying to figure out his motives.

"Yeah, and the door," he said.

I nodded. "Yeah, I noticed and I appreciate it, I do, but why?"

"Why?" he said back slowly, and then shrugged. "Because I was bored and they needed to be done, the roof does too but, more importantly at the moment, I've got something for you," he said, taking off toward Damien's room. "I figured since you are hunting again you should have your own weapon. Now, don't thank me, Damien was planning on giving you this anyway." He walked back out and stopped in front of me, placing a knife in my hand.

I looked over the old knife. The blade was serrated on one side and the hilt was some kind of bone. At the top of the hilt were three names carved: Billy, Greg, Damien. I ran my thumb over each carving; they were all so different and all expressed the personality of the person. The first one was neat and structured, almost proud in presence. The second was my father's and it was carved in all capitals, and had a sort of militant style to it. The last of course was Damien's and, like my brother, it was messy, said what it needed to and was a little rough around the edges.

I smiled. There it was, my family tree as far back as I can remember, carved into the handle of a knife. I felt tears welling in my eyes and I couldn't believe I had never seen this before. I looked up to meet his eyes.

"Thank you," I said with a heartfelt smile; he had no idea what that meant to me. He held out his hand and I passed it back. I watched him pull a knife from the inside of his boot and scratch at the hilt before passing it back. I looked at it and just under Damien's name, in neat linked writing, was mine. It was different from the rest as they were from each other and my name couldn't have been carved more perfectly. I ran my fingers over Grandpa's name again.

"That knife is passed from father to son, down through the West line. Damien told me that, seeing he was never planning on having kids, he was going to pass it to you to keep the tradition alive," said Xavier, watching me.

"William West," I said, still tracing my grandfather's name, "What was he like? Did you know him?" Xavier nodded and looked away as I looked up. I had heard so much about my grandpa, how great he was meant to have been, but nobody ever told me what he was like as a person; would he have taken us on fishing tips? Told us stories when we were younger? Or would he have been a slave driver like Dad? What I wouldn't give to have known him.

"Another time, maybe; I'm not in the mood for stories, especially that one," he said with sadness in his tone, like the story was a tragic one. I went to argue but he looked away again, an annoyed expression on his face. "Misty, leave it," he snapped before I even got a chance to speak, and walked off.

Puzzled, I looked at the knife, wondering what he knew that I didn't. I headed out back to clear my head. Sliding open the door, I looked over my backyard. I remembered how big it looked as a kid; back then it seemed like a world of its own and that's exactly what Damien and I had pretended it was. Now, though, it just seemed small and empty. I sat down on the old porch swing. I was trying to teach myself not to take Xavier's mood swings personally. I'm sure he had his reasons, even if most of the time they didn't make sense to me. I heard the sliding door open and I looked toward it. Xavier was leaning on the door frame, giving me an apologetic smile.

"Can I join you?" he said, motioning to the seat swing.

"I don't know, can you?" I replied, trying not to sound harsh, but failing. I guess I hadn't quite mastered not taking his bad moods personally yet.

"May I?" he asked in an apologetic tone.

"I guess. Since when do you need permission?"

He sat down and rested his elbows on his knees. He linked his hands and hung his head, sighing. When he finally looked up, his gaze scanned the yard. "I remember the first time I ever visited this house," he said, looking at me. "It would be twenty-five years now; I was sitting on this very swing for most of the evening, and the place looked a lot different back then. The yard was crowded, full of your family and friends. Your parents were dearly loved and it was no wonder; they were good people. Your father was like family to me, and he always treated me that way even when no one else would. There was a big table covered in a blue tablecloth." He pointed it out as he explained. "Stacked high with presents. Back then I would rarely venture from my coven and I didn't do the hunting scene anymore, but I made an appearance anyway because he asked; I was glad to hear from him. I remember the smile on his face as he came up to me and said, 'Xavier, meet my son.' There was only one other time I have ever seen him smile like that and it was followed by, can you believe it, it's a girl'!" He chuckled and looked down again, then continued, "Your father was cooking the barbeque and your mother was standing under that tree, cradling Damien, humming him to sleep."

"I don't remember my mother, she died when I was born," I said, meeting his gaze.

"She was beautiful; you look so much like her and you have the same blue eyes and brown hair. She was the kindest person I had ever met; she had the same charm as you have, and I liked her from the first time we spoke. I remember turning to your father and telling him to marry that girl the second she had walked away, and I remember the goofy smile on his face when he said 'I'm going to.' Everyone was so happy; it was the last time I can remember feeling like I belonged there, like I was amongst family finally. If only your father knew I would end up working with both of his kids! Of course, working is a relative term," he said, raising an eyebrow with that cheeky smile on his face. "Although I doubt he would have liked the thought of us hooking up. No, actually I know he wouldn't have. I've had a long time to think over things I've already done, and with just what I've had I can see that having eternity to think about the choices you make will only make you see that even little things, like being accepted or rejected, can change your life. The day I was banished for the second time, if your father hadn't taken my side I wouldn't be here now. I would have never met Damien, I never would have met you. I know that doesn't answer your question from before about your grandfather, but I wanted you to see that."

He took my hand and looked right into my eyes. "The smallest of gestures can change a lifetime of discussions. Years ago, your grandfather made his and I had to live with them whether I wanted to or not. So believe me when I say, I'm sorry for the way I act sometimes but you have to understand, some things are better left in the past and I can't stay stuck in there anymore. Right now you are my future, Misty, and that's where I need to be, just to be here with you."

I smiled as laid my head on his chest. I knew he was trying to find the right words and I knew they might never come, but he was right about one thing: little things can change a life, because this was a moment I would never forget.

He leaned down and kissed my forehead. I never wanted this moment to end, but like all good things it did. Our moment was broken as his phone rang.

"Yeah," he said, leaning forward with his whole body tensing at once. I could hear the muffled sound of a voice on the other end and caught a word or two every now and then, but it really didn't faze me that much. "Where? I'll check it out now; thanks, Joe." He hung up and got to his feet. "I gotta go," he said, kissing me on the cheek, and then he took off.

I sat there for a moment trying to process what had just happened; after that conversation all I get is "I gotta go?" Shaking my head, I got up and headed inside.

CHAPTER SIXTEEN

My back was aching from the training the night before, and all my muscles were screaming. I needed to relax. I ran a bath and grabbed my iPod from the bedside table; there was nothing in the world more relaxing than a nice bath. I got undressed and sank down into the warm water. It felt so good I could have almost moaned. Part of me still wondered what Xavier had run off to check. I did catch something about a lead, but all I could do was wait and waiting sounded great at the moment. I laid there until the water went cold and the skin on my fingers and toes had wrinkled up. I wrapped my hair in a towel and then wrapped another around me before heading into my room to get dressed again.

"Misty, great news, we've found it, Alex's hideout, Lincoln runs the place, the part below street level anyway, I couldn't get in there during the day but at night that's when all the operations happen and I bet that's where they've got Damien," Xavier said excitedly as he burst into the room. He threw his arms around me and kissed me, hard. The second his lips touched mine they sizzled, and he quickly jumped back. I would have liked to take the credit for that and claim my kisses are just that hot but, of course, there was a more reasonable explanation; at least reasonable to us.

"You had a shower?"

"Bath actually," I corrected, feeling bad for having forgotten about the rigged pipes. *It had only lasted a few hours last time,* I thought and he smiled, a not happy smile.

"Well, looks like I'll just have to keep my hands to myself, for now," he said. He was muttering to himself as he turned and walked toward the door again, but what I caught sounded like "I can't believe I forgot to unrig the pipes, so much for wanting a shower."

I couldn't help but laugh at that even though I was sure I wasn't meant to hear it. I ruffled my hair with the towel a few more times to make sure it was as dry as I could get it before I put it up. The last thing I needed right now was a cold. I decided to go for some fresh air even though it was late afternoon I was super-pumped and the good news about finding Alex added to that. I headed over to the old oak tree that stood in our backyard. Damien and I had always called it Mom and Dad's tree. Dad had told us this was the spot they had their first kiss, and it was also the spot that they were pronounced man and wife. I looked at the carving that had triggered those stories, and laughed.

Greg loves Wendy
4 eva

I didn't really know much about my parents' relationship but I knew for sure that they were in love. I collapsed at the base of the tree, unable to make the smile leave my face. There was a good chance we might have Damien back by tomorrow, assuming Xavier had a plan; Alex and this mysterious Lincoln will finally get what's coming to them, and all will go back to normal in our fucked-up lives. I sat staring at our now-overgrown sandbox and the half-buried truck; finally, I was going to get my brother back again.

"Well, well, well, this was easier than I expected." I jumped up, startled by the voice that came from somewhere behind me. I sprang to my feet and waited, looking for the owner of the voice.

"Who are you?" I asked, stepping back a few paces as a man stepped out from behind the tree. His lips turned up at the corners in what could have almost been considered a smile, and his eyes, the prettiest blue I had ever seen, focused their gaze on me. The wind played with his blond feathery hair as he examined me. It wasn't what I would call long; it was shorter than Xavier's but the longest pieces hung down past his ears. I tried to take him all in but found myself overwhelmed by the sight. I couldn't for the life of me figure out why until he smiled a real smile and I saw them. Fangs.

"Sorry, how rude of me. Please let me introduced myself, I'm Ryder," he said, his voice laced with an English accent right out of the nineteen hundreds, but in no way did he look like an English gentleman. For starters he was wearing all black, well mostly, almost like a uniform but none I had ever seen before. His shirt was gunmetal grey and straight-cut, nearly militant in style, and over that he wore a black trench coat but again, I had never seen that style before. There was a small silver cross on his collar that had some kind of detailing I couldn't really make out. He wore black cargo pants and some kind of utility belt. The belt crossed over his hips, making an X on his lower torso, and was lined with various weapons and other menacing-looking things. And, to top it off, he wore a pair of boots identical to the pair Xavier lived in. I took a few more steps back with eyes wide, not really sure what to do. "Did I startle you?" he asked, his gaze still fixed curiously on me, and I couldn't help but notice: as menacing as he was, this guy was also smoking hot! In a weird, damn obviously not human kinda way. His beauty was supernatural; not even Xavier had that kind of presence.

"We don't speak much, do we?"

I yelled at myself mentally to speak. *Come on, Misty, come on!* "What do you want?" I asked, trying unsuccessfully to sound brave. He did the almost-smile thing again and it sent chills down my spine.

"A new hunter is big news in my world, but the long-lost West returning at long last, well, that's legendary," he said, taking a step closer. "Fame has its price, though, and the bounty for you is really extraordinary."

Bounty hunter, great! "Yeah, well, you can try, vampire boy," I said, getting ready to see how much of that training stuck. I went for my knife but it was gone; great. He laughed carelessly, like he knew I was no more threat than a kitten, but I had news for him: this kitty has claws.

"Oh, you think I want the bounty? No, I have no need for such things; creatures talk and I have come to offer you my assistance. You see, I am somewhat of a specialist," he said. His expression hardly changed; I couldn't read the guy. He had no tells; he could have told me he was the king of Mars and, apart from that being really obvious, I had no way it to tell if he was lying. I had to keep him talking.

"Specialist?"

He looked me over again with that same curious look, and nodded. "Indeed. I am sorry. I didn't mean to frighten you; let us start over. I'm Ryder Kingston." He extended his hand. I looked at him, unsure if I could trust him or not but, as if sensing my doubt, he said, "It's okay."

"Misty West," I said, being brave and kinda stupid by taking his hand. His grip was firm but he pulled away quickly.

"I know who you are," he said, looking down at the burns on his hand.

"What do you want?" I asked again.

"As I said, I came to offer my assistance. It's not often rumours spark my interest and you, Misty, have quite the interesting rumour base. I just wanted to see for myself what the hype was about." Seeing how the look of curiosity hadn't left his face since we started talking, he didn't find what he was expecting.

"Well, I'm just your normal hunter, nothing special," I said, backing up a few more steps. I contemplated running but knew I wouldn't get far.

"Yes, I can see that but that only makes it all the more intriguing," he said, reclosing the gap I had made between us. His hand ran along the tree as he slowly stepped toward me.

"Well then, why help me?" I asked. My voice was nearly shaking, seeing I was unarmed and outmatched and all. Sure, there was a chance I could avoid attack for a while, but without delivering any blows of my own I was as good as screwed anyway.

"I'm what my kind calls a rogue…" he started. His charming tone made him sound so harmless, but this guy had an air to him that felt almost deadly. That was it, deadly, maybe he was like some kind of vampire assassin who had come to kill me. That was the expertise he was talking about, and the only thing this guy was going to help me with was entrance to the afterlife!

"I know what rogue is," I said calmly, but I was anything but.

"Right, of course you do. It seems the rumours are true, that you and I have a common enemy. I hate the vampire underworld and all the creatures tied to it; they're vile, evil, disgusting creatures that want nothing more than to expose us all, breaking the balance that people like me and people like you have fought so hard to enforce. It may not be intentional but if things keep going the way they are, the world will know the truth about what is really out there and it will not end well for anyone. Not human nor creature; we cannot share the same world. Past efforts prove that, and if we were to form an alliance we could make enough noise to make them think twice about even leaving their homes, especially the vampires. We need only to bide our time; soon a Rogue will take power and finally we will have everything we need to win. The war that has been raging for centuries will be over, and with hunters on our side there is no losing!"

Was this guy for real? I wasn't out to do anything apart from save my brother. Sure, as a hunter it's my job to stop creatures exposing themselves to humans, but was that even a possibility? Because the hunter would already know about it, right? The sound of the sliding door opening broke the eeriness that had fallen across the backyard and pulled me from my thoughts. *Xavier, thank god!*

"Hey Missy, you left…" Xavier started looking up as he descended the stairs, and within the space of a second he was standing in front of me looming over the other vampire. Ryder's face paled slightly, something I would have never imagined was possible, and he dropped to his knees and bowed.

"Ryder," growled Xavier, looking every bit as deadly as the other guy felt. I was kinda glad he was around.

"My lord," said Ryder, bowing his head. I looked between them; as hardcore as Ryder seemed, he knelt before Xavier silently and almost seemed afraid. I guess Xavier did have a loyal following after all.

"Get up, we've known each other far too long for that," he said, his voice still cold. I looked to Xavier as Ryder got to his feet, still averting his gaze. Can't say I blamed him. Xavier gave some pretty mean dirty looks. "What are you doing here?"

"I'm came to help my…uh, Xavier. I heard about what happened with Damien and the rumours of Misty. I remembered the West hunter was your hunting partner and I assumed, after hearing what I had, that you would have wanted her to have some protection whilst you retrieved Damien, but it was foolish. I should have known you would have everything under control," said Ryder.

"Yes I do, and Misty's more than safe with me. Your services aren't needed. I think it best if you leave," Xavier said. The formality in his voice was strange but I noticed he adopted it around other vampires; must be a status thing. Ryder shook his head and I saw the muscles in Xavier's shoulders tense. I was still trying to work out what role Ryder played in all this. Did he work for Xavier or something?

"I have not been entirely truthful. I did realise you would be here and, despite my better judgement, I came anyway. You know better than anyone I never spite my better judgement; I am meant to help with this. Please, brother, put your faith in me as I have in you. Let me help."

You could tell Xavier was considering his offer. As long as we could trust this guy, two vampires are better than one, I guess.

"Okay, but you will not even think of harming the hunter, you understand, either of them."

Ryder nodded. “Of course, it does not even need to be said,” he said politely, or maybe it just sounded polite because of his accent. Xavier gave a small nod and looked to me.

“Misty, I’ll fill our friend here in on all the details, will you wait inside?” he asked. I guess it was one of those things he didn’t want me to see, so I really couldn’t argue because chances were I didn’t want to, either. I nodded in response and turned to head back inside, but a hand fell on my shoulder and I stopped. Xavier placed the knife in my hand and gave me a serious look. “I would advise that you never forget this again: next time you won’t be so lucky,” he said quietly into my ear before letting go and turning back to Ryder.

I shivered; if I didn’t know better I would have said that sounded like a threat, but I knew he hadn’t meant it that way. I headed back inside and straight for the lounge room window. Yeah, yeah, I know, but the curiosity was killing me and it was dark enough out that they wouldn’t be able to see me spying. I could see their lips moving and both of their faces were void of all emotion; *this guy had to work for him, right?* I wanted to hear what they were saying because, just by looking at the nonviolent tone it seemed to have, I was nearly a hundred precent sure there were details in the conversation that he hadn’t even told me yet, or maybe were even about me. I watched as Ryder paced in front of Xavier as they talked.

Ryder was shorter than Xavier, but most people were, seeing that guy was a giant and all. I guessed Ryder would be about average height. I knew he wasn’t that much taller than I was, and he had a reasonable build to him as well. Sure, he hardly had Damien’s build, but he wasn’t lanky like Xavier. He looked powerful; the boy definitely had some muscle behind him. His strange attire and menacing build would really make the guy stand out in a crowd and, judging from what I had seen so far, I was pretty sure he didn’t mingle with humans often. He looked about the same age as Xavier. I would put him no more than a couple of years older; my guess, late twenties. His feathery hair had almost a yellowish gold colour, too; from back here it looked spiked in a messy but hot kinda way. I wondered if he had that little skill Xavier had to get it to stay the way they want without trying. I couldn't see his face in much detail now but it still struck me how incredibly beautiful this guy was, stunning in a deadly killer kinda way.

Ryder suddenly halted and looked up at Xavier, shocked; that was clear to see even from here. He didn't try and hide the look of displeasure as he spoke. I looked between them; the tone of the conversation had completely changed and I wished I could lip-read. Xavier clenched his fists at his sides and the tell-tale signs of his temper getting the better of him were sprouting like wildfire (yes, I had taken the time to note them all, thought it was maybe a good idea to know when to avoid a situation). Without warning, Xavier scuffed Ryder and started yelling. He looked angry as hell and even though he was yelling, I still couldn't hear a damned thing. I kinda felt bad for Ryder; he must get this a lot with a boss like Xavier. I loved the guy but I could never work for him. Ryder nodded in response to whatever Xavier was saying and Xavier set him to his feet after his little rant was done. Ryder straightened himself up as if unfazed by the outburst, and they both walked toward the house in silence.

I was getting used to the fact that vampires were stunningly beautiful. I mean, just by looking at the two walking toward the house you could see that even the ones who weren't hot were still stunning; it was so unfair! Xavier entered the lounge and walked up to me. A small smile crossed his lips as he stopped and it was actually kinda reassuring.

"Misty, will you invite our friend in?" he asked gently. I smiled and nodded, totally forgetting that vampires couldn't enter a human's home without an invitation. Xavier had gotten one from our father years ago, before I was born, but this new guy needed mine. I nodded, not really wanting to argue since Xavier still looked tense as hell.

I walked to the newly fixed front door and opened it. I wasn't really sure how this was meant to work, so I just looked to him and said, "Come on in." He smiled that small almost-smile and thanked me. Xavier led him to the lounge and turned to me. "Misty, I need you to run the holy water from the pipes for me. Here, I'll show you which ones, and please, Ryder, make yourself at home." He led me to the bathroom, closing the door behind us. He turned the shower on full blast, receiving a few small burns in the process and talked to me in a hushed voice.

"Okay, the only reason I have allowed Ryder to stay is because he's good at what he does and we could really use the backup."

"And that would be?" I asked; no one had actually told me what this guy did or who he even really was.

"He's, well, it's kinda hard to explain, he's a soldier of sorts. He was a leader of the rogue army when it was still active, around the time I was a member. The rogue army acted as the peacekeepers of the vampire world so that the hunters didn't. He's old-fashioned in his ways but effective, and I know from experience he's someone you want on your side," he said, still in a hushed tone. I nodded.

"Okay?"

"He's perfectly harmless in the sense that he won't try and feed from you, but he is honour bound and wouldn't dare anyway." He smiled at me.

"You're a rogue as well," I said, I wasn't sure how vampires worked but I was pretty sure rogues and normal vampires were on two different sides despite being the same species.

"Yes, technically, but really, I deserted the army a long time ago and have no affiliation to the ones that still remain, so yes, by rights I am, but any vampire who doesn't follow traditional ways is called rogue in today's sense. There are rogues like Ryder and me that are the real deal, and by coven law he can't be classed as anything else because of it. Rogues have a completely different regime in place and if I do take the throne I will be the first-ever rogue to take a position of power among the nobles, and it might help the rest of us fight the war that has been raging among our kind for centuries."

"War?" I asked, and he cursed under his breath.

"Never mind, I shouldn't have mentioned it," he said drily but I wanted to know now; it was the second time I had heard about a war and I was sure I had some kind of right as a hunter to know (not that I would say that to him, though).

"No Zay, tell me!"

He sighed and nodded. "Rogues are at war with everyone else. Basically, we believe that our world should stay secret and we should stop meddling with the humans, so, many, many years ago the rogue army sided with the hunters to help take care of it, which resulted in today's supernatural underworld and the precautions that have been taken to keep it secret but that doesn't matter; it has nothing to do with you. Damien has already involved himself, I'm not letting you do the same."

"Zay, we're hunters; it's our duty to keep the rest of the world safe from supernatural creatures and it has always been that way. If it kept the supernatural world a secret, kept the rest of the world safe, then I'm all for it."

"No! It has been going on for far too long now, it has nothing to do with what we are doing. I'm only involved because I was there, I helped cause it and now I need to fix it. Too many hunters have meddled and gotten themselves killed. I will not see you or your brother suffer that same fate. It is vampire business, I have to end it and you will stay out of it, that's final," he snapped.

"Final!" I repeated. I couldn't believe he had really just tried to order me! Me, of all people! "Final! You can NOT tell me what's final, okay! My whole life I've had someone telling me that or saying it's too dangerous. I'm sick and tired of people telling me what I can and can't do. I'm not a child and I'm not one of your little disciples; you cannot control me. I will decide if it is too dangerous for me or not, and I will be the one to say whether I think it a risk worth taking. It's my life, Xavier, and

I will do whatever I please with it, and you or anyone else for that matter will have no say in it! Now that's final," I snapped, finally losing my temper like I hadn't done in ages. I stormed out, slamming the door in his face.

"Misty," he called after me, his voice still muffled slightly by the door.

"No, Xavier, just leave me alone," I called back, storming into my room and slamming that door too. I threw myself down on the bed, mad as hell. I had given up hunting because I was sick and tired of living in my father's shadow, sick of him telling me what I should and shouldn't do, and I wasn't considering taking up the life just have someone else start. There was a knock at the door that I ignored. I had half expected him just to barge his way in, but he knocked again.

"Go away, Xavier, I'm so not in the mood to hear how cute I look when I'm mad," I yelled at the door. I hated how he thought he could get out of it so easily by saying something like that. I heard a soft chuckle, but it didn't belong to Xavier.

"It's not Xavier, he stormed outside and took off. May I come in?" said Ryder, pushing open my door and standing in the doorway. I knew he could physically come in if he wanted to, but it was nice to see that he actually waited for a response. I nodded, not seeing why I couldn't trust him; he seemed nice enough, if socially awkward.

"Yeah," I said, looking over to him. He walked in silently and gently closed the door behind him. He slowly walked over to the bed. I sat up, wondering what he was doing and what he wanted.

"May I?" he asked, again motioning for the edge of the bed. I nodded. For a vampire, he sure did have lovely manners. He sat down on the edge of the bed and looked at me. "I gather that what I just witnessed is a usual occurrence between the two of you?" he asked gently. I nodded again; come to think of it, we *did* argue a bit and this was the second time one or both of us had stormed off because of it.

"Yep, it's becoming a recurring thing," I said voicing my thoughts out loud.

"Don't let him get to you, love; he means well, it's just the way he is. I've known him for about thirty years now and the only thing of use I've learnt is to keep out of his way when he's in a bad mood, which is often," he said giving me a genuine smile. I think it was the first one I had seen and it was completely charming. It almost melted me on the spot: simple, sexy in an old-fashioned kind of way. I smiled back; it was impossible not to. "But I really think that applies more to me than you." He chuckled at that, then stopped, "I don't wish to sound rude but I have wondered for some time now: how does it work between the two of you? Not just you, of course, but between a human and a vampire: how could something so pure love a monster? Granted, he is a rogue and a nice guy, but as a rogue it is hard enough to be around humans, let alone live with or even date them. I've been a vampire for a very long time and I still find it hard to cope around humans. But Xavier ignores it, like you guys are just like us and it doesn't bother him at all," he said, he looked, generally puzzled, and I really didn't think he was trying to be rude; this guy came off as a no-bullshit kind of guy.

I shrugged. "I don't know, he said he is fine and that he could never hurt us, but other vampires say that it's obvious that he's struggling, although I can't see it." I looked down at my hands.

"Well, I can hardly say I blame him; stupid as it is, you are incredibly beautiful for a human and as a hunter your blood has this edge to it, even being as close as I am I find myself intoxicated by you," he said.

I smiled and felt myself blush. He said it seriously but I wasn't really a hundred precent sure that was a compliment. "Thank you, but for a human, what's that meant to mean?" I asked.

"Nothing personal, but when you have been a vampire as long as I have, you lose your sense of humanity and tend to prefer your own kind," he said with a smile. There was another knock at my door, but before I could even register it Ryder was at the window.

"What are you doing?" I asked.

"It's better this way," he whispered in a voice barely audible, and climbed out the window.

"Misty, look, I'm sorry, can I come in?" said Xavier through the door.

Still puzzled by Ryder, I answered. "I guess."

He pushed open the door, slowly crossed the room and sat on the bed. He rested his elbows on his knees and looked to me. "Look babe, I'm sorry, I guess I can be a bit of a hothead at times and I don't mean to boss you around or tell you what to do, but I'm only trying to protect you, I just don't want to see you get hurt, that's all," he said, and I could tell he was really sorry and he actually did mean what he said. Also, talking with Ryder had cooled me down a bit and made me see I maybe overreacted.

"I know, I guess I maybe blew it out of proportion a bit," I said.

"A bit?" he joked, laughing lightly. I kicked him playfully. "You still mad?"

"I can't ever seem to stay mad at you," I said with a smile.

He laid back next to me, holding out his arms for me. "Well, that's not a bad thing," he said as I rolled into his arms, laying my head on his shoulder.

"So when do you reckon we can check out that place you found out about?" I asked.

"Tomorrow night, possibly; I nearly have my full strength back and with Ryder there it should be safe enough to look around. If we find him, though, then we'll think of something," he said casually, like going in with no plan was totally protocol.

"Haven't go that far?"

"Hey, halfway is good enough for now. Hell, we might just wing it."

"Because that's so your style."

"It used to be, when I was in the rogue army," he said, smiling evilly. Rolling over so he was on top of me, he kissed me.

"Mmmm, I can't even imagine you dressed like that, but I have to admit it does look strangely good."

He smiled. "Should I be jealous?" he asked but something in the way he said it made me think he already was.

"No, I bet it would look better on you," I said. I was so glad I could finally voice my thoughts and could finally hold him and kiss him and just be with him as much as my heart desired.

"You know, I think I just might still have my old uniform somewhere. I'll have to don it again for you," he said.

"You know what would look sexier?" I asked, running my hands up his sides, pulling his top over his head and throwing it to the ground. "Halfway there," I said, going for his jeans, but he just smiled and grabbed my hand.

"No, Misty," he said.

"Why?" I moaned. Yes, I actually did. I couldn't believe he was being responsible. At the moment all I wanted was sex; was that really too much to ask?

"Because sex is different for my kind and I don't trust myself enough, I might … get carried away, just wait please," he said. I hated his sudden change of heart.

"We were fine," I protested, and he shook his head. *So much for as much as my heart desires.*

"We got lucky, let's just stick to what we're good at," he said, kissing me again. I heard Ryder clear his throat from the door.

"I'm sorry to interrupt, but Xavier's wanted…" I interrupted him before he was able to finish.

"I know," I said with a small giggle, and kissed him again. Xavier smiled and kissed me back before he pushed himself to his knees and looked to Ryder. Having him straddling me while shirtless wasn't going to help my patience in the not-jumping him department.

"Hold that thought," he said, climbing off the bed and following Ryder. My heart raced and I just laid there for a second awaiting his return, but then I heard her voice.

"You do have great choice in company don't you?" I heard Magenta state coldly from the door. I got up to see what was going on. I couldn't say I was cool with him being shirtless in front of her; it was easy to see they had history.

"It's lovely to see you too, Magenta," said Ryder.

"The pleasure's all yours, trust me." There was a pause and none of them spoke for a few seconds, then Magenta sighed and blurted out. "Rogue, Zay, really? I thought you got over that stupid rebellious stage?"

"Well, if my memory does serve, you were once rogue too," Xavier said.

"No, I was once stupid and I got you caught up in my stupidity; you, however, chose to worsen it. The day you deserted was the happiest day of my life and now this, you're running with rogues again?" she said. Giving in, I finally went out to stand with the boys. Magenta looked as beautiful as ever today, and I secretly hated her for that.

"We stick together, always," said Ryder.

"Brothers for life whether we like it or not. Besides, I won't turn my back on them now, not when they're looking up to me," said Xavier.

"I was always getting you out of trouble. Fine, I'm coming on this bloodbath you call a rescue mission," she said.

"No, Magenta, we're fine," he argued.

"Yes, Xavier, I'm coming and that's final," she snapped back. "I know things you two couldn't dream of."

"Fine, but as long as you are here you will hunt out of town, and it will be often, because you even think about," he stopped and looked at me, and we all knew what he meant by that gesture, "and I'll kill you myself, no matter what our past may have held, got it?" he growled.

"Like I said before, you're more of a threat to her than I am. Besides, it will be good for the girl to have some female company, she must be drowning in testosterone by now," she said, looking to me.

"Well, she hasn't complained yet," growled Xavier, grabbing my arm. "I'm not going to demand you come, but I'm going to tell you to walk and if you don't walk you'll be dragged," whispered Xavier to me. I didn't like his tone but he was mad and obviously needed me to be with him at the moment, so how could I refuse?

"Come in and make yourself at home," I called back to her as Ryder pulled open the door.

CHAPTER SEVENTEEN

Xavier

"Ten years, I don't see her for ten years and *now* she cares if I live or die," I said, pacing, my anger finally reaching breaking point, I punched my fist through the wall of Misty's bedroom. "I'll fix that."

"Okay, you don't hate people for no reason and I'm sure that's not love you're harbouring, what's up?" she said, watching me pace, and I didn't want to tell her because she was wrong. It was love. Well, it used to be.

"Yeah, about that, not really a story you want to tell a girlfriend," I said, finally stopping the pacing. I sat down on the edge of her bed.

"Well, as the girlfriend in question, I really don't mind. I just want to know what's bothering you, Zay," she said sweetly, her voice full of concern. But, as with other things I had refused to tell her about, this was something I couldn't bear to drag up, not fully.

"Misty, what did I say about things staying in the past?" I asked, giving her a serious look, but I knew there was no avoiding it, not this time.

"Yes, but this is something that affects us all. If you're going to lose it every time the two of you have a conversation, we will never get Damien back. Tell me, baby, please," she said.

I looked to her and nodded. I knew she wouldn't like it before I even started. There was so much about my life that I couldn't tell her, or anyone for that matter, and she knew when

I was lying so I had no choice but to tell the truth, as much of it as I could.

"It started the night I met my maker…." Memories of that night filled my head as I spoke. It was as if I was still there. I was really drunk, I remembered that much, I remember how cold a night it was, and I remembered her. She was stunning, the most beautiful creature I had ever seen, and I vowed then and there that she would be mine by the end of the night, but little did I know at the time: I was the one she had come for. With long auburn hair and eyes the exact colour of chocolate she had the attention of every guy in that bar, but she only had eyes for me. If I was sober I would have seen the signs, known that she wasn't human; I would have felt the pull of her scent and the touch of compulsion before it overcame me. But I didn't, and before the night was through my life had come to an end. That's where Magenta came into it; she found me in the alley behind the bar and knew I was in transition. To save me and any poor soul that stumbled across me, she took me back to the rogue headquarters.

I woke up a week later with no idea where I even was. I was in a state of shock. Everything felt foreign to me, my voice, my skin, my vision and the burn. I freaked when I realised I had been sitting there for about twenty minutes without taking a single breath, thought I was dead, and in I way I was right. If I had calmed down enough, the hunter in me would have known straight away that I had been turned, but of course calm was the last thing I was ready to be. Then, all of a sudden, there she was, my saving grace, Magenta.

She smiled and bent down to my level, and explained that I was a vampire and how she had found me. At the time I did the most sensible thing I could think of: I ran for it. I went to the only place I could think of, the only place I could go, back to the Wests, and life went on. After a couple of weeks, I was outed and killed Lincoln. News of what I had done spread fast, and suddenly not even the Wests had my back. The council of families was called and to my horror, William West, the man I looked up to, labelled me a threat to the hunting community and made the order for me to be taken care of.

Magenta, as she always has been, was good at finding out things that didn't concern her, and she found me and taught me the ways of the rogue. I spent the next five years of my existence devoted to her, as if she was my sire. There wasn't a thing in the world I wouldn't have done for her, and she let me believe she loved me just so she could keep me around. I was too stupid or too blind to see the truth and I fell in head first, only to be torn apart because one day, without so much as a good-bye, she left, and until now I hadn't seen her.

I didn't like the vampire I became after that. I fell in with a crowd that got me back into the eyes of the hunters for all the wrong reasons, but I was given a choice which allowed me back into the family. My hatred for her shaped who I became as a vampire and there was no way I could relive that, not now, not ever, but instead of telling her the truth about her family and about Ryder and who he really was, I told her the basics, finishing with "But even after twenty-one years, the sound of her voice cuts so deep that I would need little if any excuse to kill her," and out of all that I told her, that one sentence was the truest thing I had said.

I could hear her jealous thoughts in my mind; she thought I still loved Magenta and there was a part of me that still did, but that part only made the pain worse and only made me hate her more. Despite her conflicted feelings, Misty wrapped her arms around me and hugged me tightly. I felt guilty for lying, but she was better off not knowing the past or any of the history I had with her family. The more she knew, the worse it would be. She was worried about me and worried that I wouldn't be able to handle her being here. She cared so much and that's why I loved her, she cared so much that even when I fell into those dark places, she was on my side and trusted I would make the right choice. Her arms wrapped tightly around my shoulders and I pulled her hand to my lips and gave it a small kiss, before resting my head back into her and smiled.

Misty

I tossed and turned, dead tired, rundown and feeling worse than hell, yet no matter how hard I tried I couldn't sleep. Xavier had suggested that I have another training session with Magenta while he and Ryder gathered supplies and planned out the plan for tomorrow night. Xavier just laid there on top of the covers, hands behind his head in his boxers, looking both carefree and super sexy. How great it must be to be cool all the time. He laughed.

"Babe, lay still for three seconds and you might be able to sleep," he said, finally looking over at me.

"No, I don't reckon, it's too hot, I'm too sore and I feel like hell," I complained.

"Well, we both know how to fix that," he said. I rolled over and laid my head on his chest.

"Christ, babe, you're burning up, even I can feel that and that's saying something. Maybe we should get you to a doctor; that can't be healthy." I watched the concern wash over his face, then I looked at the clock.

"Yeah, great plan at three o'clock in the morning," I said, watching the clock tick over to three.

"Three, did you say?" I nodded, but as I did my head started to spin and my eyes got heavy. Maybe Xavier was right; maybe I did need a doctor.

"Okay, maybe I…" I managed, but that was all. My voice caught in my throat and my breathing became sharp. Xavier sat up, worry on his face as he looked at me. My ears started to buzz; every limb felt like it weighed a million pounds and suddenly a strange feeling washed over me, almost like I was a guest in my own body. I was there but had no control whatsoever. I saw Xavier fly off the bed suddenly, running to the door. He was calling out to someone but I couldn't hear a word he was saying. All I could hear was the buzz in my ears getting louder and louder. Xavier pinned me to the bed, his lips were moving, except nothing was coming out.

What was going on? I started to struggle, trying to fight him off even though I knew it was pointless, but I couldn't stop. I couldn't feel any pain, but I knew if I didn't stop I was going to get hurt. I cringed mentally as I saw the amount of force he was using to keep me pinned, almost like he was struggling. Ryder burst in and quickly swapped places with Xavier, who disappeared from the room. My head pounded and my skin started to burn. I could feel the pressure from Ryder's grip crushing my shoulder, but the only pain I could feel was the burn running through me like fire in my veins. It was like my insides were on fire, and I wanted out of my own body so bad. I could feel myself fighting him, struggling to get him to let me go. Hurting myself to get him off of me, but no matter how much I wanted to, I couldn't stop myself from doing it no matter how hard I tried. I screamed as the pain I could feel intensified and my body copied the response. But the one that was heard was a scream of frustration. With one mighty thrash, I threw Ryder off of me and ran to the door. I couldn't figure out why I was doing this; I just knew I had to. I skidded to a stop, nearly crashing right into Magenta as she blocked the door. My gaze fell on the window *what was I planning to do, jump out?* Yes, that's exactly what I was going to do, so I guess lucky for me our house was only one story so the drop wasn't that bad, but why was I thinking about jumping out the window in the first place? Ryder appeared in my line of sight and blocked the path to the window. I screamed again; the scream almost sounded inhuman, even to my ears. The buzzing got louder and the burning got worse. *What was I doing? Where was I going?* I knew there was no way of knowing that because I wasn't in control. Was I possessed? I don't remember being possessed; it's not something you're likely to forget. I felt my hand grasp something, it was cold, hard, and I couldn't turn my head to see it but I knew it was my knife.

"*Stop it now,*" I demanded of myself, but nothing happened. I watched in horror as my stance changed and so did the grip on my knife. *Stop it, no!* I knew full well I was in attack mode; I was going to fight my way out. Xavier appeared in front of me seemingly out of nowhere, but as quickly as if I had expected it, I plunged the knife into him. The knife sliced into his lower torso with ease. I knew that this knife was made to fight almost anything; even it should encounter some resistance but it hadn't because the force with which I had used it was way out of my own abilities. He ignored it and ripped my hands away from the knife before I could do any real damage.

He left the knife where it was and started saying something. I backed up a few steps, my hand going to my ears, but I couldn't hear a word. His lips were moving; it looked like he was chanting the same phrase, a spell of some kind, maybe. I looked around; Ryder and Magenta were doing the same. My gaze fell back on Xavier and I felt myself growl something at him, but still not a sound. I saw what looked like a talisman in his hand. He grabbed my arm and pushed it into my chest. It felt like something was crushing down on my shoulders, forcing me to my knees. They buckled and Xavier lowered me gently to the floor, still chanting whatever they were chanting. It was like something exploded in my mind. The searing pain was unbelievable; I managed to move my head and look up into Xavier's eyes as the burning stopped and my hearing returned.

I heard the last sentence he yelled, which was some phrase in Latin; whatever had hold of me suddenly let go and I wasn't quick enough to pull myself back together. My body went limp and collapsed to the ground, but before I had a chance to get a grip on what was going on my mind gave up and I blacked out.

CHAPTER EIGHTEEN

I slowly opened my eyes.

"Xavier, she's coming to," Ryder said as I did. I looked over; he was kneeling beside my bed. It took me a few seconds to get my bearings and realise we were no longer at my house but at the coven. I'd remember these sheets anywhere.

"What's going on?" I asked, my voice hoarse; although I hadn't done it by choice, all that screaming was hell on my throat.

"You were possessed, well, not possessed-possessed, but hexed-possessed, they're done with magick and not the type where you pull a rabbit out of a hat, serious stuff, the kind of stuff you don't want to mess with," Ryder said, his gaze thoughtful. I was starting to think I might have gotten the wrong impression of this guy.

"Somebody should have told them that," I joked, my head still killing me. Ryder gave one of his trademark almost-smiles at my joke.

"We looked all over for the hex bag, well, Xavier did mostly, but it was nowhere to be found so we suspect it was demonic magick, which would explain why they waited for when they did, demonic magick is strongest at three a.m. Some call it the witching hour. You were just lucky Xavier knew what he was doing or we could have lost you," said Ryder. Xavier knelt down next to Ryder and took my hand. *My hero,* I thought at him with a loving smile he returned. I remembered the whole thing like I was walking through a haze. I knew I had no control over what I was doing; it was like I was there in my mind but not in body.

"Oh my god, I stabbed you!" I blurted out, looking to Xavier as the memory came rushing back. He laughed and nodded like it was something that happened on a daily basis. Not something I would find funny but each to their own, I guess.

"Yeah you did, and it hurt like a son of a bitch too, trust me to give you a knife that can actually penetrate my skin," he said in a light tone. Why isn't he angry? If someone stabbed me I would be pissed.

"I'm so sorry, I couldn't stop myself, I had no control, I didn't mean to stab you," I said as the guilt ran through me. I'm not sure why I was begging for forgiveness when he didn't even seem to mind. *Maybe because, uh I don't know, I stabbed the guy and it was the right thing to do, am I missing something here?*

"Misty, you didn't, whoever was controlling you did, so there's not much use in being mad at you when I can take it out on whoever pisses me off next, because they deserved it; you don't," he said. In his own fucked-up logic that might have made sense, but I still stabbed him.

"But I…" He put a finger to my lips.

"I said it was fine, now you need to rest, unlike me. The injuries you sustained can't be ignored that easily; you'll need your full strength, seeing that they are coming after you now." He looked to the door. I could see Ryder's back in the doorway; I hadn't even seen him move.

Xavier lowered his voice. "I think it's safe to assume who was behind it and they're getting desperate. We can't stay in the same place for long, especially not here, it isn't safe, don't trust anyone," he said, kissing me on the forehead as he got up to leave the room. I looked around again, a little worried. Trusting people in my profession (well, my family's profession) was a dangerous choice, so his words didn't really catch me off-guard but they did make me think. Someone I did trust, someone Dad treated as part of the family, a guy he trusted with his life, had already betrayed us. Who's to say you can fully trust anyone these days? The low mummer of voices I had been hearing since Xavier left the room suddenly exploded to a more audible level.

"I don't have time for this, Magenta," I heard Xavier snap. Looks like she was going to get the brunt of his anger.

"Okay, well, I think we all know who is behind this and he's not out for hunters in general either," she said. I kept quiet. Xavier and I already knew the reason for that, and I wondered why he hadn't told them.

"What, you think he's targeting Wests?" asked Ryder.

"Yes, that's exactly what I think, Lincoln is after payback, he was exiled completely, neither hunter nor vampire would take him in where Xavier was welcomed back with open arms," she said.

"Well, that much I already know. Alex already told me that and said that was the reason he was doing it, but I don't understand; he should know better than anyone that I wasn't welcomed back easily. I was manhunted, no hunter wanted me around, especially not William West," said Xavier's hushed voice, and that news shocked me.

"No, but Greg and Joseph did, so do Damien and Misty. And we all know the real series of events and the reason why they have been told as they have, it was years Xavier, like it or not, you still worked for them the whole time and if I remember rightly, you…." started Ryder.

"Shhh, okay. I know what happened, I was there, but why doesn't Alex? It's not the best-kept secret," Xavier said.

"Look at the facts, Xavier. They all match up to the widely known story. The reality is that only us who were there know the truth, and because of that they killed Greg, they have Damien, and they want Misty, they're taking everyone who believed in you away, like you did to him. Then they'll deal with you. William West was by far the greatest hunter I have ever known, do you really think he would let something like that get around?" asked Magenta.

"Makes sense, it's what I would do," said Ryder.

"No, I had to do it, they don't, it can't be the reason.... then it is all my fault, all this time I've been putting them in danger, why didn't we know about this sooner?"

"Because we haven't seen you in years. You could have never known this was going to happen, if you hadn't abandoned us we might have seen it coming," said Ryder.

"We had to, I told you leaving was our only choice. When both sides want your head on a platter, you high tail it the hell out of there and you never look back. I'm not ever going to. The brotherhood is dead, I betrayed my family's trust to ensure you lived, William would never have let that get out, and neither will I. So we have to find them and take them out before they get the chance to find out something no one should ever learn. We move in tonight. I'll get someone to watch Misty, we can't risk hand-delivering her to him," said Xavier.

I'd heard enough. I had no idea what was going on and, really, there were some huge holes in Xavier's story already, but this only made them bigger, and it made me think could I trust him? There was obviously something they knew that I didn't, and I would find out what it was, but for now if they're going after my brother there is not a damn thing they can do to stop me from coming. I threw myself out of bed way too fast and was hit by a wave of nausea. When that subsided they were still talking the logistics of the plan, and I was going to stop them.

"No," I said, bursting in, still really uneasy on my feet but I knew it would pass. They all looked at me, surprised, and I could see the realisation that I had heard their secret conversation cross each of their faces as soon as they made it.

"Misty, this is not something I'm willing to negotiate," snapped Xavier. Out of them he looked the guiltiest. Magenta just stood there with a cocky smile and Ryder was expressionless as usual. Xavier's glare bore into me; he knew me well enough to know what I was objecting to and he damn well should.

"I don't care. I'm coming, Xavier. I will not just sit here like always, helpless, while you all go and rescue Damien. Alex killed my father and he's planning to kill my brother, it'll be a cold day in hell before I let that arsehole live to see another day," I retorted, putting as much resolve in my voice as possible. They all looked at me with very different expressions once again, and it stuck me what unlikely accomplices they all were. Xavier's eyes met me with disapproval, Magenta's with amusement and Ryder's – well, it was always kinda hard to tell with him, but he had that almost-smile on his lips and he kinda looked proud.

"Misty, your shoulders. You must be in pain," said Xavier gazing over at the bruises forming on my shoulders, which you could easily see because I was still in my pyjamas.

"Stop trying to distract me! This is just as much my fight as it is yours. It's my family, Xavier; I would die for them," I snapped.

"No, you're not. I will not be the one who puts you in that kind of danger," he growled back. I knew this was going to blow up but there was no way I was going to back down on this, not ever.

"Well you don't really have a choice, do you?' I said, holding his gaze unflinching.

"Yes, I do. I say you're not cut out for this. You have to be strong in both mind and body, and I'm not convinced that at the moment you're either. We have no idea what to expect, Misty. What we're going to be up against when we get there is not just after you, but me as well, so they will be ready to use deadly force. There is no length too far that I won't go to, or haven't gone to already, to save both you and Damien. Have you ever seen someone rip someone to pieces with their bare hands? I have and I've done it myself. This isn't training anymore! You don't have a second to watch, a second to be scared or a second to think in situations like that, you act. You're injured; that could cause you to be a second slower than normal. That second will get you killed and you wouldn't even see it coming. I need someone who will react then think, but I can't trust you will; they have your brother and god knows what they have done to him, but you can't freeze or he dies. Tell me that you could watch Damien being torn to shreds, and still be able to save yourself and him if you could. Tell me that and mean it, and I'll let you go," he growled.

"Xavier," growled Ryder in response. His tone was deadly but unnecessary because there was no length too far I wouldn't go to save my big brother, either.

"No, I want her to answer me. Can you promise me you won't just be another casualty, Misty? And if it all went south, could you watch Damien die and live with that!" he yelled at me. I shrunk away from him slightly. I didn't want to show weakness, but I knew what he was capable of. But I didn't know about me; could I live with myself? I shook my head. I couldn't promise that, no one could, but even if that was the price I had to pay I would.

He wanted the truth; he'll get it. "No," I said quietly.

"What was that?!" he said in that harsh voice. Ryder growled again and stepped in between us, but I never looked away from Xavier's dark emerald gaze.

"Enough, you've proved your point," he snapped, getting up in Xavier's face.

"No! Okay, I can't, but I'm willing to take that risk," I yelled back suddenly. Xavier's gaze shifted to Ryder.

"Well I'm not; you're not coming," he said, glaring at Ryder for a moment longer before he left the room. I just stared after him. The nerve of him acting like it was his decision what I do with my life! I should be able to choose who I want to risk my life for, not him!

"Arrr," I screamed as the frustration built up. I wanted to follow him and punch him right in his stupid face, but I knew I couldn't for two reasons. One: he wouldn't even flinch so it wouldn't be satisfying and I really needed it to hurt him, and two: it would just break my hand. Instead, I stormed toward the lounge room. I threw myself on the couch as roughly as I could. I wanted, no I *needed,* to hurt something, so being a little rough on the couch was a start. I was in such a huff I didn't even realise Ryder had followed me. Carefully, he moved my legs to make a space where he could sit down. I glared at him but he looked at me, his expression unmoved, as if I had merely looked at him.

"Wow," he said, looking at my shoulders. He raised a hand and placed it over one of the bruises; it fitted perfectly. I slapped his hand away. I wasn't in the mood to be touched; besides, they kinda really hurt.

"Oh, wow, I'm sorry," he said, again unfazed. "But that just shows how hard it was to keep you down." A subject change was not what I wanted right now; I wanted to rant, yell and scream but it wasn't Ryder I was mad at, and he had just stuck up for me, then come to see if I was okay. Well, I assumed that's why he was here. I had to cut the guy a break even if it was only a half-hearted one, so yeah, I could deal with a subject change.

"Yeah, well, you didn't really have a choice did you?" I said coldly.

"Misty, Xavier is just protecting you; like I said, he has his ways and you're not making it easy for him," he said, switching the subject back. Well, so much for that!

"ME! I'm not making it easy for him?" I gave a humourless laugh and continued. "Look, Ryder, I don't care how much of a bad idea you think it is or he thinks it is for that matter, really I don't. Alex killed my father and now he has my brother, that's all the family I have left, and if Xavier thinks he can scare me into to changing my mind he has another thing coming. Misty West doesn't scare easily, buddy."

"You two really are perfect for each other, you know that? You are two of the most stubborn people I have ever met. You would both rather fight than talk and die than take a second to think it out first. Sooner or later you're both going to realise how childish you're being, because you are, really. If there is one thing I've learnt, it's that there is always more than one right answer to life's questions," he said.

"Except when there isn't," I responded. He just looked at me. I wasn't going to argue with him, too. I had made up my mind.

"Okay fine, brood and fight it out, see where that gets you."

"You know what I think? I think I like you better when you have a job to talk," I snapped.

"You don't want me to talk to you, fine, I do not feel like playing into your childishness anyway," he said coolly. We both sat there quietly for a few minutes and, strangely, most of my anger had dissolved or had unfairly been projected at Ryder, who was looking rather bored, and even though he didn't seem upset that I had lost it with him, I still felt terrible.

"I'm sorry," I said suddenly.

"Think nothing of it. I think it better for all of us if you vent at someone who actually has his emotions under check and is not in any way emotionally unstable," he said.

"You provoked me?" I exclaimed, working it out. He pissed me off on purpose to calm me down.

He nodded. "I would have done the same for Xavier but no one wants him venting his anger, not even me, although it would be better for you guys to talk it out rather than scream at each other."

"Yeah, I know," I replied. "But he just makes me so mad!"

Ryder smiled a small smile and went quiet for a second. "When he cools down enough for you to talk it out, try not to mention that your bruises fit my hands perfectly, please," he said with a laugh, lightening the mood.

"Well, I think you're scared of the wrong person, Ryder," I said, shoving him playfully and laughing.

"Oh, please forgive me, Miss Scary Hunter, don't slay me, have mercy," he said in a flat tone.

"Nope, you've done it now, I'm afraid I'm going to have to," I replied, fully aware that he was more scared of – well, I can't really see this guy being scared of anything really, especially not me.

"I'm shaking," he said with a smartass smile on his face, the first of those I had seen and, just like his actual smile, I loved it. "Please Misty don't hurt me."

"Smartass," I said, slapping him. He pretended it hurt, doubling over dramatically, and I resisted the urge to kick him off of the couch.

"Never do that again," he said as he straightened up and fixed me with the most devilish smile I had ever seen. "I might like it." My jaw dropped, like right to the floor I was so shocked, and I slapped him again harder this time.

"Xavier would kill you if he heard that," I said, remembering the slightly jealous tone in his voice when we were talking about him earlier.

"Yeah, well, I'm still alive so I'm taking he didn't, thank god," he said with a laugh.

"Okay, I give in, really what's up with the look? It's really anime," I asked and shrugged.

"What? I happen to think it looks quite good, thank you," he said.

"Yeah, true, but it's just different. What ya think, should I give it a try?" I asked, raising an eyebrow at him. He looked me up and down, then laughed.

"It takes a particular type of person to pull this off and look this good, and honey, you just aren't me. For starters you have boobs, rather nice ones at that." I slapped him again; it was starting to hurt my hand.

"You are really pushing your luck, boy," I said. I couldn't help but laugh; I really had misjudged this guy.

"Okay, but seriously now, that fact and many others put you out of the running to pull this off. I'm sorry but you'll never look this good," he said, straightening his collar and smiling. I laughed harder than I had in ages. There was a whole other side to Ryder I would have never guessed existed, seeing how the guy gave off the whole death on legs vibe, but I could get used to it, and part of me really wanted to get to know this guy.

"Oh my god. You're so on yourself," I joked.

"Hey, now that is offensive," he said with a laugh.

"No denial, I see, and what happed to the quiet, sweet rogue from before?" I asked, and he shrugged.

"That was all part of my evil plan to lure you in, mwahaha." He gave an evil laugh that was really awesome, then cleared his throat. "I mean, you know, he's around." His smile was entrancing, cheeky but evil, the kind of smile that made you smile back and instantly cheered you up. I felt a sigh coming on but stopped it before it happened, thankfully. He was cute, funny and nice, but I would be having him killed if Xavier saw me flirt back.

"No, really, I'm sorry. I'm just trying to cheer you up and if anything I've said has offended you, I do apologise. Just don't dob me into your boyfriend or your brother, both very bad choices. Most likely ending with me dying and although it's long overdue, it's not really on my to do list at the moment."

"Really? Because all I would have to do is…" I took a deep breath and he dove for me, covering my mouth, knocking me backwards.

"I'm sorry I have to do this but you leave me no choice; are you going to scream?" I shook my head. "Good, because I rather like living," he said with a laugh. A growl echoed in from the hall and both our eyes flew to the door. Ryder let me up as a loud crash shook the wall. Without hesitation we both sprang to our feet and darted into the hall. I watched Magenta pick herself up from the floor where she had landed, and crouch as Xavier entered the hall. He looked mad, madder than usual, and she was ready to attack. Fear was evident on her face but she wasn't backing down. He said nothing but the look alone was enough to say he was going to kill her, but why? Ryder and I watched as he made his way across the room toward her; we had to do something.

"Xavier, no," I protested. He stopped and turned to me. The look in his eyes was wild. I had never seen anything like it before. I tried not to cringe. The look brought tears to my eyes. He growled in my direction but Ryder jumped in front of me, snarling back. This was the first time he had really scared me. Xavier froze; he looked at me horrified, as if he only just realised what he had done. Magenta fled the room and Ryder pulled me into his arms, still growling at Xavier. Xavier's eyes faded back to green and he took a step towards us, but stopped. Ryder put himself between us and normally I would have protested, but not this time. Xavier looked down; regret washed out his features and just like that, he was gone.

I wanted to chase after him. After seeing the hurt look, I wanted to see if he was okay, but that was just crazy. What was I doing; he could have killed me!

"Shhh, I'm sure he didn't mean it, he would never hurt you… I wouldn't have let him," Ryder said quietly, stroking my hair and holding me tight. I just stared at the door. It wasn't like I had never seen him like that before, but this time it was different. There was something else there, something in his eyes, a true killer. I pulled from Ryder's grip and gave him a half-hearted smile to say thanks before I went to lie down for a while. What was going on? What had Magenta done? I couldn't help but picture the look on Xavier's face after he'd growled at me, and I couldn't help but feel responsible for causing him pain. I had made him feel like a monster and that's why he fled. Even though my more rational side knew I had done nothing wrong, I still felt guilty. I laid there for a good ten minutes, guilt tearing me apart.

"Guilt is a vitamin deficiency," said Xavier quietly from the door. "Well, unknown guilt is."

"What, you a doctor now?" I said harshly; even though we had both calmed down I wasn't sure I was ready to talk to him yet. He gave a soft chuckle.

"No, I saw it on *House* once," he said. We were both quiet for awhile, and I wouldn't even look at him. "I'm sorry, but that kind of thing is going to keep happening and I'm going to have to keep apologizing and breaking my promises, because it's in my nature to be violent. Not just my vampire nature either, and I can't change; lord, I've tried. Maybe Magenta was right, I am just another danger to you," he said.

"What? No Xavier, I know you're a spaz and it's cool that you lose it sometimes, really, I know deep down that you would never hurt me," I said, sitting up.

"But I could and I was going to. If Ryder hadn't jumped to your defence I would have. I saw the fear in your eyes and the tears, I'm sorry," he said. It was dark, but I could see his shape leaning against the door frame.

"How many times are we going to have to go through this? I trust you," I said. "You just have to learn to trust me, too."

"As long as I'm a vampire and you're a human," he said, quieter than a whisper. I wasn't even sure it was meant to be out loud.

"Xavier, I wasn't crying because you scared me, and as for the whole human thing, we both know that's easily fixed; turn me," I said.

Okay, that was the first time I had even thought about being turned; I guess it was my only option if I wanted to be with Xavier, and for some stupid reason I did. Eternity without the complications of being human didn't sound that bad, right?

"Not an option," he said.

"Why not, is the thought of spending eternity with me really that bad?" I snapped.

"No."

"Then why, Xavier?" I said.

"The thought of ending your life to make you into this sickens me. Do you really want to be like this? Being a vampire isn't fun, it isn't glamorous like you've seen in the movies. I wouldn't wish this on anyone who had a choice, let alone you, so why would I kill my own girl to curse her with it?"

I got up and walked over to him. "You're so frustrating," I said. I was kinda glad he had said no, because truthfully, I didn't want to be a vampire, I liked being human and if he had said yes, he would have called my bluff.

"And you're not?" he said, smiling smugly.

"Urgh," I complained, rubbing my temples, "you are going to be the death of me someday."

"Let's hope not," he said, leaning down to kiss me. I gave in. I was tired of fighting, but I knew it was far from over no matter how much I wanted to yell and tell him how stupid he was, that we could make it work, but eventually we both knew it would be our only choice if we wanted to stay together, but that was a long way off.

"You're so sexy when you're mad," he said, pulling me from my thoughts. I smiled as he kissed me again. His hands roamed the small of my back as his lips traced along my cheek and down my neck. Soft kisses sent chills through my whole body; he stopped but didn't look up.

"Can it wait, Ryder?" I heard Ryder stop at the doorway and sighed.

"It's dusk, we should really get going," he said. Xavier stepped back and looked down to me.

"Find that knife I gave you, I'll get changed and find us a car," he said. I smiled ecstatically. *I won, I really won!*

"Thank you," I cried, throwing my arms around his neck and kissing him again. He looked to Ryder.

"Don't let her from your sight," he said after we broke apart. Ryder nodded and took my hand, pulling me from the room.

CHAPTER NINETEEN

I decided to go incognito and dressed in black. Black top, black pants, black shoes, even a black hair tie, and I felt super-ninja. Part of me knew that black on black looked good on no one (well, maybe the one exception was Ryder, because it most certainly looked good on him). Vampires pointed and whispered as we passed. It wasn't hard to tell what they were talking about. We stopped at the doormat express, I'm sure that's not what it's really called, but that's the name I'm giving it. Ryder stepped onto it.

"God, I hate this thing," I said, stepping on and latching onto Ryder. At least this time I knew what to expect. The sun was setting as we crossed the yard to the drive. The view was breathtaking. Ryder didn't speak as we stood there, but he had that kick ass look on his face. The kind that said "mess with me, come on, I dare you." Xavier had said fighting is what he did best and if we were right, there was going to be one hell of a fight.

A flicker of a coat blowing in the wind caught my eye and I looked down the drive. I did the only thing I was capable of doing: I stared. I watched as Xavier rounded the corner into the drive. He was dressed in an outfit similar to Ryder's. I watched every step he took as if it were in slow motion. He wore black three-quarter cargo pants with that same strange belt, except his had a chain running from that to his cargos. His shirt was identical to Ryder's except his was white and he wore it mostly open; only the last few buttons were fastened. The black trench coat fluttered as he walked and the studs on the combat boots gleamed in the setting sun, two sleek black and chrome bikes in tow. He stopped in front of us and thanked the two guys that led the bikes. I hadn't even seen them until then. He got on one of the bikes and started it, then smiled. *Oh my god,* I thought, then sighed. Not even attempting to stop it.

Ryder stepped over the other bike and said something to Xavier. I registered his voice but not what he said, I just couldn't. Xavier looked so natural in those clothes and him next to Ryder was a sight too good for one girl to process. *I think I died and went to rogue heaven.* I watched as his amazing green eyes lit up and those soft kissable lips formed that cheeky smile. My brain was still registering his beauty in slow motion but I couldn't care less.

"Misty, woohoo, earth to Misty," said Xavier, his voice suddenly snapping me out of it.

"What?" I asked.

"Welcome back," he joked, patting the seat behind him. I smiled, but that was all I could manage. I stepped over the bike and wrapped my hands tightly around him.

"Hang on," he said taking off. *I was planning to* I thought, still not able to verbalise my thoughts. We rode at an amazing speed, weaving in and out of traffic; I closed my eyes and kept my head down like I always did when Xavier was driving, but I couldn't ignore the unimaginable thrill of the whole situation. Man, I missed being a hunter. We stopped at this hall outside of town. This was a place I had been hundreds of times when I was a kid, and this whole time it was a supernatural epicentre? I looked at the notice board. It said singles night, a good cover, I guess. Xavier got off the bike and I followed. I couldn't help myself. I gave into to my desire and jumped him; hey, there was always the off-chance one of us wouldn't be walking out of here tonight, so better now than never. I pushed him against the wall, not being at all gentle, and kissed him hard. One hand roamed his hair and the other slipped inside his shirt and down his amazing body. He kissed me back with a passion that should only be saved for the bedroom. I guess he was thinking it too.

"Hey guys, not really the time nor place," said Ryder from behind us. I pulled away breathless. I wanted him so bad; how long was he expecting me to wait?

"God, I want you," said Xavier, giving me one last longing look as he pushed open the door. The inside of the hall was packed, and something told me they weren't here for singles night. We crossed the room and headed out back. It was dark and eerie quiet, away from the crowd. We stopped in a long dark hall that seemed to stretch on forever.

"Okay, one of these doors leads down. Find it," he said to Ryder, who took off straight away, no questions asked. Xavier looked to me with longing in his eyes; I guess my little display had gotten to him. "Wait here," he said, giving me one last kiss before taking off as well. I leaned against the wall. *I don't want you to get hurt but I'll leave you all alone in a dark hallway, in a place full of scary monsters!* I thought as looked around. The place was just as creepy as it was when I was a kid. I guess now I knew why.

"Well hello, pretty lady," said a man who seemed to materialize out of the darkness. I looked at him and he blinked two sets of eyelids. Okay, so not human. "You here for the singles night, beautiful?" he asked. Great; he sees a poor little human that has stumbled onto something way beyond her imagination and needed to be dealt with, or eaten.

"Yes, and I'm with someone, sorry," I replied.

"Me too," he said, stepping closer.

"And it's not you," I added for clarification, because he didn't seem to get it. I looked around *and that somebody better get his arse back here right now!*

"Now, don't be like that, girlie," he said, flicking his forked tongue. *Great! A reptilian.*

"Back off, you scaly son off a bitch," I said, reaching for my knife, I bet it worked just as well on reptilians as it did other creatures, seeing I couldn't quite remember how to kill them.

"Sorry that took so long babe, the loos were atrocious," said Ryder in his charming English accent, taking me into his arms. He looked to the creepy thing disapprovingly. "Can I help you?" he said. I noticed his fangs were extended, which I must add was rather odd. The guy looked him up and down, then shook his head. It wasn't hard to see he had picked Ryder for a vampire right away.

"Good, now where were we?" he said, kissing me suddenly, ramming both of us into the wall.

The creepy reptile guy left, muttering, "Fucking vampires!" as he did.

Ryder pulled away quickly. "Sorry, it was quickest way to get rid of him, no one likes to watch a vampire feed," he said. I nodded and that sounded good in theory, but I shouldn't have enjoyed it that much.

"Yeah of course," I said, still kind of shocked that he kissed me, and he was one hell of a kisser.

"But now I see why Xavier likes that so much, you taste as good as you smell," he said and I smiled, not really sure how to respond to that.

"Found it," said Xavier. I quickly pushed it out of my mind.

"There was a reptilian, Ryder scared it away," I said suddenly, at a rather impressive speed.

Ryder shot me a warning look, and it was a good thing Xavier was looking at me curiously so he didn't see it. He looked to Ryder. "Good job," he said with a smile. I guess he thought I wanted him to praise him, and I smiled nervously.

"Okay, great, let's go save my brother," I said, a little too excited. Don't get me wrong; I was happy that I was going get him back. But that kiss was going to eat me up inside. I was going to tell him the moment we were all safe.

We walked down the dark hallway that the room's trapdoor had led us into. We hadn't passed a single door and there was only one way in and out of this place. Xavier walked by my side and Ryder close behind; I saw a door at the end of the hall.

"Look," I said, pointing to the door as we stopped. There was a light shining from underneath it.

"Damien," Xavier whispered; he must have picked up on his thoughts. He went quiet again and closed his eyes. "Damien!" he called as he opened them.

"Xavier," I scolded, "what if Lincoln and Alex are in there?"

"They're not," he said, jogging to the door and kicking it open. We walked in and there he was. Damien was tied the same way Alex had tied us. Except he was tied with both chains and rosary beads, a good foot off the ground. He was all bruised and beaten and his lucky brown leather jacket was covered in blood, his own most likely. A lump rose in my throat; he looked a mess. He looked up at us, his green-blue eyes expressionless, and his short, dark blonde hair sat flat on his head, instead of its usual spiked style. He looked pale and fragile and he was so skinny; he had lost a lot of weight.

"Bout time," he said, his deep voice huskier than usual. He looked to me. "Missy, what the hell are you doing here?" He didn't give me time to answer before he looked to Xavier. "What is she doing here? What the hell are you wearing? And why is there a rogue with you?" Xavier rolled his eyes; same old Damien.

"Are we really going to play twenty questions or would you like us to save your ass," he said.

I ran for my brother, breaking the rosary chain, Xavier broke the other. He fell to the ground landing on his feet, barely. He straightened himself up and I threw my arms around him, pulling him in tight and never wanting to let go.

"What are you doing in a place like this, Missy?" he said, pulling away he so could look at me.

"I'm a West, Dee, hunting's in my blood," I said, and he smiled at me. Even as beaten as he was, Damien had the warmest smile, the type that could make you feel better in an instant, if you got the pleasure of seeing it.

"I was afraid of that," he said, coughing and nearly collapsing. Both me and Xavier dove for him, keeping him up right. I let him drape his arm over my shoulder and we turned to walk for the door, but instead of leaving we all froze.

"Well, well, well, all in the one place, that was easy," said Alex from the door.

Xavier crouched and growled like he was going to pounce and attack him, and Ryder did the same. Damien straightened up at the prospect of a fight even though he was in no condition to; my brother hated looking weak.

"You're outnumbered, jerkoff. There are four of us and only one of you," said Damien with a cocky tone in his voice. Alex smiled and pulled a gun pointing it at me. *Not again!*

"Don't you touch her," growled Xavier. Alex stepped forward, grabbed me and pointed the gun to my head. *Why do the bad guys always grab me!* He smelled my hair, which was super creepy and really disgusting.

"Now, doesn't she smell tasty?" he said as I reached for my knife, but he grabbed it first.

"Now, now, Misty, we wouldn't want you to cut yourself with so many vampires in the room." He adjusted the gun. "One move and I'll blow her brains out," he warned. I saw Xavier slide a gun across the floor to Damien, who grabbed it and, with a speed that was almost inhuman, pointed it at Alex.

"You shoot and it will be the last thing you ever do," warned Damien. I thought I had come to rescue him? Alex grabbed my hand and ran the tip of the knife along my palm; both Xavier and Ryder tensed up.

"It's such a waste really, bleeding a beautiful girl dry, and to do it in front of her brother," he said in a mocking voice.

"Hurt her and I swear," growled Damien. Ryder breathed out and retook his crouch; both his and Xavier's eyes darkened. Xavier's fists were clenched and his hands were shaking.

"Cool it," ordered Damien as he looked to Xavier. He snarled, baring his fangs; a soft rumble of a growl could be heard in his chest. He seemed to be stopping himself.

"Does her blood bother you, vampire? You want it, don't you? Crave it; you want to drain her of it? You can taste it now, can't you Xavier, it's been there tempting you and you need it," said Alex, as I watched Xavier's eyes follow a drop of blood that dripped from the knife to the floor. He snapped out of it somewhat.

"Never," growled Xavier, his voice gritty and rough through clenched teeth. Alex tried to turn me around but I took advantage of the move and kicked him in the balls. I ducked out of the way as he shot the ground, doubling over in pain. I ran to Damien's side and Xavier didn't spare a second; he grabbed Alex and smiled evilly.

"Well, well, Alex, I promised that this would happen. Finally I have you, and because you're an evil old bastard and you made me wait, you can bet this is going to be slow and painful," he said, grabbing him by the throat then slamming him to the ground.

Alex spat up blood. "Have mercy, just kill me," Alex begged.

Xavier smiled that crazy smile. "Mercy? Sorry, that word's not in my vocabulary." He looked to us; his eyes already showed his sanity slipping. "Run, now!" he snapped, growling. Damien grabbed my hand and dragged me from the room. I heard Alex's screams as we ran down the hall.

We waited in the now-abandoned hall. Half an hour had passed since we left Xavier to deal with Alex, and I could believe he was truly doing as he threatened. Damien cradled me in his arms as we waited. It was so good to finally have him back. Xavier entered the hall and stopped. He was drenched in blood and he collapsed to his knees with his head in his hands; *was he crying?* I pulled away from Damien and made my way over to him. As I got closer I realised he wasn't crying; he was laughing.

"Xavier?" I asked. His head shot up, his once-emerald eyes were now black and his smile was twisted, evil. He got to his feet, taking a few steps toward me, and before I could blink I was being pinned against the wall off the ground. He smiled up at me.

"Don't worry, babe, it only hurts for a little while," he said, turning my head. I closed my eyes, expecting a bite, but instead I fell to the ground hard. I looked up to see Damien pinning Xavier to the ground with a knife to his throat, and Ryder standing beside them. I was impressed with the speed with which they had taken him down.

"Xavier, snap out of it, dude, do not make me kill you," said Damien putting a little more pressure on the knife. Xavier's eyes fluttered and changed back to green.

"Damien?" said Xavier as if he was waking up from a dream "No, I didn't?" Damien let him go and he looked over to me and breathed out a sigh of relief. He got that shocked look on his face as he remembered what had just happened and what he had done to Alex. He broke down for real this time.

"Dude, it's cool, you can't control blood lust, we all know that," said Damien, patting him on the shoulder.

"Xavier?" I said, walking up to him.

"No, stay back," he said.

"Come on, Xavier."

"Keep back, you don't know what he's capable of," warned Damien, taking a step forward again.

"Yes I do, and I trust him," I said to reassure my brother.

"Why?" Xavier said, looking up at me. "How could you? I just nearly killed you and you can't imagine the horror that I created in that room, but I enjoyed it, bleeding him dry, watching him suffer." I knew he was trying to keep me away, but Alex deserved every bit of it and more. I smiled at him gently. "Why are you smiling? It disturbed even me," he asked, looking confused.

"Alex killed my father, tortured and kidnapped poor Damien and he hurt you. Death, in my eyes, was a get out of jail free card, no matter how painful it may have been," I said.

Xavier shook his head in disbelief. "I will never get you, Misty," he said. I walked up to him, slipping the blood-covered shirt off his shoulders so I could hug him.

"You already have, hook, line and sinker, and you always will," I whispered, then kissed him.

"Whoa! No, no, no, hold up!" yelled Damien, pulling us apart. Unlike Xavier, Damien had no quarrel being rough with me. "What the hell is going on here?! And what do you think you're doing?" he said looking to Xavier. Xavier smiled but said nothing.

"What's it look like?" I asked, but it was rhetorical.

"Every brother's worst nightmare," he said, shooting daggers at Xavier with his eyes. Damien was up to his old tricks again. *How I missed them.* "My sister and me best friend playin' tonsil hockey! That's what it looks like!" he snapped. I smiled. Xavier was lucky he was Damien's friend, because the worst he was going to get was verbal abuse. Damien shoved him with enough force to make him stumble, which again was impressive.

"You hurt her and I swear that I'll slay your ass so fast that you'll think your still alive, until your head falls off," he warned.

"Good to have ya back, bro," said Xavier with a smile.

"No! I'm not your bro. You broke the bro code, dude, uncool," he said. I knew we were never going to hear the end of this.

"Come on, man, you can't blame me? Your sister's hot," said Xavier. Damien drew his gun and shot him. I gasped, shocked, as the echo of the shot bounced around the room. Xavier was blown backwards clean off his feet and fell to the ground. I couldn't believe it; he shot him!

"Oh my god! Damien!" I scolded as Xavier sat up; Damien looked pretty pleased with himself.

"Man, that kills, asshole," complained Xavier. Relief rolled over me as he pulled shards of silver from the wound. "Totally uncalled for."

"Yeah, well, fuck you, Drack!" Damien huffed, putting the gun away. I shook my head and patted my pockets. My knife was gone. *I can't leave that!*

"My knife," I said and ran toward the trap door. I walked down the hall toward the door, not really wanting to enter. Xavier appeared in front of me, stopping me in my tracks.

"What are you doing, running off like that, down here of all places; I wasn't joking when I said there is a mess in there. Look, you just wait here; let me get it," he said, walking off. He stopped, as the sound of the door opening made us both jump. I saw a figure at the door; they were pointing a gun at Xavier. Panicked, I reacted without thinking.

"Nighty-night, vampire," said a familiar voice and I dove in front of Xavier as I heard the gun fire.

"No!" yelled Xavier as I felt the bullet pierce my chest; the figure fled as I fell to my knees.

"No! Misty no, babe, hold on, honey," said Xavier, dropping to his knees right beside me. My head started to spin. I felt tired, kind of groggy as I looked down to the wound in my chest.

"Xavier, I…" I started, but I could taste blood and I knew that was never a good sign.

"Why did you do that? I'm immortal, you're not," he said. I could see his eyes start to glisten.

"People do crazy things for the ones they love," I managed to get out, and tried to smile at him.

"You shouldn't have," he said. I was falling deeper and deeper into the darkness with every second and Xavier could see that. "Hold on babe, stay with me, it's going to be alright, don't worry," he whispered as he pulled me into his arms and stood. A tear rolled down his pale cheek and stained it red because his tears weren't water, they were blood. Every movement hurt as he ran and I started to cough; the blood was choking me.

"Xavier…" I said as the darkness consumed me.

"Stay with me, babe, everything's going to be okay," he said, his voice was getting quieter with every word. "I love you, please don't leave me, hold on," he cried. His voice seemed so far away, so quiet, as I slipped deeper and deeper into the darkness.

CHAPTER TWENTY

Damien

"I'm going to kill him!" I said as I paced the floor of the place that had been my personal hell for the last two months. I looked over at the rogue no one had bothered to introduce to me, and stopped. He was pacing the floor as well. Man, it felt good to be free to again, to be able to move. Every joint was sore and every muscle screamed at me to sit down, but I couldn't. There was so much I needed to do, and the thought of making Xavier pay for even thinking about getting it on with my sister made freedom oh so much sweeter. Now all I needed was a good diner-style hamburger and some lollies, and life would be perfect. Pain ripped through my stomach as it growled. I felt violently ill for a second as a wave of nausea washed over me. Man, I was hungry. *Speaking of food,* I thought.

"Man, I'm hungry, what's taking them so long. I swear if they don't hurry up I'll turn to cannibalism," I complained. The rogue shrugged and continued pacing. I looked toward the door and Xavier appeared. He had Misty in his arms and her body was limp. *No!* I ran for them as fast as my aching muscles would carry me.

"What have you done?" I yelled; this time he really would die if she was hurt. I took her limp, almost lifeless body from his arms, cradling my poor baby sister close to my chest. *Come on Misty, please, baby girl, wake up.*

"Get her to a hospital," he demanded, and motioned for the rogue to follow him; they both took off. My strength wavered for a second as I looked down at her; she was so pale and her skin was cold, but she was still breathing. Blood gushed from a wound in her chest, covering her shirt and mine; she'd been shot. I ran out of the building and looked around. *There has to be a car somewhere.* An old piece of shit Honda caught my attention; it was the only car in the lot and it would be easy to hotwire. *It will have to do,* I thought, sprinting as fast as my legs would carry us; I gently sat Misty down and looked around for something to break the window. Normally I would break in more carefully, but careful was the last thing on my mind at the moment. I gave up quickly, bringing my elbow back and breaking the window. Pain shot through my arm as I knocked away the bigger pieces and reached in, unlocking the back door. I carefully placed Misty in the car and climbed in the passenger side. The glass cut up my jeans and stabbed into my legs as I did. I winced but pain was nothing to me at the moment; I had to save my baby sister.

I ripped open the dash, finding and connecting the wires I was looking for. The car revved to life. I wasted no time chucking it into reverse and speeding backwards, before quickly turning and jamming it into first. I sped down the road doing well over the speed limit, well over what I had expected this piece of shit to do, yet it still wasn't fast enough. If I only had the Stang we would be there by now. It took another five minutes to make it to the hospital, and Misty was eerily still. I pulled up outside the door. I think it was an ambulance bay, but I didn't really care. I had to get her in there; she had already lost a lot of blood. I gently got her out of the car and burst through the doors of the ER.

"I need some help over here," I yelled, catching the attention of everyone around. The room soon turned into chaos, people running everywhere, yelling things, just moving too fast for my shocked state to process. I laid her down on a gurney they had wheeled over. Everything was a blur but I could see a man in scrubs yelling orders to the nurses, but his voice wasn't registering. They rushed her off and I just stood there watching. I went to follow; but a nurse had her hand on my chest, pushing me back.

"Sir, you have to stay here," she said.

"Misty, but that's my sister!" I replied, feeling weak and helpless for the first time since my father had died.

"No, please, let the doctors handle it. Everything will be fine. Please sir, follow me," she said, leading me to a room. She looked at the cuts on my arms and legs; I had almost forgotten they were there.

"Are you okay, sir?" she asked but I was still in shock; it took me a few seconds to reply.

"Yeah, I'm fine," I said. She shook her head and turned to another nurse that I hadn't even noticed standing there.

"Go get him a blanket, I'll get him cleaned up, I think he's in shock. Sir, can you follow me." I nodded because I couldn't think enough to argue, and followed. She led me to a cubicle. The pain was starting to hit me and being chained off the ground really takes its toll on your body; every joint screamed in pain. In the last three months I had suffered beatings like nothing you could imagine; of course, if I had gotten free he would have regretted it. Hardly any sleep and barely enough food to keep a normal human alive. One nurse put a blanket across my shoulders and I looked to the nurse who was dressing my wounds. She was hot, I mean like naughty fantasy hot. Normally by now I would have tried my best to pick her up. Probably started referring to her as sugar or even grabbed her ass, if I felt like being classy, but I couldn't even find a mental striptease, I was so exhausted. Now that's saying something. I was at breaking point, tired, hungry, worn out, and worried sick, *Man, this night should end.*

I went back and sat in the waiting room. She handed me a couple of dry biscuits and offered me some coffee. I nodded and gave her my best attempt at a charming smile, but I really didn't feel all that charming at the moment.

"Black," I said when she asked how I wanted it, and she walked out. I pulled the blanket tight around me as I looked at the messy stack of Chick's Bibles sitting on the table in front of me and bit into the sorry excuse for a biscuit; I groaned. There had to be a vending machine or a cafeteria around here somewhere. The nurse placed a steaming Styrofoam cup on the table in front of me and I thanked her, sitting back in my chair. I laid my head back, leaning over the back of the chair. My eyes were heavy and I had to fight the temptation to sleep. I looked down at the coffee, wondering if it would help, but decided I needed something a whole lot stronger. *What am I thinking? Screw coffee! I need bourbon or scotch, anything as long as it's alcohol and strong,* I thought, running my hands through my hair as I rested my head in my hands for a moment. Xavier better hurry and get his stupid Dracula ass here, he has some serious explaining to do about a lot of things. I closed my eyes; I wasn't going to sleep, I was just going to rest my eyes until the doctor came back.

"Damien! You awake?" Xavier yelled in my ear. I jumped, nearly falling off the chair.

"Yeah, I was just resting my eyes," I said, half-asleep still. My voice was a dead giveaway that I was lying but give me a break; I've had a long couple of months.

"Do people normally snore when their resting their eyes?" asked the blonde rogue who I now realised was a pom.

"So what, a man can't rest his eyes whilst snoring anymore?" I snapped, trying to wake myself up properly. Xavier rolled his eyes, chucked a couple of dry-looking sandwiches into my lap and took a seat across from me. I wasted no time digging into the sandwich, and took down half of the first in just two bites; they tasted so good.

"How's Misty," he asked. I just looked at him and tried to resist the urge to snap, *"Well, she just got shot, so how do you think she is?"* but I settled for something nicer.

"Well, I don't know, do I look like a doctor, Drack? What I want to know is how she got shot in the first place," I snapped, taking another bite. Okay, well, I didn't say it was going to be much nicer.

"It was meant for me but Misty took the bullet," he said with a humourless laugh. Funny? I didn't think it was that funny either. "God knows what it had in it, it could be anything. If it was V-tox it could have seriously nasty effects; that stuff's not meant for humans."

Ya think, I thought, glaring at him. I didn't want to be rude and talk with my mouth full.

"Why did she push you out of the way, anyway?" I said finally, not really caring much for manners.

"I don't know, I asked her that myself," he said. What wasn't he telling me? He should know better than anyone, I don't like surprises because they always end badly.

Oh and by the way we are going to have a nice long talk about the you hooking up with my little sister thing and I can't promise you that it won't involve guns, I thought directly at him. I waited for a response. I had one of what we called the West family abilities. I could communicate telepathically if the other person allowed it. But in order for it to be a two-way conversation they had to have the ability for it to work. It kinda works like a UHF radio; you have to be tuned into the right channel for it to work. I can also propel my thoughts into people's minds, willing or not, so it helps on missions where Xavier and I have to split up and it's also a very cool party trick. Joseph reckons that the reason Xavier can read minds as a vampire is because he had that ability when he was human but it's not an uncommon power for a vampire to have, especially royal ones.

What's there to talk about dude, I'm with your sister, I love her, she loves me, what more do you want, his voice said in my mind. I hardened my gaze and looked at him, screwing up the wrapper in my hand.

I don't want anything, how could you dude? You know how weird it's going to be if you break up? And if you hurt her it's my job, no, my right to kill you, and besides this means I now officially do not like you, it's like a rule that I not like Misty's boyfriends.

He sighed out loud and shook his head. *Well, I don't really plan on breaking up with her any time soon, or at all actually. Dude, you have no idea what this is, I think it's the real deal.*

We're not doing the whole chick flick moment, okay, I know you girls like gushing about your feelings but keep them to yourself, the less I know the better, but I'm watching you, dude, you are officially on the big brother radar, effective as soon as Misty is around us. I warned there was no way he was getting off the hook for this one. I was going to make his life a living hell as soon as everything was back to normal. He smiled and laughed; the pommy rogue looked to him, expecting him to explain what was funny, I guess.

"Well, thanks for that Dee, sweet of you to care," he said out loud. The pommy rogue gave him a confused look. I guess he didn't know Xavier could read minds, but I will admit it's so funny to see the looks on people's faces when we only gave snippets of a conversation.

"Who the hell is the pommy rogue?" I said, looking at him. My curiosity finally got the better of me.

"His name is Ryder," said Xavier. His tone was disapproving, but I didn't really care. You would think by now he would have realised that I don't really give a rat's arse about what he thinks.

"And I'm English," the rogue corrected. *I think I like pommy rogue better.*

"Yeah, same diff, you're a pom, I'm a yank, and once upon a time ago he was a yobbo, what the difference English, poms, it's all the same to me," I said, leaning back in the really uncomfortable chair; man, these things sucked. He looked at me just as disapprovingly as Xavier had; well, I guess we're never going to be BFFs.

"Forgive him, Ryder, he's.... well, he's Damien ,and that's really the only excuse I can offer you for the way he acts; he takes some time to get used to," said Xavier. *Damien, apologise,* snapped Xavier, giving me a death stare.

No, I'm not apologising for being me, if he don't like it he doesn't have to listen and just for that I'm going to keep calling him a pommy rogue, I thought back.

Your mouth is going to get you killed one day, he replied.

Well, you're well on the way to getting yourself killed, I felt the need to catch up somehow. You have more enemies than you can count and the only reason they haven't killed you is because you're nuttier that a squirrel's turd and there scared you'll get them first. I gave him a smartass smile, knowing I had won.

People wonder why I'm crazy, they would know if they could only read your mind. Being trapped in a dark empty space all day can send a man off the edge, he thought, returning my smile. Okay, maybe I was a little quick to judge on that. I gave him an evil look.

You're lucky we're in a hospital, I thought, wondering: if I shot him through my scrunched-up jacket would it muffle the sound enough to not draw attention? But then again, he's not worth ruining my jacket over. He smiled and laughed to himself, but I wasn't joking. I was so going to kill that boy one day; it wasn't an if really, but a when. We sat there not really talking for a while. *I wonder if I could get away with resting my eyes again, just for a few minutes.*

"We're going to have to…" started Xavier, but I interrupted him. I knew exactly what he was going to say.

"No, we can fight our own battles. Besides, we tell him about this and he'll have both our hides, for once I would like him to think we are capable of doing one job without screwing everything up," I said.

"Damien, we're only human, dude," he said. I looked at him waiting for him to correct himself.

"No, I'm only human, you… you are the reason we are always in these kinds of messes and to make things a whole step worse, you dragged my poor, sweet baby sister into one!" Oh yeah, I was going back there.

"ME! No! Going to Misty was my last option. You knew that you couldn't right this by yourself, but still you tried anyway. If you hadn't been so stubborn, like you are being now, and just admitted for once that you're not bulletproof and you needed help, none of this would have happened. You vanished off the face of the earth! You know what Joseph and I went through to get even a lead on you, but we got nothing, you should be thanking your lucky stars that it was Lincoln that captured you because if it had been anything else you would be six feet under right now. Death isn't pleasant; take it from someone who's already been there and done that. What you have to somehow get through that five inches of skull into that hunk of grey matter you call a brain is that you're not superman, we saved you, not the other way around," he snapped, getting to his feet.

As if out of instinct I did the same; no one shapes up to Damien West. Xavier always tried to intimidate people by standing over them. A fact he couldn't help, but he never has or ever will stare me down.

"What do you want me to do? Leap into your arms and cry my hero?" I asked, raising my voice. Xavier's eyes were darkening. He was getting pissed off but that was good because so was I, though I didn't have the little tell-tale signs.

"You are a moron, do you really think that's...." he trailed off.

"Is everything alright in here?" asked the quiet voice of a very confused nurse. Xavier looked away.

"Yeah fine," he said, slumping down into the chair he stood up from.

"Peachy," I grunted and sat back down as well, staring at my boots.

"Okay," she said and left the room.

We sat there in total silence. Even my thoughts were limited to whether or not Misty was going to be okay, or on what I could scrape up to eat, because I was still starving. Finally, after what felt like hours, the doctor walked in.

"Misty West's family," he said, looking down at a chart. We all got to our feet and eagerly looked at him. He shrank back a bit, but in our defence we were a pretty intimidating bunch.

"How is she?" I asked.

"Is she going to be alright?" added Xavier.

"At the moment she's stabilised, but she's still in a coma. There was no head trauma and no real reason why she fell into it in the first place. It has us all stumped but we're doing all we can to keep her comfortable, and hopefully she will wake naturally. We're running tests on the bullet she was shot with just in case, but I'm afraid there is nothing more we can do. I'm meant to ask in the case of a shooting, what happened?" he said, looking from me to Xavier.

"We were mugged," I said, thinking it would be a believable enough excuse. "I tried to catch the shooter but they overpowered me."

He looked me up and down. "They overpowered you?" he said questionably. I nodded. Okay, I guess it was kinda hard to believe someone could overpower me; I wasn't exactly the weakest-looking guy in the world even with the fact I had been practically starved, but maybe I could use that to my advantage.

"Yeah, you got a problem believing that?" I said, putting a threatening edge in my voice. He shook his head quickly.

"No, of course not, muggings happen all the time," he said, his voice wavering a little.

"So, can we see her or not?" I asked.

"Immediate family only for now, sorry," he said. I raise an eyebrow. *What, can't he see the family resemblance?*

"Well that's no problem; I'm her brother," I said.

"And I'm her husband," lied Xavier, and I gave him a dirty look.

"Well, it's fine for you two to come." He looked to the blonde pommy rogue.

"I'll wait here, shall I?" he said, sitting back down in the waiting room chair. We followed the doctor to a room. He pushed the door open and motioned for us to enter. I walked in the room and looked around. It was like most other rooms in the hospital. White walls, those tiles that look like plaster with holes in them and those bright, flat lights that are the same shape and size as the tiles. I looked to Misty; she was hooked up to all these different machines. The steady beep of the heart monitor was the only thing that broke the silence. I stared, horrified by what I saw. All that ran through my mind was that I was going to lose her. I had basically raised this girl, her first word was Damie, I was her big brother. I should have protected her, I'd promised I would, yet here she was. She was all the family I had left. I had to do something.

I thought about what the doctor had said. It was nothing they had ever seen before but that doesn't meant it wasn't something we hadn't; there was definitely more than holy water in the bullet, but what? I knew there was only one way we were going to find out. We had to get the bullet for Misty's sake, and to protect people from trying to deal with stuff they aren't meant to even know about. It was my responsibility as a brother and as a hunter to retrieve it, but how? I looked to Xavier who was sitting in the chair beside her bed.

"We're going to need that bullet," I said.

He looked up at me. I could swear he was on the verge of tears, big girl. "That would be in the lab by now and dude, last time I checked, places like that are restricted."

I smiled a cocky smile, starting to think he didn't really know me at all. "Has that ever stopped me before? I'll find a way," I said, getting up.

"Damien! Dude, don't do anything stupid," he called after me as I walked out. I formulated my plan as I walked. I knew I would need a security pass to get in to the lab and there was only one way I knew how to get one.

After almost five minutes of searching I had to change strategies; if I couldn't find a security guard, I would have security find me. I knew it wouldn't be hard. I had been thrown out of my fair share of places for being too rowdy, and this was no exception. I tend to be a little rowdy at times, especially when I've been drinking, and with what Xavier and I do for a living I spend a lot of time in and out of this hospital and, well... a lot of time drinking, so they had little patience for my attitude. *I could tip a gurney, nah, done that before...* I see Dr Leeann Davis walking my way. Now, she was a doctor I would gladly get sick for. She rolled her eyes when she saw me standing in the hall blocking her path. She could play hard to get as much as she liked; I knew she wanted me.

"Hey sugar, come for your monthly dose of vitamin Dee," I said smugly, stepping in her way as she goes to pass.

"Mr West, they still haven't caught you yet?" she said, giving me that smile doctors and checkout chicks give when they say "have a nice day." I laughed, fixing her with my most charming of smiles.

"Nah, baby, they can't catch me," I said, and she rolled her eyes again.

"What you in for? Wait, let me guess; alcohol poisoning?"

"Now don't be like that, sugar. I've been a good boy. Want to help me break my streak?" I asked with a flirty smile.

"That's Dr Sugar to you, now please, I have work to do," she said. I stepped out of her way. Fight all you will, doctor, I will have you.

"Oh I get ya, hey doc I think I need a check-up, I'll be waiting in that room with my pants off, so you can give me an oral exam," I called after her as she walked away. I heard her give a quiet chuckle.

"Sorry Mr West, better luck next time," she said and kept walking. I watched every step as she walked away. *Oh yeah she wants me.* Out of the corner of my eye I saw a guy leaning against the wall, staring at me. I hadn't noticed him until just now and he kinda gave me the creeps. I turned away. *Let it go, Damien, he's probably sick or something,* I thought as I looked for something to attract the attention of the guards, but I couldn't concentrate. I could feel that guy's eyes burn into the back of my head. I knew it was probably just me being paranoid but I had to say something. I wasn't going to be able to stop myself any longer.

"Hey buddy, I got something of yours on?" I said, turning around only to see he was no longer against the wall but right behind me. "Well, you got a problem?"

He just looked at me; his strange coloured eyes seemed to change colour as he slowly grew to my height. He smiled. His teeth were all twisted and moving like weeds in his mouth; he was a shifter and right before my eyes he was becoming me.

"Not yet, you haven't," he said in a voice that was similar to mine but maybe not as deep yet. It tackled me to the ground, ripping off my lucky jacket and throwing it to the side, "I'll need that, Damien doesn't go anywhere without his lucky jacket," it said, clawing at me with messed-up hands. I dodged the claw and the thing went feral, biting, punching and pretty much doing anything that would give it the advantage. I heard a tear before I felt the pain. Without even looking I knew it had just ripped open the skin on my stomach and, worst of all, I knew its claws had just ripped right through my favourite Van Halen tee shirt. It stopped for a second as I looked down at my shirt, which now was ruined. Blood ran onto my jeans from the scratch that had accompanied the redecoration of my favourite shirt. *Okay,* maybe that's a little deeper than I first thought but it wasn't all that long. I shook my head and glared at the monster. *Okay, now it's personal.* I overpowered him with one mighty and kinda painful heave, pinning him down and punching him as hard as I could a few times. Really, I was just trying to see if I could return the favour and redecorate that thing he called a face. Which, I might add, was getting handsomer by the second. But of course I only knew how to make two colours, black and blue.

"Man, did you pick the wrong day to mess with me, shifter boy," I said as it tried to fight me off. I looked around quickly. I needed silver and sadly that wasn't the kind of thing you just found lying around. If this was a normal day I would have at least four items of silver on me and if I didn't it would be with the hunting gear, and again all my gear I was in the Stang. I looked around. *What can I use?* I thought, trying to keep it pinned while I thought. Then I remembered the one item of use that they didn't strip me of, my belt. I knew a silver-studded belt would come in handy someday. I ripped it off, getting the most disgusted look from the shifter. I shook my head as I pulled the shifter to his feet, ramming him face-first into the wall and forcing his hands behind his back, sort of like a cop would in some kickass action movie. I bound his hands using the belt with the spikes facing inwards. He screamed in pain as the metal burned into him as I pulled tighter on the belt, keeping his face rammed against the wall. Silver was toxic to shifters, so it was really only a matter of time now.

"What do you want?" he cried out after a few seconds. That caught me off guard; I was just about to ask him the same question.

"What do I want? You're the one who was trying to steal my identity and my lucky jacket; shifters don't steal people's things unless there trying to be them for a while, meaning you had all intention of taking me out first," I said.

I noticed that my little show had grabbed the attention of a passing couple, who quickly turned and swiftly headed for the elevator. Well, this was going to get me the all attention I wanted, but not any that I'm likely to use to my advantage at the moment. I ripped the last bit of my shirt that was holding it together and threw it the ground. I lifted its head and rammed it against the wall again when it didn't answer me. "I'm waiting," I said, getting impatient. I had no way of killing it and I'm sure he knew that, and even I knew that in a matter of seconds someone was going to come up here to stop me so I was wasting my time, but I had to at least try. If anything, I could poison him so he died slowly.

"What for, hunter? I saw you, thought it would be a good way to get a quick change and into a hunter of all things, but not just any hunter, a West to be exact, ya know, what kind of respect I would get if I had just managed to pin you for a second?" His eyes were darting around the hall.

"Don't lie to me, shifter, lying to me is a very bad idea."

"I'm not," it replied smugly. I shook my head and sighed.

"Wrong answer," I said, pulling it from the wall and throwing it to the ground. I looked over it and it already partly looked like me. Then it hit me: of course I had a way of killing it. I loosened the belt from its wrist. Keeping it pinned with my knees, I put the belt, with greatest of difficulty, around its neck. I pulled a little tighter on the belt and it let out a strangled scream. Yep, that was the exact result I was looking for; I eased up a bit so it could answer.

"What are you doing here, shifter," I asked, keeping it pinned with my boot. I could see blood trickling from its wrists where the belt had previously been.

"I told you," it said, pain evident in its voice. I booted it and it curled into a sort of foetal position.

"I can keep this up all night," I warned, booting it again. It coughed up blood; the silver was working, "But can you?" I asked, leaning over it and pulling the belt tighter. It gagged and coughed, struggling for air as the metal burned into its skin.

"Freeze," yelled what I could only imagine to be a security guard from behind me. "It's only Damien, call off back up." *How insulting,* I thought as I booted the shifter again, this time not stopping. "Take him down," I heard one command as someone tackled me. The belt flew from my hand as I crashed to the ground. I fought him off as I attempted to slip the security pass off of his belt and into my pocket; I gave up when I had it. I looked around; the shifter was gone and, sadly, so was my belt.

"What the hell was that?" he asked, keeping me pinned to the ground.

"Shifter," I said in a natural tone. Most people at the hospital knew the truth about what Xavier and I do, hence the reason I got free medical treatment and probably, best of all, they didn't hand me over to the feds or keep me in their file system. I saved the hospital from a bunch of murderous ghosts that construction workers disturbed when renovating an old wing. Lucky for the people who did manage to escape that they were in a hospital; otherwise it would have been pretty bad. As it was, the situation was pretty nasty. I guess it was also lucky for them that I happened to have been in the free clinic that night, and no, it wasn't something nasty. I was just getting some home fix-up jobs looked at; turns out it pays to have medical training before trying to perform stiches. As soon as I heard the words ghost and hostages I couldn't resist the urge to step in, but everyone who was there knows if it wasn't for me, there would have been way more deaths than there were.

"You're kidding, right?" he said, realising that for once I wasn't actually drunk.

"Nope," I said and for once that wasn't a lie.

They shook their heads. "Look we don't want to do this to you, but this time were going to have to turn you in, we can't have you attacking people on hospital grounds," said Mike, the head of security at the hospital, who had just happened to be my only backup the night I saved the place. He'd learned about hunters directly from the source, and if he wasn't wasting his life here I would have said he'd make a decent one.

"Dude, chill. I was doing you all a favour, trust me. Look, I'll go, you don't even have to say I was here," I said, pulling myself from the other's grip and grabbing my lucky jacket. I turned and walked down the hall, waving over my shoulder.

I saw two more block my path. "Make sure he leaves, he's crafty, that one," said Mike as the two guards grabbed me, lifting me off my feet and carrying me down the hall.

"Hey, hey, watch the merchandise," I yelled as I struggle to free myself. "Hey, big, tall and stupid," I said, still unsuccessful in freeing myself from their grips without hurting them in the process.

One looked over at me. “Yeah, I’m talking to you, I’m giving you about two seconds to stop manhandlin’ me before someone gets hurt,” I warned. They stopped and threw me out the door. I landed with a thud. “Yeah, that’s what I thought,” I said as I looked up to see Xavier and the pom standing in over me.

CHAPTER TWENTY-ONE

"What happened to you?" asked Xavier as I got to my feet.

"A shifter tried to steal my identity," I replied, brushing my jeans off. They both gave me a puzzled look.

"It steal your shirt too?" asked the pom. I was really starting to dislike this guy.

"Probably not, Damien always manages to rip some item of his clothing off in a fight," replied Xavier, both of them acting like I wasn't even standing there.

"Don't lie, you love it," I joked, and Xavier rolled his eyes.

"It's one of Damien's many annoying talents," he said, still ignoring me.

"It's more of a skill really," I said, knowing I was still being partially ignored. I slipped my lucky jacket over my shoulders and pulled out the security pass. I walked to stand next to the rogue. The cut along the bottom of my torso had stopped bleeding and it wasn't as big as I first thought; might leave a nice scar, though. "Along with quick fingers," I said, waving the pass in front of them to grab their attention. Then I quickly slipped the rogue's wallet from his weird pocket to prove my point, and stepped back. They both looked at me, waiting for me to get to the point. "Sleight of hand; while everyone's looking over there, something's happening over here, cha-ching" I said, holding up his wallet and smiling. He patted his pocket, stunned.

"How'd you?" he asked, trying to work it out. I had become extremely good at pickpocketing, so that not even a vampire could tell I was doing it.

"Like I said, I'm good," I said, chucking his wallet back. He caught it in one hand and slipped it back into his pocket.

"Okay, enough showing off, I know what you're capable of but we still need that bullet," said Xavier. *Buzzkill,* I thought.

"Well ,the labs are on the far side of the hospital, third floor, you two can like bust in at super speed, get in and out before anyone knows what hit them," I explained, hoping that I wouldn't have to do much in this plan. Xavier passed me a gun and shook his head.

"Good plan, use our powers in broad daylight, no one will notice that at all," he said in a dry voice.

"It's night, dude," I replied in a smartass tone.

"Don't you think I know that?" he snapped. "It's a saying," Okay, someone's touchy tonight.

"Fine, I'll do it myself, you just wait out here with the pom, and I'll do the heroics as usual," I said, tucking the gun into my jeans and walking back into the hospital. Okay, all I had to do is get in and out without being noticed, sounds simple enough, right?

"Dee, wait," Xavier called after me, but I was already gone. I walked in and looked around. I saw the security guard I didn't want to see leaning on the desk. *Shit!* I put my head down and walked a little faster. *Please don't see me, please don't see me!* I had tried to outrun this security guard a number of times but failed, I swear that guy could be in the Olympics. I made it to the stairwell unseen, *totally ninja.*

"Freeze," I heard him yell*, Okay, maybe not.* I pushed open the door and took off, bounding the stairs two at a time. He caught up way too quickly. *Detour,* I thought, taking the closest door I could find and sprinting down the hall. I pushed past a doctor, sending his charts flying as I sprint through the crowded hallway, but the guy was still hot on my tail. I pulled open the door, slammed it behind me and bounded the steps once again. The door had given me a few seconds lead but I knew he would soon make it up. *This dude can't be human.* My lungs burned as

I bound the last few steps. I pushed myself to go faster as I hit the hallway again. I tipped everything I could to slow him down. All I needed to do was make it down this hall and up one more flight of stairs. I made it to the stairs but I was stuffed.

I knew there was no way I could stop now, I had to push on. I took a deep breath and kept running. I heard his footsteps behind me, and they were closing in. I figured I was slowing down or he was speeding up; my best guess was first option. I bounded the last flight of steps, using the rail to stop myself from tripping on my own feet. Out of nowhere, the guard grabbed for me. I jumped out of the way and he tripped on the steps. Somehow I managed to keep my footing, and ran for the door. That was the break I needed. I pulled open the door and sprinted down the hall to the lab, pulling the pass from my pocket as I ran. I skidded to a stop, swiping it quickly as I did. I watched him pull the door open, take one look at what I was doing and run like hell. I looked at the lock that was still loading, and tried to catch my breath. *I'm getting too old for this shit,* I thought as the unnecessarily slow loading lock beeped and I pushed open the door. I threw myself in and slammed it, then grabbed a desk and dragged it in front of the door. I leaned against the desk to catch my breath. *Ha, finally outran him!* A rustle caught my attention. I pulled my gun when I realised I wasn't alone, but really, when I thought about it, of course I wouldn't be. There was a young girl and an older guy, both dressed in lab coats, standing there staring at me. I had caught my breath just enough to talk.

"Right, I want the bullet that was removed from Misty West now," I yelled, cocking the gun. The girl nodded. "As for you, in the cupboard," I demanded, pointing the gun at him. He did as he was told. There was bashing at the door; it wasn't going to hold for long I had to hurry it up. The girl passed me the bag with the bullet in it; it was whole and just made of lead with a silver tip, by the looks of it, which was strange.

"Thanks, sugar, now I really hate to have to force a lady such as yourself into a supply closet, but I'm kinda pressed for other options, so if you don't mind," I said, gently gesturing to it with my gun, and she nodded again, backing herself into it. I looked around quickly, coming to the realisation that I was trapped. I couldn't see another door or even a window I could escape from. I hated to admit it, but it was time to call in back up.

Yo, Zay dude I need a little help here, I thought, concentrating and hoping that Xavier heard me.

Really? Wait, I must have been picking up someone else's thoughts because I could have sworn that you just asked me for help, wow. Even the voice in his head was a jerk.

No time for your shit at the moment, I need a way out and I need it five minutes ago. I looked at the door as the desk slid forward bit. I threw myself against it, using all my weight to keep it there. *Make that ten minutes ago,* I corrected.

I'm on my way, where are you? he asked finally.

The lab and ya can't use the door, were going to need our own personal exit.

Dude, that means...

I interrupted him. There was no time for arguments. Sure, I loved my sister and would do just about anything for her but I didn't really feel like going to jail, and there would be no getting out with a record like mine.

I don't care what it means, just do it! I snapped. I looked toward the far wall as it crumbled. I shielded my eyes as brick dust went flying everywhere. I opened them to see Xavier and Ryder walking out from the dust, and the gaping hole that they had entered from. *How did they do that?* We're three stories up and there was no ledge.

"In the words of a world's most modest hunter, I'm good," he joked. Security rammed the door again, jarring my entire body. *Not good.*

"Okay, chit chat time is over, let's go," I said, walking to the hole in the wall. I looked at it. It was as good of an escape as any except there was one problem: I couldn't make a jump like that and live.

"New plan, you kill everyone, and we just walk out the way we came," I said, looking down; it was worth a shot. Xavier rolled his eyes and nodded toward the hole in the wall. The rogue jumped out, his long coat flickering as he fell. Xavier smiled evilly at me; I knew what he was thinking and took a few steps back, shaking my head.

"No, hell no!" I said, backing up even more. With a speed that made it impossible for me to avoid him, he grabbed me and slung me over his shoulder, then jumped. I felt the wind rushing around me as we fell. He landed in a crouch but before I even had time to think, he had taken off again. I looked over to see the rogue running next to us. *Hell no, this has gone long enough.*

"Stop!" I yelled and they skidded to a halt, putting me to my feet. "No!" I yelled, pulling the gun from my belt.

"What is it?" Xavier asked, looking around.

"Do, not, manhandle me!" I growled, taking the few strides forward him, and rammed the gun up under his jaw. "If you want to not live to see another day, I would never even think about throwing me around like that ever again or I'll…" he interrupted me before I could finish my rant.

"Kill me," he finished. I heard the rogue laugh and I pointed the gun at him.

"Just because I don't know you, don't mean I won't hurt you so bad that you'll be split three ways from Sunday," I snapped.

"Yes, with lead bullets, good luck with that," said Xavier. I turned back and fired a few rounds into his chest but the bullets just fell to the ground; they wouldn't even penetrate his skin.

"What the hell did you give me lead bullets for?" I snapped.

He shrugged. "So you can't shoot me."

"Well, mission accomplished."

"Okay, if you're over your little tanty, we can work on what to do next," he said, but we both already knew the answer to that; there was really only one answer.

"Joseph," I said, admitting defeat, and Xavier nodded.

"I'll get us a car," he said, taking off down the road. I sat on the curb, totally and absolutely stuffed. I didn't think I had ever been this tired in my life. My mouth was dry and my throat burned like I had swallowed fire. I could have killed for a drink. I guess that's what you got if you ran the entire three floors of a hospital. I looked over to the rogue who was standing there quietly looking up the highway.

"So, what brings you hunting with the best of us," I said, looking up at him.

"I have my reasons," he said, not looking back at me. He kept his gaze fixed down the road.

"Like?" I probed.

"Like, the reasons that I have," he replied coldly.

Man, he can hold a grudge "Okay, no need to be shitty. Note to self: don't talk to that guy," I said, turning away. I knew I probably could have said that in my head, but I have never been good at processing what I said before I said it. I saw him look down at me out of the corner of my eye.

"I'm sorry, I'm just having trouble deciding whether or not to take you seriously, I heard about the fearsome Damien West, the single most vicious killer we as a kind have ever known, and you get here and you're just a human. I could kill you so easily and you would never even know what hit you," he said, sitting down as well.

"You could try," I corrected. The guy could have given me a little credit; I would have put up at least a bit of a fight. "What did you expect me to be like… like Xavier?" I asked.

"Well, yes," he replied.

"I'll let you in on a little secret. This life screws with your head. Makes you do things you didn't even know you were capable of doing. If you don't learn to see the funny side, all you end up seeing is darkness and Xavier, sorry to say, is not so living proof of that. I do my job to live, I don't live to do my job." I patted him on the shoulder as I got up and started walking.

"Wait, what are you doing?" I heard him call after me.

"Walking," I said as he appeared next to me.

"We're not waiting for Xavier?" he asked, looking down the road.

"Well, I'm not, but you can do whatever the hell you want. I'm not your keeper."

He nodded as we both kept walking. A dark blue GTO came to a sudden stop next to us and the passenger side door opened. "Need a ride?" said Xavier.

I ran my hand along the bonnet. "Nice, where'd ya flog this from?" I asked as we got in the car.

He just smiled and spun the car around, before taking off down the highway. The normally hour-long drive took us about half an hour, and with everything else going it felt like no time before we were pulled up outside of the old gas station. I got out and walked inside. I turned away as I saw a girl leaning over the counter in a skimpy tank top and miniskirt. I swear, if she had just bent over a little more it would have been a panty party up in here. She turned and smiled at me. *Well, well, well, hello there*, I thought as I looked her up and down. My smile faltered when I realised that she wouldn't be more than seventeen on a good day. I shook my head and headed upstairs. *That's so not fair*. Joe walked up a few minutes later.

"Hey Joe," I said, actually really glad to see the old guy.

"Don't you 'hey Joe' me boy! What the hell were you thinking? Wait, you weren't thinking, were you?" he snapped, walking up to me. On second thought, maybe not so much.

"I'm sorry, okay, you can yell at me as much as you want, but first we need your help," I said, pulling the bullet from my pocket.

"It's Misty," added Xavier from behind me. Joe looked from me to him as I held out the little plastic bag.

"What have you two done?" he asked.

"No, nothing, the bullet was meant for me, but Misty took it, she's fallen into a coma, we think the bullet caused it. God knows what was in it, but I'm sure it's more than a little silver and holy water," said Xavier.

Joe took the bullet, inspecting it. Most families that hunt make their own bullets and each have a little mark of identification on them in case another hunter finds one. Ours was a small W, but seeing our bullets are designed to explode on impact, it didn't really matter.

"Great job boy, you've really out done ya self this time!" he snapped, shaking his head at me, and walked into the other room like it was entirely my fault. There was no "I'm glad to see you're okay kid," or "It's good to have you back, boy," nope, just "you've really outdone yourself this time," what a loving uncle I had. "I'll see what I can do, it's going to take a couple of days at least, so you guys can crash here if you want and, by the looks of Damien, that's what you need," he said, sticking his head back in.

"What? I'm fine," I said, knowing full well that was a lie.

"You look dead on your feet, boy, get something from downstairs to eat, then go to bed," he ordered. He always treated Xavier and me like we were kids, but I couldn't argue with him; he has been like a father to me since my Dad had died.

"Ya got nachos," I asked, looking toward the stairs. He nodded and walked off. "Love me some nachos," I said, more to myself than anyone walking toward the stairs.

"Oh, and Damien, close up shop while ya down there," he called out to me as I walked downstairs. I look at the time. It was late, well past eleven, which made me wonder what kind of parent lets a girl out dressed like that at this time of night? I made my way downstairs and locked the doors. Normally at this time of night only trucks come through anyway. I grabbed a bottle of Coke from the fridge on my way to the counter to pack up the till. I skulled most of the bottle before I even got there, but the thirst that burned in my throat didn't fade, not even a little; maybe I was coming down with something. I locked up the money, fixed myself some nachos and headed back upstairs to see if Joe had anything a little stronger than Coke.

"Hey Joe, what you got for a man to drink around here?" I called as I walked over and examined the dusty old books on the shelf while munching down the nachos. If I wasn't so lazy I would have fixed myself something proper to eat, to try and regain my strength and all, but nachos and whiskey just sounded better and easier. The bookcase was filled with old journals, various lore books and books that I couldn't tell you what they were about if I wanted to. I heard Joe laugh.

"How cute, the boy wants a man's drink," he said, walking out into the kitchen of his apartment.

"Ha, ha, come on man, the booze," I said.

"Cabinet, on the wall to ya left." I continued looking at the dust-covered bookshelf. Back in the day hunters kept journals (of course, this was before the internet) with everything they've faced in them, all the symbols and chants one may need in case a fellow hunter needed to know how to kill something they hadn't faced before. I looked at the names on the spines. Dounmouth, Peterson … I paused, looking at the last two journals. Connor and West.

No, it couldn't be, I thought pulling the book that said Connor from the shelf; Connor's not a hunting family. I opened the book; it looked really old. I looked at the date on the first entry: May 19th, 1831. I closed it, looking over the other journals. West, Connor, West, Connor, there were tons of them, all from the same time.

"Oh praise the lord, it is a miracle, Damien West is looking at a bookshelf," said Xavier as he walked in the room.

"What? I was just looking at these books, they have ya last name on them," I said. He walked over to the liquor cupboard and got out two shot glasses.

"Oh man, that's scary," he said sarcastically. "I'm sure I'm not the only Connor in history."

"Clearly," I said, looking at all the journals, tempted to read them.

"Dude, I never thought I would be saying this to you but, you think too much. I'm an out of family, remember; that book probably belonged to my uncle or something. My family has been hunting just about as long as yours." He poured out two shots. "Here, drink this, a couple of these and you'll be right."

"Yeah, I guess it's not totally unbelievable that there were other out-of-family Connors," I say, walking over and talking the shot from him.

"To another not so successful mission," he toasted in a dry tone.

"And pray that next time we'll get it right," I said before I downed the shot. Not even the burn from the whisky dulled the thirst that burned in my throat. Placing the remainder of my nachos on the counter, I grabbed the bottle and skulled what was left. This time the burn from the whiskey overpowered the dry burn that was already in my throat. Xavier stared at me wide-eyed as I realised maybe that was a silly thing to do. *Why did I do that?*

"Dude," he said snatching the bottle from my hand as if he couldn't believe I had just done it, "what did you do that for?"

"I was thirsty," I said, knowing that some time pretty soon I was going to become fairly drunk.

"Clearly," said the pommy rogue from the doorway. *When did he get here?*

"Just great, Dee, now I'm going to be watching your drunken ass all night," he snapped.

"Not if you join me," I said, motioning to the cabinet. I reckoned between the two of us we could polish its contents off.

"Dee, you know that me and the drink have had our flirtations over the years, but for once we need to be on the ball and ready, just in case," he said.

"Suit yourself," I said, walking over to the bookshelf and grabbing one of the books that said West on the binding. I sat down.

Xavier grabbed the empty bottle and put it in the bin. I turned the book over in my hand. By the looks of it Joe read this one a lot, because it was one of the few without a thick cover of dust. I opened the book and looked at the name on the inside cover. *Joseph West.* I smiled. Maybe that's because it's his, I thought, starting to read the first page. It was dated back twenty years ago.

CHAPTER TWENTY-TWO

May 27, 1988.
Trinity,

What to say about Trinity, average demon, well maybe not. My first solo case still unsolved. No matter what trap I set she still slipped from my grip, hexes, spells, charms, nothing works; we may be looking at an unheard-of breed of demon. My latest failure happened in front of the entire hunting council. It was called to decide the fate of a good friend and partner of mine, who had been turned into a vampire. He had returned after some years and still insists on hunting; it was the first time this case had seen trial. He got two first string votes so I think he's safe for now. I had heard rumours that Trinity had planned to get her hands on Xavier, corrupt him to help her, so I rigged the place so tight that no demon was getting in or out without a hunter noticing, but despite the fact, all windows were covered by salt lines and the doors maned by devil's traps, all the usual hunters protection charms and the works. It was all for nothing. Nothing worked and she had been in and out without anyone noticing. Further research will need to be done and warnings will have to be spread. I will bring down that evil bitch if it's the last thing I do.

I unfolded all the pages that were stuck in place; they were just on hexes and stuff he had researched. I looked over at the other page; it had the date and the heading was wolves. It was just facts about them, how to kill them, you know, the basic stuff, nothing like the page before. I flicked through quickly, noticing the stuff about that demon was always different, like he was documenting progress, rather than instructing. I put the book back on the shelf. I was starting to get overly bored and slightly hypo, meaning the whiskey was taking effect. I was waiting for it to hit me. I knew it would soon; the buzz was unmistakable.

"Xavier, come have a look at this," called Joe from another room. He left and the pommy rogue followed. I didn't bother to follow because, even sober, I didn't have the head for science-y stuff. I laid my head back and closed my eyes. The room had started to spin. I decided that getting up was probably going to make it worse, so I kept still. I heard the tapping of the computer keys, even the low hum of the computer itself. *Wait a minute, that is the other room, dude you hearing things.* The chirping of a bird in a tree across the road told me that maybe I wasn't. I tried to think back to what had happened when I was being held captive by Lincoln, but I could hardly remember a thing. Most of the time they kept me drugged; I spent most of the time so spaced out I could barely think. I remembered waking up a number of times, groggy, confused as hell and dazed, but I started to wonder if whatever was in that bullet was the same thing they had used on me, and if that was the case, it either wears off or we can find some kind of antidote, it should still be in my system, right? My thoughts drifted to Misty laying there in that hospital bed and I couldn't help but feel responsible.

The room started to rock even while I was sitting and I knew the night wasn't going to end well. Xavier and the rogue entered the room. *Just keep ya mouth shut, don't talk, don't move and you're not going to make a fool out of yourself,* I coached myself. I knew that bit of advice wasn't going to be very useful because it's hard enough to stop myself from doing something I wanted to do when I was sober, so it's almost impossible when I'm drunk.

"Anything," I said, feeling the booze hit me and hard. I tried to keep my thoughts clear and think straight, but it was becoming challenging.

"No, not yet, he'll keep working on it though," said Xavier, pacing the room. Watching him was making me dizzy.

"Will you sit still," I snapped.

"Why this bothering you, Dee?" he said, stopping for a second only to start up again. My thoughts drifted back to Misty. I stood up and it felt as if the world dropped out from under me. I staggered a bit but steadied myself. Okay, standing just made everything a whole lot worse.

"What are we going to do?" I said ready to take action and save my sister.

"You're not going to do anything for the moment, at least until morning, and we're going to work this out," he said.

"And how are you gonna do that, Drack? Huh?"

"Look, Damien, I'm not arguing with you while you're drunk," he said, pushing me down into the chair.

"I'm not drunk, yet." *Pretty close, though.*

He shook his head. "What if once again, because of us, some innocent civ pays the ultimate price and in this case the innocent would be Misty? Could you live with that?"

"Don't worry, Damien, I'm going to fix this, I'll find a way."

"That's not what I asked."

"I'll find a way," he snapped. "I won't lose her." I tried to bite my tongue but I couldn't help myself; it was like what I wanted to say was being propelled out of my mouth.

"You shouldn't have her in the first place! I know you and all you're going to do is hurt her. If not in one way it'll be another, and I won't let that happen to her. She's been through enough in her life," I snapped.

"Well, you haven't exactly been the world's best guardian angel," he argued.

"I've tried, you don't know what it's like to have to do what I've done, all you have to watch out for is ya self, you have no idea the burden I carry."

"And what would that be?" he said smugly.

I got to my feet again. “You’re pushing your luck, Drack,” I said.

He stopped and turned to me. The green of his eyes had darkened so I could tell I hit a nerve. “Well, do something about it,” he challenged, stepping closer and backing me into the wall behind us. “Fine, you’re pissed I’m dating your sister, but I love her, Dee, and whether you like it or not I’m not going anywhere, and unlike you and her father I’ll be there for her no matter what, not only when I feel like it,” he said, getting up in my face.

“Shut up,” I growled. I reach for my gun, debating if shooting him would give me the satisfaction I needed.

“What? The truth hurts, huh?” he asked. I tried to shove him out of my face. Which I should have realised would be useless; it was like shoving a wall. He shoved me back into the wall. My head crashed against it and I let myself slide down it. The spinning was worse now and I could feel myself falling in and out of consciousness. He knelt beside me.

“There’s a change coming, get used to it,” he said, before I finally blacked out. I woke up on my bed in my room. I sat up, *I’m going to kill him,* I thought, looking around. Strangely, I felt fine; my head didn’t hurt or anything.

“Dee, breakfast’s ready,” called Misty from the kitchen. *What the?* I thought, going to get up, but I couldn’t. I looked down to see what was holding me to the bed, but nothing was there. I was laying on my bed fully dressed, boots and all, that when I realised those boots had been destroyed New Year’s Eve, a year ago. I was dreaming. I always had weird nightmares when I felt guilty about something, or if the booze didn’t agree with me. The kind of nightmares you know you’re having, but no matter how hard you try you can’t wake up from them. Suddenly, it was like I was watching it rather than experiencing it. Misty walked into the room with a plate of my favourite blueberry pancakes in her hands. She always had done sweet things like that when I came home from hunts.

"Merry Christmas, Dee," she said, looking over to the bed. I did the same only to see myself fast asleep. I looked at the time on the clock; it said ten AM. I remembered this; I wanted to be there for Christmas but I had a big case that I couldn't ignore, so after it was done I drove all night just to make it. I had only gotten back about three hours earlier, and Misty had been sound asleep.

"Oh," she said, sitting the pancakes on the dresser next to the door and pulling the door shut. "Sweet dreams," she said before the room went black. The door opened again. I looked around. I was in Dad's old room going through the trunk in the secret compartment where he kept all his hunting gear. Misty was leaning on the door frame.

"Hey Damien, I was wondering," she started.

"Not now Misty, I need to find those old crosses of Dad's," I said, not even looking up at her.

"Oh cool, how long you home for?" she continued.

"Not long," I heard myself grunt at her. I remembered this case, zombies in Arizona if I recalled correctly. I looked at her and I noticed the calendar on the wall. It was her birthday? No, I don't remember forgetting her birthday.

"Okay, well, I was wondering if maybe be we could do something special today, or just hang out."

"Misty, I'm busy," I snapped.

"Come on Dee," she begged.

"You arsehole, look at the date, screw the hunt, it's her birthday dude!" I yelled at myself, feeling terrible because this had actually happened, I did remember this after all. I had only realised what the date was after I was back in Arizona. I watched myself grab the crosses from the trunk.

"Misty, not now; this is important," I said, pushing past her and leaving the house. I heard the rumble of the Stang's engine as I took off. I looked to Misty; she was crying.

"Jerk off" she yelled and leaned against the wall. I walked up to her and ran my thumb across her face to wipe away her tears, but of course it did nothing, she didn't even know I was there.

"Happy birthday sis, I am a jerk and I'm sorry, maybe Xavier was right, you do deserve better." The room went dark again. *Great,* I thought. I was starting to see a pattern; what I had seen so far was all based on my own memories but my brain was adding the parts I didn't see to torture me. I looked around as the light faded in. I was at the coven this time, and this could have been a number of times, because we stayed there when our hunts brought us close to town. I saw Xavier sitting at the bench flipping through an old lore book.

"Meant to be a white Christmas, maybe you should go home, I'm sure your sister would love it. I was planning on spending it at the bar anyway," he said, looking over to me. I was sitting at the table, pieces of my dissembled gun scattered in front of me as I cleaned them. Oh yeah, I remembered this because it had only happened last Christmas.

"No, look, once we get the call from Joe we're out of here, I'll spend New Year's with her."

"Dee, she's family…" he started, but I interrupted him.

"Christ, Xavier, if I want to hear your whiny self-help shit, I'll ask," I snapped and continued cleaning the gun; he shook his head and went back to the book. It went black.

You have got to be kidding me! Okay, I get it, I'm a jerk and a terrible brother. No, I'm a terrible person. I already know what I am but that doesn't mean I want to face it, wake up already! The scene started to change. I wasn't letting myself off that easy. *No, please.*

"Nooooo!" I screamed, shooting up in bed; I was in the spare room at Joseph's again, *Thank god.*

CHAPTER TWENTY-THREE

The light shone brightly outside the window and my head pounded as I turned away from it. *I hate hangovers.*

"Morning, sleeping beauty," said Xavier from the door. I lay back down.

"Go away," I mumbled.

"Someone looks a little worse for wear this morning, Joe said get your ass up," he glared at me, "and hurry, the world doesn't revolve around you." He walked off.

Shitty, looks like someone woke up on the wrong side of the coffin this morning, I thought, rubbing my aching eyes.

"I heard that," he yelled from the other room.

"You were meant to," I yelled back, cringing from pain. Xavier's sudden hostility toward me kind of shocked me. Yeah, we fight like any normal people forced to spend a lot of time together do, but normally, no matter what I say or do, he just shrugs it off. Hell, I even shot the guy on a regular basis and he just laughed it off. Now all of a sudden it was like he hated me, and as far as I knew I hadn't done a thing to him. I was going to sort this out now; neither of us could work like this. I dragged myself out of bed and into the lounge. Everything felt somehow unnatural, like I wasn't in my own skin, which was just weird. I shrugged it off; maybe it was the hangover. I sat down, and Xavier shot me a dirty look and turned away.

"Xavier and I identified the substance to be a kind of anaesthetic, specially designed for people affected with the vampire gene. It is stronger than any known human one and we're guessing from our tests that the amount in the bullet was enough to sedate a vampire for at least forty-eight hours, so used on a human, it could be decades." He stopped and took a deep breath. "The virus fights it, that's what causes the sedation, but the human immune system can't, it won't. We have two choices one; hope it wears off and two inject her with the virus,"

I just looked at him. "Is there another way," I asked.

"Well it's not meant to last because it's used for vampires, if the hospital can't wake her up, then we can't either," said Joe, I could see this was hard for him; she was his niece, after all.

"Injecting her with the virus, that means turn her, right?" He nodded.

"In theory, yes," he replied, and I didn't like that sound of that.

"And if we wait?" I asked.

"Like I said before, we have no idea how long it would take for it to wear off, because the human body can't process it like a vampires can. That being said, there is a chance, slim but a chance, that if left long enough it will attack Misty's immune system and she'll have no way of fighting it."

"She'll die, so how long we guessing before that happens?"

"Hoping never, but if it does we should start to see the signs of it in two to three weeks and in that case again there's no way of telling how long she'll have." The room fell deathly silent.

"So I have to choose between killing and, oh, killing her?!" I asked.

"Damien, I know it's tough, but it's your call," said Joe. I stopped; this was all my fault. If she hadn't come looking for me none of this would have happened. No! If Xavier hadn't dragged her into this she would still be at home safe, not faced with death. I knew how Dad would react in this situation. Turning Misty goes against every rule in the book, but could I live with the guilt that I could have stopped two of my family member's deaths? All I knew was that I had to save Misty, no matter what it took.

"Fine, turn her," I said. The words felt like acid as they left my mouth.

Joe nodded slowly. "You sure about that, boy? It's not a decision to make lightly," he asked.

Truth was I wasn't, but I couldn't let her die. "I will not live to see my sister's funeral, she's all I have Joe, I would rather her be undead and still here, than six feet under."

"So how you want to do this? I have some old venom we used for hunting back there, or there is always the natural way," he said. I nodded, thinking about it for a second; I could kill two birds with one stone if I let Xavier do it.

I turned to Xavier. "I want Xavier to do it; I know Misty would want it that way."

"No," said Xavier coldly.

"No… What? Why?" I asked, confused.

"I won't, I can't," he said.

"What do you mean you can't? Of course you can. You've done it before."

"It's not that I physically can't; I won't take her humanity. I can't do that to her," he said.

"Are you deaf? Didn't you hear? She is going to die if you don't, Xavier!" I snapped. I couldn't believe this.

"She'll die if I do. Vampirism isn't nice and it's not something you can turn on and off, either; she'll be stuck like it for eternity, this is not a choice and it's not better than dying," he snapped.

"At least she'll be kind of alive! I won't lose her. Xavier, if you care about her the slightest bit you'll do this for her, for me," I practically begged.

"No, what if she would rather be dead than be turned, huh? Damien, what if after you save her she asks us to end it? I've seen it happen before. Will you be able to kill her then? Because I sure as hell won't be able to and I can't live with the guilt of knowing I've just condemned her to a life she hates," he snapped.

"I would never hurt her, vampire or not," I said.

He gave me a dirty look. "Find another way."

"We have other ways. Xavier, you're not the only vampire out there, hell there's another one in this room, and then there's always Joe's way. I would prefer if you did it just for Misty's sake, but don't you think for a second that'll I'll give up on your account; if this means saving her I'll do just about anything," I snapped at him. I was well and truly sick of his attitude right about now. His eyes turned black.

"No, this is not happening and anything that wants to try has to get through me first," he snarled, looking to Ryder as if giving him his warning.

"You are such a selfish prick! You'll let her die just because you'll feel bad, well boo fucking hoo, Xavier. It'll be a cold day in hell before I let you stop this and if that means that I have to dust your ass here and now, so be it. You say you love her, well prove it, save her," I yelled; we were both on our feet by this point. I heard a rumble of a growl in his throat as his fangs extended. He was readying to attack. *Fine, if he wanted to play, we'll play,* I thought, looking around for a cross, holy water or anything I could use as a weapon against him. Before I could move he punched me, knocking me off of my feet. The force threw me back into the wall. Picking me up, he lifted me high off the ground just like he had when I'd met him.

"You have no idea the choice you're giving me! I get to choose between killing her or leaving her in a state worse than death. It's killing me, Damien, it really is, but it's not our choice to make and I will not do this to someone again!" he yelled, reading my face, waiting for me to show fear or give into him.

"Put me down," I said in a strong voice; showing any weakness only provokes him. His black eyes seemed to bore into my skull; they were empty, evil like they weren't even his anymore. "NOW!" I demanded. He didn't break his gaze. I needed to snap him out of it before he did something we'd both regret. I knew that maybe it was pointless and I was probably wasting my strength, but I figured it would, at least, jolt him out of it enough for him to come to his senses. I stowed my boots into his stomach. To my surprise he dropped me and stumbled backwards. I fell to the floor, almost amazed that that had worked. I picked myself up. Normally hitting Xavier was like hitting a wall, pointless because you're the one that ends up with a broken hand or foot in this case, but not this time. He straightened up and glared at me.

"How'd you..." he asked.

"You said that we'll have to go through you, so bring it Drack," I said, maybe a little more confident than I should have been. I knew I was about to get my ass kicked back to last century but Damien West never backs down from a fight, ever.

"Fine, it's your funeral," he said, lunging at me again. I got out of the way, dodging his attack with a speed I didn't think I was capable of at the moment. Ryder went to step in and Joe grabbed his shoulder.

"Leave it boy, let them get it out of their systems here where we can control it," he said.

Xavier went to grab me. Again I dodged his blow, and I punched him instead. He went down for a second but recovered, quickly popping his jaw back into place. He swung at me again and I ducked under his arm, stepped behind him, pulled his left arm behind his back and twisted his wrist. I twisted it harder, watching in shock as he lowered himself to the ground; this was actually hurting him. *I am on a roll today!* I heard a loud crack as the bone in his wrist snapped. He groaned in pain and I loosened my grip for a second, regretting it as soon as I did, because that second was long enough for him to twist around, swinging his leg out, knocking me off my feet. I landed hard on my back. He pinned me to the ground, delivering a couple of blows to my face. I hardly noticed the pain but I knew that was probably because of adrenalin. I managed to kick him off of me again and go to get to my feet. There was a blow to my back as wood shattered around me. Xavier was holding what was left of one of the chairs. *Son of a bitch!*

But still that didn't stop me from getting to my feet. I needed the advantage and since Xavier wanted to fight dirty, so would I. I spear-tackled him and we both went crashing through the table.

There we were, rolling around in a power struggle, punching, kicking and doing everything we could to keep the other down. I reached for a shard of splintered wood with every intention of staking this bastard. I guess Joe had seen it as well and quickly grabbed the scruff of my shirt, while Ryder grabbed Xavier, pinning his arms behind his back.

"Now boys, play nice," said Joe, yanking on the collar of my shirt.

"Play nice? That arsehole dislocated my jaw and broke my wrist!" yelled Xavier, struggling to break free from Ryder.

"Well, you hit me with a chair," I said almost immaturely.

"Okay, enough, now that was long overdue and now we have everything out of our systems you boys are going to kiss and make up," said Joe, looking between us. I looked down at my boots. My throat burned and my mouth was dry and I could feel the after-effect of that fight sneaking up on me. I gave my head a quick shake, trying to stop the spinning and the confused feeling that was running thought it. I shrugged out of Joe's grip as the burning worsened.

"Fine, but I'm not apologizing," I said, my voice coming audibly hoarser than usual. My heart was pounding faster and faster, like it was going to explode from my chest.

"You alright kid?" asked Joe. I nodded, *Dude, relax, you were just in a fight with a vampire, it's just catching ya, it'll pass.*

"Damien, maybe you should sit down," suggested Ryder, and that kinda took me off guard.

"I'm fine," I snapped. "Now come on; we have to save Misty."

"No," said Xavier.

"No?" I repeated.

"Yeah, you heard me, no," he said back.

Rage washed over me. I could kill him! How could he do that? I felt an unnatural rumble in my chest as if… well, if I didn't know any better I would have called it a growl escaped my lips. They all just stared at me. *What was going on?* I was going all primal on them, I needed a moment to gather my thoughts and clear my head.

"Maybe I'm not alright," I said, sort of centring myself. All of a sudden it was like everything in the room hit me all at once. My eyes darted around the room, looking at things that I hadn't ever noticed before. I even became more aware of the others in the room, especially Xavier and Ryder. "I'm going to go get some fresh air," I said, taking off downstairs. I rushed outside into the cool morning breeze; it felt good on my burning skin. I ran my fingers through my hair and strolled toward the newly updated, old-fashioned looking bowsers. I collapsed down between them, trying to get a grip on myself.

My mind was still racing. Taking in everything in great detail. Every action, every breath, everything; it was all thought out faster than I had ever thought before. Not that I have ever needed to think them out before. I had never been one to over think things, I'm more of a not think at all and just wing it type of guy, so this was new and I didn't like it. My mouth went dry as that annoying burn filled my throat again, but at least this time I knew I wasn't thirsty. I looked around, scanning the woods, wondering what had made the sounds I was hearing. There was a crack of a stick breaking, and my attention shot to where the noise had come from. I looked through the thick woodland across the road. My eyes watched something I couldn't see, but somehow I just knew it was there. The sound of another stick breaking caught my attention further. I tried to snap out of it. I even tried taking a deep breath, but that didn't help at all. I caught the smell of something amazing. It smelled so good it was almost mouth-watering. The smell alone soothed the burn in my throat and I knew straight away it was what I needed. I sniffed the air, which seemed like a mildly weird thing to do.

I suddenly rose to my feet and knew exactly where I was going. I wanted whatever it was I could smell so badly. Without stopping to think I started to run, faster than ever before. The smell grew stronger as I got closer, and so did my need. I needed whatever it was I was chasing, and I was powerless to deny myself. As I got closer the smell became almost irresistible, and then an animal came into view. It was a deer of all things, and I couldn't for the life of me work out why I was trying to catch a deer. I ran through the trees as if I knew where I was going, as if this whole crazy act I was putting myself through wasn't all new to me. I was hunting it and it felt natural, wild and crazy but free. I liked feeling like a predator stalking my prey, it empowered me and the smell entranced me. It all seemed so natural. I caught up with the bounding animal, pouncing onto its back, bringing it down. It kicked and struggled under my weight, but I had it pinned. It wasn't going anywhere. The predator in me smiled. It was a side I didn't think I had but it was consuming me, overriding my better judgment.

I hadn't wanted to catch a deer but here I was, and I knew it was the source of the amazing smell and I still wanted to so badly, but it made no sense. The smell of the woods mixed with the sweet smell I was craving, making it somehow sweeter still. The combination pulled my mind into a haze, dazing me. The accelerated thud, thud, thud of its heartbeat excited me, drew me in. The smell was so strong now I could taste it. Being a hunter it was a taste I was familiar with, considering the number of times I'd been punched in the face over the years. Then I realised what I smelt. What I wanted to taste. It was blood. The thought was repulsive, but somehow the idea of tasting it didn't seem bad, but almost good. I couldn't tear my eyes away from the thin stretch of skin that covered its pulsing jugular. The burn ached in my throat, it was no longer a need, I had to do it. I had to bite it. It was all I could think about; it consumed me. I lowered my head sinking my teeth into its neck. The rich metallic liquid filled my mouth, soothing the burn in my throat. The animal struggled as it died and the rapid thud, thud, thud of its heart slowed to a stop. That snapped me out of it and suddenly I realised what I had just done. Blood stained my lips as I stared down at the deer in horror. I wiped my mouth and looked at the red liquid on the back of my hand. A part of me still wanted more, and that made me feel sick to my stomach.

My stomach heaved as I turned away, bringing it all back up. I panicked and ran for Joe's, somehow knowing my way back even when I had hardly paid attention coming out here. I burst thought the door and sprinted for the stairs at a speed that scared even me. I stumbled up the stairs, not able to get my footing with the speed I was going, and stopped at the top; my chest heaved and for the first time in my adult life I was terrified. All three sets of eyes focused on me.

"There's something wrong with me," I said. Joe's eyes were blank as he looked over me. I knew full well I still had blood on my face and down my shirt, but I couldn't have cared less at the moment. I looked at my hands as if they weren't my own and Joe roughly grabbed the back of my head, yanking it from side to side and then did the same with my wrists.

"Who done it and where?" he yelled at Ryder and Xavier, still searching me for something. Xavier and Ryder's eyes went blank as they shrugged. They both looked kinda shocked, even the rogue.

"He hasn't been bitten. Trust me, we would have noticed the change. They don't just happen overnight," said Xavier, but he didn't look entirely sure about that.

"And beside he's still human, well partly at least. He has a heartbeat and he smells like a human," added Ryder.

"What's going on?" I said, my voice coming out as if I was out of breath. My chest tightened and my head was spinning; I started to freak out again. The room was filled with that same smell from the forest, except stronger this time. A steady thumping echoed in my head. It was too much to take in. The sights, the sounds, the smell, I couldn't handle it; I could feel it consuming me again. My head was spinning out of control and my throat burned, it burned so bad.

"Damien!" cried Joe as I felt every ounce of energy I had drain from me. I grabbed his arms tightly, my breathing laboured. As quickly as it took over I snapped myself out of it, but the effort it took caused me to fall to the floor. I was so tired all of a sudden. Joe kneeled down next to me; his lips were moving but the only thing I could hear was a steady thump, thump, thump. My vision blurred and my eyes grew heavy; everything just seemed to melt into nothing as I fell into the deepest sleep I had ever had.

CHAPTER TWENTY-FOUR

I woke up to the same dry burn in my throat, and the light burnt my eyes. There was a massive hole in my memory, like I had been on a huge bender. The last thing I remembered, I was fighting with Xavier. How did I end up in bed? I had thought I fared well in our little fight but I guess not; I didn't even remember who won.

"Well, the dead wakes, how are you feeling?" asked Xavier, leaning on the door frame. I hadn't even noticed him standing there.

"Like death warmed up," I said, my voice hoarse. *What did he do, try and take out my wind pipe? Cheap shot old friend,* I thought.

"Yeah, I wouldn't joke about that if I was you," he said, commenting on my comment not my thought.

"What, why?" I asked, not really in the mood for his games this morning. I felt like shit.

"Don't you remember?" he asked, answering my question with a question. I hated when he did that. I shook my head; he was already pissing me off. I could feel my temper flaring up already.

"If I knew, I wouldn't have to ask you," I said in a matter of fact tone.

"Damien, we think you transitioned…" he trailed off, probably because of the look on my face.

He said what now! "I what!?" *This can't be happening.*

"We think you've been turned into a vampire, we don't know h…"

I interrupted him. "What?!" I though he was messing with me, he had to be. He shook his head.

"It's true, dude. Tell me do you feel like yourself this morning? Is there a slight burn in the back of your throat? The sun through that window just a tad bit hot? Have you got this mildly, um, unwanted feeling, like you just don't belong here?" he asked.

I nodded. *How'd he...oh hell no!* "Yeah?" I stammered.

"Yeah, well, the burn is because of the thirst. The sun would be photosensitivity, and that feeling only gets worse, and last but not least, the other feeling comes from protective wards and religious items around this place. And that, my friend, is what it feels like to be a daywalking vampire in a hunter's house."

I just stared at him; this was not happening. There was no way I could have been turned. I wasn't bitten, but everything he said added up. The hunter in me knew he was right; it was the only logical explanation. "We don't know how it happened but just try not to freak out. It's a big difference, I just..." he looked away.

"What? What is it?" I probed, not liking where this was going.

"I just have never seen anyone have this kind of reaction to the venom. It happened too fast, and the person normally falls into a, well, 'sleep' while transitioning, but you didn't. It started before you passed out, you even experienced blood lust. I think the weirdest thing is how it affected you. I know the normal kind of effects, paleness, fangs, eye colour, but this, I just feel bad for you," he said.

I felt my anger rising again. I was trying to stop it flaring as a twinge of fear washed over me. How I looked was who I am, and I liked the way I looked. I had worked really hard at creating my look, an expression of who I was, which is totally awesome and maybe even a little badass, but more importantly, this mug often proved a hit with the ladies and in the twenty-six years I have had the pleasure of using it, it had never let me down. He looked up and threw me a hand-held mirror, shaking his head as he did.

"Really, I don't know what to say dude, I'm sorry, look if you want, but trust me it isn't pretty." He looked away again.

I took a deep breath, raised the mirror, looked myself in the face and… To my surprise I looked exactly like me. Well, there were small differences; my skin looked smoother and the tan I had worked so hard to keep was gone. The strange greenie-blue colour of my eyes seemed intensified somehow, and for the first time in my life, my short dark blonde hair was sitting perfectly spiked without water or hair gel. I opened my mouth to see if the fangs I had been expecting to see were there, but nothing. My teeth were normal. *What kind of vampire doesn't have fangs?*

"But of course you look exactly the same, sad really," he said, a smile beaming on his stupid face.

"Prick," I said, throwing the mirror at him; it hits the wall and shattered. He laughed and took off. "Ha, I can catch you now," I called after him, playing into his little game.

"You wish," I heard him reply from somewhere on the other side of the house. I dragged myself out of bed, kinda grateful Xavier was just being a dick, but I suspected not all of what he had said was a lie. I felt strangely light on my feet, some may even have even called it graceful, but they would regret it if I heard them. I gathered up some clean clothes and got changed. As I walked into the lounge, the feeling of being unwelcome intensified and it was almost like a pressure inside my head. It was as if something was screaming for me to leave; the bare skin on my forearms burned like I was sunburnt and I found myself turning away from the crosses that hung on the wall.

I couldn't believe how much this sucked. I remembered all of the crosses, all the protection spells and charms designed to keep everything unnatural out, and it only made me realise Xavier was right, it was going to get a lot worse. Joe grabbed for his neck as I entered the room, and I shook my head as he smiled.

"Ha, ha. We're funny, aren't we," I said coldly, hoping it wasn't Joe I had attacked.

"Never be too careful boy," he said, passing me a book.

"What do you want me to do with this?"

"Oh yeah, you don't know what one of these are, do ya boy?" he joked.

"Yeah that'd be right, pick on the high school dropout," I said as I looked at the page he had the book opened to. The title was *Lamia Infirmitate,* which was Latin and roughly translated to "vampire sickness" in English. I looked up at Joe, who motioned for me to keep reading as he spoke.

"We think it may be what you've got, not contagious, which means that you were infected with it on purpose." I continued reading, it was all in Latin, but a certain passage caught my eye. Basically it explained that it was discovered in a small village outside of Rome. There have been at least a dozen cases documented, but it's suspected there have been many more undocumented cases. Like the flu it attacks the body, changing it, giving the affected person temporary vampirism. In all cases that had been seen, the effects wore off. There have been no survivors and so far no cure had surfaced. A lot of remedies were listed but from what I could tell, all cases have proven to be fatal. After full transformation the victim has two weeks before the effects wear off.

Fatal! The look on my face must have said it all. I was going to die. I knew it had always been a possibility. I'd spent the last few months thinking each day might be my last, and it hadn't worried me. But no one had actually said it and had me believe them, even if this time it was just a few short sentences in Latin.

"Your case is different, those affected with it died while they had the flu and use the limited immortality to survive the duration, but you boy, you are still alive. Well, technically, your heart's still beating. This may not even be what we're up against, but I wanted you to know the possible outcomes. Besides, that's a very old journal, I figured there might be a cure now, so over the last week I've been searching nonstop for it," said Joe.

I wanted to say "You think? The thing's written in Latin" but, wait! Did he just say week? I had been out that long? All my thoughts turned to Misty, suddenly I didn't care so much about me.

"How's Misty?" I asked. I wasn't going to argue the time frame. I wasn't an idiot and Joe wouldn't lie to me. I noticed Xavier and the pom enter the room; the looks on their faces said that nothing had changed.

"Stable," replied Joe. Looking at him now, I could see how tired he really was; all these things must be running him ragged.

"Can I go see her?" I asked, unsure why was I asking. Of course I can. Well, maybe; what if I was a danger to her now? To everyone? What if I was one of those psycho newbies that can't control themselves? The ones that were so much fun dust. The looks on their faces said they were worried about the same thing too. My temper flared up; how dare they judge me! It was me we're talking about. I could do this and I would rock whatever creature I happen to have been turned into to the greatest of my abilities. If I got to be a vampire for a week, then Damien West would be the best damn vampire this world had ever seen. Move over Drack, there's a new sheriff in town.

"Maybe not the best idea, give it a couple of days," said Xavier.

"Yeah, well, I can't do that. You see, I live by this rule, which entails that I do the opposite of whatever you say, so that means I'm going today, now even," I said smugly. Xavier shook his head and sighed.

"Fine, you can go, right now," he said.

Boy, he is so stupid sometimes. "Well, if you insist," I replied, walking toward the door, but he blocked my path.

"Damien please," he pleaded. I shook my head.

"I thought you did the opposite of whatever he said?" said the pommy rogue. I really didn't like him.

"Well, they're my rules, I can change them whenever I want," I stated matter-of-factly.

"Well, we're playing by my rules now, and guess what? You're out," said Xavier.

"Hell no! Move, Xavier, before I move you," I warned. He tensed up, readying to fight if he had to. Normally taking Xavier down physically isn't an option, but seeing I had some kind of super strength, I thought I could take him.

"You'll have to move me," he said again, trying to stare me down, and all that was doing was pissing me off.

"Suit yourself," I said, bringing my fist back, but something caught it. I stopped, realizing it was Joe.

"Enough, both of you. If Damien wants to see Misty he can, we can't stop him," he said and I smiled, getting almost childlike joy from beating Xavier. Xavier's eyes darkened; he never really liked not getting his way.

"Thank you Joe," I said, a smug smile on my face.

"But," he started, pausing for a second; here come the conditions. "I don't think it's good to be going out in your state. I trust you boy, and if you think you can handle it that's good enough for me, but that being said, you step one foot out of line and I give Xavier and Ryder full permission to take you down, by whatever means necessary, and you will do as Xavier says or, I swear boy, I'll pump you full with so much holy water that you'll think you're god. Do you understand me!" he said firmly.

"Too late, he already does," remarked Xavier, and I shot him a deadly look.

"Shut it," Joe snapped, before looking back at me. "Got it Damien?" I nodded; there was no point arguing because I knew Joe had ways to keep me here whether I liked it or not, especially now.

"Fine," I agreed, and he nodded for us to leave. Walking outside, I looked down the highway; *I wonder how fast I can run now?* Xavier and Ryder walked to the GTO, ignoring me again. I looked around; it was like seeing the world in a whole different light. The sun felt strangely warm on my skin. I looked to my arms for a second; it was like my natural tan was back, except this was oilier and fake looking, but still pretty cool.

"Defence mechanism," said Xavier as he stopped by the car. I looked up at him. "Vampires haven't always been able to come out in the daylight, the oil in the skin protects us from burning too fast." said Xavier.

"Every vampire has a different tolerance and it would seem that yours is rather low," says the rogue. Both Ryder and Xavier pull up their sleeves. Ryder's darkens slightly while Xavier's doesn't change at all. *Great,* no more doing the mechanics on the Stang shirtless, that always was a hit with the ladies. I tried not to let it bother me. I wasn't catching on fire or whatever vampires do in the sun, so I didn't care, that much.

"We should run." I really wanted to test out this speed and stamina upgrade. *Try and catch me now, stupid inhuman guard.* Xavier shook his head.

"No," said Xavier, leaning on the open driver's side door.

"Why not?" I asked.

"Because I'm lazy, get in the car," he said, getting in himself. Ryder followed suit but I stood there debating whether I should do it anyway. "I said get in the car, Damien," he snapped. I glared at him, remembering Joe's words. I walked over to the car. I didn't know how many more orders I could take before I shot the guy. I got in and we sped off down the road.

It felt good to finally be on the same level as Xavier, more to the point to be able to kick his ass without wasting my bullets; those things were expensive to make. I could tell Xavier didn't share my enthusiasm, and I knew why. He was still pissed that we were going in the first place; you'd think the guy would be thrilled to see Misty since, you know, she's 'the one." But I guess if he cared for her even a quarter of what I did it would kill him to see her like that; she's my little sister and I needed to be there for her.

The hospital seemed particularly busy for a small town and I wondered if they had gotten over the fact we had smashed a giant hole in the wall. I had heard a possible cover story was that a bunch of oxygen tanks had exploded; bastards owed us anyway. The three of us walked through the sliding doors and what happened next made me stop in my tracks. I watched as every female in sight stopped and stared at me. Xavier and Ryder didn't even seem to notice this strange phenomenon, but I sure as hell did. I walked slowly after them, overwhelmed by the attention. I was kidding myself into thinking that I did have a reaction of the opposite sex, but I sure as hell had never caused this kind of reaction before.

"Hey," I said, passing a fine little nurse whose reaction had been similar to the rest of the women in the room. She just smiled and giggled; I was totally a rock star. *This is awesome!*

"Damien," I heard a sweet sexy voice say, and I turned around to see Dr Sugar standing there, looking as fine as ever.

"Hey sugar, on a first name basis now?" I asked cockily. She only smiled and bit her bottom lip. She walked up to me, placing a flirty hand on my forearms and leaning up to whisper in my ear.

"Call me Leanne."

"Okay, sugar, I can do that."

"I was thinking about what you said the other day and maybe I could give you that exam you were after last time," she said, removing her hand, "because in my professional opinion you do look a little hot." *Oh, boohya!* There was no way this was really happening. I must be dreaming, because seriously, she'd been rejecting me for months. I always knew she'd give in.

"Hell yeah," I said as she twisted her fingers into mine and began to lead me off.

"This way big boy," she said in the single most alluring voice I have ever heard. I got three steps before someone grabbed my shoulder. I knew who it was without even looking at him. Xavier. I tried to twist from his grip but it was pointless.

I glared at him over my shoulder. "Remove the hand before I do," I warned. I wasn't gonna let him ruin this on me. He shook his head and smiled at Dr Sugar.

"Can you give us a moment?" he said in a charming tone.

"Sure thing, handsome," she replied walking off.

"What the hell did you do that for?" I snapped at him.

"Damien, you can't just go off with every pretty face that throws herself at you."

"Why not?" I asked. It was what I normally did; beggars can't be choosers, right?

"Because scent is a vampire hunting tool, as you know, that provokes lust; lust and lunch can become the same thing when you don't know what you're up against. Sex is different for vampires, sometime vampires can get sexual pleasure from feeding so it's often associated pretty closely." he said. I suddenly felt sick; I really didn't like the thought of that. "So unless you're hungry, I would suggest you turn yours off because you reek of it," he said, letting me go and walking away.

I just stared blankly at him, I couldn't smell a thing but I sure as hell wasn't hungry; I'd rather starve, something I never thought I would hear myself say. I guess his words triggered the off switch because all my groupies returned to what they had been doing, confused looks on their faces. Xavier was meant to be such a ladies' man in his time, but now, well, he really stinks at it, talk about cock blocking! He has to be the worst wingman ever, even though he's helped me pick up a number of chicks in the past; ruining my chance with Dr Sugar just erased all of them. We made our way to Misty's room and shut the door behind us. She was stirring. I rushed to her side.

"Damien?" she asked, still half asleep; we must have woken her.

"Hey, Mist, how you feeling?" I asked, taking her hand and using my foot to drag the chair behind me closer to the bed.

"I was shot, Dee, how do you think I feel?" she said, and I couldn't help but laugh. Xavier knelt by the other side of the bed and she looked over to him. He smiled, cupping the side of her face in his hand. She smiled back; it had been a while since I had seen that truly happy expression on her face.

"Hey," she said. He leaned up and kissed her gently on the forehead.

"You scared me half to death, you know that?" he whispered. His eyes roamed her face. He was looking at her like she was the only woman in the world. It was sickening really; I didn't want or need to see their mushy display of affection, so I looked away.

"You're already dead," she joked.

"Oh yeah," he said softly; she laughed.

"Are you feeling alright, Damien?" I looked back to her. "You look pale."

"I'm fine. You shouldn't be worrying yourself about me, you're the one in hospital," I said smoothly. She smiled, closing her eyes again.

Are you going to tell her? asked Xavier's voice in my head.

Not just at this second, no. This wasn't the time or place to break the news I very well might be dying.

She'll realise something's wrong, she's a smart girl.

Then we'll cross that bridge when we get to it, I argued. He wanted to add something else, I could tell, it was written all over his face, but my phone rang, saving me from his mental lecture.

"We're in a hospital, Damien," snapped Xavier. I pulled it from my pocket and left the room.

"Hello," I said walking down the hall towards the exit.

"It's Joe, I need you back here now, you'll never guess who is distributing the vampire flu." I nodded, hanging up the phone and taking off down the road.

CHAPTER TWENTY-FIVE

Misty

I opened my eyes; the room was dark so they had trouble adjusting.

"Ah, Miss West finally we meet," said a voice from somewhere in the shadows, then a man stepped forward. He was tall, maybe even taller than Xavier; he was also well built, maybe even a little on the heavy side. His dark brown hair was cut into a longish crew cut and his eyes were so dark you could nearly call them black. He was well dressed and walked with an unnatural grace for a man of his size. His handsome face was pale, but his expression could only be described as evil. "Let me introduce myself, I'm Lincoln," he said as he slowly strolled toward me. "You've caused quite a stir in our world, my dear."

He stopped next to me, taking my face gently into his large hands so I couldn't look away from him. "Who knew Xavier's one weakness would be so very beautiful, but do not fret, I don't wish to hurt you or your brother for that matter, Xavier's the one I'm after. You see, he took my life, now I have to return the favour."

"No, you don't. Haven't you ever heard the saying 'an eye for an eye, leaves everyone blind'?" I was getting better at putting on a brave front. His smile turned to one of amusement.

"You're a smart girl, brave and selfless; none of those traits will help you right now," he said, his voice suddenly becoming firm. He let go of my face, taking a few steps back.

"It doesn't have to be this way. Damien is going to kill you when he…" he interrupted me.

"He won't let's just say I'm keeping him preoccupied," he said, the amusement creeping back into his voice.

"Xavier will come after me, when he finds out you have me," I warned, running out of threats.

"Oh I'm counting on that my dear. I also know Xavier quite well, and I know it won't take long for him to realise that it isn't you in that hospital bed, and when he does we will be ready for him." He said this with that pure evil smile on his face once again.

"We?"

"Yes, we," said Magenta, stepping out from the shadows. She walked to Lincoln's side and he put his arm around her. "Sorry about shooting you before, it was meant for Xavier but this has worked out far better."

"Why are you doing this?" I asked, unable to believe she was in on it the whole time; she seemed so nice.

"Now, don't get me wrong, Xavier's a good kid but some things are just more important," she said.

"I won't let you get away with this!" I cried, realising just how helpless I was. Lincoln removed his arm from Magenta and strolled back over to me.

He grabbed my hand and kissed it softly, then tsked, "My dear sweet Misty, you don't really have a say in this now, do you?" he said, subtly nodding at Magenta, who shot me an evil look.

"Sweet dreams," she said coldly, before knocking me out once again.

Xavier

A wave of relief washed over me as I watched her drift back to sleep. The last week had been hell; I spent the whole time thinking I would be forced to do the unimaginable to save her. As I watched her sleep I couldn't shake this strange feeling, like something wasn't right about her. Maybe it was just me being stupid, but I was sure something wasn't right. I watched her fall deeper into sleep. A strand of her soft brown hair fell across her face. I smiled as I brushed it back, expecting the sweet scent that drove me crazy, but it didn't come. I looked closer at her and suddenly imperfections I should have noticed the moment I saw her became clear; like how her tan seemed darker than normal, her eyes a different shade of blue. I tried to read her thoughts, which in the past had always been challenging, but this time I could do it with ease. They all seemed fake, almost like they had been fabricated to suit me. I dug deeper; it wasn't easy but I found what I was looking for. A voice deep down in the back of her mind, and it wasn't hers.

They never mentioned I would have to stay in the same room as a psycho hunter and a homicidal vampire; I really have to learn to read the job description. I got up from my chair and stepped back from the bed, looking to Ryder.

"It's not Misty," I say fast and at a frequency anything but a vampire wouldn't have been able to hear. He raised an eyebrow. I nodded toward the machines the Misty imposter was plugged into. "As soon as I grab it, unplug them," he nodded. I counted down from three, then grabbed her. We both move so fast that it wouldn't have seen us coming even if it had its eyes open. I put my hand over its mouth as it tried to scream.

"Where's Misty?" I growled, baring my fangs. I removed my hand enough for it to talk.

"Don't hurt me, have mercy, I was only doing my job," it pleaded.

"Again that word, someone should spread it around that that word isn't in my vocabulary. So I'll ask you again, where, is, she?!" I pushed down slightly on the imposter's windpipe, not enough to crush it, but enough to cause soundless pain. Lucky for it I've gotten better at controlling my strength. I stopped so it could answer, but it said nothing. I felt rage welling in the pit of my stomach; I have always been a hotheaded person and it takes very little to piss me off, but since I had become a vampire it took a lot more to control it. That crazed feeling washed over me.

"Don't push your luck, Shifter, I'm not in the mood to be nice," I snapped, feeling a growl rumble in my chest.

"Lincoln has her," It choked.

"Is he going to hurt her?" I asked.

"I don't know."

"What does he want?" I growled.

"You, he wants you."

"Where is he?"

"I don't know," it said again.

"Don't lie to me, lying to me is a very stupid thing to do," I warned.

"Really, I don't know, I've never met the guy, I'm just doing a job, please I'm not stupid, I know who you are, I would tell you if I knew, believe me I would." Its face was riddled with fear. It brought that twisted smile to my face the way it always does. I dug through its terrified thoughts and, lucky for it, it was telling the truth. I loosened my grip.

"I'm giving you to the count of two to change your shifter ass back and get it out that window," I said, turning away. I have never liked watching a shifter shifting. "One. Two…." I turned back around and it was gone; now we had a new problem; Misty was gone!

"Okay, I need you to erase any evidence of us ever being here today and I need it done fast. I'll meet you in front of the hospital in ten," I said to Ryder. He nodded and disappeared out the window. I waited a few minutes, planning it out in my head before following. I walked back around to the main entrance and inside. I made my scent as potent as I could, which sadly wasn't quite as strong as Damien's had been, and walked up to the desk where a young nurse was looking at a computer screen.

"Hey, I was looking for my girlfriend's room, would you be able to tell me where it is?' I asked.

"Name," she said looking up to meet my eyes.

I focused on her and smiled charmingly. Needless to say, it wasn't the first time I've used my scent or my looks to get my own way. "Misty West," I said, directing everything I had at her. She stared at me and gave a small laugh.

"Yeah, um, huh, right Misty," she said, typing away on the computer. I back off a little so she could think. "Thirty one B," she said. I smiled again, cranking it right back up to ten.

"Sorry to be a pain, but would you mind terribly showing me where it is?" I asked. trying to look clueless. She nodded, getting to her feet straight away.

"Sure mister … um…" she paused.

"Young," I said as we start walking.

Lucky bitch, look at this guy, hot and totally charming why can't I get a guy like this? I heard her think. My smile widened; scent wins again.

"Here we are Mr Young," she said

I smile, pushing open the door. "Please call me Lance," I said in seductive voice. She smiled and turned to walk away. I looked in the room.

"Um, excuse me miss?" I said and she turned back around eagerly.

"Yes, Lance?" she asked.

"There must be a mistake, this room's empty," I said, quickly withdrawing my scent and backing right off. She looked in the room as she woke up from the haze.

"They must have moved her, I'll check her chart."

The hospital quickly went on lockdown after that and I played the part of distraught boyfriend for the cops, giving them my fake cell phone number as I left.

"Please, you hear anything call me," I said before walking outside. That had taken longer than I'd expected, and I found Ryder leaning against the side of the building.

"Finally, you said ten minutes Xavier, what is that in your time? Because I have been standing here for thirty minutes," he said, looking pissed off, which was rare for him.

"I said ten minutes, I didn't say which set of ten minutes I was talking about," I said and he shook his head.

"Where's Damien? He can't still be on the phone," he asked, and I had to agree no one could hold a conversation with that man for that long. I concentrated and mentally scanned the area for his thoughts but I couldn't hear them.

"There's only one way to find out," I said, pulling my phone from my pocket and dialling his number.

"Hello," said Damien on the other end.

"Hey, I just thought I would let you know that I just kicked some shifter's ass at the hospital, it was awesome," I said dryly.

"Cool," he replied, sounding confused.

"No, Damien, it wasn't, because that shifter was wearing a Misty suit and I got it to tell me where she was. Lincoln has her, dude! So where the hell are you?" I yelled into the phone.

"Son of a bitch! Look, meet me at Joe's, I know where he is," he said, hanging up.

I resisted the urge to throw my phone again. I turned and walked toward the car, grabbing the parking ticket from under the window wipers and shredding it before I got in. Ryder got in as well and no sooner had he closed the door than I spun the tires and tore off down the road toward Joe's.

CHAPTER TWENTY-SIX

I weaved through the traffic to get there as fast as I could. Lincoln wanted my attention; well, now he had it and I'm going to make him regret it. The car came to a screeching halt outside Joe's as I pulled the hand brake on and took off inside without even closing the door; I bounded the steps two at a time, trying to get there faster.

"Where?" I asked as I reached the top; both Damien and Joe turned to look at me.

"Back Ally, black market. But we're on the hit list, we go there and we'll be dead before we even get out of the car and we're no good to her dead," said Damien, seeing the look on my face. He always tried to save everyone, he wanted to be the hero of his own little tale; normally I agreed with him, but not this time. There was only one person I was worried about saving and if it meant drifting to the dark side to do it, so be it. Damien, meet your worst nightmare; nothing will be able to stop me.

"I don't care, I'm going to get her and I'm going now, whether you like it or not!" Damien smiled; I take it that was the answer he was hoping to get.

"Atta boy," he said, grabbing his gun and taking my side. The one thing I'd learned about Damien is that he never turned down a fight.

"Welcome to the dark side, brother," I said, and he gave me a confused look as he tucked his gun back into the waist line of his jeans, but just shrugged it off. We had both been to Back Ally a number of times. Some of the things you needed for this profession you can't just get anywhere, and Back Ally is where the lowest of the low do business. The stuff that goes on in the shadows there is enough to scare someone for a lifetime; only the evil and the strong even make it through the gates alive.

"If we're going down," I said, looking to Damien.

"We're going down hunting," he finished. I could practically feel his excitement. Joe just shook his head.

"Well, I can see it's pointless trying to stop you boys from going, but I have something that will help you," he said, getting up. "I got my hands on these a few years back." He walked from the room and returned a few minutes later with a box. It was old and encrusted with jewels. The lid had some kind of symbol I didn't recognize on it. I watched as he put it on the table and opened the lid; I looked at the twin blades resting in red velvet.

"The fallen weapons," I exclaimed in amazement. I'd heard countless stories about the fallen weapons, and until now I was sure that they were just legends. The story goes that when the first angels fell from heaven, they created these weapons to get revenge. There are four that I know of, Lucifer's pistol, Lilith's crossbow, Sorath's ring and Gabriel's blades. The story goes that there were twenty of them originally, but they were all destroyed by angels. These weapons are rumoured to kill anything. He passed one to me and the other to Damien. I examined the knife in awe; the blade was serrated and red. It almost looked like glass, and was so thin it seemed like the smallest of taps could easily snap it. The hilt looked to be made out of bone, with wings carved into the bottom. The blade seemed to light up as it touched my skin. I dragged the blade gently across the back of my hand just to test it; it cut through my skin like it was nothing. Maybe the stories were true, and if they were, I was going to be putting this knife to good use. There was no way to get any mortal vehicle near Back Ally in one piece and I was fresh out of immortal ones, so were going to have to do this the old-fashioned way. Damien thanked Ryder and told him the road ahead was going to be dangerous, and there was a good chance that we weren't going to be coming back. He was right; it was dangerous and the odds were against us, but I would give my life a million times to save hers.

After an amazingly short argument, Damien agreed to let Ryder come with us. I knew he would. Ryder's a warrior; it's was the only life he knows. I tucked the blade into my belt, hoping it wouldn't slice straight through. After a few goodbyes to Joe we took to the trees, running faster than I have run in a while. It felt good; there were no distractions and no need to stop. If we kept up this pace, we would be there by midnight. The sky darkened to dusk and that faded into night. The wind whipped though my hair and tore at my clothes, but it felt so free. For just a second I got that childlike joy that my skills brought, but the feeling was short lived as we slowed to a jog, then to a walk, before finally coming to halt in front of the secret mountainside entrance. Like Atlantis or the entrance to the Bermuda triangle, this wasn't a place you could get into unless it wanted you to. I looked to Damien, then to Ryder; taking a deep breath, I stepped through the entrance.

I waited on the other side and for a few moments I stood there alone, looking around the dark, sordid alleyway. Here it was always night, always dark. A place like this wasn't for the faint of heart; it shed new light on being afraid of what was in the dark. Damien stepped from the entrance, followed by Ryder. We had no idea where to find Lincoln but that didn't matter. I would kick in every door until I found him if I had to; nothing was stopping me now. We slowly strolled to the darker end of the alley. People stopped as we passed; the presence of hunters always disturbed a place like this; they all wanted to know what we were here for. I looked around at some of the faces watching us as we passed. Many I knew, and many knew a side of me that belonged in these streets.

"What you looking at?" Damien asked a couple of passing vampires getting too nosey for their own good. I felt a growl rumble in my chest as we kept walking. The evil that littered these streets deserved everything that we could throw at them, and as much as I wanted to tear them all into tiny shreds, I knew I couldn't. I had more important things to deal with. A blockade stood up ahead waiting for us, huh? I guess they really didn't want us back there. We stopped in front of them; normally we had no right to start a fight and we left when we were told but not today, today they were going to get the fight they were waiting for.

"Hunters aren't welcome here, that includes you," said a skin walker as he blocked our path. I looked at the group of monsters that made up the blockade then looked back to the skin walker, who I knew was named Lucas; he was a pack leader we'd helped out once before. In fact, at one point or another we had helped most of these creatures. I didn't even try and hide my hatred for them.

"Since when has that included us?" I asked, knowing no matter how many of them there were, we were still the dominant force in this fight.

"Just turn around, Xavier, I said you're not welcome here," he growled.

"Now that's saying something," said Damien. Lucas looked between the three of us as I felt my fangs extend.

"You're all vampires!" he said, shocked. That announcement made Damien laugh.

"Ha, give the dog a bone, who's a clever boy," said Damien in a voice you would use to praise a puppy. Lucas growled more savagely this time, tensing himself. I did the same. I wasn't afraid of a mutt.

"Move!" I demanded sharply.

"No."

"Fine, this is how it's going to work I'll fight you for it, I win, you die, any questions?" I said, not giving him any other options.

"I'm not letting you through. You want to get past, you're going to have to go through me," he snarled, starting to shift.

"If you insist," I said and attacked before he even had a chance to fully shift. I tackled him, going straight for the jugular, and with one quick slash I tore out his throat. I didn't have time to play around with these idiots. He fell to the ground. Blood covered my hand and arm, which wasn't helping my anger control situation; were-animal or not, it still smelt good. Supernatural blood was the sweetest. I cricked my neck and looked around at the rest of the group. Their faces were riddled with fear and their thoughts were scattered.

"Who's next?" I asked, sucking my fingers clean, and they all just stared wide-eyed. They cast worried glances at each other; it had taken me just under a second to take out their leader, so with the three of us it would be over in a minute. Damien drew his blade and Ryder crouched, preparing to go primitive like I had; they cleared a path and I straightened up.

"Wise choice," I said as I stepped over Lucas's body and walked through them.

Damien got up in one creature's face quickly, just to see them jump back, before laughing and following. I regained what little self-control I could and used it not to laugh; that was just too easy. Ryder and Damien kept their distance from me as we walked, but I didn't really blame them for that. If I had just seen someone do what I had, I would want to give them a wide berth as well. News of what I'd done travelled fast and everyone cleared the street as we passed, which was fine by me; the less I had to see of those scumbags the better. We stopped at the end of the alley; this part was pitch-black dark, and only the evilest things go on in there until now.

"Well, here we are," said Damien, stopping next to me. It was almost like another world beyond the darkness; who knew what we'd find when the light was gone?

"How are we going to find him?" asked Ryder from the other side of Damien. I looked around; people down this end of the alley didn't seem as worried about our presence as the others did. I grabbed the first poor fool who came within my reach, scuffing him and bringing his face to mine. I extended my fangs once again.

"Lincoln?" I snarled. It smiled at me. I couldn't even tell what it was, evil elf, maybe?

"At the very end, last door, if you can make it there that is," it sniggered and I threw it to the ground. It scurried off. Without hesitation, I stepped into the shadows.

"Xavier, wait," I heard Damien call after me, but I wasn't stopping; I had heard stories about what goes on in here but I knew there was nothing more they could do to me. I was already soulless, dead and crazy, so really, what else could they do? Damien and Ryder caught up to me quickly; they were looking around more warily than I was. I growled at a few creatures in the shadows, as they watched us pass.

"Dead man walking," hissed a voice before snickering and shuffling deeper into the shadows. I have only been in this place a few times and I can't even begin to explain the horrors I saw, but this time it was quiet like they were waiting, watching, hiding, except the kind of things you find in here don't hide from vampires or hunters. The alley came to an end and a door loomed in front of us. It was all that stood between me and Misty, so needless to say it didn't take long to get it open.

"Lincoln, I'm here, do your worst!" I yelled as loudly as possible.

"All alone, Xavier?" said Magenta, stepping from the shadows. Just seeing her made my blood boil. I should skin this bitch alive for all that she'd done.

"Not exactly," said Damien, standing next to me. Ryder took my other side.

"You're…" she said, staring at Damien wide-eyed. Once again, his reputation preceded him.

"Your worst nightmare bitch," he said, grabbing for the knife. I crouched, ready to attack.

"Oh, I've wanted to do this for so long," I growled, then faltered when a familiar scream broke my focus. Both Damien and I looked toward the hall where it came from. We knew we couldn't both go; someone had to stay and help Ryder

"Go get your girl," said Damien, lunging at Magenta. I nodded and ran down the hall following the sound of Misty's scream. I felt all the rage, all the anger I'd been trying so hard to keep control of, release as I pushed myself to go faster.

"Misty!" I called out, not knowing how much further I had to go until I reached her.

"Xavier!" I heard her call from behind a door at the end of the hall. I kicked open the door, bursting in. The first thing I saw was her. She was tied up, all beaten and bruised. My hands started to shake and my breathing quickened. My mind focused on a familiar face; my fangs extended and something else took over. I pulled off my jacket as my eyes scanned the room. Just the thought of crushing Lincoln's skull in my hands excited me, even though I knew it shouldn't. At that moment I'd never felt less human, and it felt good.

Misty

I couldn't see Lincoln any more.

"Misty!" I heard Xavier call out to me from somewhere in the building. *Oh no!*

"Xavier!" I called back. I looked around again and I knew he would be here any second, I had to warn him. "Xavier, it's a trap," I tried to yell, but my voice was muffled by a hand.

"Shhhh, now, play nice or I won't even give him a fighting chance," whispered Lincoln before he stepped back into the shadows. I struggled to break free; in only a second Xavier was going to burst through that door and Lincoln would kill him while I watched powerless to do anything to stop it.

Everything slowed down; Xavier kicked the door in and I looked over at him. His normally emerald eyes were now black, and seemed to glow in the dim light from the door. His pale skin contrasted with his dark shirt that almost blended into the back ground. I gazed over him and saw there was a confidence in him, even in the way he stood, that I hadn't seen before. I smiled at my saviour. I had never been happier to see someone in my whole life, but he had to get out of here before….

"Xavier, my old friend," said Lincoln, stepping into view.

"Lincoln," replied Xavier, walking into the room. They started to circle one another in a deadly dance.

"You look good. What it's been forty years now?" he asked.

"Yeah, well, you look like shit, Link," said Xavier coldly.

"Maybe that's because that last time you saw me I was still human. Still vibrant and alive, but now look at me. I'm a monster, an undead creature of the night."

"You always did talk way too much, Link. You want revenge, here I am, take it," challenged Xavier.

"And you always were the mouthy one," replied Lincoln, and before I could blink there was a loud crash and Xavier had Lincoln pinned to the wall.

"Yeah, but now I back it up," he snarled. Lincoln shook his head and kicked him off. Xavier lunged for him again and they grappled in a deadly power struggle. It was hard to tell who was winning, but I was praying it was Xavier. I watched as Xavier went flying through the air and crashed to the floor. As he landed Lincoln was on him, stomping one foot down on his neck.

Xavier choked. Only a vampire could kill another vampire like this; I couldn't watch.

"You haven't changed. I have the home field advantage. This is my court, you're just playing on it," Lincoln yelled. I felt tears run down my cheek. *Fight him, Xavier, do something*! Xavier grabbed his foot, tripping him, and quickly jumped to his feet, pulling something from his back pocket. Lincoln did the same but as he did, Xavier bought his hand across his throat so fast I couldn't even tell what he'd done. Lincoln grabbed for his throat as the flesh around the cut burned; Lincoln's wound wasn't bloodless and it definitely wasn't pretty.

"Looks like I changed the rules," said Xavier, plunging the knife into Lincoln's stomach and pulling it back out. Lincoln fell to his knees. "Game over, Link," said Xavier, kicking him over. Lincoln crumbled to dust before he even hit the ground. He turned to me, and his eyes returned to their normal emerald state.

"Misty," he said breathlessly, looking at me lovingly. My tears quickly turned to tears of joy as he ran over and untied me. He took me effortlessly into his arms and the refreshing chills that his touch caused ran down my spine as he spun us around; he set me to my feet.

"How are you?" he asked, staring deep into my eyes.

"A lot better now that you're here," I said as he brushed a lock of hair out of my eyes, pulling me into him again.

"I swear if you ever do this to me again…" he said with so much relief in his voice, it made me smile. He loosened his grip so I could see his face again.

"You'll kill me?" I finished.

"No, I could never; I'll just have to find some other way to punish you," he said with that cheeky smile I loved.

"I like the sound of that," I said, standing on my toes to reach his lips. He leaned into my kiss.

His kisses were hungry like they'd never been before, filled with such passion, such intensity. I heard someone clear their throat from behind us. We broke apart and Xavier let me go. I looked over to see Damien standing at the door; my smile widened, which I didn't think was possible.

"Damien!" I cried, running up to him and practically throwing myself into his arms. He caught me, pulling me into a bear hug, and spun us both around.

"Missy, I was so worried," he said, giving me another big squeeze before letting go. I looked at him; his normally tanned skin looked pale and his bluey green eyes seemed more vibrant. My brother had always been handsome but now he seemed flawless, kinda perfect, a lot like Xavier, a little too much like Xavier … *oh. my. god.*

"You're a vampire!" I said, taking a step back in shock.

"Only temporarily," he said casually.

"Finally a sensible reaction," said Xavier, walking over to me. I pushed him playfully and hugged my brother again.

"It's good to see you, vampire or not," I said, and Xavier took my hand as I let go.

"Did you get her?" he asked Damien, but Damien shook his head.

"She got away," he replied, sounding kinda deflated. Xavier's face went expressionless for a second, but he calmed down quickly.

"Well, get her next time," he said simply. "For now, let's just go home." He put his arm around me and the three of us walked outside, and no one dared stop us. I guess word had already spread of Lincoln's death and who had caused it. I could tell Xavier liked that he was now widely feared. He lifted me into his arms and pulled me into to him so tight, it was almost like he was scared I was going to disappear, but I wasn't going anywhere. He kissed me softly on the forehead.

"You might want to close your eyes; it's going to be a bumpy ride."

EPILOGUE

Things after that soon went back to normal; Damien and Xavier went back to hunting but they only took on small jobs closer to home, and for the first time in a long time, I had what felt like a real family. If you had told me before this all started that in the next month my entire life was going to change I would have died of laughter, but looking back now I wouldn't change a single thing even if I could. I was in a stable relationship, reunited with the family I had thought had lost for good and I was happy, truly happy. Who would have figured?

"Damien, turn the music down!" I yelled from my room, kicking the wall.

"Ah, nah!" he yelled back, the booze evident in his voice.

"Oh my god, you suck!" I screamed over *Sleep when I'm dead* by Bon Jovi, before storming outside. I sat under mom and dad's tree. I smiled as I looked around the backyard. It was such a beautiful night even though there was a raging two-person party going on inside. The stars glittered against their dark backdrop and the air was nice and warm for a change. I looked up as the muffled music from inside became clearer and the song changed. I smiled as I realised it was my favourite song, Ronan Keating's *This I Promise You.* Xavier stood in front of the open glass doors, arms crossed over his chest, smiling in my direction. I felt my cheeks burn hot, and a smile crossed my lips as he walked over to me. He staggered a little as he bounded down the stairs. I giggled. It didn't surprise me even a little to see him so unsteady on his feet. The party inside was a celebration of a hunt well done, which in other words meant they managed to finish it without stuffing up somehow, and seeing that the two of them have been celebrating since about lunchtime, I would have been surprised if he was sober.

"Can I have this dance?" he asked, pulling me to my feet and not even giving me a chance to answer him. I took his hand and he pulled me in closer to him. I laid my head on his chest as we swayed to the music. I pulled away slightly to meet his eyes and he looked down at me adoringly; a tightness filled my chest.

"What are you doing out here?" I asked. His steps faltered a bit before he laughed softly.

"Do I need an excuse to want to see you now?" he asked, his voice laced with a slight smugness that I assumed was alcohol-related. I shook my head.

"No, if I had it my way we would never be apart," I answered. He gave me a cute lopsided smile and spun me under his arm before pulling me in close again. He pulled me closer still and started to sing.

"And when I look into your eyes all of my life is before me." I laughed as he dipped me over his arm, twirling me in extravagant moves that without him I wouldn't have been capable of. He pulled me back in close and looked me in the eyes as he continued to sing. *"And with every beat of my heart I give you my love completely, my darlin, this I promise you."*

The look on his face said he meant every word, even though he was only singing the lyrics. I smiled and laid my head on his chest again as I listened to him sing. He sang every word like it was written just for me, and at that moment there was no place in the world I would have rather been than with him.

"I wish this night would never end," I said dreamily.

"All things have to end, Misty, that's the way of life," he said softly.

"Not for you they don't." I started pulling away so I could see his eyes. He looked down to meet mine. "For everyone else they do, but for you anything can last forever."

"You make it sound like that's a good thing, Misty. Youth and beauty only hold value because they don't last. Having eternity makes it easy to see life is fragile and all good things must come to an end sometime, or it's pointless," he said, leaning down to kiss me. The kiss was tender but my heart wasn't in it. I was caught on his words. I loved him, that much I knew for sure, and even the thought of that love ever fading, not existing anymore, hurt more than anything I had ever experienced. He pulled away when he realised I wasn't kissing him back. I stopped moving. I could feel the moisture in my eyes and the tears burned slightly but stayed hidden.

"What if I don't want it to end?" He stopped, taking a step back; even through the drunken haze I could see the wheels in his head turning.

"What don't you want to end?" he said, worry creeping into his voice.

"You and me, love, happiness… life." I trailed off.

"Babe, it doesn't have to," he started, then fell silent, realising what I was saying. "Don't," he said quietly, looking away.

"I love you Zay, and I want to be with you forever, this doesn't have to end for us, not now, not ever."

"Misty," he said quietly again, still not looking at me.

"I never want to leave you."

"And you won't have to; we'll work something out, we'll make it work," he said; slight agitation was creeping into his voice.

"Xavier you know what I'm going to ask," I said as softly as I could manage. He looked up from staring at our feet; it was easy to see he was mad. He knew what I was going to ask, alright.

"I can't believe you're going to ask this now," he said, not trying to hide his agitated tone.

"You knew I was going to ask eventually," I said softly. He rubbed his fingers across his eyes and sighed.

"Misty, please, not now, we'll talk about it when I come back," he said, his voice softening. I just stared at him. *Wait!? What? When he comes back.*

"Where are you going?' I asked.

"Damien and I have a case lined up, and the reason we never told you is because it's dangerous and I don't want you involved," he said. I started to argue with him but he stopped me. "And I don't feel like arguing with you so give it a rest," he said. His tone was gentle but it had an edge to it that told me that I should keep my mouth shut on both issues; besides, I didn't feel like arguing either. Admitting temporary defeat, I laid my head on his chest once again. His grip around me tightened as he leaned down to kiss me. The kiss held no anger but was soft, gentle and filled with love. We both knew this wasn't the last time we were going to have this conversation, and as long as we were together it was going to keep coming up; be it tomorrow or ten years from now, but everything just felt way too good tonight to ruin it by arguing. Instead, we danced under my parents' tree in the moonlight, allowing our lips to meet and just enjoying it while we could. With him in my arms I had everything in the world I needed. For now.

CPSIA information can be obtained at www.ICGtesting.com
Printed in the USA
BVOW001410010513

319573BV00002B/677/P